The Alchemist of *Genoa*

David Breakell

POWER HOUSE BOOKS

DOWER
HOUSE
BOOKS

Copyright © 2025 David Breakell

David Breakell has asserted his right under the Copyright, Designs and Patents Act 1988 to be identified as the author of this work. This book is a work of fiction and while some historical figures are portrayed, along with the historical events and facts with which they are associated, their roles in the story are entirely imagined.

All rights reserved. No part of this publication may be reproduced, stored in a retrieval system or transmitted, in any form and by any means without the prior permission of the publisher nor circulated in any cover or binding other than that in which it is published, nor resold without similar conditions being imposed on the purchaser.

First published by Dower House Books in 2025

ISBN 978-1-0683647-0-9 / eBook 978-1-0683647-1-6

Cover design by Ann Weinstock
Typesetting in EB Garamond and IM Fell by Kerry Ellis

Cover painting: Giovanni Battista Moroni, *The Tailor* (detail), National Gallery, London, reproduced by permission of Alamy Limited.

Map of Genoa by Nat Case

www.davidbreakell.com

"A powerful master is Sir Money: born with honour in the Indies where everyone is its friend, it comes to Spain to die and then is buried in Genoa."

–Francisco de Quevedo, Spanish poet

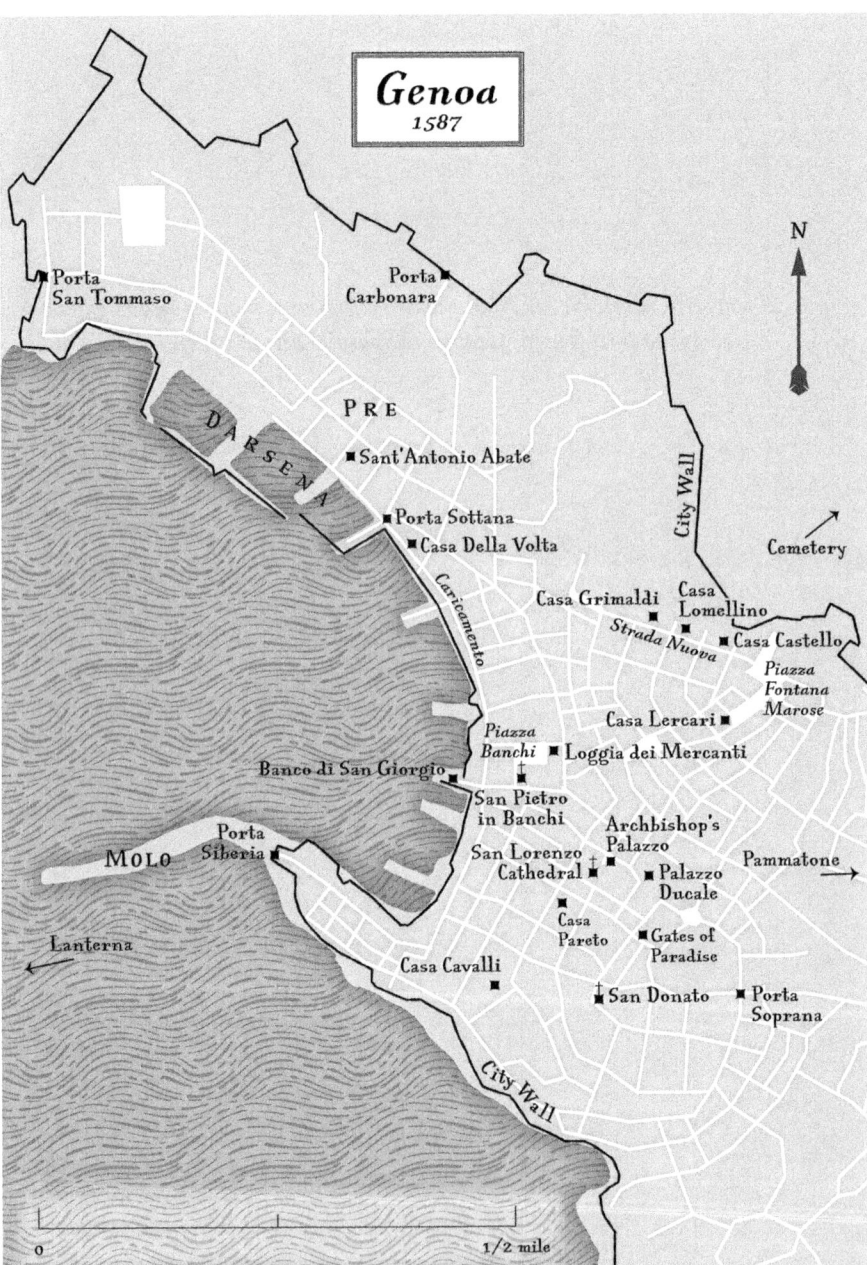

Cast of Characters

("F" against a name indicates a fictional character)

THE ENGLISH

Robert Beale: Clerk to the Privy Council. Married to the sister of Ursula, Lady Walsingham.

Montague Belltower: nephew to Thomas Sutton. Known familiarly as Monty. A member of the Wool Merchants' Guild. (F)

Sir Francis Drake: sailor, circumnavigator of the globe and a privateer in Queen Elizabeth's naval forces.

Robert Dudley: 1st Earl of Leicester, Lieutenant-General of Elizabeth's armies in the Netherlands and a Privy Councillor. In earlier times, a contender for Elizabeth's hand in marriage – and her heart.

Queen Elizabeth I: twenty-nine years after her accession to the throne, the Virgin Queen is now in her mid-fifties. The defeat of the (first) Spanish Armada is still over a year away.

Thomas Sutton: a London-based banker and merchant, his wealth based on his Yorkshire coal interests. Founder (some years later) of Charterhouse School in the City of London.

Sir Francis Walsingham: Principal Secretary to the Queen and a Privy Councillor. Elizabeth's 'spymaster'.

Ursula, Lady Walsingham: wife to Sir Francis.

Septimus Winterhey: Master of the *'Mary Gale'* (F).

THE SPANISH

Felipe (Philip) II: King of Spain and Portugal and ruler of a global empire. Member of the Hapsburg dynasty. Now in his sixtieth year.

Don Juan de Idiáquez: aged thirty-seven, the king's Principal Minister for Foreign Affairs and a member of the triumvirate of three ministers called the "Junta de Noche", that effectively ruled the Spanish Empire under Felipe. Previously ambassador in Genova.

Miguel de Oquendo: Naval officer and captain of the king' ship, the *"San Felipe"*. A year later, he would be a squadron commander with the Armada.

Don Balthasar de Zúñiga: Spanish emissary, sent by Minister Idiáquez to Genoa to negotiate loans for the king's war effort. (F)

Sebastian: Felipe's manservant.

THE GENOESE

Domenico Castello: head of Banco Castello. Known familiarly as Nico (F).

Lisa Castello, nee Della Volta: orphaned daughter of Cristoforo, and wife to Nico (F).

Alessandro Castello: Nico's younger brother and business partner. Known familiarly as Sandro (F).

Vittorio Castello: father to Nico and Sandro, retired silversmith (F).

Ferrucio Lercari: banker and moneychanger, senior partner in Banco di Liguria (F).

Giovanni Lercari: Ferrucio's younger son, familiarly known as Gino (F).

Cardinal Antonmaria Sauli: Archbishop of Genoa.

Father Guido Vacchero: senior priest at San Lorenzo and confessor to Lisa Castello (F).

Julia Visconti, nee Della Volta: aunt to Lisa and a 'merry widow' (F).

MINOR CHARACTERS

Adriana: a courtesan and close friend of Bianca Bastone (F).

Ambrogio Di Negro: Doge of Genoa, head of the Republic's governing body, the Grand Council.

Andrea De Marini, head of an ancient family and father to Nicoletta (F).

Bianca Bastone: a courtesan at the "Paradiso", nicknamed 'Blackbird' (F).

Paolo Brozzi: a novice priest at the cathedral of San Lorenzo (F).

Lorenzo Cavalli: host to Monty Belltower during his stay in Genoa (F).

Nicoletta De Marini: a novice nun at the convent of Santa Maria (F).

Fabio: a young urchin, working 'below stairs' at the cathedral (F).

Jan Huysmans: Flemish merchant, Trades in spices in Genoa (F).

Battista Lomellino: banker, on the board of the Banco di San Giorgio, syndicate partner of Nico Castello (F).

Lina Luzzati: the proprietress of the "Paradiso" (F).

Sergente Luca: officer of the Ducal Guard at the Lanterna, Genoa's lighthouse (F).

Sister Maria: a nun in charge of Sant'Antonio Abate, a hospice in Pre district (F).

Giovanni Mazzini, Nico's clerk at the Loggia (F).

Capitano Merello: an investigating officer in the Ducal Guard (F).

Bernardo Pareto: a dissolute young nobleman (F).

Benedetto Saluzzo: Treasurer of the Banco di San Giorgio (F).

Simon: a fisherman in Genoa harbour (F).

Sergente Spazio: a non-commissioned officer in the Ducal Guard (F).

Leonardo Tasso: a lawyer, adviser to Nico Castello (F).

Dottor Vannone: a doctor from the city hospital, the Pammatone (F).

Gildo, Luca, Lorenzo, Marco, Maria and Paola: members of the Castello's household staff (F).

The city is generally referred to in the text of the novel by its name in Italian, Genova (hence Genovese, rather than Genoese). However, in the author's notes, chapter headings and when spoken of by the English characters, is it called Genoa, the equivalent in English.

Genoa along with most other catholic countries, although not those in the Eastern Orthodox tradition, adopted the Gregorian calendar five years before the story is set, in 1582, at the instigation of Pope Gregory. Protestant countries like England did not follow suit at the time. The dates indicated for chapters or scenes set in England reflect the applicable dates under the Julian calendar, which she maintained until the 18th century.

Chapter One
SCYTHING LANE, CITY OF LONDON: 9TH FEBRUARY 1587

He was struggling to keep awake. Dimly, through his exhaustion, he wondered if he was becoming incoherent. His host hadn't interrupted the report: no word or gesture to indicate his reaction. Taking a breath, Beale ploughed on.

"Oh, it was the sight of that crimson petticoat that stunned us all, brother. She just stepped out of her black gown and stood there in her undergarment, still as any statue. You could hear the sudden intake of breath. An affront to all who saw it. And to our faith."

The listener's expression barely changed, just a slight narrowing of the eyes.

"Then Master Bull stepped forward and asked her forgiveness, which she gave him straight back. Her ladies – those my Lord Kent had consented to be present – began to weep. She spoke to them in French. As I heard it, she counselled them not to mourn but rejoice at her deliverance. They bound her eyes with an embroidered cloth and retreated to the back of the stage. She knelt before the block, stretching her arms out wide and said, *'In manus tuas, Domine.'* Master Bull steadied himself and raised his arms high. I prayed it would be swift, one blow. Not much to ask, surely? He struck the back of her head. Who knows if it killed her, she did not stir. He swung again: this time true. But even then, her head was not fully severed from the neck. And so, he went a *third* time. At last, merciful heavens, it was done." Beale swallowed hard. His hands were shaking, despite the warmth coming from the hearth.

"At first there was silence among the crowd, until Bull held her butchered head aloft crying 'God Save the Queen'. A few muttered 'Ayes' but their voices died away, struck dumb by the sight. I swear her lips were *still moving*, though no word came from them. When Bull realised, he looked at the head as if to stare it out. But at that very moment, it dropped from his grasp. He was left holding just her blood-soaked wig.

Her shaven head rolled across the stage toward us. The eyes staring, the lips *still* trembling. Some lawyer fellow standing in front of me, stepped back in recoil." Beale jerked backwards, hitting the chairback. "Trod on my foot," he muttered, almost to himself. His narration was punctuated by a log in the grate sputtering and crackling.

His brother-in-law still made no interruption, and Beale was forced to resume.

"So, Dean Fletcher stepped over the headless body, calling out, 'Thus perish all the Queen's enemies.' My Lord Kent echoed him. Those were the only ones to speak. Bull and his assistants made to take her from the stage. But even then, it went awry. As they raised her body, her little pet dog scampered out from under the dress. It had been there all the while. It stood in the pool of blood, between the head and body of its mistress, not to be moved or quieted. Its pitiful whining taking away all dignity from our proceedings."

Beale coughed to clear his throat. "And so, the hall was emptied and the stage taken down. The Sheriff ordered the castle locked and all those who had witnessed the event detained there for the while, lest word get out into the town. Paulet instructed that all her clothes and possessions be burnt. Someone was told to wash the wretched dog. We took her to the remotest cellar in the keep. The physicians examined the body and removed the organs. They declared to us, my Lords Kent and Shrewsbury, Master Paulet, the Sheriff and myself, that her heart was sound. Lest it become a holy relic, we buried the heart deep below the castle wall, where none could assay its whereabouts. Orders were given that her head and body be embalmed and placed in a lead coffin. My Lord Shrewsbury said he would dispatch his son to Greenwich, to give Her Majesty a report of these events. He looked sorely distressed as he spoke. I thought I had seen tears in his eyes earlier, before the deed was done."

Beale's host nodded slowly, as if that were the reaction he had expected.

"So, mindful of your instructions, I left Fotheringhay before Lord

Talbot could set off. I had a mounted escort and fresh horses in readiness, stationed along the route. Darkness fell before we reached Wellyn, but we kept on by such moonlight as there was. We rode like the devil was behind us, to be sure we made London ahead of the young lord. It was barely three in the morning when we reached Bedlam Gate. Never was I so glad to be inside the city's walls, brother."

Beale slumped back in his chair. His eyes went upwards to the shadows flickering on the ceiling. There was a brief silence in the room when all he could hear was an owl hooting somewhere, its night-time hunt obviously successful.

His host hauled himself into a standing position. Stiff-legged, he stepped across the hearth and put his hand on Beale's shoulder. Beale almost flinched. But Walsingham's expression had softened.

"Thank you, Robert. A full account. You deserve to rest after your long journey. But I fear I must ask you to perform one more errand for me this morning. Go to the Bishop of London, inform him of this momentous news."

Beale blinked. "You mean, now?" It was still dark outside; dawn would not come for two hours.

Walsingham shook his head. "You can rest upstairs awhile, then change your attire, take some breakfast. Call on him afterward. But do *not* tell him all you have told me. Bishop Aylmer only needs to know that the Warrant of Execution was carried out yesterday. That Mary Stuart is dead and in her coffin. That Lord Talbot is gone to Greenwich to inform the Queen this morning. If he presses you for more details than this, Robert, say you are not authorised, commend him to me."

"And what should the bishop do, then?"

"Say to him this. The Council wishes him to proclaim the great news, ring the church bells of London, in celebration. The people should know, and soon. Better that we announce it to them, than they hear of it through the spreading of rumours."

Beale dragged himself to his feet, reluctant to leave the fireside. Then, touching the buttons of his doublet, he remembered.

"Oh, there was one other matter. I should have mentioned it before, perhaps." Reaching inside his doublet he drew out a rather crumpled document. "We searched her apartments of course, as you instructed. There was nothing. But Paulet found this item on her person, sewn into that red petticoat no less."

Beale handed the paper over. Walsingham unfolded it carefully.

"Paulet and I, we could make nothing of it. Meaningless words and numbers, My Lord Shrewsbury seemed keen to take possession of it, but I told him I was instructed to take any papers we found to you directly. I said that you would know what to do with such a puzzle."

A single nod from his host. "You did the right thing, Robert."

LATER THAT MORNING, a Friday, the bells of London began their ringing. Their discordant madrigal penetrated the depths of Walsingham's house. It seemed that the bellmen at the Fen Church and those at St Dunstan's in the East were trying to outdo one another. Soon their song was joined, from just across the street, by St Olave's solemn peal. From church tower to church tower, the news was spreading through the city's streets. Like water from a bucket, running along the mortar channels in a brick floor. The Scottish Queen is dead, the bells said.

Walsingham hobbled away from his paper-strewn desk and sat by his study window that overlooked St Olave's churchyard. Trying to ignore the spasms in his gut by fixing his mind on the rhythm of the bells. But moments later, he was bent over almost double, his face creased up. He cursed out loud at the floorboards beneath his feet. After a time, the stabs of pain receded and he leant back in the chair, breathing hard through his mouth. He reached for a small glass on the side table, swallowing the contents in one gulp. He waited for the potion to take effect. The pains still came back, but less sharply this time. Finally, mercifully, they subsided, and he was able to move around freely. There was a knock at the door and Ursula came into the room.

"Will I see you at dinner, Francis?" He noted the sound of resignation in her voice.

"I will try, my dear."

"Can the affairs of state not wait for just one day? Remember Doctor Baily's instructions, that you should have as much rest as possible."

"Physicians," muttered Walsingham.

"Then do it for me, as your wife."

He knew that Ursula could be as strong-willed as he, when the circumstances required. "My dear," he gestured towards the desk, "this cannot be deferred. But I will endeavour to finish directly."

Ursula's gaze moved to the empty phial on the side table by the window.

"You know I do not like you to take so much of the opiates."

Walsingham held her reproving gaze. "I have been in some discomfort, my dear," he said, dragging his fingertips across his forehead. In truth, the pain had been excruciating, even the simple act of passing water was beyond him this morning, but that information he kept from her. Ursula had more than enough to deal with at present.

"All the more reason to rest."

"Perhaps so. Once I have put certain matters in hand, we can all go down to Barn Elms for a few days." Walsingham smiled at his wife, but she did not respond in kind. He could tell that she was not fooled. The prospect of a few peaceful days in their Putney home was, they both knew, some way off.

"We will have to see how Frances fares in the coming days."

"How is she this morning?" He was almost afraid to ask.

Ursula looked askance at him, her voice rising with frustration. "How should any young woman be, first losing her husband, and then the child she was carrying? Go upstairs and speak to her yourself."

Reproached, he raised himself from the desk and reached out to touch her sleeve. She retreated inches out of his reach, and stood still, half-facing the door. He slumped back down in the chair, defeated by it all. When he next looked up at his wife, her face had crumpled, tears running down her cheeks.

She looked at him. "Forgive me husband, I do not mean to speak harshly, but..." She could not finish the sentence. Walsingham stood up and this time, took her in his arms. He held her tight, trying to quell the shudders running through her body. As she cried openly, he wondered at the way Providence appeared to have deserted them, at this of all times.

First, the news had come of Sir Philip's death, after an apparently minor wound in the fighting at Zutphen. Their daughter had returned from the Netherlands, immobilised by grief. They feared for Frances' health and that of the baby she was carrying. And with reason, for some weeks later the child, a little girl, was born dead. And now, to add another burden to their distress, it turned out that their son-in-law's estate was vastly in debt, debts for which Walsingham had agreed to stand surety. It was all too much, too quickly. Feeling the weight of Ursula's pain, Walsingham confessed to himself that, with all that pressed on him and his family, he had taken refuge in his work. It occurred to him as he held her, that his wife had no such diversion.

When Ursula gently released herself from his embrace, he glanced at the desk. For a moment, he felt pulled in two directions. But she was right, as always. Mary Stuart would plot no more. Addressing the aftermath of her execution could wait, at least for the moment.

"Let us go together and sit with Frances," he said, guiding Ursula towards the study door.

HUSBAND AND WIFE sat at their dining table. Neither had any appetite. Walsingham idly fiddled with his spoon. Ursula broke the silence. "So, have you heard how the Queen responded to the news?"

"First reports are that she screamed at Talbot and then at Burghley. But you know how changeable she can be. Here was a decision she had put off for years. And now she finds she cannot reverse it."

"Best then that the Council remains united, steadfast."

Walsingham did not reply, but she persisted.

"And our citizens? How have Londoners reacted; do you know?"

"Oh, judging from my first reports they have received the news well. Rowdily for sure, some looting and damage here and there, but their hearts are with their Queen."

"Thank heaven for it. If the commoners' response was otherwise, no doubt she would blame *you* for stirring up riot and rebellion."

"That is what I am *for*, my dear. That is my employment. To undertake the tasks that she would not, to take the blame where she *could* not."

Ursula did not laugh.

That afternoon, Walsingham returned to his study. He went to the document that Robert Beale had retrieved from Mary Stuart's petticoat. After nearly an hour trying to read the coded message, he admitted defeat. Doubtless it was a Spanish cipher and there was only one man in London who might be able to break it. He summoned his manservant.

"Tobias, go to St Andrew Undershaft. A fellow called Thomas Phelippes lives there, above the Golden Cockerel. Just by the entrance to Leadenhall Market. Tell him I would be grateful for his attending me here." The servant turned to go. "This evening, Tobias," Walsingham added, unnecessarily.

Chapter Two

THE MERCHANTS' LOGGIA, PIAZZA BANCHI, GENOA: TEN MONTHS EARLIER

Nico Castello thought he had made himself clear. Not clear enough, it seemed.

Jan Huysmans frowned, shading those cool Northern eyes. "You know I'm good for the money."

He shook his head. "That's not in question, Signore."

"What then? You've loaned me similar amounts before. And look at these." Huysmans passed over the pouch with its sample of peppercorn. "No doubt about the quality."

He didn't need to look at the contents. "Yes, but the price is too high."

"Are you telling me my business, Signore Castello?"

"I'm just saying what I'm prepared to risk in it. That's *my* business."

Huysmans closed his fingers in a fist and flexed them outwards. "So," he said, after a pause, "what's your best offer?"

"I can do it at four hundred ducats. Not a lira more, though."

The merchant blew air out of his cheeks. "At that price, my seller will walk away."

"I suggest you see if he does."

Huysmans tilted his head to the side. "Do you know something I don't?"

"I just believe you'll struggle to make a decent turn on his asking price."

His client muttered under his breath and grabbed the pouch, raising it off the table. But he didn't stand up. He turned his head and looked out towards the market stalls in the Piazza Banchi. "So, if I can get it at four hundred, you'll give me the *cambio*?" Still holding the pouch in mid-air.

"Surely."

Huysmans pushed his chair back. "Give me an hour."

HUYSMANS DIDN'T NEED AN HOUR. When he returned, his expression told Nico that the offer had been agreed. While Nico's clerk, Mazzini, recorded the credit in a leather-bound ledger, Nico chatted with his client. Once the paperwork was in order and Huysmans had signed the *cambio*, Mazzini handed a short note to young Lorenzo, the straw-haired boy standing next to the *banca*. Lorenzo stepped out between the stone columns fronting the Loggia, onto the pediment. He cleared his throat and, like a choirboy at Mass, intoned what was written on the note, to the onlookers in the piazza.

"In the year of Our Lord fifteen eighty-six, on the fifteenth day of April at Genova, Jan Huysmans promises to pay four hundred ducats, at two ducats to the Flemish guilder, to whomsoever is nominated in Antwerp by Domenico Castello and Partners. Payment to be made no later than the fourteenth day of July of this same year. May Christ the Saviour be your Protector."

Nico watched Mazzini counting gold coins into a leather pouch and with a bow, presenting it to Huysmans. As his client walked off to pay the pepper merchant, he reflected on what he had told, or rather not told, the Dutchman. *What do you know that we merchants don't?* Well, like Huysmans, Nico knew the recent selling price of pepper in the Antwerp market. It would have been a decent profit at those prices. But unlike his client, he also knew that Huysmans' seller was in a hurry. And for good reason. By next month at the latest, prices would surely fall, pushed downwards by the sheer volume of cargo coming from the East. Even if a couple of Portuguese boats failed to make it, the result would be the same. Huysmans would be grateful to him when the time came. Not that he expected thanks for being good at his profession. Huysmans' gratitude would be expressed by repayment in full, on the due date. And by entrusting Nico with more of his business next time.

It was after midday. Business in the Loggia was slowing down. He signalled to his clerk that it was time to close. Young Lorenzo, with a show of military precision, folded up the cloth which covered the *banca*. The cloth was adorned with the bank's emblem, like a heraldic design. The Cross of St. George on the chief and below it, three castellated towers in chevron formation. Like three columns of silver coins on a blue tablecloth. The castle towers were a reminder of Nico's family name of course, but the image also suggested the dependability of the bank.

The market crowds were thinning as Nico crossed the piazza, followed by his small team. Mazzini carrying the weighty ledgers; Lorenzo, his young arms stretched around the abacus; and Nico's two guards, Luca and Marco, bearing the bullion chest between them. Lighter now by four hundred ducats. The small column turned out of the piazza and headed up Vico dell'Amor Perfetto.

By this narrow, shaded street, which Nico took every day, you could walk from the Loggia on Banchi to his house on Strada Nuova, from buzzing marketplace to gracious residential street, in less than a quarter of an hour. But in between, you passed through one of the city's less reputable districts. The buildings along Amor Perfetto, a street named by someone with a dry wit, housed many of the city's brothels. In the shady *carrugis* leading off it, whores openly offered their services to the passers-by.

As the troupe reached Vicolo Salute, the steepening gradient slowed them down. Two women emerged from a corner house. One of them called out suggestively, commenting on the muscles on Nico's guards. The whores would have known that Nico himself was no prospect as a customer. Not that he took a moral view of their trade. For all the Church's railing against the sins of the flesh, fornication was just part of human nature, was it not? Looking embarrassed, Marco was about to wave the two women away, but Nico laid a hand on the young guard's raised arm. Drawing a few coins from his purse, Nico handed them over to the nearer of the two. His reward was the look in her face, and then a slight bow of the head as she pocketed the dole. "Not every time, mind," he said, moving on. Marco, knowing otherwise, exchanged glances with Luca.

Many of his fellow bankers would return to their residences by carriage, even though it meant a circuitous route, along Via San Luca and circling around San Siro. They would say that Amor Perfetto was not wide enough for their horses. True perhaps: but Nico sensed the real reason. Rather than have desperate humanity pricking their consciences, most of them preferred to look the other way. But then they, and their forefathers, had always been wealthy men, unlike himself. He always felt some unspoken need to acknowledge that, against the odds, Providence had favoured him. And he knew the people of these streets, the base of the city's pyramid, even if he had climbed far above them. That didn't mean taking unnecessary risks, of course: Luca and Marco always went heavily armed, as did Nico himself.

As they crossed Via Maddalena, the scene slowly changed. The higher you went, the more respectable the residents. Finally, they turned right into Strada Nuova. Marco and Luca paused, puffing and blowing as they put down the currency chest for a moment. After the dank smells and grubby tenements a few streets below, the air up here was almost sweet. This broad avenue represented the present boundary of the city's expansion inland, as it crept towards the hills above Genova. Between the great houses, you could catch glimpses of the orange groves above them, newly in blossom. Nico's own property, acquired just two years earlier, was at the eastern end of the street.

HAVING ASSIGNED them their duties for the afternoon, Nico left his team in the lobby and headed upstairs to the *piano nobile*. He entered the *salotto*, the smaller room where he dined when not entertaining family or guests. Two places were set for the meal, as usual. But, just as usually, his brother Sandro was late.

Nico had long since ceased to look to his brother for a major contribution towards running Banco Castello. Their father, Vittorio, had no doubt known, when the time came to hand over his business to his two sons, that the younger one had no talent for work, only for enjoying himself. Sandro seemed content to sit back and watch as Nico turned their father's silversmith business, with its sideline in small credit transactions, into a fully-fledged merchant finance house. But traditionalist that he was, Vittorio had been unwilling to endow Nico with sole ownership. Even so, rare was the morning when Sandro took a turn in the chair at their *banca*. If he turned up at all, he would stand around and make jokes with the customers. And when he wasn't down at the

Loggia, he spent his time carousing with the younger members of the Doria clan.

The demon whispering in Nico's ear told him that his brother was being indulged. It scarcely helped that God had seen fit to distribute fairness of features between them in unequal shares. Both were striking men in their way and Nico was a hand's breadth taller than his brother, but Sandro was notably handsome. And he had a full head of dark, curly hair, whereas Nico's was already receding from his temples. At the same time, the angel talking into his other ear reminded Nico that work was, for him, easier than social intercourse whereas for Sandro the opposite was true.

Nico was eight years older than his brother and, in the days when he had been a sturdily built youth and Sandro a little boy in need of his brother's protection, Nico would never hesitate to defend him against all comers. That was the way it had been, the Castello boys against the rest of the world: the priests at San Giovanni who taught them; the other boys in their school; or the older street ruffians who claimed that the district of Pre was their fiefdom. The Castellos were immigrants from Bergamo, here in Genova under sufferance, and the people of Pre were not going to let them forget it. Now, fifteen years on, things were rather different. Over the years, the ordinary people of Genova had gradually taken to the Castellos. In the Piazza Banchi, Nico was known, though not to his face, as *"the Alchemist"*, the man who had turned the base metal of his humble origins into the gold of a respected banking business, with a grand house on Strada Nuova to match. The envy of the lower orders, which usually attached itself to the conspicuous wealth of the merchant families, somehow had not followed him, perhaps because people felt that underneath, the Castellos were not so different from themselves. The reverse of that coin though, was that the old banking families, the Grimaldis, say, or the Pallavicinos, were inherently suspicious of the Castellos' success and made a point, when conversing with friends and neighbours, of bemoaning their limited social connections.

Nico was half-way through his main course, when Sandro appeared. A healthy glow on his features and a hint of perspiration. A morning spent outdoors.

"Well, you are here finally. I said we should review the accounts this afternoon?" was Nico's opening gambit.

"Don't recall," said Sandro, grinning. "Why not ask me how my morning went?"

"Well, since you weren't down at the Loggia, I hope it was a profitable one in other ways?"

"I'm sure my presence isn't necessary. Any more than yours. Why do you pay our clerk so much, if you can't trust him to do business without you?"

"I *do* trust Mazzini actually, but he's not ready to manage without my being present," said Nico. "Besides, if a prospective customer turns up, I want to see him face to face."

"But you could set limits for Mazzini's discretion. If a customer presses for better terms, he could always refer to you. The Grimaldis' manager conducts their business in the Loggia: why not us?"

"The Grimaldis' business has many facets, not just the exchanges they make in the Loggia. For us though, what goes on down there represents our entire livelihood. I just believe that our authority and presence are necessary to protect it. No banking business ever succeeded with absentee owners."

This was an argument the brothers had had before and would have again. Plates of cold meat, cheeses and olives were brought in, and Sandro started wolfing the spread down hungrily. They continued their meal in silence, until he returned to Nico's earlier question.

"Well, I was out riding with the Lomellinos and..." he paused, noticing Nico's expression. "But this is business, dear brother, as much as pleasure. The Governor's son was invited too. After all, we need to build good relations with his family. No doubt *some* of our neighbours would try to discredit us with the Dorias behind our backs." Sandro tilted his head in the general direction of the Grimaldi residence. "If they got the chance."

Nico admitted - to himself - that the business of diplomacy was probably better suited to Sandro's particular skills. His easy charm and good looks tended to open doors.

"Anyway, Giovanni Doria told me that his father was with the Spanish ambassador for several hours yesterday. There are rumours that the Spanish are preparing an armada to attack England."

Nico had heard the self-same story circulating in the Banco di San Giorgio that morning. He speared a piece of fruit, then responded: "Let's hope they stay that way, Sandro, rumours only. Wars aren't good for business. At least, not if they last too long."

"Don't worry on that score. Apparently, the ambassador expects it to be a short, sharp campaign. If the Spanish land an army there in numbers, what can the English really do? It's like a wasp attacking a bull."

Nico smiled at Sandro's quip. "I don't *worry*, I merely weigh up the bank's best interests. But, if I were Governor Doria," Nico placed his hand over Sandro's, stopping the loaded fork mid-way to his brother's waiting mouth, "I wouldn't be so sure of the outcome. Don't underestimate the wasp. If it stings hard enough, the bull will run off."

Chapter Three

CARICAMENTO, GENOA: LATER THE SAME DAY

As she walked, the young woman looked along the avenue to her destination. The sun, sinking on the western horizon, made the stucco walls of the Banco di San Giorgio shimmer with light. Amidst the mass of rigging and masts, the banking house was like a signal beacon seen through bare trees. It was a fair walk from her home to the bank and Lisa was impatient to get there. Feeling constrained by her skirts, she gathered up the folds of material in her fingers. As she lengthened her stride, she left her maid Maria trailing in her wake.

Caricamento, that crescent-shaped thoroughfare which divided the port from the city, was bustling on that spring evening. Horsemen rode by, sometimes a carriage. Families were out walking, taking their ritual *passeggiata*. Some of them knew Lisa Della Volta personally and greeted her. Other couples glanced as she strode past in the opposite direction: the husbands covertly admiring her face and figure, their wives, noticing the discreet glance, tut-tutting at her unseemly haste. Fifteen feet below the promenade, between the arches of Sottoripa, Genova's traders plied their wares. Fruit and vegetables, leather and cloth, the cries of the street-sellers, and the flutter of pigeons as they scoured the market debris.

But Lisa paid no attention to the sights and sounds around her that afternoon. Her mind was focused on one man: her father. She clutched the brief message she had received, asking her to attend at the bank. She had been foolish to worry about the length of time since his last letter.

The mail from New Spain could take many months. Besides, he would have been travelling great distances between stops, on that far-off coast.

Cristoforo Della Volta had left Genova, nearly a year ago, in a galley bound for Cádiz. There, he had transferred to a Spanish carrack, which took him across the Western Ocean to New Spain and the Vice-Royalty of Peru. The parting of father and daughter at the quayside had been full of tears. Her mother, Anna, had died when Lisa was just four and thereafter, she was anxious whenever he left the city. Even now at eighteen - and still unmarried, unlike many of her contemporaries from the convent school - she still felt his absence keenly. Her father argued that he often travelled on the bank's business, but even he could see her point. This journey was of quite another dimension from his occasional visits to other Italian cities or even Madrid. To try and soften the blow, he reminded her of the significance of his mission. Appointed *prottetore*, he would report to the treasurer of the San Giorgio on the silver wealth of the Spanish Empire. She was proud of his important role, but it did not alter her feelings of abandonment.

Given the inevitable length of his absence, Della Volta arranged for his widowed sister, Julia, to travel up from Livorno and stay with Lisa in the family home. Julia's late husband had bequeathed his wife a house in the centre of the city, but also the lease of a waterfront property in Livorno which, so far as Aunt Julia was concerned, was vastly to be preferred. She obviously regarded her brother-in-law's Caricamento residence as being inadequate compared with the comforts she enjoyed there. Lisa was less than enamoured with her temporary guardian. Julia was far less tolerant of her niece's spirited independence, and made it clear that in her opinion, Lisa had been seriously indulged by her father. Lisa spent her time devising ways to circumvent the restrictions on her movements imposed by Julia. She knew that she should have shared the message from the bank with her aunt, but decided to escape the house before Julia could ask where she was going. She took Maria as her escort, to provide some sort of excuse for the unannounced departure.

As she walked, she recalled her father's last letter, written from the Panama coast. She had read it so many times that she could almost recite the contents. He described the region so well, the sticky heat, the sudden storms of the jungle interior, the tedium of travelling alongside the mule trains as they hauled their silver burdens towards some outpost of King Felipe's Empire. His letter included two small sketches of star clusters which were unfamiliar to her. Cristoforo took a keen interest in the heavens, the celestial not the spiritual kind, and had taught Lisa to know her constellations. Some of his enthusiasm had migrated to his daughter.

But most significant from her point of view, his letter had concluded with the fervent hope that the ardours of this voyage would merit a substantial bonus from the bank's grateful shareholders. And that would mean that Lisa's dowry was secured: a good marriage could thus be made. He had no wish to see his only, much-missed, daughter enter the convent as a novice. May it be so, she had said to herself.

LISA ARRIVED in front of the banking house and paused again, to allow the wheezing Maria to catch her breath. She could feel a soft breeze from the sea cooling the beads of perspiration around the nape of her neck. She looked up at the frescoes on the bank's frontage, gleaming in the late sunlight. Saint George on his white horse, fearlessly spearing the dragon. As a four-year-old child, Lisa had allowed herself to believe that the hero thus depicted was a likeness of her father. The first time she had said this, Cristoforo had laughed loudly - until he saw her pained expression and picked her up in his arms and kissed her. How many evenings would Lisa's nursemaid, or in the early days her late mother, walk with young Lisa along Caricamento and down to the Bank to meet him at the end of his day's work? If her mother came too, the return journey was always a jostling for position to hold Papa's hand. Her parents played a game of shutting her out, but Lisa was persistent and eventually her tiny fingers were encased in his grip, which to her felt all-powerful and reassuring.

The vision faded and Lisa stepped inside the doorway, followed by Maria. There was always a small crowd at the entrance to the San Giorgio, but the group of guards noticed her. A woman visitor to the Bank, never mind a young and beautiful one, was a rarity. She ignored their stares and looked around for Carlo, her father's old retainer. He would have recognised her immediately, but it seemed he was not at the Bank today. After a few moments, one of the group of guards, a young fellow with dark curls, approached her and gave a curt bow.

"Lisa Della Volta," she began, almost swallowing her words, "to see Treasurer Saluzzo." The guard knew the family name, of course. Signore Della Volta was a deputy treasurer of the bank. But rules were rules; he fumbled with the register to check Saluzzo's appointments, whilst Lisa fanned herself. "Please hurry."

Nodding, he shut the book and escorted Lisa and her maid up the marble staircase to the first floor. He deposited them in a dimly lit anteroom outside Saluzzo's office. After a few minutes, which seemed much longer to Lisa, Saluzzo himself came out from his office and greeted her, somewhat showily she felt. Motioning to Maria to wait for her, Lisa walked through the double doors. She had met the Chief Treasurer just twice before but was instinctively suspicious of his charm. The setting sun was streaming in through his office windows and Lisa had to shield her eyes, after the gloom of the anteroom. Saluzzo walked back behind his desk and motioned to her to sit down, but Lisa was already talking before she reached the chair.

"I was *so* thankful to receive your message, Signore Saluzzo. It has been many months since I last heard from Papa. I was beginning to …"

Lisa saw his eyes briefly shift to his left as she spoke. She followed his glance to the corner of the room, her eyes adjusting to the light. To her surprise, Saluzzo already had another visitor, a priest.

The visitor rose from his chair and stepped towards her. In a reflexive movement, Lisa curtsied. The priest stretched out his bony right hand and motioned her to rise. Puzzled by his presence, Lisa looked questioningly at Saluzzo as she took the chair next to him.

"This is Father Guido, who has come from the cathedral," Saluzzo said, though without elaborating further. "Tell me, Signorina, when did you last hear from your father?"

"I… had a letter from him, sent from a port called Nombre de Dios, but that was several months ago."

"Indeed yes, we understand he left there and sailed to Cartagena. That was where he was residing when…"

"When…what, Signore?"

Saluzzo's fingers were toying with the small badge of office pinned to his doublet. "I am afraid…that is, we have received a report from our Ambassador in Spain. It seems that …Cartagena was attacked two months ago." Lisa could feel her body stiffen; her hands gripped the arms of the chair. "A flotilla, led by that English pirate that the Spanish call *'the Dragon'*, sailed in at dawn. The English took the city in a single day. There was a … terrible cannonade before it was taken. The Governor's mansion was badly hit. That was… where your father was staying."

Saluzzo looked uncomfortable, seeing those golden-brown eyes glowering at him. He started talking more rapidly. "One cannon shot landed on his quarters. It must have been over in moments. He cannot have felt any pain..."

But already, Lisa was not listening. She stared out of the window to the sea beyond the harbour. The setting sun glared back at her. Nothing came. No tears. She shut her eyes and breathed out slowly through her mouth.

Saluzzo's ingratiating voice re-entered her consciousness. "Be assured Signorina, the Bank will do everything we can to assist the family. Cristoforo Della Volta's memory will be honoured by this institution."

Lisa looked blank. She had never much concerned herself with her father's business affairs - or the family finances for that matter.

Catching her expression, Father Guido intervened. "With respect, Signore," he said, glancing at Saluzzo, "I think it is a little early for Signorina Della Volta to be discussing such things. She needs time: time to grieve for her father - and to pray for his immortal soul."

Lisa stared at the priest's gaunt face, finally registering the possible meaning of his last comment. "Did he not receive absolution?" she exclaimed.

His hollow cheeks forced themselves into an awkward smile. "There would have been no time, my child. But God is all-seeing. Your father died a true martyr, killed in the honourable battle against these... heretics. Why, their guns even destroyed the newly built cathedral!"

Lisa did not appear to react and deciding to leave his religious zeal for another time, Father Guido took her tightly clenched fist in both hands. "My child, your father will find his true place in heaven among the Saints." Lisa gazed deeply into the priest's face, seeking answers. "Come with me, Lisa. We will pray together. The true faith will be your great comfort in this dark hour."

At first, Lisa did not move, and the priest squeezed her knuckles gently. She slowly stood up. Leaning heavily on his arm, and with a mere nod of farewell towards the mute Saluzzo, she allowed herself to be led by the priest out of the room and down the marble staircase. Maria followed them down the steps, terrified at her mistress' distressed state. When they reached the bottom, Father Guido turned and dismissed the maid with a few whispered words. Taken aback by the force of his expression, Maria reluctantly trudged homewards alone.

It was not far from the Bank to San Lorenzo Cathedral, perhaps four hundred paces, but Lisa had no sense of time or distance as she and the priest walked through the narrow, ascending streets and alleys. The pair arrived at the church's west door as the twilight finally faded. Once inside, he guided her to a side chapel to the right of the Choir. Lisa kneeled and he led her in prayers. After some time, he paused and stood back, considering the young woman as she repeated the time-honoured phrases over and over. Her eyes were firmly closed as if the light was bright

Finally, their prayers of intercession were concluded. he touched her elbow, motioning her to stand.

"Tell me Lisa, is there anyone with you at your father's house?"

"Oh, yes," she said, as if only now remembering, "my Aunt Julia has been staying with me."

"Then I would like to meet the lady. I will escort you home and you can introduce me."

Father Guido crossed the aisle, with a bow towards the altar, and opened an unremarkable door in the north-west corner of the cathedral. Beyond it, a flight of stone steps led down, not to the crypt, but to a narrow passageway wide enough for one man. It passed anonymously under the street which flanked the cathedral's northern side and arrived at another set of steps which led up to a corner of the courtyard adjoining the archbishop's palazzo. At the opposite corner of the courtyard was an ornate oak door. He rapped on the iron knocker and was admitted by one of the archbishop's servants.

The Coadjutor Bishop, Antonmaria Sauli, was halfway through his mid-day meal. He was sitting alone at the centre of a table in the archbishop's dining room which, without asking anyone's approval, he had assumed during the archbishop's recent illness. A large man, Sauli was in his mid-forties but looked older, with his puffy eyes and several chins - which the collar of his richly embroidered surplice failed to disguise. Father Guido apologized for the intrusion, but the bishop waved his free hand, as if directing him to be brief.

"Your Grace, regarding the Della Volta girl, I met her last night at the San Giorgio, as arranged."

Sauli merely prodded his food with his fork.

"Needless to say, she was distressed by the news of her father. After prayers at San Lorenzo, I escorted her back to the family residence. I met her aunt, Julia Della Volta there. She is Signorina Lisa's closest surviving relative."

"Did you manage to learn anything from her?"

"The girl wished to go to her room, so I had the chance of a private word. According to the lady Julia, the estate will be very small. The property is merely leased, but it has about twenty years to run. Otherwise, very little apart from his personal effects - and whatever honorarium the San Giorgio may decide to award the family."

"And her relationship with her niece?"

"I already had the impression from the girl that she and her aunt are not on the closest terms. As for the aunt, she appeared somewhat put out by the inconvenience."

"No doubt she is less than overjoyed at the prospect of having to maintain her niece."

"Yes. She suggested the signorina might enter the convent. I had the impression that would not be the girl's wish."

"Which is why my plan is to be preferred." Sauli's self-congratulatory tone indicated to Father Guido that it was best merely to listen.

"Signorina Lisa will marry - as soon as it can be arranged. And, in the meantime, you will stay close to her, be her constant adviser. Tell her aunt that, at this delicate time, she should see no visitors, saving yourself. Once you have become her principal support, we can approach the gentleman I have in mind with the marriage proposal."

He took a sip of his fine Montalcino wine from a jewelled goblet. He continued reflectively, "So the estate is small..."

"Indeed. But then, the girl is fair of face. Exceptionally so, I would venture."

Sauli looked at his wine glass, wondering how much weight to attach to the priest's opinion on female pulchritude. "That may be enough."

"May I know the intended husband?"

"I expect you to keep this information in confidence. We intend that the girl should be married to Domenico Castello."

Father Guido kept his facial expression impassive, as he considered the idea that Sauli had just imparted. The Della Volta family, while of honourable descent, had fallen on leaner times whereas the Castellos were mere immigrants from Bergamo, but were rapidly becoming one of the wealthier families in the city. "A prestigious union indeed, Your Grace. No doubt Signore Castello will wish for sons to continue the family line."

"No doubt he will, but our main interest is that Signore Castello and his kinsmen should be better friends of the Church than in the past. The Della Voltas are loyal members of our congregation, and they will help bring him into the fold."

Guido would have liked to continue the discussion, but the bishop did not seem in the mood to converse. Further questions would have to await the time when Bishop Sauli wanted to progress his plan to the next stage.

After a few moments' silence, he raised another issue.

"And what news of Archbishop Pallavicino? Has the fever eased at all?"

Sauli paused before responding, as if struggling to call to mind a piece of news that he had heard in some unremembered place. Eventually, he raised his shoulders in a shrug. "He is no better. I fear that His Grace has but a few days remaining in this mortal world." The bishop's words were solemn, but the voice betrayed no distress at the prospect of his superior's likely demise.

Father Guido instinctively crossed himself. The bishop copied the priest's gesture perfunctorily and returned to his wine. Taking the hint, Guido bowed and departed.

Chapter Four

CATTEDRALE DI SAN LORENZO, GENOA:
THREE WEEKS LATER

Nico didn't make a habit of being on intimate terms with the clergy. "God is everywhere, son, not just in church," Vittorio had once said to him, when his father found the eight-year-old Nico out in a lie. Nico attended Mass on Sundays – and made regular donations of a size fitting to a man of property – but that was the limit of his present involvement. So, a written invitation from a priest called Father Guido, apparently one of the senior clerics at the cathedral, to discuss a confidential matter left him wondering what they would have to discuss. No doubt a donation for the altar fund or some such.

But it was imprudent to refuse, so one Friday morning he found himself being admitted to the archbishop's palazzo close by San Lorenzo and escorted to an anteroom, where his host was waiting.

Father Guido didn't have the well-fed appearance of the priests who conducted Mass when Nico was in attendance. Although his face was unlined, his hair had turned grey, prematurely it seemed. His features were gaunt and his slight, almost skeletal, frame contrasted oddly with his deep, sonorous voice. Nico wasn't one for small talk, so it was a relief to find that Father Guido wanted to get to the point straight away.

"I asked you to be kind enough to attend me here because I wanted to discuss something of an intimate nature."

"Of course."

"That's to say, the prospect of a marriage contract."

"Between...?"

"Ah, I mean for *yourself*, naturally."

Nico let out something between a laugh and a cough, failing to cover his surprise. He had always said, if anyone was peremptory enough to ask, that he was too busy to find a wife. In truth, he knew he was neither well-born, nor especially handsome, and while he was not closed to the idea of marriage, the bank and his desire to build it into a major force in the city, had long ago taken precedence.

"Permit me to explain. The Coadjutor Bishop has taken a young lady, one Signorina Della Volta, under his shielding wing. The girl's mother died many years ago. Her daughter – still unmarried - has attained eighteen years. And now she has been orphaned after the untimely death overseas of her father, Signore Cristoforo."

As the priest paused, Nico recalled where he had once met the girl's father. That was at the Banco di San Giorgio, where Cristoforo Della Volta was a deputy treasurer. That was over a year ago. And now he remembered that the San Giorgio had subsequently sent the man on some mission or other to New Spain. That hadn't turned out so well, obviously.

"Bishop Sauli is of the view," Father Guido continued, "that the young lady should at least have the opportunity for matrimony. Unfortunately, ah, the dowry is not large, but her family is after all, distinguished. So, the bishop felt that, with you being one of the city's leading *merchants* but without ah, heirs as yet, it might be opportune for you to consider an alliance with her family?"

Nico half-listened as the priest extolled the eminence of the Della Volta clan. They were one of the *Alberghi*, he recalled, those old families that had been designated by Andrea Doria many years before as constituting the city's ruling class. Much as Nico resented the way people attached such importance to rank, he could see the advantages of such a marriage. No money there, perhaps, but an unimpeachable name. The bank would certainly benefit from the connection. Whereas if he had sought an alliance with, say, a daughter of one of the wealthy merchant dynasties, people would always whisper that he had married his fortune, rather than making it for himself. And finally, this young woman was effectively under the guardianship of Bishop Sauli. The man was surely on the threshold of assuming Archbishop Pallavicino's mantle, since it was rumoured that the incumbent was not long for this world. No need to antagonize the bishop, therefore. He could at least consent to a meeting with the family, even if it came to nothing.

And so it was that, a week later, Nico found himself back in the archbishop's palazzo with Father Guido. On entry to the meeting room, Nico saw that the priest was not alone. Nico had been informed ahead of time that he was to meet the young girl's aunt, her closest surviving relative. The lady was seated beneath a window, a dark outline against a lit background. But as Father Guido turned to introduce her, she rose and lifted the veil back from her face. Brushing past the priest, and then stopping in front of him, she made a perfunctory curtsey in the general direction of Nico.

"Julia Visconti, Signore Castello. Visconti is of course my late husband's name. But I am a Della Volta," she added in an imperious tone, implying that that explained everything that needed to be said. "Lisa's poor father was my older brother."

Nico bowed deeply. "My sympathies for your loss, Signora," he said, not delineating whether he referred to husband or brother.

Signora Visconti was a lady of early middle years and, in so far as Nico was any judge, rather overdressed. By the city gossip, Paolo Visconti had died leaving his youngish widow a moderate fortune, but she was rapidly working her way through it, entertaining lavishly, and was now selling off his prized horses.

The aunt took another chair closer to Nico and settled herself into a pose, topped by a glued-on smile. She sat playing with her fan, from time-to-time correcting Father Guido on minor details of her niece's short life and looking along her aquiline nose at Nico. Supposedly, she was at the meeting to protect young Lisa's interests, but Nico sensed that the lady had but one thing on her mind – his money - and what the marriage might mean for both women. No doubt she had already considered the prospect of her niece leaving the embarrassingly modest Della Volta house on Caricamento and moving into Casa Castello.

"Not as grand as those on Strada Nuova perhaps, but it's a good house," she was saying, "with four floors, overlooking the harbour. You would easily be able to sell the lease, if you were so inclined, Signore."

The Della Voltas had once held sway from a grand palazzo on Piazza Cattaneo, in the old city, but years before had lost much of their fortune after a collapse in alum prices. Cristoforo Della Volta had been forced to take this waterfront house at the northern end of Caricamento, embarrassingly close to the border with Pre district. In effect, the lease of the property was the Signorina's dowry. But to Nico, who had made his own wealth, the dowry was of limited importance. And, as brother Sandro would no doubt say, a union such as this would help propel the Castellos into the higher echelons of the Republic.

After more praise had been heaped on the young orphan by both the aunt and the priest alike, and Signora Visconti had made some half-hearted enquiries about Nico's own family – he sensed the shudder in her shoulders when he mentioned his father's humble trade – the conversation started to peter out. Finally, Father Guido brought the discussion to a head. "Signore, signora, may I summon the notary so that we can draw up the *sponsalia*?"

Signora Visconti signified her agreement, a trace too quickly, with a thin smile in Nico's direction. But Nico raised his eyebrows a fraction. "I would first like to meet the young signorina. We have yet to be introduced, after all."

The lady blinked, apparently surprised by his request. Nico knew that often the practice was for the contract of marriage to be drawn up long before the couple had even seen one another across a room, much less been introduced. But, after a confirmatory glance towards the priest, it seemed that Aunt Julia was not about to quibble.

"Very well, Signore Castello. I suggest we all meet at my house, Casa Visconti. Shall we say, Saturday at noon?"

"But what if she's as ugly as sin?" Nico asked his brother, while preparing to leave.

Sandro, who was helping Nico on with his doublet and making sure that the shoulders were well smoothed down, stayed concentrated on his task. "Then you'll be well suited, won't you?"

"Alright, no doubt I asked for that, but…I mean: how will I *know*? No use going to father and asking him. He always says women are a mystery."

"Ah, so you're asking me, an unmarried man?"

"I didn't like the aunt much…"

"You're not marrying the aunt." Sandro stood back to admire his handiwork with his brother's attire. "And this is the man who unerringly knows when he can trust a customer with credit. What's happened to that instinct of yours?"

"Somehow, this is different. Look, why don't you come with me? An extra pair of eyes…."

"Be careful. Might decide to marry her myself."

Casa Visconti, one of several fine houses along Via del Giustiniani in the Old City, was rather like its widowed owner - a bit overdressed for Nico's taste. Remodelled many times, castellations on the parapet, niches with classical friezes, columns around the portico intertwined with serpents, it scarcely seemed to know what century it belonged to. Once admitted, the brothers were shown into the *sala principale*, which had a similar fondness for ornate plasterwork. There were some impressive paintings here and there, but Nico noticed one or two areas on the walls where it seemed portraits had previously hung. Beneath one of these blank spaces stood Father Guido, looking rather out of place amidst the finery.

After several minutes' wait, with only Sandro's chatter and the priest's monosyllabic responses puncturing the silence, Julia Visconti entered the room and greeted her three guests, taking in the depth of their bows. "And so, Signore Castello," she said, turning to Nico, "let me introduce my niece." She glanced behind her. "Lisa?" she called to the figure in a simple cream dress, pausing in the doorway.

Nico looked in the same direction. His gaze was met by a pair of wide-set eyes, not dark as he had expected, but almost the colour of burnished gold. And he *knew*.

LISA SAT IN HER BEDROOM, facing her mirror and getting ready for the guests to arrive. Her maid Maria was fussing around her, but she had good-naturedly banished Aunt Julia to the *sala* rather than be forced to listen to yet more instructions on how she should behave. For the first time perhaps, she could approach her aunt on equal terms. After all, by the end of today's festivities she would be an official bride to be, formally engaged to one of the city's leading bankers.

The exchange of faith rings, *the anellamento*, and the vows the pair exchanged with it. The biggest day of her young life thus far. Catering for all these guests and the other necessary expenses had been costly – needing a loan from Aunt Julia – but it was the tradition that it was held at the future bride's home. Signore Castello - she must stop calling him that - Nico had thoughtfully offered to host the ceremony instead, but she had insisted, family pride dictated, that it be held in the house on Caricamento.

To complement her only formal silk dress, she picked out an oval pendant, encrusted with emeralds, which had been Nico's first present to her. Emeralds were intended by the giver to signify chastity and good health, as she well knew, but their soft lustre also seemed the most fitting adornment to the dress, as well as showing off her auburn tresses to best advantage. As she placed it around her neck, she wondered that she and Nico would share the same wine cup, would experience their first kiss and begin to sense the intimacy of husband and wife. Earlier in the week, Aunt Julia had even suggested that, after the exchange of rings, Signore Domenico would be within his rights to expect his future bride to share his bed. But when Lisa consulted with Father Guido on the matter, he indicated that such a view was considered old-fashioned, and that the Signore would surely wait until after the wedding itself.

In any case, Nico had been a somewhat shy wooer. Following the old custom, Nico had deputed his brother Alessandro to deliver the stream of engagement presents that he had bought for Lisa, after the families had signed the *sponsalia*. She recalled the first time that she met her prospective husband at Aunt Julia's house, in the company of his younger brother. As the initial, awkward meeting had progressed, she'd felt a moment of disappointment that it was Nico and not Sandro, with his easy smile and dark, good looks, to whom she was becoming engaged. And then, each time Sandro paid a call to the Della Volta house with another extravagant gift, he was charm and jollity itself. Nico, judging by their brief acquaintance, was of a more sober temperament.

But now she had banished those feelings, ashamed of her own superficiality. Nico was not the most handsome man to some eyes, it was true, but there was something in the way he stood, the way he spoke when addressing her aunt which spoke of his strength, his belief in himself. It was perhaps admiration, rather than attraction she felt, but it was a start, she told her mirror.

And what a start, compared with the fate which had lain in store for her just a few short months ago. Life had closed in on her after that fateful day at the Banco di San Giorgio. Those dismal weeks being bullied by her aunt, punctuated only by the bouts of grief that washed over her, had seemed like a foretaste of what would surely follow. The remainder of her days locked inside nunnery walls, alone and uncomforted. But then, just when all seemed lost, she had been summoned to Father Guido's study.

His news, that a marriage had been arranged for her, had come like a deliverance. Surely the saints were watching over her. And indeed, he had frequently reminded her that it was very much due to the beneficence of the church, and to the newly appointed Archbishop of Genova in particular, that Lisa could look forward to the blessings of matrimony. Not only that, but to a position as the wife of an eminent and wealthy citizen. Wondrous indeed. The only aspect which she had not fully understood, indeed still did not, was his comment that Signore Castello would need her devotion and guidance to become what his elevated situation required of him, a pillar of the Church and the Republic.

But she had been altogether too excited to question the priest's declaration. The fact that she could begin preparing herself for her new station in life, had washed the other thoughts aside. That she would still be living under the watchful eye of Aunt Julia in the meantime, was a small price to pay. Besides, there was an end in sight to that. The sponsalia had been signed by both families. And now, today was the formal engagement in the presence of witnesses. And in just another month, in early July, the wedding itself.

It seemed that even Archbishop Sauli considered the marriage propitious: as a mark of his favour towards Lisa, just yesterday he had sent her a betrothal gift, a copy of Jacopo de Varezze's "Golden Legend". She had placed the book of saints' histories, with its beautiful engravings, on top of the *canterali* in her bedroom.

The sound of Julia calling her from below prompted her out of her reverie. She placed her ruff around her collar. Glancing at her mirror, she decided she was ready.

NICO AND LISA emerged through the great west door of the Cathedral, her arm on his. Despite the uncertain weather, most of Genova had turned out to line the streets. Everyone wanted a glimpse of the pair making their first walk together as a married couple, part of the *domiductio* of ancient tradition.

As they progressed towards Campetto, the men whose workshops populated the nearby alleyways downed tools to stand outside for a moment. In Via Scudai, the craftsmen hammered on the wooden shields hung above their doors, beating in time to the march of the wedding party. Even a few squalls of rain had descended, to bless the couple with good fortune. "*Sposa bagnata, sposa fortunata,*" as some onlookers tritely remarked to their immediate neighbours, gesturing at the skies. The unseasonably wet conditions persisted as the wedding procession wound its way through the streets up to Strada Nuova. As they skirted a puddle, Lisa whispered in Nico's ear: thank goodness for her new zuccoli with their high heels which had kept the hem of her beautiful wedding dress out of harm's way. Nico smiled but didn't say anything in return.

Custom, and Lisa's footwear, dictated that their journey through the city's streets was not a quick one. Apart from the occasional exchange, there was little conversation between them. But, as she reflected, they were effectively strangers. It would take time. For a moment, she wished Nico had his brother's gift for idle chatter.

At last, the procession reached the entrance of Casa Castello. Or Palazzo Castello, she should say. Goodness knows, it was large enough. Nico stretched out his right hand to escort Lisa up the sweeping staircase which led from the courtyard to the principal floor of the house. As she put her hand in his, she could feel her fingers trembling. He squeezed them encouragingly.

As they negotiated their way up the staircase, Lisa tried to concentrate on the wedding breakfast ahead. The grand *festa* in which she would meet all her new relatives and her husband's friends. The event at which she would be the focus of attention and would be expected to lead. In a way, the ceremony at the Cathedral with its high formality, had been the easier ordeal. She looked to her left, across the inner courtyard, at the broad columns which formed its borders and the four storeys of stucco and galleried landings above. This was the house of which she would now be *donna di casa*. Her introspection was brought to an abrupt end as she and Nico entered the *sala*, to the acclamation of over a hundred guests. San Lorenzo's nave aside, it was the largest room she had ever stood in and everyone in it was focusing their attention on her.

It seemed like she had been introduced to the whole of the assembled company, group by small group, before the pair finally sat down for the wedding meal and their guests followed suit. Hers and Nico's chairs were in the centre of the head table, but on her other side, she found herself next to her new father-in-law, Vittorio. Opposite her were Sandro, Aunt Julia and Father Guido.

Once again, there was little chance to converse with Nico without being overheard, and he did not seem especially inclined to talk. It was all quite intimidating, but at least the delicious red wine was calming her nerves. Whenever she reached for her wine cup, for yet another exchange of toasts, it seemed that Sandro had replenished it. Soon she was even laughing with old Vittorio, who complimented her on her appearance. At least he seemed to approve of his son's choice of bride, even if he struck her as being, well, a man with a very earthy way of talking. His homilies were starting to grate when thankfully, her new brother-in-law came to her rescue.

"Excuse me for interrupting, Padre, but I'm sure Lisa would appreciate being escorted by her husband around her new home?"

"That would be wonderful," she said.

Vittorio spread his hands to indicate his permission for her to leave his company.

Nico leaned across the table towards his brother. "But you take more of an interest in these matters, Sandro. You would explain the household so much better than I," she heard him say.

Sandro laughed. "I'm sure that would not be proper, dear brother. Lisa expects *you* to conduct her, to signify her position."

Lisa felt herself starting to blush, until she realized that the brothers were joking with one another - and teasing her.

While Sandro discreetly instructed the maidservants to slow down the serving of wine and sweetmeats, Nico took his bride's arm and escorted her out through the main doors of the *sala* to meet the rest of the household staff, now assembled in the lobby. Then onwards, past the private dining room and Nico's *studiolo* to the north wing, where Sandro resided and where Aunt Julia would soon have her own rooms. They then came to the apartment which would be Lisa's own, newly and sumptuously painted in golds and pinks. It was beautiful, but to Lisa the most surprising part was her private bathroom, which was decorated with richly glazed tiles. An unimagined luxury. As the final stop on their tour, they came to the double doors leading to Nico's own rooms.

She preceded her husband into his apartment. She was surprised to find the room had the minimum of ornament. The few pieces of furniture around the room were of the highest quality, but they betrayed little of the man who lived in it. Immediately opposite the main door was Nico's bed with its four carved legs and a canopy endowed with gold damask drapery. To her immediate left, a daybed simply fashioned in wood and close by it, high-backed chairs for Nico's visitors and a side table with glassware and a jug for drinking water.

On either side of the bed proper, on the flanking walls, were the only other items of furniture, a new pair of matching *cassoni*, expensively executed in walnut and chestnut. Nico had mentioned to her some time ago that he had had the chests especially commissioned for the wedding. The scenes of the Annunciation and the Nativity depicted on their panels were expertly carved in wood. He noticed her looking at them.

"You might like it if one of them was placed in your room, Lisa?"

Lisa recalled that some years ago, her father had inherited the sole remaining *cassone* in the Della Volta family, now more than a hundred years old. It was made in the traditional Venetian style with painted panels, not carved wood as was the current fashion, and depicted the story of Solomon and Sheba. The gilt was showing its age these days and the paint had long faded, but it was a reminder of her family. She mentally resolved to have it brought over from the Della Volta house to place in her own bedroom, but she kept that thought to herself. "Would it not be a shame to separate this pair and frustrate the artist's fine conception?" Her confident tone of voice surprised even herself. The wine must have been stronger than she thought.

Nico shrugged. "I am sure that Del Varga would not care," he observed, referring to the artist, "so let it be your choice."

He removed his sleeveless jacket, tossing it carelessly over one of the chairs, and slouched on the daybed. Lisa wondered how long before the awareness that these were their first moments alone as man and wife would dawn on her apparently distracted husband. An easy intimacy would, she realised, take time but she longed for that informality she had known with her father, to whom anything could be said, no topic however trivial would be ignored.

Searching for an opening to Nico's thoughts, she spoke of her nervousness on arriving at the Cathedral. It was a way of hinting at her anticipation of their wedding night, shortly to be upon them, but Nico did not take the bait. In her preparations for marriage, she had discussed many things with Father Guido, but he was obviously not qualified to give practical guidance on marital intimacy. Reluctantly, she had turned to Julia. "Oh, that'll soon pass. Besides, when you have children to bring up..." her aunt had said, with a knowing look.

Perhaps if she walked across to the main window: a joint look at the sunset might reignite conversation. She was vaguely conscious that she was swaying, it must be her precarious heels. Walking past the edge of the bed, she steadied herself by placing her left hand on the bedcover.

It was only then she sensed that Nico was immediately behind her. His hand came to rest on her shoulder. Before she could speak, he had turned her around to face him. His lips came down on hers, impatient, hungry, as with his other arm he pulled her closer to him. After their lips finally parted, she leant backwards, breathless. But his arm had relaxed its grip on her waist, and she fell back onto the bed, plunging into the feather mattress.

"Not so fast, husband, let me undress at least, I …" she began, with a laugh, but the sentence was never finished.

Chapter Five
GREENWICH PALACE, NEAR LONDON: FEBRUARY 1587

By the time the river launch reached Greenwich Palace, the morning's wintry skies had cleared, but there was no warmth in the sun. Walsingham stepped through the river gate and crossed the courtyard. Once inside, he was ushered into the audience room. No sign of any other member of the Council.

He was kept waiting over an hour until Elizabeth swept into the room attended by her ladies in waiting. He recognised the predatory look on her face.

"And so," she announced to Mistress Blanche Parry, but intended for his hearing, "here comes another of the conspirators. Master Secretary, have *you* come to ask our forgiveness too?"

Several Councillors, Burghley included, had sent grovelling apologies to the Queen, accepting that the Council had overstepped the mark in carrying out her Warrant of Execution. So much for unity. But he sensed that, in scorning him so publicly, almost humorously, she was treating him differently from the rest. At least, he hoped so.

"Majesty, I have come in part to discuss Sir Philip Sidney's funeral. You will recall it takes place on Thursday?"

If the wind was taken out of Elizabeth's sails, she did not show it.

"Ah, of course. You will understand that the dreadful events of the last few days had quite taken it from our mind."

He ignored her excuse and gave the Queen a summary of his plans for the memorial service. There would be seven hundred notables attending at St Paul's. A ceremonial procession marching to muffled drums, with the funeral carriage and horses draped in black, bringing up the rear. A grand public event with the Queen at its centre. Mourner-in-chief.

When he had finished, the Queen thanked him for his efforts, seemingly satisfied with the arrangements.

"But I should have enquired about the widow. How is your daughter - Frances, is it not? I am sure she will need all her strength on the day, faced with this fresh reminder of her untimely loss."

Walsingham was used to the Queen's supposed feminine sensibilities. "Madam, I am sure she will cope. Though it has been a hard winter with the loss of her baby so soon after Sir Philip's death. We pray that she will take solace from the service, and the pain will ease over time."

Feeling uncomfortable, Walsingham decided it was time to move on. "If we may talk in private, there are some other matters I must discuss with you."

The Queen's eyes widened. "If you *must*, I suppose I can spare you a little time."

She dismissed her ladies and, as they departed the room, busied herself with sniffing at the scented pomander on her left sleeve. They adjourned to the room next to the Queen's bedchamber. Elizabeth walked over to a window overlooking the bend in the river. She gazed out beyond the Thames, to the marshy land on the north bank where her hunting dogs were kept. Keeping her back to him, Walsingham noted, as he closed the doors. She finally turned round, her eyebrows arched in enquiry.

"Madam, you asked if I had come to apologise. In the matter of Mary Stuart's execution."

Elizabeth sucked in her cheeks, making her cheekbones appear more prominent, but did not interrupt.

"Certainly, there are consequences we should discuss, matters on which you might seek my counsel," he began, "but that was not my purpose."

Her face reddened with anger. "Then you are no better than the rest of them," she spat out, "and besides, Davison knew my mind. When I signed the Warrant, he knew it should stay in his safe keeping. Instead, he betrayed me."

"William Davison is your loyal servant, Madam. Had he understood that was your intent, he would not have presented it to the Council in the manner he did."

Elizabeth scoffed. "If that is the truth, then he is a fool. And so are you, for believing him."

Perhaps she was right in that at least. "If I am at fault, Madam, it is for believing that what I most desired was indeed true. That at long last, after nineteen years of plotting and scheming against your Majesty, the Scottish Queen would be called to account for her crimes."

She marched up to him, putting her face close to his, her fan raised high as if she would strike him with it. "Her crimes, yes. But Mary was a sovereign prince. And you and your nice fellows, you took off her head!"

Walsingham resisted the temptation to raise his voice. He spoke slowly and deliberately. "Had I been there, I would have taken up the axe myself."

"An axe, yes! You *have* it there. Not even by the sword, as befitted her rank!"

"And I would have done so a thousand times before this, Madam, had you acceded to my advice. Your crown itself was in peril."

Elizabeth started striding up and down. "Have I not risked my crown all the more, by killing the holder of another?" She was at full pitch now, somewhere between self-pity and fury.

"Madam, Mary Stuart committed crimes against your person and your faith. There is no doubting the justice of the matter." He paused, counting the seconds. "And just as important is that last week, she was your mortal enemy. And this week, you have one less such enemy."

Elizabeth threw her fan on the floor. But it was more in frustration than anger. Best to wait it out. After a lengthy silence between them, she turned to face him again.

"And so, it is your contention, Sir Francis, that this..." she could not bring herself to say the word, "...has made my realm safe. Is that it?" Her cheeks were still flushed, but she was now arguing with him, not merely shouting at him.

"Saf*er*, Madam. Saf*er*. Your safety is my constant goal." He bent down and picked up the discarded fan. Offered it to her. She took it, with the barest perceptible nod.

"Very well, Sir Francis."

The heat slowly left her face. She walked across to a chair and arranged herself in it, spreading her palm across the overskirt of her gown. What do you think of the pattern, by the by? Is it not fine? You did not comment on it when you arrived."

He complimented her on the ludicrously expensive dress. But since she was apparently in a spending mood, he decided to try a different subject. "Madam, one small matter."

Elizabeth closed the fan with a snap.

"You recall my letter to you regarding the Intelligencers?" he continued.

Elizabeth shut her eyes momentarily, no doubt recalling his recent request for funds.

"Indeed, I do. You seem to think that your Queen is a fountain of money whose sole purpose in life is to support your little intrigues and adventures."

"I am appreciative of your contributions, Madam, but the Service is costly to me. I truly cannot afford to continue for much longer."

"But you keep watch on half the world! You will soon need a larger house than Scything Lane, just to keep your records in." She looked pleased with her own joke. "Besides, I cannot afford it either."

"Majesty, there is no expense so vital, no service more important, than intelligence."

"Lord Burghley tells me you have thirty agents placed across Europe. They cost me the earth already - and now you ask for more."

In fact, Walsingham had over fifty intelligencers working for him, but there was no point in correcting her statement.

"There are many dangers to watch for, both at home and abroad," countered Walsingham, "and without their work, we would never have uncovered the Throckmorton Plot, we ..."

"Yes, yes, yes," said Elizabeth with rising irritation, "I understand that, but must it cost so much? Five thousand pounds?"

"It sometimes takes more than thirty pieces of silver to get a man to betray his brothers in arms." Momentarily, he reflected on the comparison between his modest request and the heavy demands made on the Queen's purse by Lord Dudley. The English army in Flanders was achieving little in return for the hundreds of thousands of pounds expended. That argument was not likely to be well received either. But it was too late to retreat now, he thought, regretting his decision to raise the subject.

"Madam, the acquiring of knowledge is never bought too dear. Knowledge of our enemies' intentions is *beyond* price."

Elizabeth's voice became a loud whisper, the menace clear. "It is certainly beyond *my* price. You seem to have forgotten that it was the hasty actions of you and your fellow Councillors that have brought us to this pass. My enemies have been sorely provoked and now you ask for money to repair the damage you've done. This audience is at an end."

She marched towards the adjoining bedchamber as Walsingham bowed in the direction of her rapidly departing figure.

As he sat in his launch returning to the Tower, his team rowing hard against the current, Walsingham offered up a little prayer of thanks. Thanks that he was returning safely to Ursula and Scything Lane. Perhaps he was indispensable after all.

A WEEK LATER, Walsingham was granted another audience with the Queen. Accompanied by two mounted escorts, he rode through the arch of Temple Bar and into the Strand. As the street broadened out, the jagged rows of teeth that were the gables of Whitehall Palace came into view. The Queen had moved her retinue up-river from Greenwich only the previous day. He was thankful: half a day spent travelling back and forth on the river was the last thing he needed now, with all that pressed upon him.

His horse clattered past the Charing Cross and through the gates of the palace. The yard was a buzz of activity: courtiers arriving and departing, servants scurrying with messages, the palace guard changing. Walsingham dismounted, leaving his horse in the care of his escorts.

He walked down the Long Gallery to the Audience Room. When he entered, the Queen was standing on the far side by a window. She was deep in conversation with the Earl of Leicester, his fellow Councillor. Walsingham, always plain in his black robes and white ruff, paid little attention to matters of fashion. But even he noticed that, by her own standards, Elizabeth looked every inch the monarch that day. Her high-standing collar trimmed with pearls and lace, her voluminous silver dress also studded with beads, and enough jewellery to... well, to finance an army. He coughed and the Queen, who had been smiling at Dudley, turned her head.

As she saw him walk towards her, the smile faded. "It seems I must endure *all* my Councillors today."

"Majesty, I would not presume on your time were it not for certain matters which it would be reprehensible to keep from you." Walsingham paused in his step, calculating that the one thing the Queen could not resist was a secret.

Putting down her fan, the Queen turned towards him. "Very well, let us move to business. What is it that will not wait?"

"Madam. I came here to discuss the issue of Spain." He paused, but the Queen merely waited for him to continue. "As Your Majesty is aware, we have known for some time that Philip is building new ships. From his harbours all around the peninsula, the reports are the same."

"Well, he's enlarging his navy," argued the Queen, with that familiar trace of petulance in her voice, "it is a long way across the Ocean Sea from New Spain, after all. He's decided that he needs escort ships to protect his treasure from Drake and Hawkins. Or perhaps he intends to assault the rebellious Netherlands by sea, eh Robin?"

Robert Dudley looked doubtful. "Parma's forces don't need naval support. Sadly, it is us - and the Dutch - who could use some reinforcement..."

Walsingham cut his fellow Councillor short. "Madam, these are not ocean-going escort vessels, so far as we can tell. We therefore doubt they are intended for New Spain. But you are perceptive, such a fleet could indeed be used against the Dutch rebels."

The Queen smiled back at him in self-satisfaction.

"...But even so, that would scarcely be comfortable for us, poised as they would be, less than a day's sail from the Thames Estuary." The smile faded from the Queen's face.

Walsingham continued, "In any event, I believe the fleet Philip is building has a different purpose. Philip may use it to enforce your overthrow. The catholic nobles here may not object if he tries it."

"We already knew from the Throckmorton Plotters that he wished me killed. But he's not tried again, these three years." The Queen tapped her fan on the window frame. "So, do you have new information?" said Elizabeth.

"Many small pieces of intelligence have come in," said Walsingham, "and over time, they have combined to make a narrative. But the most recent..." he reached into his doublet and extracted a document, "was a letter. The original was in a difficult Spanish code, but after a few days of study, we have managed to assay its hidden text. It comes from the king himself."

Taking the uncoded letter from him, Elizabeth began reading the text aloud. But as she engaged with its contents, her voice tailed off and she read silently to the end. She passed the document to Dudley.

"And the sovereign whom the author addresses as 'Your Majesty?'"

"None other than Mary Stuart."

Walsingham waited for the explosion to arrive. But Elizabeth remained calm. "How would you know that?"

"Because, Madam, of how the letter was discovered. You'll recall that at various times we have intercepted secret letters to or from the Scottish Queen, from various sources."

"But this one eluded you until now, did it?"

Walsingham held her gaze. "That was because it was secreted about her person. It was sown into her undergarment. The one she wore ...at her execution."

Elizabeth shut her eyes momentarily. Opening them, she looked again at the letter. "So, it is genuine," she muttered.

"Just so. And the fact that in it, the king assured her that the Army of Flanders would be stood down for the time being. Which has since come to pass, as Lord Robert will no doubt confirm. So yes, I am convinced that it is genuine."

Dudley intervened. "When Philip talks of the English Enterprise, he refers to their removing Your Majesty and putting Mary Stuart in your place."

The Queen jumped at his remark. "Ah, but Mary Stuart is dead. And Sir Francis, you told me that her death would make us safer, did you not?" she added, turning back to Walsingham.

"Madam, I did. Nor have I changed my view. If Philip *does* seek to invade us, he will find the catholic nobles less minded to support your overthrow than they once were. Especially now there is no obvious candidate to assume your throne, save perhaps a Spanish one. But of course, when he wrote this letter, Mary Stuart was still alive. And it will be some weeks before he comes to hear of her death. We have embargoed the ports to slow the news from getting abroad. Which gives us some time."

"Time? Time for what exactly?"

"Time to prepare our defences for the assault that will almost certainly come." Walsingham glimpsed Dudley nodding in assent.

"But now he has no figurehead to presume to our throne. Would he not abandon the folly?"

"I believe he was using Mary Stuart for his own purposes. He would not especially care *who*, so long as a new ruler can bring this country back into the Popish fold. He could choose any of his children to assume the throne, and make the Duke of Parma his Regent, for example."

"And your evidence, save for this letter?"

"He is scouring Europe for arms, he is building ships in every navigable river in Spain, he is spending every silver dollar that his new territories can supply as soon as it arrives, and if the funds run short, he simply borrows from his Genoa bankers...."

"By preparing our defences, Sir Francis, you mean building defence works along our coast, raising the muster in the shires, augmenting our navy. All of which we must pay for. A fortune - and all for an assault which may never come."

Elizabeth walked over to the royal chair and sat down, as if emphasising her prerogative to make every decision alone, whatever the views of her advisers. Walsingham's patience began to desert him.

"Madam, with every month that passes their fleet grows bigger. If we wait indefinitely, it may be so large that our entire resources, including the privateers, cannot defeat it."

After a long silence, Elizabeth turned to the Earl. "Robin, you must bring our troops back from Flanders without delay."

Before Dudley could respond, Walsingham intervened. "Madam, your assessment is right, our defences must be strengthened, and urgently. But not with the Earl's squadrons, I submit. The rapid removal of our contingent would merely arouse the Duke of Parma's suspicion that we had obtained intelligence of their plans. Currently, he is unaware of our state of knowledge - that gives us a valuable advantage. And our withdrawal would make it easier for his Army of Flanders to cross the Channel unhindered. Quite apart from our treaty promises to the Dutch. So, I urge you not to change Lord Dudley's dispositions. Rather it is the Council's view that we must strike first, *before* we are struck at."

"And, if not by the Earl of Leicester's forces, how exactly," said Elizabeth, "would you propose that we *strike?*"

"By sea, madam. It is Sir Francis Drake's plan, and the Council fully supports it, to attack the Spanish in their harbours. His flotilla will have the advantage of surprise. Moving swiftly, he would catch them with their breeches down."

The Queen laughed, appreciating the crude humour.

"We propose he attacks Cádiz, where there's a substantial merchant fleet. Not a place the Spanish would consider an obvious target. Less heavily defended than, say, the naval harbour at Lisbon. And further from England."

"Attack merchant ships?" Elizabeth looked doubtful.

"Yes. And quayside stores. Philip's armada can't sail *anywhere* without huge supplies to support them. Until they're on English soil, there'll be nothing to live on, save what they carry with them. Take away his dinner and you take away the soldier."

The Queen hesitated, instinctively looking at Dudley for reinforcement. There was a pause. Walsingham prayed inwardly.

"It seems to me, Madam," said Dudley finally, "that attack is our best defence. The Spanish do not need to be told we will defend our island to the death. But they don't expect us to attack them in their own country."

Walsingham pressed home. "All of this is about *time*, madam. Every day that we can delay Philip's preparations is another day to prepare our defence. The defence of your realm."

He paused: they had not told her any of the details, but she knew enough to decide the principle. She seemed almost persuaded, if he judged her demeanour correctly. Perhaps simple greed would clinch it. "And then," he added, "there is the Silver Fleet. It should arrive from New Spain this summer and if Drake is there, poised with his flotilla, we can seize some of Philip's treasure into the bargain."

The Queen snapped her fan shut. "*If* I agree, how many ships does Drake need?"

"He has already raised a squadron of sixteen privateers, but Your Majesty would need to support him with perhaps ten more."

Elizabeth winced. "That is too much," she said, "but we may be able to spare him, say, half that number. And he must not sail until I have reflected further. It is my decision alone."

Walsingham's face expressed disappointment, but it was a mask. He had calculated that another six warships would be more than sufficient. Attacking in narrow harbours required a fleet-footed squadron, not an armada of vessels getting in each other's way. "As Your Majesty disposes," he said. "I will send word to Drake, so he can start preparations immediately. And then await your command."

It was time to leave, before the Queen changed her mind.

But when he got home to his study, he looked again at the Spanish letter. Something was needling him. That was it, the reference to the banks. Even if Drake could seize more Spanish silver, Philip would just borrow the money. His bankers in Genoa would provide it. England would be just as vulnerable as before.

Chapter Six
THE ALCÁZAR PALACE, MADRID: MARCH 1587

Lifting his head from the pillow, the old man squinted at his clock. The tiny oil lamp encased in its gilt frame was sputtering, but if he leaned closer, he could just make out the hour. It would soon be Prima, the first Mass of the day.

Pulling back the bedspread, he swung his legs out and planted both feet on the floor. Placing his knuckles on the edge of the mattress, he tensed his arms and levered himself upwards. Wincing with every step, he hobbled from the tiny bedroom into the sparsely furnished apartment with which it connected, leaning on the nearby furniture as he went. He forced himself to keep moving. The pain must not distract him during prayers.

His young manservant entered the room, carrying his breakfast on a tray. Sebastian had been in his employ for less than a year but seemed to understand instinctively his master's simple needs. Sebastian announced that after prayers, Jean de L'hermite would pay him a visit. This at least was good news. Jean was the only person who seemed to know how to alleviate his gout. True, the Dutchman was overly fond of wine, but so were many others from his country.

"In that way," he observed, as his manservant buttoned his plain black doublet, "the Flemish are like the English." Sebastian, who had yet to accompany his master beyond the borders of Spain and Portugal, merely assented.

"I stayed in England for a year as a young man, you know," he said, as Sebastian affixed his ruff. "It is a green and beautiful land. But the people: nothing but drunkards and pirates. Our Dutch friends like drinking too, but they at least are men of culture. As their great painters testify."

His duties over for the present, Sebastian withdrew. Left alone to his reminiscences, the old man recalled his wedding in Winchester, all those years ago. True, Mary Tudor was even plainer than her portrait had suggested, but she was a staunch believer. Ah, what could we have achieved together, if only she had borne me a son? Spanish arms, English ships: an unbeatable combination. We could have conquered the whole world, thought the king.

BUT WHEN HE returned from Mass, there was no sign of de L'hermite. Instead, his foreign minister, Juan de Idiáquez was waiting for him. Idiáquez looked more than usually animated, if that were possible. The man was indispensable, but if only he were a little less *excitable*.

"So, Don Juan. Has our *flota* landed at Cádiz?"

Idiáquez shook his head. There was no indication it had even left New Spain. "Forgive the intrusion at this early hour, senor, but I have received a message. From Don Bernadino in Paris," he added, as he handed over the letter. The king had recently introduced the rule that he was no longer to be addressed as 'Majesty' but simply as 'Senor'. He sensed that Idiáquez still found it difficult to adjust to this relative informality.

The couriered note from their French ambassador was in code, but Idiáquez had made a translation, which he also passed to the king. Felipe sat down, somewhat gingerly, and reached for the necessary spectacles.

Holding it close to his face, he spotted the date in the top corner. "Written only ten days ago. What does Don Bernadino consider so urgent?" he asked. But before Idiáquez could respond, he became engrossed in the letter. His eyes narrowed when he reached the third paragraph:

'Your Excellency should be advised of the most disturbing news. I have it on the authority of their Ambassador Stafford, that the English have had Mary

Stuart executed. The murder took place two weeks ago, on the instructions of their Privy Council. Stafford believes that the Council did so against Queen Elizabeth's wishes, although she had signed the Warrant of Execution previously. It seems she did not intend the Warrant to be carried out, merely kept locked away. But Secretary Walsingham gave the gaolers at Castle Fotheringay his orders in any event.

This is but a brief note: I will dispatch more details as soon as I have them. In the meantime, please advise His Majesty of this shocking development. Given its import for the Enterprise, I have sent a similar note to the Duke of Parma, in the Netherlands.

May God grant His Majesty the power to avenge this wicked deed.

Your servant,
Bernadino de Mendoza.'

His Most Catholic Majesty, Felipe II, King of Castile and of Aragon, Ruler of Portugal and the Netherlands, King of Naples and all Sicily and Emperor of New Spain and Peru, struggled to his feet, steeling himself for the fight. "These murderers," he said, his body shaking. "A sovereign queen. It is unspeakable." He glared at Idiáquez, breathing heavily.

"This crime must not go unpunished, Sire," the minister responded, lapsing back into formal address. "The Englishwoman, she is the daughter of the devil. We must destroy her - and her Councillors - at the earliest opportunity."

But Felipe was in no mood for such a discussion. Behind the magnifying lenses, he could feel his eyes watering.

Not wishing to expose himself in front of Idiáquez, he turned away in the middle of his response. "But first, there must be a proper period of mourning. We will pray for the immortal soul of that poor lady." And with that he headed back to the Royal Chapel, to get down on his long-suffering knees again.

THREE DAYS' mourning is surely more than sufficient for a mere Queen of Scotland, thought Idiáquez as he strode along the draughty corridor towards Felipe's apartments. He decided to test Felipe's mood again and was pleased to find that the king was calmer, his mind focused. Hours of prayer had obviously expunged the emotion he had felt on receiving the terrible news. After their greetings, he watched Felipe shuffle across the room, deliberately skirting the furniture. Disguising the stiffness in his gait as best he could, Idiáquez noted. Now, if we are ever to do it, is the time. A couple more seasons and the king would be too old, too infirm.

"The English Enterprise, Don Juan," Felipe began. "As I see it, the death of Mary Stuart complicates matters. We have lost our intended successor to Elizabeth's crown."

"But senor, if I may...."

Felipe cut across him. "I mean it could jeopardise our relations with Rome. His Holiness supported our placing her on the English throne. Now she's gone, what does that say for the loan he promised us?"

Idiáquez had pondered the same question privately, but now his sovereign needed a display of confidence, not hypothetical problems. "Pope Sixtus may accommodate us with *financial* support, but that does not give His Eminence the right to dictate your majesty's *policy*. The proposed loan terms do not stipulate that Mary Stuart is made Queen of England. What if we were to install another candidate of Your Majesty's choosing? Will the Pope condemn us, after we have rid the world of that heretic queen? Would he invade England himself?" Idiáquez scoffed. "With what armies?"

"But without his loan, how can we launch the invasion?"

The old caution, he thought. The king seemed determined to find obstacles. "Rest assured, senor, the finances need not be a stumbling block. After all, the *flota* from New Spain will surely make port later this season. And if, for whatever reason, it is delayed, we can ask your bankers in Genova to cover the costs for the short term...."

"Well, it seems we cannot wait for His Holiness, so you had better pursue the banking option. Sound them out."

Idiáquez bowed his head briefly, by way of accepting his instructions. As he raised his head, Felipe was hobbling over to the window. Idiáquez followed him. For a moment, both men observed the sylvan scene in the Campo below.

Felipe mused aloud. "So, Don Juan, with Mary Stuart gone, who should rule England now?"

Idiáquez decided to leave that question unanswered for the moment.

"Perhaps if my *son* were to marry an English noblewoman," Felipe continued.

"An *excellent* plan, senor, but I do not think that at this critical moment we should be distracted by the question of the Crown Prince taking a wife, given his tender age." Felipe's only surviving son, who bore his father's name, was just nine.

"Then we must consider another candidate. England cannot wait a *decade* for her salvation from heresy. Isabella at least, is of full age."

Idiáquez realised that the king was just as set on the destination as he was: it was merely that Felipe needed to be steered towards the right course. "An English husband might seek to govern her," he pointed out. Felipe nodded in agreement.

"Senor, the Infanta can achieve her own destiny in God's good time. But I submit we need not search high and low for a candidate." Idiáquez paused for effect. Felipe stared at his minister, questioning.

"With Mary Stuart gone, surely your own claim is the most compelling?" Idiáquez continued. Before his master could reply, he had gone down on one knee. "As the greatest monarch in the world, you are beyond doubting the person to lead that sorry country back to the True Faith."

Smiling but saying nothing, the king ushered his minister back to his feet. Idiáquez knew better than to fill the ensuing silence.

Finally, the king spoke. "It is true I can claim descent from the Plantagenets. You'll recall that John of Ghent was my ancestor?"

"So, it could be said your claim to the English throne *precedes* Elizabeth's. And I believe that England and Spain were allied back in those times. That is, before Henry Bolingbroke seized King Richard's crown."

"That is also true."

"And of course, senor, you *married* Mary Tudor."

"I did - and in an English cathedral."

Idiáquez beamed at his sovereign, sensing his growing confidence. But it seemed Felipe had another objection. "It is true, though, that I agreed to relinquish my claim by reason of the marriage."

The minister ignored the point, a mere technicality after all, and reverted to the core of the matter. "But Mary Tudor has been dead these thirty years, God rest her blessed soul. And has been succeeded by a bastard heretic. One who sponsors pirates and murders princes. Surely, it is nothing less than our *sacred duty*?"

"The more we discuss it, the more it seems the proper course."

"And surely *now* is the time, senor, with half the English nobles incensed at Mary Stuart's beheading. Is it not the moment to rally them to our cause?"

Eventually, Felipe spoke with firmness. "It is, Don Juan, it is. If ever there *was* a time, this is surely it."

Idiáquez forced himself to look suitably stern. "As Your Majesty decides. Once the armada is made ready to sail the Enterprise can succeed, and even more gloriously than was first conceived."

"Agreed. We will discuss this matter again, Don Juan, and soon. Work must restart on provisioning." Felipe took his minister's hand and clasped it firmly. "You simply *have* to find the money."

Idiáquez bowed and withdrew. Striding down the corridor, he smacked his clenched right fist into his left palm. Jean de L'hermite, coming in the other direction, saw him do so but kept his expression unreadable. Idiáquez could not resist smiling at him.

Chapter Seven
CASA CASTELLO, STRADA NUOVA, GENOA: MARCH 1587

Nico turned to the maid who was waiting at table that morning. "Is my brother at home, Paola?" he asked, as he passed her his hat.

"I believe Signore Alessandro is out presently," she said, blushing. "But I will tell the Signora that you have returned, Signore."

Paola was a recent arrival in the household. Shy, but quite pretty. He wondered if she had already succumbed to Sandro's charms.

Then he remembered: Sandro had gone to Governor Doria's palazzo, as a guest of the young prince. He sat down and waited for his wife.

After a couple of minutes, he heard the tap-tap of a pair of zuccoli on the floor tiles and the rustle of silk skirts. His bride of nine months entered the dining room. Would there be a time, he wondered, when his pulse no longer quickened when he saw her? The cascade of dark auburn hair, the arms held just so, the turn of the head. But it was her eyes, above all else, which held your gaze. Genova had many beautiful women, but none he could recall with those eyes of pale gold, flecked with amber. The eyes of a lioness.

"I suggested to Sandro that he should defer to you," Lisa said, when Paola had served the meal. "Regarding the Prince's invitation, I mean," she added, "but he said you were content for him to represent the family."

Nico was content enough. He had no great love of ceremonial dining with the Dorias, but these days it seemed his regular presence at these functions was expected. Sandro, by contrast, seemed eager to take part.

"Less time playing the courtier and more time devoted to our business, would be welcome," he responded, "but yes, I'm happy he takes his share of these engagements."

"They seem to be becoming more frequent," observed Lisa. Nico recalled that a week or so earlier, her aunt Julia had implied that the Castellos' increasing presence at court was entirely down to the Della Volta name. Julia clearly regarded her niece's marriage as a regrettable step down the social ladder. Thank goodness the lady would be heading back to her villa in Livorno in a few days' time.

"Where are your thoughts?" asked Lisa, her hand touching Nico's.

"Oh, excuse me, I was just...reminding myself of what needs to be done this afternoon."

"Was it a busy morning at the Loggia?"

"No, but the Netherlands merchants are back in town for the Easter Fair, so things should get busier. And your morning?"

"I went to a workshop in the old city with Sandro, looking at some marble pieces for the garden. On the way back, I went into San Lorenzo. For confession."

Nico didn't comment. He had never acquired the habit of confession, a practice which was less widespread in his youth. To his way of thinking, Lisa was too reliant on her confessor. She was married now and should pay more heed to her husband.

"Father Guido asked if we could help them with a donation. For the missionary priests they're sending to the Netherlands. Of course, I said we would."

Of course. "So, am I to be the patron saint for any cause?"

"I *know* you have been generous to their orphans' fund, Nico, but the missionaries need our support too. It is difficult, dangerous work."

"Then they shouldn't put themselves in harm's way. Who decreed that we should send priests into the middle of a war?"

"But they are doing the church's work. Helping Catholics who are in danger."

Nico shook his head. "That's not what I hear. The missionaries denounce anyone they deem heretical. Force them to renounce their faith. In truth, they're there to help the Duke of Parma crush the Dutch rebels."

"Who tells you this?"

"Merchants from Antwerp and Bruges. I hear their tales of woe whenever they're in Genova."

"So, you would rather help foreigners than our own church?"

Nico shut his eyes briefly. "No, that isn't it," he said.

"So, what is your objection, then?" said Lisa.

He gave her a steady look. "I don't believe that our church is putting its strong arm where it's most needed." But before she could continue the argument, he raised his hands. "Be that as it may, I *will* make a charitable donation."

For a moment Lisa looked pleased, until he added, "But not for any of the archbishop's little schemes. Whatever sum you promised Father Guido, I'll double it. But I'll give it to the city hospital instead. That way the Pammatone can complete their new wing all the faster. Tell the Father that some of the money can be used to build a chapel there."

The golden-brown eyes glowered at him. "But what of your duty to your church?"

"Duties, duties. All I ever hear is what we, the congregation, should do to help *them*. Never do I hear what the church can do to help its congregation." He heard his own voice, sounding ill-tempered. He knew he should tone it down, but he was angry now.

"Oh, and what help do *we* need exactly?"

"Not *us,* Lisa. I don't mean *us*. Just walk around the city. If you look, you can see the people who truly need help."

"Then you won't support me?" she said angrily, standing up.

"Leave the Netherlanders to find their own way to God. Who are *we* to say they should follow *ours*?"

Lisa glared at him, apparently unable to come up with a riposte. Then she threw down her napkin and headed for the door. Nico caught her arm as she passed next to his chair. Wriggling free from his grasp, she fled the room, her heels clattering down the corridor to her apartment.

Nico banged his fist on the table. The vibration toppled his wine glass and the contents spread across the tablecloth. He set off down the corridor after her.

Reaching her door, he heard the sound of her receding footsteps on the other side. He reached for the handle, but Lisa had locked the door. He lifted it slowly back and forced it down again at the same instant as he slammed his shoulder into the door.

The door swung inwards, hitting the return wall with a crash. He stepped inside and strode through to the bedroom. Lisa was standing next to her bed, with one hand holding the bedpost, as if to steady herself. Her cheeks were flushed, the lips slightly apart. Something in her expression told him she was not unhappy that she had made him lose his temper.

As he walked towards her, she turned away. He grabbed her by the waist, forcing her to turn and face him. They stood still, just inches apart, glaring at one another. Then, in a sudden movement, he pulled her towards him fiercely. His lips came down on hers. At first, she resisted him, leaning backwards, but then he felt her body soften, and she returned his kiss.

THEY LAY ON THE BED, limbs entwined, drifting in and out of sleep. It seemed that the argument earlier – and for that matter, their meal – was forgotten.

Lisa raised her head off the pillow and rested on her elbow, surveying Nico. Conscious of her movement, Nico half-opened his eyes. She smiled back.

"Perhaps we should argue more often," he joked.

"Perhaps we should." She prodded his chest. "But what about my request?"

Nico opened his eyes wider. "Still? Is it so important to you?"

"I wouldn't have asked if it were unimportant."

"But why so?"

"Why? Do you not think our church a force for good in the world?"

Nico wasn't going to answer that. His thoughts on the matter probably wouldn't be appreciated. But though they talked about the church's mission, he sensed that her impulse was more personal, it went much deeper.

"Have you always felt that way? I mean, since childhood?"

Lisa was hesitant at first, but eventually the reminiscences started to come.

"I was too young to know much about Mama's faith, but she made me say my prayers every night. She put a small Madonna beside my bed...but it's a hazy memory."

"And your father? After your mother passed on?"

'Oh, he carried on with our prayers together, for a while at least. He would tell me that Mama was looking down at us from Heaven.

That was a comfort. And yes, he took me to Mass. But when I was ten or eleven, I realised he was not so observant himself. I would tell him what the priests at San Luca had said, and he would politely listen. But he seemed more interested in what was being said or written elsewhere, the news about discoveries, the stars, even the clouds. He tried to interest me in those things too..."

Lisa shifted on the bed, sitting up and hugging her knees. "He explained that sometimes there were arguments between these men of science and the church. But it was possible to love God *and* be interested in what was being discovered. For myself, I felt these discoveries were interesting, but they didn't explain the big questions. Life, death, Heaven and ...the other place. Only the priests talked about those things. That's still the case, you know, when it comes to it."

Nico didn't see how that meant whatever the church did was to be approved of and supported. But he didn't say as much. "Alright, let's say that Father Guido and his fellow priests have an important job to do, here in the Republic. But why should they spend their resources trying to convert foreigners back to the Faith?"

"But how else will the heretics see the error of their ways?"

"And why is that so important to us?"

She rose from the bed and grabbed her robe. "If you cared for me at all, you'd understand why. Or had you just forgotten what they did to my father?"

She rushed across the room and into her bathroom, locking the door behind her. Nico decided not to damage two doors in one afternoon.

Left alone, he reflected on how his boyhood experience of the church was so different from Lisa's. He recalled how the priests had stressed the importance of charity and the blessed state of the poor. But no such charity seemed to find its way to the actual poor. Certainly not to his father's door, or any of his neighbours, so far as Nico could tell. Indeed, from the modest sums that Vittorio Castello earned as a silversmith, he was expected to make significant donations. Nor did he seem to resent doing so, despite the fact they were expected rather than appreciated. Nico remembered telling his father that the priests were more interested in Vittorio's lire than in the sincerity of his repentance. Vittorio gave him several cuffs to the head for impertinence. And his father had a strong arm. Nico had made himself rigid, so as not to show the pain of the blows. Once Vittorio had calmed down, he explained to Nico that it didn't matter what the *priests'* purpose was, it was the

Lord's purpose that mattered. Nico didn't know how his father could be so sure of the Lord's mind. To Nico, the evidence of what was foremost in the priests' minds was clear enough. A view which had not been changed by his experience as an adult.

But as he acknowledged to himself, his antipathy towards the priests at San Giovanni, their parish church in Pre, wasn't so much about their apparent indifference to his family's struggle. It was more personal than that: his harsh treatment in the church school, the beatings and punishments, the humiliations from other boys who jeered at his immigrant status, the denial of kindness. Not so different from life outside school, but, with all their talk of a loving God, the priests scarcely lived up to their own pronouncements. Today, the very different, respectful way in which he was treated by the church was merely the consequence of his rise to wealth. Their seeking large donations from him was just as much a business transaction as the work he did in the Merchants' Loggia. The fact that a material part of these donations came from the profits of his trades with Protestant merchants didn't seem to disturb the clergy too much. But he could see that Lisa's loyalties would prevent her from seeing it that way.

The bathroom door opened. Looking at Lisa's expression, he decided they had had more than enough theological discussion for one day.

Chapter Eight

GRESHAM'S EXCHANGE, CITY OF LONDON: A MONTH EARLIER

"Ten per cent? Why, that's usury," the merchant protested.

"I think you will find, Master Falconer, that it is nothing of the sort. You are of course, welcome to assay the market. If you can obtain better terms from another house, then I wish you good fortune."

The black notebook was snapped shut. Thomas Sutton pulled on his calfskin gauntlets, ready to leave the Exchange.

Sutton's prospective customer touched his arm. "A mere figure of speech, Master Sutton, I assure you. Excuse the hasty response. I am sure we can find agreement."

Sutton took in the nervous smile. Slowly, he removed the gauntlets again.

The Exchange's bell struck for the close of business just as Sutton managed to get his usual terms accepted by Edward Falconer. The compact was duly entered in Sutton's notebook, in his small, ornate hand. The parties shook on it, as if old friends. Sutton repeated that, on receipt of the executed pledge on the following Monday, he would make the agreed advance. Payment direct to Falconer's troublesome creditor, in gold coin.

As he stepped out of the Exchange moments later and headed west along Chepesyde, Thomas Sutton gathered his ermine collar tight against the February wind. To a passer-by, only the piercing blue eyes and grey sideburns would have been visible above the fur-lined cloak and below the turned-down hat. It was a short step from the Exchange to the house he was renting in Bread Street, but Sutton scuttled along, the quicker to reach the blazing hearth that would be awaiting his return. Why did folk ever assert the nonsense that London was warmer than his native Yorkshire?

MONTAGUE BELLTOWER - OR MONTY, as he preferred to be called – was a large-framed man with a shock of ginger hair and an unkempt beard. His was an open, trustworthy face which most times bore an easy smile. That and his sociable habits were assets that helped him in his chosen trade of wool merchant. Monty had also been fortunate in having, in Thomas Sutton, a well-connected uncle. Sutton, one of England's richest merchants and banker to several Privy Councillors, had taken Monty under his wing when his improvident father had died. Monty had mined Sutton's substantial connection to get brokerage appointments, especially from wealthy landowners with fleeces to sell.

Monty had arrived a few minutes early, his curiosity piqued no doubt. As the fellow Yorkshiremen greeted one another, Sutton noticed the young man's face was beginning to round out. The bloom of youth was still there, but good living was softening him up a bit.

"Master Belltower, you look prosperous enough. Or is it that you've seen the inside of too many ale pots?"

His visitor laughed, slapping Sutton on the shoulder. "No, uncle, I have been a prudent fellow. But as a matter of fact, I am *rather* peckish. What do you say to supper at the *Three Tuns*?"

"Doesn't your wife provide a good table at home?" queried Sutton. For a moment, the younger man's face lost its smile. Domestic life was not exactly to his taste, the banker guessed. Although it had been a good marriage that Monty had made, to a wealthy widow, Sutton had heard that it was no love match.

Sat in a corner of the Newgate tavern less than an hour later, he watched Belltower make short work of the fish stew - it being Friday - and even shorter work of the wine. Sutton, barely hungry, teased his own platter with his spoon.

"You were saying that it's hard to move wool at present."

Belltower shrugged. "It's been a difficult season. The money isn't there after last autumn's harvest. The merchants are still nervous." Another pull at his wine.

"I understand, Montague. But don't despair. I asked you to come and see me because I might have the opportunity you're looking for."

Belltower leaned forward across the table, pushing his goblet to one side. The casual expression disappeared from his face.

Sutton continued. "A few investors and I, we're proposing to sell English wool abroad. Prices on the continent are stronger than here, as you'll know. So, if we ship a *large* enough cargo, we will make enough profit to cover the cost of the shipping charters."

"How large?"

Sutton gave him an indication. The ruddy eyebrows shot up.

"And so, when it comes to conducting the trades, naturally we thought of you. You're one of the leading wool brokers in London. Or at least, you were when I last enquired."

The younger man grinned. "I am your man for that. And I know *exactly* where you can purchase the finest fleeces. Hungry sellers, all of them."

Sutton glanced at the wine pitcher. He gestured to the barmaid for a second flask.

"So, where do you propose to trade the wool? Antwerp?" said Belltower, once his glass was refilled.

"Normally, we would. But the Dutch rebels are blockading the River Scheldt. So, the Adventurers have decided on Genoa."

"Genoa?"

"We believe it's where we'll get the highest prices. You would sail with the first shipment. Once you've settled the trades, agreed the prices, you can sail home. The balance of the cargo would be shipped there in stages, over the rest of the summer. On terms agreed by you, beforehand. Of course, it would be preferred if you could stay there until their August Fair and oversee the later deliveries as well."

Belltower looked doubtful. "I haven't been to Genoa before."

"I know that. But you've visited other Fairs, Bruges and Lyons, I recall? I've been to Genoa's Fairs a couple of times myself. Fine city. So, I can give you a few guiding points. And of course, some useful introductions."

His guest took another gulp of his wine.

"So, would it be a problem to leave hearth and home for a season?" Sutton asked, wondering if the rumours about Belltower and his wife being estranged, weren't in fact true.

But the younger man shook his head. "Oh, no, that's not a

concern, Uncle Thomas. I was just thinking that I don't have much of the Italian tongue."

Sutton laughed. "A small difficulty. I didn't either, when I first went. Got by on Latin and a bit of French mostly, until I picked up the local language. You will too."

Seeing Belltower's expression, he continued. "But here's a notion. Occurs to me that we've a few Florentine gentlemen in the Guild. You could always meet them for a little conversational practice. I'm sure that would smooth things over, you would soon have enough Italian to get by."

Belltower looked relieved. "Sounds a splendid commission. Happy to take it on."

Sutton clapped him on the shoulder. "Excellent fellow. The Adventurers will be relieved to have their business in such capable hands. Oh, and I forgot to mention, when you're in Genoa, they will want you to negotiate a few purchases for the Guild. Silk, spices, the sort of things that Genoa excels in."

"Sounds better and better."

Chapter Nine
CASA CASTELLO, STRADA NUOVA: EARLY APRIL 1587

Sandro made a play of bringing Nico and Lisa out into the garden "now the weather was warmer". As they walked, the scent of orange blossom wafted down onto the terrace. He led them to a spot at the garden's western end which Lisa hadn't particularly noticed before. Sandro had designed the formal terraces to complement the house, but this area had been obscured by canvas while the work was going on. They came to a halt in front of the scaffolding.

Lisa looked curiously at Sandro. After a few moments, he said, "We have something to show you, Lisa."

The two brothers stepped forward and with a flourish lifted the tarpaulin over the poles and lay it down in front of her. Revealed was a niche in the terrace walls around which, newly constructed, was a stone archway in classical style, with portico and pillars. And around it was a small border, newly planted with rose bushes and sweet herbs.

"Oh, Sandro, it's delightful," she said, stepping forward to embrace him.

Sandro stepped back. "Well, it's your husband you should thank. It was his idea. Although I helped with the design."

She turned to Nico. "I didn't think you paid that much attention to the garden," she said, returning to his side and putting her arm in his.

"There's a new plaque we've placed in the wall," Nico said,

pointing it out. "I thought you might like to have some words engraved on it - in memory of your father?"

She did not conceal her surprise at the suggestion. "Nico, that's...that's so thoughtful of you. A lovely idea."

"After all, there's no garden at your old home. But you can see Caricamento from here. There's your house," he pointed.

She scanned the horizon, turning leftwards. "And you can see the San Giorgio too, from here."

While Sandro pointed out to Lisa some other features of the new terrace, Nico reflected on how things had gone with their marriage over what was now just ten months together. It had not been an easy adjustment for either of them, although winter at last seemed to be turning into spring.

Lisa was not at all like his mother, the only other woman he had seen at close quarters in her domestic life. Of course, their circumstances were so different. But he had been unprepared for the storms which interrupted their otherwise happy existence. Arguments which often seemed to revolve around the church. Most times, he was able to bring her around, but that didn't mean she had changed her opinion, just that she'd accepted his was different. The surprising thing was that Lisa never acknowledged that she should ultimately defer to him, her husband after all. She was not cowed by his much greater experience; the difference in their years didn't seem to count. For a young woman, not yet twenty, there was quite some steel in there, he concluded.

Not that he would have wanted a sheep-like partner, the fact that she had her own views and regarded them as being as valid as his own, that he could respect. It made for a bumpy ride, but better that than years of unruffled calm. That didn't stop him being surprised – sometimes caught out – by her tenacity.

Perhaps all young women from families like the Della Voltas behaved this way, although he thought that unlikely. It seemed that Cristoforo Della Volta had brought Lisa up, after his wife's death, to be independent of thought and action. Having lost his only son at birth, Cristoforo had seemingly fitted her into both roles. Aunt Julia had hinted on several occasions that Lisa had been indulged by her father and that it was Nico's duty to curb her, make her into the proper, obedient wife of a citizen. Like most of Julia's utterances, he paid it short shrift.

Sandro and Lisa finished their inspection of the new garden and with a glance at the clouds building over the mountains behind

Genova, which presaged a spring shower, the three of them headed inside for their midday meal.

In the *salotto*, they found that a courier had delivered a letter for Lisa. From Aunt Julia in Livorno.

"What does it say?" asked Nico, noting her darkening expression as she read down the page.

"It seems she has run out of money." There was a certain exasperation in Lisa's voice. "Apparently, she has mortgaged the Visconti house and now the bank is wanting to take possession of it. She says she has sold everything that she realistically can but is now at the end of that road."

Nico shook his head, glancing across the table at Sandro. "Why didn't she come to us before? We could have helped with the bank."

Lisa scowled, as though the answer was obvious. "Because she would never ask you. A matter of family honour."

There it was again, thought Nico, pride based on the family name outbidding all other considerations. Even if Lisa didn't get on that well with her spendthrift aunt, she clearly approved of Julia's stubbornness in the face of hard reality.

"So, what does she want, that she's so reluctant to name?" he said.

Lisa shook her head. "I hate to ask, Nico, you know she can drive me into a choler sometimes."

"Ask what?"

She breathed out audibly, steeling herself. "Can we have her stay with us for a while? Just until we can sort her affairs out. We've got the guest apartment on the floor above Sandro's."

Nico shrugged. "If you can bear it, I can."

Lisa touched his hand on the table. "Thank you. You realise I'll have to make it sound that she'd doing *us* the honour, by staying here?"

A COUPLE OF WEEKS LATER, Nico and Sandro were both down at their *banca* in the Merchants' Loggia. The Easter Fair was upon them and the hunting season over, so Sandro was spending more of his days sharing business duties with Nico. Or was it that he preferred to be out of the house rather than share it with Lisa and her aunt? Fortunately, Julia had been a model of good manners since her return from Livorno. But it was early days yet. Nico was waiting for the condescension which would no doubt surface at some point.

Business was steady that morning and the brothers had plenty to occupy them. Suddenly, there was a commotion in Piazza Banchi. Shouts rang out from the other side of the market. A cluster of pigeons on the parapet of San Pietro della Porta flew out from their temporary perches and arched towards the cathedral. Nico could see people yelling, gesticulating at one another, the ones at the back of the crowd straining their necks to see what was going on.

He sent young Lorenzo to find out what was afoot. Minutes later, the youth was back in the Loggia, breathless and excited. News had just arrived from the harbour. A Genovese galley had berthed this morning, back from Spain, and its crew had spread an astonishing story. Cádiz has been put to the torch, they said. Was it Barbary raiders, asked Sandro? Or the Turk?

Lorenzo shook his head. Who would believe it, that English pirate, Il Drago, was the culprit. He swept into the harbour unannounced, only raising his standard at the last moment. When he fired his cannon, Felipe's galleys ran away, leaving their merchantmen defenceless. To be pounded to pieces by his culverins. And the Spanish army cowered behind the city's walls and watched, as the bully sailed away with his plunder.

The initial commotion died down and people fell into conversation. What did it mean? Where would Il Drago look for his next victim? The banker at the table next to theirs speculated as to where that might be. Barcelona, perhaps? Lisbon, more likely, suggested Nico.

Sandro wondered. "But what about Genova itself? The Governor has allied himself to Spain, remember."

Nico was doubtful. "Why would Il Drago want to antagonise us? Better to befriend us and hope to loosen our alliance with King Felipe."

Sandro's eyes drifted towards their neighbours in the Loggia. Turning around, Nico saw several of their fellow moneylenders were hurriedly closing their stations. That would merely make matters worse, he thought. Customers would start to worry that there would be a stop on credit. That the *cambisti* might even cease to honour their trades. As if Nico's suspicions had been transmitted to them, some of the crowd surged forward towards the *bancas*. One table on the edge of the piazza was overturned with a crash, coins spilling everywhere, as the weight of the mob behind pressed on those at the front. Tempers rose and scuffles started breaking out. The spectators at the back roared the participants on.

Minutes later, men armed with pikes ran into the piazza. The Doge's Guard in their scarlet uniforms. Like a line of red ants heading for the centre of an anthill, the Guard forced their way through the mob and separated the combatants. Slowly, the crowds dispersed, their entertainment over. An uneasy calm set in, as merchants and money-changers gossiped in smaller groups.

When the buzz had died down, Sandro asked his brother, "Just how did Spain lose this battle, in the heart of its greatest harbour? Perhaps the story is right: Drake didn't follow the rules, didn't raise his flag."

Nico shrugged. "Whether he did or didn't, we'll never know for certain. In any case, what people *believe* happened is all that really matters."

As Nico saw it, the real question was: what damage had been done to Felipe's war machine? Had he suffered a mere wasp sting, or was it a more serious injury? If the reports of prizes taken and dockside stores burned were accurate, the king's loss was substantial. Not that that would deter Felipe from making war. Far from it. Likely, it would have the opposite effect. And so, his demands for credit from his bankers would ratchet upwards.

That much was clear, then. The result of this plundering was that Spanish borrowing would increase. And, as night follows day, credit would get tighter all round. The price of money would have to rise. He made a mental note to review the requests for credit he'd received in the last few days.

The second important question was whether Felipe could afford to repay a larger level of debt. And thankfully, that was only a question for those *cambisti* who provided credit to the king. Nico was glad he was not among them.

Chapter Ten
THE ARCHBISHOP'S PALAZZO, GENOA:
APRIL 1587

Recently enthroned as archbishop after the premature death of his much-loved predecessor, Antonmaria Sauli sat alone in what was now *his* dining room. But the prelate was not thinking of his new responsibilities to his flock, the citizens of the Republic, as he cut into his second roast quail. He was reviewing the letter he had received several weeks' earlier, from Madrid. From the king's foreign minister, Don Juan de Idiáquez.

The door opened and Father Guido entered the room. Judging by the letter, Idiáquez had given the archbishop a delicate mission and Father Guido was, inevitably, the man Sauli had selected to assist him in it. Even so, the archbishop found it hard to warm to his subordinate. Physically, the man was his opposite. A complexion like sour milk, the cheekbones hollowed out, his forearms all sinew and bone. Sauli understood that Father Guido fasted regularly and flagellated himself to excess. But these were the times. Sauli kept his disgust with such practices to himself. The man was far too useful.

"Senor Zúñiga has arrived," announced the priest. Sauli bowed his head slightly, acknowledging their previous discussion. This was the Spanish emissary that the archbishop had been expecting, the one whose impending arrival was mentioned in Idiáquez' letter. He paused, as he cut into his meat.

"Very well. Say to him that I am engaged on pressing matters, but I am agreeable to interrupting my duties for a brief consultation." Sauli chewed on the next mouthful. "Bring him to the library in say, fifteen minutes. And attend us at the meeting."

Thus dismissed, Guido bowed and exited.

Deciding he had had enough of his dinner, Sauli folded the Madrid letter and headed for the library. This room was the glory of his palazzo. Hundreds of ancient texts, separated by the occasional devotional painting, adorned its panelled walls. He selected a suitable volume and opened it at a middle page. This would do. He placed it on one of the library desks and lowered himself into a gilded chair. He adopted a studious pose. By the time there was a knock at the door, he had almost become distracted by what he was half-reading: one of the lesser-known Christian martyrs was coming to his inevitably bloody end. A few moments later the door swung open, and Father Guido announced his entry with a polite cough.

"Don Balthasar de Zúñiga, Your Grace," he said, turning to the visitor behind him with the suggestion of a bow. Looking discreetly over his book, Sauli took in his guest. The Spaniard was dressed in black from head to foot. With his spare frame on long, spindly legs, he looked like some enormous insect. He had a smallish head which, combined with his dark complexion, made his oversize ruff appear even more prominent. Having stood to greet Zúñiga and to receive the Spaniard's kiss on his jewelled finger, Sauli eased himself back into his chair and motioned to his visitor to sit opposite him.

Zúñiga's tall, gangly presence initially conveyed an air of authority, but the effect was offset when he spoke. A thin, reedy voice with a variable pitch. Father Francisco, the priest in residence at the Spanish ambassador's house, where Zúñiga was lodging, had confided to Father Guido that the household had already nicknamed him 'the Cicada'. Guido had deemed that piece of gossip too childish for the archbishop's ears.

When Sauli enquired of Zúñiga's journey, the Spaniard regaled him with the privations of travel. Evidently, he was no sailor: even the short sea crossing from Barcelona seemed to have taxed his limited tolerance. Zúñiga went on to describe, in tedious detail, the extent of his delegated authority from the king. After a few minutes, Sauli held up his hand. He had no time for such legal trivia.

"Senor, *please*. Your minister, Don Juan de Idiáquez, has taken me into his confidence as to the purpose of your visit."

Zúñiga inclined his head in acknowledgement.

"Who in Genova knows of your arrival?" Sauli continued.

"I paid my respects to Governor Doria, yesterday morning. Naturally, I did not disclose our objective. I said merely that I was here to brief our ambassador on affairs at court."

"I trust the Governor did not think that curious. *Our* ambassador returned from Madrid just a month ago."

"Circumstances can change in a month."

"Indeed, they can. We hear that the Englishman, El Draque you call him, has visited great destruction on the port of Cádiz?" Sauli was pleased to note that his question had put the Spaniard off balance.

"Your Grace, I am sure you understand that these rumours do much harm. I said as much to the Governor."

"I can *assure* you I don't spend my time listening to idle gossip. In any case, I was informed of it by Don Juan's letter, which I have here." The *presumption* of the man, Sauli thought.

"Whatever you and I may do or say, Senor," the archbishop continued, "this news has been all over the city for two weeks. Genova *floats* on a sea of gossip. It is the lifeblood of her commerce. I see little point in futile attempts to maintain secrecy. Better to let the affair blow over."

By his expression, Zúñiga seemed reluctant to bow to the inevitable.

"But what of the damage done by El Draque?" continued Sauli, careful not to disclose the limits of his own knowledge.

Zúñiga waved his hand in a gesture of dismissal. "The attack was of no serious consequence. A few ships were seized or damaged, some quayside stores were burned, but the prompt arrival of our armies soon persuaded the cowardly Draque to abandon any hope of attacking the city itself."

Sauli was unconvinced. This was the same comforting line that had been peddled by Idiáquez, in his letter. "No doubt it was but a minor annoyance to King Felipe, but you will understand our concern that the English pirate, God strike down the heretic, could assault such a great harbour with impunity."

"His attack, without raising his colours, was an outrage. But the criminal will not find his way back to England so easily," insisted Zúñiga. "The Captain-General and our fleet will surely destroy him."

" '*They sow the wind and shall reap the whirlwind*', as of course the Good Book tells us. So, shall we move on? How do preparations for the Enterprise stand?"

"We are nearly ready. Construction of our armada is well advanced. But we need more weapons to be purchased. And supplies."

"Which is where this loan comes in, no doubt. How much would His Majesty require?"

Zúñiga looked nervously across at Father Guido.

"The Father assists me in *confidential* matters, so you should have no concern about his presence. Naturally, to assist you, we need a little more information."

Zúñiga's response was stiff. "Don Juan has authorised me to borrow up to five million ducats."

Sauli sucked in his cheeks. "A sizeable sum."

"But would be repaid as soon as the *flota* arrives. Or alternatively, when Pope Sixtus commits to his promised loan."

"As for His Eminence's position on the Vatican loan, I am not of course at liberty to talk about that." Sauli smiled, as if to imply his intimate knowledge of the secret negotiations in Rome.

"So, who should we approach, Your Grace? How do we stand with Senor Grimaldi?"

"I'm afraid that Signore Grimaldi will drag his feet. I gather there are certain problems with existing loans. As I explained in my letter to the Foreign Minister, fresh capital - and a fresh face – will be required, in my view."

"Possibly Lomellino's house? Or the Pallavicinos?"

"Signore Lomellino is a possible choice, but there is a newly established bank, the Banco di Liguria, looking to make its name. The Lercaris – a distinguished Genovese family – are behind it. Such a transaction - such a client - may prove irresistible to them."

"Then let us meet them. The Minister indicated that you also have considerable sway with a ...Banco Castello?"

Sauli raised his arms off his chair. "Don Juan is most generous in his remarks. But yes, we have our allies in that camp too."

"Tell me about this Senor Castello."

"Not from a respectable family, I regret to say. But a shrewd character. The people call him "*the Alchemist*". A man who comes from base beginnings like them," the archbishop sniffed, "but one who has transformed himself into finer stuff."

"His sympathies are with the Enterprise?"

Sauli recalled the popular saying that Domenico Castello would trade with the Devil if there was a profit in it. But he only laughed inwardly at Zúñiga's question.

"They *can* be, Senor Zúñiga, they *can* be. But the undoubted privilege of lending to His Royal Majesty may not be sufficient to be certain of Signore Castello's support."

"Are there no bankers with principles?" Zúñiga exclaimed.

"I suspect that Signore Castello's guiding principle is not to lose his *money*. But I believe we can secure him, if the terms are right."

"Then please arrange an interview. I will impress on him the importance of the honour we bestow on him."

And that will make *such* a difference, thought Sauli, rising from his chair by way of dismissing the Spaniard.

Once Father Guido had escorted the envoy out of the room, Sauli picked up the correspondence he had been reviewing earlier.

There was a second letter, underneath the one from Idiáquez in Madrid. It had arrived a few days ago, but instead of putting it in a drawer, Sauli had kept it by him, so that he could gratify himself by looking at it from time to time. As he re-read its contents, a smile broke out across his face. His appointment to the College of Cardinals, confirmed by Pope Sixtus' own hand. Finally, this was his reward - and it confirmed the Vatican's belated recognition of his efforts, after being prompted by the Spanish minister over a long period.

But what would the Spanish expect from him in return for their support? His help in securing the secret loan from Pope Sixtus was part of it, no doubt. But as he looked at the scrappy signature on the Pontiff's letter, Sauli knew that getting a single lira out of that cunning old peasant would be a considerable challenge. Sixtus would play for time, and his maximum advantage, as he always did.

No, if Minister Idiáquez wanted the money quickly, the focus would be on the banks, here in Genova. This city was the doorway leading to the Enterprise and he, Sauli, held the key.

Chapter Eleven

IN THE BAY OF BISCAY: APRIL 1587

Monty Belltower stood at the bridge of the *"Mary Gale"* alongside her master, Septimus Winterhey, as they tacked around St. Matthew's Point. Two other ships, the *"Kateryn"* and the *"Clement"*, followed in her wake. This careful manoeuvre by the small flotilla, and the first sight of land since departing Plymouth, relieved the tedium of their voyage down the Sleeve. What was the attraction of a life at sea to a man such as Winterhey, Monty wondered.

Under the main deck and down to her keel, the *"Mary Gale"* was stuffed with her precious cargo, staples of the finest Cotswold wool. As were the other two ships. Monty's brokerage fee, assuming he could carry off the task the Merchant Adventurers had entrusted to him, would be substantial. And that was important for several reasons. The financial reward was only part of it. First and foremost, he had to justify the trust placed in him by Uncle Sutton. Without his uncle's influence, Monty knew he would not have landed such an important commission.

But there was another reason at the back of Monty's mind. His wife, Jane. Not long married, Jane was older than him and a wealthy widow. A good marriage, as his family - Sutton included - kept reminding him. Good for whom, he wondered. It was certainly no dream of romance and Jane had the habit of letting him know, without saying so, that it was her money they were living on. It stuck in a proud Yorkshireman's throat. Like grit in an oyster.

The "*Mary Gale*" turned south-west, leaving the coast of Brittany behind them, and the flotilla had soon cleared the offshore islands. Two days later, halfway across Biscay, they took a more westerly course, to keep a safe distance from the rocky north-western coast of Spain.

The days became warmer, the winds lighter, but the progress slower. The occasional French merchant ship came into view, but no contact was made. Monty was soon bored and accepted Master Winterhey's offer of cards, to pass the time. They played Bezique, the captain steadily winning and Monty losing. But after a couple of days, Monty scooped a large windfall. There was a pause in the card-playing after that and, while Winterhey and Boatswain Verney busied themselves with the charts, Monty took his exercise on deck.

In his wanderings, he often came across the cabin boy, whom the sailors called Joe. The lad was in his mid-teens, had dark eyes and a shock of near black hair. A face with no scars, physical or otherwise. Joe hadn't had time to acquire them. His skin colour was light brown, unlike the ruddy, weather-beaten faces of his fellow crewmen. Joe was always busy: running errands below deck, scampering up the rigging to check the horizon, learning new skills from the crew, with whom he seemed popular. Monty's curiosity was piqued; he asked Boatswain Verney about him. "Italian lad, a runaway," was all he could get out of the man.

On a listless afternoon, when there was little point in hoisting more sail, the crew were enjoying a brief spell of enforced idleness. Monty found Joe squatting on deck, his back to a mast. He was reading a book. That was surprising, given that most of the crew didn't have their letters. Only a few could do as much as write their own names, Monty suspected. Looking over the boy's shoulder, the text seemed to be in Italian. But the few words and phrases he'd picked up from the Florentine merchants in London weren't anywhere near enough to translate even a sentence of it.

"What is it you're reading, young man?"

The lad looked up. Then he closed the volume and passed it to Monty. He looked at the short title, trying hard not to read it aloud. But his face must have betrayed his efforts, for Joe explained, "*Il Decamerone*. Ten people leave the city together, escape the plague. Each one tells a story."

Monty had not paid much attention to his letters at school, but some faint memory was stirred by Joe's description. He decided to steer the conversation away from literature where, he feared, his limited knowledge would be easily exposed.

"And where is your home city, Joe?" he said.

The youth didn't respond but took the book back from him. Time to practice a little Italian, he told himself. "*Dove sono*, Joe?" he said, aware of his halting pronunciation. How pathetic to feel embarrassed in front of a mere boy.

But it got a response. "*Sono di Genova*," Joe said, a hint of pride in his voice.

Feeling a little more confident, Monty pressed on. "*Allora, quanti anni hai?*"

"*Diciassette*," Joe said, with a scowl of defiance.

Seventeen. A boast, Monty guessed. The lad's voice had broken, but he looked no more than fifteen, perhaps sixteen. "And what are you doing on this boat?"

The lad shrugged, as if it was obvious what he did here. Monty decided to persist.

"Mi chiamo ...Montague."

The boy looked but did not respond.

Monty repeated it. "*Monta-gue*. How do you say - in Italian? *Montecchio*?"

Montecchio, as a name, seemed to impress the lad more.

"And your name, Joe, *in italiano*?"

The youth breathed in. "Giovanni. Giovanni Lercari." Obviously, too much of a mouthful for English seamen, compared to 'Joe'.

"Can you read English books too?" Monty asked.

The boy shook his head. "Only a little. The Master showed me his Bible."

"Perhaps we can help one another. I would like to read Italian better."

Monty went back to his cabin to find a suitable volume from his very limited collection. No poetry or plays there, the choice fell between *The Art of Angling* and Markham's *Country Contentments*. In the end, he plumped for the latter. Its occasional line drawings of the huntsman's quarry, the stag, the hare, the fox and the boar, should make Monty's explanation of the English words easier.

Over supper with Winterhey that evening, he raised the subject of the cabin boy.

"Ah, you've been talkin' with Joe?" the master said. "A stowaway. It was on the journey back from Genoa, last season. Found him hidin' down in the hold. Smart lad I'd say, from a good family even. Can read and write. Seems he just wanted an adventure, to go to sea." Winterhey spoke as if he was quite fond of Joe.

"And you couldn't return to port?"

Winterhey shook his head. "We were 'alf-way to the Rock afore he were discovered. I promised I'd find him a Genoa-bound boat in England, or take him home the next charter I got, but he didn't seem too worried. When we was back in Plymouth, I offered to find a family for him to lodge with, but he didn't want that neither. Said he would stay with the "*Mary Gale*" until we returned and since then he's sort of become one of the crew."

"But now he's going back?"

"Yes, I'm sure he has grievin' parents somewhere in Genoa. I'll speak to the authorities when we make port."

MONTY BELLTOWER WAS on the bridge several days later, when Boatswain Verney was at the wheel. Verney nodded in the direction of the starboard bow. Cloud was piling up on the western horizon. "We'll be in for a blow," he said, "...might have a rough night." He yelled some instructions to the second mate. The crew started taking loose stores to the lower decks. Anything that couldn't be stowed below was lashed to the rails or the masts.

Monty took his evening meal with Winterhey, as usual. Several times, conversation was interrupted by their plates sliding across the table. Their supper over, Winterhey went to check with Verney that all was well up top. For Monty, there was nothing to do but retire to his cabin. The roll of the boat was getting steeper all the time, or so it seemed. And the wind was howling. But even so, he fell asleep almost immediately.

It seemed that only minutes had passed when he was jolted awake. He had rolled across the bunk and hit the bulwark. Fumbling in the dark, his eyes latched onto the glow from the gangway lantern. It was banging against the planks of the deck above. "Jesu, we're going over!" he muttered, and hurled himself out of the bunk. Then he heard the boatswain's yells from up top. A call to arms. He scrambled up the steps.

Reaching the top, he forced the door open, but the onrush of wind nearly threw him back down the gangway. Gripping the door jam, he pulled himself outside. Immediately he was drenched in freezing spray. Beyond the ship's sides all was black, the sea and sky indistinguishable. For a moment, Monty thought he saw the flash of a sail, one of the "*Mary Gale's*" sister ships he assumed. Winterhey was on the bridge, screaming orders to the men up top. Verney was next to him, fighting with the wheel. He guessed that Verney was trying to turn her, so they could run before the wind.

As his eyes adjusted to the darkness, he saw men strung out like rows of spiders on the yardarms high above him. They were struggling to reef in sail, clinging to the juddering timbers each time the ship ploughed into a deep trough. One of them lost his footing. He was holding on by his hands, his feet cartwheeling in the air trying to locate the rigging beneath. Monty suddenly realised it was the cabin boy, Joe.

The "*Mary Gale*" yawed as a huge wave smacked into her, amid-ships. A scream from aloft, as Joe's grip loosened. For a moment he was flying above the deck, his limbs spread wide in a star shape. Then his ankle struck one of the lower spars, turning him on his back. He was still dropping, though trying to grasp any rigging within reach.

It seemed to take forever for Joe to fall. But then he was down, down in the surf washing over the port side, close to the ship's rail. Monty scrambled down the main deck, holding onto whatever he could, his feet nearly swept from under him by the rush of seawater. Finally, he made it to Joe. The lad was floating in two feet of water, his body jolting against the rail with each wave. Either stunned or dead, Monty couldn't tell. Grabbing Joe around the waist, he tried to drag him up the deck towards the bridge. Another wave swept the starboard side, taking them with it and slamming them into the port rail. As the water receded, Monty was down on his knees, coughing up seawater. He grabbed Joe and set off again, but the pitching of the ship threw them back towards the fo'csle, just as if they were scraps of paper.

Through the roar, he heard Winterhey yelling from the bridge. He looked up and spotted a coiled rope under the master's arm. Winterhey had lashed the rope to the bridge rail and stood poised to throw it. Monty beckoned with his free arm and Winterhey hurled the rope in his direction. It fell short, but stretching out he could just reach it. He coiled a couple of lengths around the boy's belly and himself. Getting a good purchase on the rope was next to impossible, but he secured it with all his remaining strength. He raised an arm towards Winterhey.

The master started to pull on the rope. But the surging water held Joe and Monty back near their starting point. Seeing their halting progress, Boatswain Verney lashed the wheel to the bridge and joined Winterhey. The two men hauled together, slowly winching Monty and Joe up the deck. It took mere minutes to drag them the thirty feet or so to the bridge, but to Monty it seemed like hours. One final desperate scramble and he was gripping the rail of the bridge steps. Winterhey took the wheel and gestured to the Boatswain to get the pair below decks. Verney put Joe over his shoulder and carried him down the steps, Monty stumbling behind him. Reaching the cabin, he sank down to his knees, staring into the gloom. All he could hear was the incessant roar of the wind, punctuated by a thump as another wave smashed into the ship. But after a while these sounds faded, and he drifted into sleep.

Chapter Twelve
THE ARCHBISHOP'S PALAZZO, GENOA:
APRIL 1587

Nico walked along Campetto, wondering why he had been invited to an audience with the archbishop himself. Perhaps Sauli would press him for another large donation to the fabric of the cathedral. Nico felt he had already given San Lorenzo more than enough to ensure his smooth passage into the afterlife. But the archbishop's appetite for commissioning expensive adornments to his church seemed limitless.

He passed the narrow Vico Scudai, where the shield-makers and weavers had their premises. At one time, his home had been near there, after Vittorio had moved the family out of Pre. By the time Nico left school, his father had rented a separate workshop, in the rooms underneath San Pietro in Banchi. But wherever they were, from Nico's schooldays until he was on the threshold of manhood, his father had been a distant figure. He spent all his hours in the shop, working on metal pieces. Earning the wherewithal for Nico's mother, Emilia, to feed the family and bring up two boys.

Vittorio had assumed that Nico would carry on the family business – Sandro was still too young for his possible future to be considered - but Nico's apprenticeship as a silversmith did not go smoothly. He was too impatient, Vittorio told him. Sensing his father's disappointment at his progress, he looked for other ways he might assist him. Given his schooling and his apparent talent for numbers, his mother suggested Nico could help by maintaining the business records, for which Vittorio had a limited appetite. And Nico, who felt all at sea when he had his father's tiny hammers and chisels in his hands, did not need to be told how to reckon up receipts and payments. Vittorio was happy to be free of this burden, and soon Nico was spending much of his time, quill in hand, re-ordering and expanding the scrappy ledgers that his father had kept.

It was a natural extension of Vittorio's trade that he lent small amounts to some of his customers, usually against the security of the items that were deposited with him for refashioning. The rate of interest he charged was equivalent to the rates charged by the *cambisti* in the Loggia. Over time, this business grew, and soon Vittorio was lending small sums to trusted customers, whether they wanted their silver pieces worked on or not. But for a customer he did not know that well, he would require the deposit of a saleable item of appropriate value.

It did not take Nico long to reorganise the debits and credits from these loan transactions in the new ledgers. And even less time to realise that his father was making almost as much from lending, which didn't seem to involve any physical skill or effort, as he did from his craft. Not one to keep such thoughts to himself, he presented his father with his calculations. And followed that with the obvious conclusion: that Vittorio should spend less time in his workshop and set himself up as a fully-fledged moneylender, a *cambisto*.

Vittorio laughed at his son's presumption and carried on hammering away at a decorated plate. "All well and good, Nico, but those *gentlemen* over there," without looking up, Vittorio gestured with his small hammer towards the Loggia, "have a good deal more capital behind them than I." Nico could sense his temper rising, frustrated at his father's apparent lack of ambition. After a few minutes, Vittorio put down his tools and looked at his son. "Besides, you're wrong to say there's no skill involved in lending money. The skill is in spotting the customer who might not pay you back," he selected a small chisel and laid its tip on the plate with a precise movement. "... and not lending to him."

Absorbed in reminiscence, Nico found he had arrived at the cathedral. The usual stream of penitents was entering and leaving by the west door. He sidestepped the queue and passed through the archway leading to the archbishop's palazzo. The iron grille was opened and Nico stepped past the guard and into the cloister. A young novice arrived to escort him to Archbishop Sauli. From the grand entrance hall, they entered a reception room. The novice's voice trembled as he announced Nico.

At the far end, facing the doorway sat the archbishop, squeezed into his chair. Nico bowed stiffly at the doorway and then approached Sauli, who extended his right hand for Nico to kiss the ring. To his right, in a lower chair, was a man he did not know. Dressed in black with an elaborate wide ruff.

"Let me introduce you," said the archbishop gesturing towards the man, "Signore Domenico Castello. His Excellency, Don Balthasar de Zúñiga."

Zúñiga stood up and exchanged bows with Nico. "Senor Castello, a pleasure to meet you," he pronounced. The formality of his manner was rather undermined by the high-pitched, reedy voice.

The archbishop addressed Nico. "I should explain that Senor Zúñiga is an emissary from the Spanish Court. You will pardon our brief communication about this meeting, but the subject is a rather *delicate* one." Sauli paused before continuing.

"As you will appreciate, Signore Castello, His Catholic Majesty, King Felipe, has many burdens and responsibilities in ruling a great empire and, I should add, in defending the Church from the many enemies that assail her. That burden is sustained by the tributes that flow from His Majesty's dominions around the world, in particular the silks and spices of the Orient and silver from the Vice-Royalty of New Spain. However, His Majesty finds he must outlay significant expenditure *before* the next tranche of the income to which I refer, arrives in Spanish harbours." The archbishop paused, glancing at Zúñiga.

Zúñiga took the prompt. "His Grace is correct. His Majesty has authorised me to make the necessary arrangements for short term credit. We have asked you here, Senor Castello, as I am advised you are a *substantial* financier. In short, His Majesty graciously invites you to participate in such business." Zúñiga paused, no doubt expecting Nico to express his humble gratitude. But Nico merely held his gaze.

Zúñiga's eyebrows arched. "And so... I would be grateful, Senor, if you could indicate the terms that you would propose, for providing credit to His Majesty."

"How large a credit, if I may ask?"

The Spaniard opened his palms outward. "Let us say, one and a half? Million ducats," he added, as if that were superfluous information.

Nico kept his expression impassive. It was larger than he would have guessed, indeed it was greater than any single advance that Nicolo Grimaldi was rumoured to have lent the king. "Your Excellency, before I could consider possible terms, I would need to know a deal more of the circumstances."

"Senor Castello, I merely mean to ascertain whether you are *willing* to offer such a loan and at what rate of interest," Zúñiga responded dismissively. "What could be simpler?"

Nico touched the widow's peak of his hairline with his index finger. "Well, with respect, almost anything. In the first place, are you in discussions with other bankers to arrange separate credits? I assume that you are."

Zúñiga's eyelids flickered. "I am not accustomed to discussing His Majesty's affairs in this way," he protested.

"You need not tell me *which* banks you are negotiating with, or any confidential details of course. But I do need to know if the king intends to borrow elsewhere, in addition to this loan. And if so, how much is the proposed debt in total."

"I may say," Zúñiga replied with a sniff, "that His Majesty's current needs are *considerable* and will no doubt involve several banks. It is not a question of how much he requires, but rather if you are willing to be one of the lenders?"

Seeing Nico glance in his direction, the archbishop intervened. "I think, Don Balthasar, it would assist Signore Castello greatly if you could indicate in general, what total size of credits you would be intending to raise here in Genova, if you can be a *little* more specific."

"And, if I may add, Your Grace, for how *long* His Majesty needs to borrow the funds," Nico said, with a smile.

Zúñiga leaned back from the table. "Well, overall, His Majesty is seeking around five million ducats. As for the loan period, we anticipate repayment within six months, although I cannot be precise. As you will appreciate, senor, it depends on when the silver fleet arrives in Spanish waters."

"Yes, I see that. And, to what use will this advance be put?"

Zúñiga looked down his long nose at Nico. "A matter of state, Senor Castello. Naturally, I am not at liberty to discuss it with *anyone*, outside the Consejo de Finanza."

"A final point, if I may. There's the question of security for the loan."

"Security?" Zúñiga looked affronted. "His Majesty is willing to execute *asientos* for his promise to repay. That should suffice."

Nico did not respond. While he was comfortable with the ensuing silence, Zúñiga clearly was not.

"And so," the Spaniard said, drumming his fingers on the table, "what of your terms?"

"My terms?" Nico echoed. "You appreciate that I will need time to consider. But please express my thanks to His Majesty, for the invitation." He placed his hands on the arms of his chair, about to stand up.

Zúñiga looked surprised. "But surely some indication, Senor Castello? This opportunity will not be open to your bank indefinitely."

Nico took his hands back off the chair arms. "I will consider it, but I cannot give you my answer today, Senor Zúñiga. One and a half million ducats is, let us be clear, a large sum of money. And then there's the absence of collateral."

Zúñiga spluttered, his reedy voice rising even higher in pitch. "*Collateral*? His Majesty's word is the finest collateral any lender can require."

Nico spread the fingers of his raised right hand. "Perhaps I should have said *additional* collateral."

Zúñiga's face reddened, and the archbishop intervened. "Your Excellency, I think we can do no more at this stage. We should allow Signore Castello time to reflect on this important matter."

Zúñiga, looking as if he would like to assault the banker for his presumption, clenched his jaw tight.

Sauli turned to Nico. "Signore Castello, I would be *most* grateful for your consideration of the honour afforded to your bank by Senor Zúñiga's invitation. Also, I would stress the importance that both the Church, and Governor Doria I am sure, would attach to the tangible support that you can provide to His Majesty."

"I will consider it carefully, Your Grace." As he stood up, Nico added, "But can I assume there would be no question of the loan breaching the Church's usury laws? Whatever terms might be set for the interest?"

The archbishop scowled. "I think you may assume so," he said eventually.

"Then, if we were to proceed, I would be grateful for a dispensation from Your Grace. For the record, merely." He bowed and made his leave.

The double doors closed behind him. As he walked down the

corridor to the lobby, he could hear Zúñiga's high-pitched outbursts through the wall, as the Spaniard yelled at the archbishop.

"So, what did the good archbishop want?" Sandro asked Nico, as the brothers took their midday meal a couple of hours later. They were alone, Lisa having gone with Julia to visit her aunt's ailing relative.

Nico summarised his meeting at San Lorenzo.

"An honour to be asked," Sandro said, when Nico had finished.

"It is?"

"Why ever not?"

"Because, for all we know, our fellow bankers may have declined this particular honour."

"When did you start basing your decisions on the views of your competitors?"

Nico smiled, acknowledging that Sandro had scored a point.

"I plough my own furrow, Sandro. But let's not run away with ourselves. One and a half million ducats is a huge sum, more than we've ever lent a single borrower."

"But this is the *king* we are talking about. I agree, the sum is large, but we could form a syndicate, sell down part of the loan?"

"Perhaps, but we can't be sure who would participate. Grimaldi certainly wouldn't join anything *we* begin. In any event, I don't really like syndicates: I prefer to keep the business we undertake for ourselves."

"I agree that's preferable. The king would be grateful to us alone."

"Oh, *gratitude,* yes. I wonder how long that would last when he had spent the money."

"But when he comes back for more, as he surely will?"

"Then we would have to decide whether to throw good money after bad. *Never* be in that position, Sandro. As the good Copernicus tells us."

Sandro leant back in his chair, reflecting. "What does he mean to spend it on, do you think?"

Nico speared a piece of salad onto his fork and chewed it slowly. "War."

Sandro's face froze for a moment. Then he smiled. "Perfect. A desperate borrower. We can set any terms we like."

"Of *course* we can, Sandro. And the king would sign *anything* we put in front of him. Whether he intended to honour it or not."

"I hope that you at least said we were willing to discuss terms?"

"I gave no indication either way."

"Why ever not? Think of it. The Castellos, bankers to the king!"

"I think more about our capital. I don't wish to lose it."

"Aren't you being a pessimist?"

"Why so? Others have lost their fortunes in lending to the Hapsburgs."

"I accept the Fuggers did all those years ago, but they took excessive risks. Whereas old Grimaldi has done very well out of the Spanish business. Why not us?"

"*Signore Vittorio* Grimaldi would be transacting *this* business if he thought he would do well out of it. The fact the Spanish have asked *me* suggests that he isn't."

Sandro had no immediate riposte. The room was quiet for a time as the brothers finished their meal.

Despite himself, Nico resumed his lecture. "And besides, what do you know of banking risk, brother? You spend most of your time these days gallivanting with the Dorias."

Sandro's face reddened. "Yes, I spend time with the prince's son. Is it not important that their family has a favourable view of us? I promote our reputation, Nico, whenever I can. I scarcely think that to be time-wasting."

He stood up, as if to leave, but then carried on the argument. "And what should I say to young Doria, when he asks me why we won't support Spain, when our competitors have? One day, he will inherit his father's title, remember."

"Tell him that... what this Republic needs is strong bankers. Not ones that lose their capital, lending to foreign princes. Gianandrea Doria knows this. So will his son, when he becomes our Prince."

"I accept there is risk. So, price it accordingly. What if Felipe *was* slow in paying? At the rate of interest we could charge, let him take all the time he needs. This isn't just lire and soldi we're talking about, with the ruler of the Hapsburgs as our customer."

"It isn't?" Nico laughed. "Of *course* it is, Sandro. Anything else is mere vanity."

Sandro started pacing up and down. "Why, the Governor himself could go on his knees to you, Archbishop Sauli could promise you sainthood, all you can see is the money you can count. Don't bother to answer," he concluded, as he marched out of the room.

"Who's promising you sainthood?" came a voice behind him. It was Lisa, who had just returned to the house.

"Oh, Sandro and I were just having a discussion."

"Yes. I could hear you from down in the courtyard."

"A business concern, nothing that need worry you."

"And I'm not included in such matters, of course."

Nico failed to suppress a sigh. "This is a banking issue, Lisa, nothing more or less ..."

"Indeed. Well, I pray that one day my husband will be as willing to trust his wife, as he is his brother." She turned to leave the room.

Nico grabbed her arm and spun her round, bringing her angry, beautiful face close to his. "Lisa, it is not a question of trust." He relaxed his grip. "I will tell you of course, if you wish." He stretched out his hand to stroke her cheek, but Lisa pulled back.

She settled herself on a dining chair and waited. Nico stood opposite her, his hands holding the back of a chair.

"This morning, I was invited to the cathedral," he began.

Lisa raised one eyebrow. "I don't suppose the archbishop wants a loan."

Nico looked heavenwards. "No, indeed not, but the Spanish do. Archbishop Sauli introduced me to an emissary from the Spanish Court. He is seeking a large loan for King Felipe, over a million ducats in fact."

"And you said yes?"

Nico shrugged. "The archbishop would wish me to, of course. And so would Sandro, as you heard just now. But I think I will decline the request."

"Is it wise, to refuse the Spanish?"

It was a question Nico had asked himself on the way back from San Lorenzo. "Well, safer in my view than saying yes. Their emissary will be disappointed by a refusal, but I can play the courtier if I need to," he reassured her. In truth, saying no to Zúñiga was simply the better of two bad situations. Either way, the consequences were unlikely to be that easily managed. But there was only one real choice.

Chapter Thirteen
OFF THE NORTH PORTUGUESE COAST:
THE SAME DAY

Sensing daylight, Monty opened his eyes. His outer clothes had been laid over his trunk to dry out. Standing up, he could feel the ship still pitching and rolling, but less severely. He dressed and hauled himself up on deck. Winterhey beckoned him up to the bridge.

Monty looked to the horizon on each side. The sea was charcoal-hued and the foam on the wavetops looked like shreds of torn canvas. But it was empty. No sign of the *"Clement"* or the *"Kateryn"*.

"Scattered by the storm," observed Winterhey, reading his thoughts.

"How is young Joe?" he asked, after a brief silence.

"Fine. Sprained 'is ankle and bruised a few ribs, but nothin' seems broken. He's a light body. Fallin' into three foot of movin' water must've saved him from worse."

"That's good to hear."

"He'll want to thank 'ee for rescuin' him. Would've been swep' away otherwise."

To Monty, it was his first storm at sea, but it seemed that to Winterhey this was business as usual. A windy day for a West Country sailor.

After breakfast – despite the depressingly familiar fare, Monty was ravenous – he stepped below decks and found Giovanni. The lad was resting against a mast, sharing some food with a couple of crewmen.

One ankle had a large bandage around it. His companions withdrew to a respectful distance as Monty approached.

"And how is our student?" he asked Giovanni, in Italian.

The smile was broad. "*Molto bene, signore. Grazie a voi.*"

But beyond that comment, it seemed that Giovanni didn't want to revisit the events of the previous night. After a while he said, "You have a family name, Signore Montecchio?"

"Why, yes. It's Belltower."

Giovanni's eyebrows knitted together. "Bello Toro?" he ventured.

"Bell. Tower. In Italian, it would be, er – *Campanile*."

Giovanni's mouth opened. "Campanile?"

"That's it."

The open mouth became a smile. And then the boy was laughing freely, his hands flapping.

"Campa-*nile*, campa-*nile*," he repeated.

Monty was laughing too, though he didn't know why. But now he was a fixture in Giovanni's mind. Each time their paths crossed, Giovanni would mimic the sound of bells. Monty didn't fret about being teased in this way. A big man with ginger hair gets used to being the butt of others' jokes. Even an impudent youth.

As if in compensation for his teasing, Giovanni gave Monty an affirmation of their closer friendship. "My family - and my friends - they call me Gino."

"Very well then, Gino. And my friends call me Monty."

"Monte, Monte," said the youth, committing it to memory.

Later that day, Monty was back on the bridge when there was a yell from the topsail yard above. He followed the lookout's pointing arm and spotted a sail on the horizon. Winterhey recognised her rigging. It was the *"Clement"*, her survival a cause for cheering all round.

The two ships battled on through powerful seas. On the following day, there was still a heavy swell, but the clouds had lifted. No sign of the *"Kateryn"*, but Winterhey's instructions had been that if they were scattered, the flotilla should reassemble off Madeira.

They arrived off the island later that afternoon and dropped anchor. Monty asked how long they should wait. Winterhey scratched his beard. "Not too long," was his response, "if she's still afloat, the *"Kateryn"* should make it to port without us and if not, well, our waiting here won't make a penneth o' difference to them poor souls."

The next day was spent on more repairs, until Winterhey decided they had tarried long enough. He called for the anchors to be hauled in.

They set a course north-eastward towards the jaws of the Mediterranean. A westerly breeze filled the sails, and they fairly skipped over the water.

Winterhey said, "We'll need every ounce of speed. Don't want to cross paths with those Spanish galleys from Cádiz."

"What if you sailed closer to the African shore?" Monty asked.

A shake of the head from the master. "That's fine, when we reach the Straits. Portuguese territory, that is. But out 'ere, best not to get too close to the African side. That way," he gestured towards the starboard bow, "Barbary pirates could find us. Slit all our throats for a prize like this."

Instinctively, Monty looked at the empty eastern horizon.

"So, if it's all the same to you," Winterhey said, his smile displaying the gaps in his front teeth, "we'll take the middlin' course. And trust to our luck until we're in the Straits."

The following morning, Monty talked again with young Gino. Before the storm, the youth had held back regarding his home life, but their shared danger had lowered his guard. It was clear that he came from a gaod family, as Winterhey had surmised. Gino was a little vague about his father's occupation, but he seemed to be some sort of merchant, so far as Monty could tell. Gino attended school at the cathedral before jumping on the *"Mary Gale"*, although he didn't seem to have enjoyed it much. Had he been the age he had previously claimed, he would have already left school, Monty realised, but he didn't embarrass the lad by bringing it up.

"Your father will be relieved to have you back home, safe and sound," he said.

Gino raised his eyebrows, an expression of doubt.

"You're worried he'll be angry with you - for running away?"

No reply. Monty suspected he had hit home.

"I tell you what. Master Winterhey and I, we'll take you to your father's house. We can explain. I'm sure all will be well."

The lad looked hopeful but not convinced. "My father, he wants me to become a priest."

"And what would *you* like to do?"

Gino looked above their heads at the masts and rigging. "I want to be a captain. Have my own boat and sail the seas."

Monty thought Gino must have Cornish blood in him, to feel that way after the storm they'd been through. "Your father will be very thankful that you have returned, maybe he'll grant you anything you wish."

The lad shook his head. You don't know my father, Signore."

MONTY WAS on the edge of wakefulness when he felt the ship change tack. As his senses came into play, he heard movements and shouts up on deck. He remembered that Winterhey had said the evening before, that they would make port the next morning. He pulled on his boots and headed up to the main deck.

Most of the crew were there: impatient no doubt, to reach Genoa after weeks at sea. Looking over the bows, all he could see at first was an uneven blue line: a narrow border of land between sky and sea. As they edged closer, he was able to pick out some features of the harbour. A man-made promontory of boulders, topped by a lighthouse, jutted out into the sea protecting it from the prevailing weather. Beyond that, the line of a second pier, leading from the eastern side of the bay - on its landward side, the tops of dozens of masts.

Master Winterhey joined him at the rail. He gestured towards the lighthouse, as they passed it. "*The Lanterna*. I recall bein' told that, at one time, you had to pay a toll just to keep her burnin'. Now, there's an oil-burner lit all the time." Painted on the sandstone column of the lighthouse, and facing inwards towards the city, was a shield bearing a red cross on white ground.

"It's like England's flag?" Monty said.

"Their Cross of St. George is the same as ours," agreed Winterhey, "but I suspect theirs were first. There's an old joke," he added, "that English sailors took the same flag to avoid fights with the Genoese navy." He laughed. "That's probably what it is, though, just a story."

Tacking back behind the breakwater, the two ships approached the second pier. "This is the Molo," continued Winterhey, gesturing to their starboard side. "This is where we berth, so if you'll excuse me."

On deck, all was furious activity as the crew prepared to dock. Sails were furled and tied, the mooring ropes ready to throw onto the pier, the lower portholes all closed. As soon as Boatswain Verney had made the *"Mary Gale"* secure, Winterhey was ready to disembark. Monty needed no urging to follow him down the gangway. He felt unsteady on his legs at first, but it passed after a few minutes of walking along the Molo. He was not a little relieved to be back on dry land.

The pair walked towards a massive stone barbican, which barred their way to the city itself. *Porta Siberia,* Winterhey informed him. An archway stood at its centre, bridging the narrow space between two squat, castellated towers. Inside, Winterhey paid his port dues to the Harbour Master. He told Monty that this was also the place where their cargo would be held until they had cleared the shipment through customs.

They left the Siberia and continued along the quay. When they reached its end, a broad, curving promenade, identified by Winterhey as the Caricamento, ran to their left dividing harbour from city. On the harbour side was a low wall. On its landward side, a long parade of houses, many four or five stories high. So different from London's narrow houses, with their irregular gabled roofs and jetties. And slate-roofed, not a thatch to be seen anywhere.

Their next stop was Banco di San Giorgio. Monty remembered Uncle Sutton's description of her. "No ordinary bank, Monty," Sutton had said. "She issues bonds and lends huge sums to the Republic of Genoa. In return, the grateful city grants the Bank the right to collect – and keep - all Genoa's customs duties. And she manages the Exchange Fairs, each quarter." The San Giorgio was, in short, banker, clearing house, treasury and tax collector for the city-republic, all in one.

The San Giorgio's offices were housed in a gleaming white palazzo, the largest building on the waterfront, which thrust itself out from the shoreline on stone foundations. Its front elevation bore a large fresco on the stucco. St George slaying the Dragon. The holy knight was wearing gold armour, the dragon, silver. Monty caught up with Winterhey, who'd seen the building many times before.

Once inside, they ascended a broad marble staircase and entered an enormous hall. Its ceiling was higher than most London houses, Monty commented. The room's sheer size disguised the number of people within. Customs officials of the San Giorgio with scribes at their side and merchants, shippers and agents clustered around the many desks, or just milling about.

Finding an unoccupied customs man at one desk, Monty presented his papers for importation of the cargo.

"You have sailed from *England*, Signore?"

"Yes, from London."

The man's eyebrows rose a fraction.

"Is there a problem?" Monty asked.

The man shook his head. "No difficulty, no. You may trade freely. But there are of course some formalities. And some levies to be paid."

The 'formalities' were extensive, so by the time they left the San Giorgio. Monty was feeling famished. They decided to stop at a taverna on Caricamento. As they entered, Monty noted the array of food on display, seafood, brightly coloured vegetables, spice jars. The pungent smell of unfamiliar herbs wafted out from the kitchen. He ordered some pasta which came in a green sauce, with herb-laden bread and a tomato salad. After his shipboard diet of broth, porridge, dried beef and stockfish, it felt like a feast. And the wines - despite assurances, he decided not to touch the water - were light and fruit-scented, not like the heavy bordeaux wines he knew in England.

The meal over, they walked back along the Molo, Winterhey to return to his ship and Monty to collect his travelling trunk.

"Where to next, Winterhey?" asked Monty.

Winterhey shrugged. "Well, I don't want to return to England in ballast, Master Montague. So, I'll be here for a few days, lookin' for freight business."

"Remember, I'll be returning to London myself after two or three months. Once I've traded our cargo, I'll be making purchases. Not as bulky as wool, but I'll need a suitable ship."

"Aye, so you said. Well, t'other way I can play it is to take on some local cargo, ship it down the Italian coast and then return to England via Genoa in a few months' time."

"That would suit me well enough."

"I will let you know what I do, either way. Where are you staying, Master Montague?" Winterhey enquired.

"My uncle has arranged accommodation for me with a merchant he knows called Lorenzo Cavalli. He lives somewhere up there," said Monty, pointing with his left hand past the black and white tower of the cathedral.

"Well, be careful what you pay those caravani, to transport your trunk to the gentleman's house," Winterhey advised as they parted.

But the dock porters had the monopoly on porterage business in the harbour, so Monty felt he had little choice but to agree the exorbitant fee that the morose-looking man demanded. They climbed steadily uphill, through broad streets initially, and then along narrower, darker alleys. Soon, Monty was wheezing from the effort. Perhaps the porter's fee was not so unreasonable after all. The man stopped in front of a large house and pounded at the door. Above it was a carved portal of elegant design, but the facing was cracked and chipped.

Lorenzo Cavalli was an elderly gentleman with a snowy white beard, but his cheerful face and his exuberant greeting of his guest belied his years. Once questions about the voyage were satisfied, Monty was shown into two connected rooms, with a bed in the second room. Compared to his bunk on the *"Mary Gale"*, the bed looked huge and inviting.

Kicking off his boots, Monty lay down and stretched his feet out, dangling them over the end of the bed. After the constant motion of the ship, it felt good. Silently, he thanked Almighty God for his safe passage from England. It was only early evening, but before he could resist, sleep overcame him.

A GENTLE KNOCK on his door woke Monty early the next morning. A pair of Signore Cavalli's maidservants entered his room, struggling with their burden. Thoughtfully, Cavalli had arranged for a copper bath to be brought for him. Soon afterwards, they returned with ewers of warm water to fill it. After a leisurely soak, Monty dressed in fresh linen and joined his host downstairs for breakfast. After demolishing the meal, Monty set out down the hill, armed with Signore Cavalli's directions.

Passing the San Giorgio on the waterfront, he spotted a small market square set back from it, which fitted Cavalli's description. This must be Piazza Banchi, he concluded, judging from the little church which took up its entire southern side. The central marketplace was crowded, business in full swing. Traders dealing in cloth, alum, spices and leather, sellers seeking buyers and vice versa.

Threading his way through the crowds to the far side of the piazza, he came to the Loggia dei Mercanti, the Merchants' Hall. Inside, its occupants were sheltered from the sun and cooled by the harbour breeze which filtered through its open columns. There sat the bankers who were financing the trade going on around them. Each institution had its own table where business was conducted, its *"banca"*. He recalled Uncle Sutton saying that the location of a *banca* within the Loggia was dictated by some unspoken hierarchy, reflecting the proprietor's place in the pecking order. But how to track down his quarry?

Monty leant closer to the man standing next to him in the crowd. "Excuse me, would you point out Signore Domenico Castello?"

His neighbour, an elderly man, looked at him curiously. Monty wondered if he was deaf, or he had not followed Monty's usage of his native tongue. He tried again, at the same time as gesturing towards the Loggia. "Signore *Castello*? Per favore."

The man was obviously surprised at Monty's ignorance. "Ah. *Certamente*. Le signore, la," he added, pointing. Monty looked in the general direction of the man's arm. It led to a table in a corner position. Behind it sat a man he assumed was the proprietor, quill in hand. Next to him a young lad with his head bowed over the table, watching closely what was being written. Monty pointed towards the seated man to get confirmation.

The old fellow shook his head, smiling. "No, no, la. *La*." Monty looked again and noticed what he hadn't seen before: some way back from the *banca*, a younger man wearing an ivory-coloured doublet.

His neighbour touched Monty's sleeve and added, in reverential tones, "You are looking at the *Alchemist*, Signore."

Chapter Fourteen
THE MERCHANTS' LOGGIA, PIAZZA BANCHI: EARLY MAY 1587

Nico observed the *straniero* crossing the piazza. The man's style of dress said he wasn't a local. His skin was pale, although reddened by the sun. He was tall, heavily built, with a mane of reddish hair. A Viking, he joked to himself. From Northern Europe certainly, by his appearance. He was threading his way through the busy market. But he didn't seem interested in the goods being offered for sale. He was looking up at the buildings around him, as if seeing the city for the first time.

He watched as the 'Viking' spoke to an old man in the crowd. The citizen gestured in Nico's direction. The stranger thanked his informant with a slight bow of the head and entered the Loggia. He stopped a couple of paces in front Nico.

"Signore Castello?"

Nico looked up. "Domenico Castello, signore. May I be of assistance?" He raised himself from the chair and gave a bow, which the man returned.

"Montague Belltower. From England. Here, for the Fair." The man's pronunciation was dire, but the Italian was passable enough to understand. Better than my English, that's for certain, Nico thought.

"Welcome to Genova then, signore. So, you have travelled from London, I imagine?"

"Arrived just yesterday."

"Indeed?" Nico attracted the attention of his young clerk. Lorenzo jumped into action and brought over a folding chair and embroidered cushions for the visitor. Followed by a jug of chilled wine, diluted with water. Once the Englishman was sufficiently fussed over, Nico waited for his visitor to explain himself.

"Signore Castello, I am a member of the Wool Merchants Guild of London. You have heard of us, perhaps?"

Nico raised his hands, as if acknowledging a small miracle. "Signore, the reputation of your house arrives before you." He was embellishing a little, but it was nevertheless true that the Guild was known throughout Italy for the quality of its fleeces. It was surprising to Nico that the English didn't seem interested in bringing more of their wool here. At least this Englishman had troubled to make the voyage.

"Well, you are generous, signore. But perhaps you will know some of my patrons better. I am here on behalf of the Merchant Adventurers. It is Master Sutton of their Company who has arranged it all."

Nico leant back in his chair, regarding his visitor. Sutton's name was certainly known, not something you could say for many merchant families from that unfamiliar country. England was perhaps a small pond, but Sutton was a big fish in it, so far as Nico had heard.

"So, Signore Castello. I've brought with me a large consignment of our finest fleeces, for the weavers of Italy. I'm approaching you because we will need to lodge the proceeds with bankers who have correspondents in London."

For Nico, though, it was too early in their conversation to get down to business details. "Interesting, most interesting. But tell me first, how was your voyage from London?"

Monty sucked in his breath through his teeth. "Glad to be off that boat, I can tell you. I'm no sailor, Signore Castello, but that was a rough passage, alright." Monty's ensuing description was accompanied by sweeping arm gestures, to illustrate the mountainous seas that had assailed his little flotilla. Nico wondered if he was exaggerating for effect. But then Monty told him that one of their vessels, the *"Kateryn"*, was still missing. Presumed lost.

Nico crossed himself. "My commiserations. Those poor souls. But at least *you* came through the tempest unscathed."

He decided to try the Englishman out with the rumours that had recently been circulating in the Loggia.

"Perhaps I should mention some recent news, in case you were unaware of it. It is said that your fellow countryman, 'Il Drago' they call him here, has attacked Cádiz by sea. Had you heard?"

He watched the Englishman's jaw drop. *Obviously not.* The man blustered. "Il Drago, who might that be...."

"I believe that the Spanish call him 'El Draque'. Perhaps that name is more familiar to you...."

"Drake," muttered the Englishman, suddenly catching on, "*Sir Francis* Drake."

"*Esattamente.*"

There was a few moments' silence as his visitor digested the news. "Are they sure this was Drake?" he managed.

Nico opened his palms outward. "I don't think there is much doubt. He sails in, no colours aloft, raises them at the last moment, he fires his cannon, destroys many ships and stores. He seizes a few prizes, he sails out."

His visitor shook his head, his upper teeth biting his lower lip. Not a report that delighted him, clearly.

"Our ship visited Plymouth before we crossed to the French coast. We were told Drake was expected to arrive there any day. That he was sailing down with a flotilla. But nobody knew his intention. I assumed he was headed for somewhere in the Indies. Certainly, not Cádiz."

Nico sensed that the man was being frank. Merchant to merchant. "*Naturally*, but here in Genova we wonder if this means war between your country and Spain."

The Englishman glanced around them, to see if they were being overheard. He leaned closer. "If it were to come to that," he said, "how would we stand, here in Genoa?"

"Well, our Governor, Gianandrea Doria, is a friend to King Felipe, as you probably know. As were his forefathers. For many years, the Dorias have led Genova's fleet in the service of the Hapsburgs. It was our navy that tipped the scales in Felipe's favour, against the Turk back in '71? But these days, the Governor is a little less inclined for such foreign adventures."

"How so?"

"Perhaps he thinks more towards the future now. He's nearing fifty and sadly, four of his sons have not survived childhood. So, he is more indulgent of the two remaining ones. And less inclined to send them off to fight Felipe's wars. He also knows these campaigns aren't popular with our citizens."

"But what of the banking families? How would they view it, if Spain went to war with us?"

"For us, Signore Montague, war is an expensive luxury. In peacetime, our financial dealings with Spain have greatly benefitted Genova, it's true. But regrettably, it has not always been a blessing for the lenders. Quite a few of them are still counting the cost of previous wars."

"And merchant business?"

"Oh, business will slow down for a while. Then, when it restarts, prices will likely rise." He opened his palms. "War and trade, it's an unstable mix."

"But I mean, how would someone like *me* be regarded in the city? An Englishman. Might my business be unwelcome here, after this news?"

The man appeared genuinely concerned, not unreasonably perhaps. Nico gave him his broadest smile. "Spain has powerful friends here, as you may imagine. So, you may find your reception, in some quarters at least, is a little… *cooler* than normal. But remember signore, Genova, she trades with the *world*. That will not be changed by a disagreement between two other countries. Our business with London will go on. The *cambisti* will see to that."

The Englishman leaned back in his chair, finishing his second glass of wine in a gulp. "That is good to hear, Signore Castello." But his tone of voice did not suggest he was much reassured by the answer. And in truth, despite his breezy assessment, Nico wondered if there would soon be hints coming from the treasurers of the *San Giorgio*, that out of prudence, the *cambisti* should scale back their business with the English.

Let's get away from this subject, he thought. "My business occasionally calls me to other capitals, but I have yet to visit London, of which we hear so much," he said.

"Perhaps I can persuade you to visit us, signore. I am sure that a visit to London would be worthy of your time," suggested Monty.

Time, thought Nico, as the Englishman was talking. He glanced over his visitor's shoulder, out into the piazza. The sun was now just past its highest point and for a spring day, it was unseasonably warm. Traders, moneychangers and customers alike were beginning to flag. *Time to go.*

"May I suggest we can discuss these matters in more detail tomorrow? Shall we say here, around five in the afternoon?" The invitation was rapidly accepted.

As the Englishman stood up, it seemed that another thought occurred to him.

"By the way, do you happen to know a Signore Lercari?"

"*Ferrucio* Lercari? Of course. He is a banker, a *cambisto*, like me. Often you will find him here, but...," he glanced around the Loggia, "... not today it seems. Did you wish to meet him?"

"Well, not in his professional capacity just at the moment," Monty said. "A personal matter, you understand."

Nico didn't, but it would be rude to pry.

Ferrucio Lercari was one of the few heads of the old merchant families who treated Nico as an equal, despite their utterly different backgrounds. He had recently told Nico that, having established the Banco di Liguria with his cousins, he now realised what Nico had achieved to make Banco Castello the success it was. A simple matter of respect for a worthy competitor.

"If you like, I could send word of your arrival to his house?" Nico suggested to Monty.

"Well, I don't know the man, he will not know my name so," he paused, "...it might be simpler if I explained the matter to you."

Nico encouraged Monty to resume his seat. "Be assured of my discretion, Signore Belltower. How can I help?"

"He has a son, I believe."

"Ah yes, Luca. He also works in the family bank."

"I meant his younger son, Giovanni?"

Nico stared at the Englishman, genuinely surprised. "Giovanni? I regret to tell you that Signore Lercari's son went missing, oh, it must be nearly a year ago now. The family have not seen him since. They have not completely given up hope, but it seems unlikely he is still alive."

There was a short silence. "But excuse me, why do you ask?" he continued.

Monty pressed his palms together. "Because I believe the boy is very much alive."

"Why so?"

"He stowed away on an English ship in the harbour. Before he was discovered, they were halfway back to England."

"But how do *you* know this?"

"Giovanni himself told me. On the boat that brought me to Genoa, the *"Mary Gale"*. He has been with her all that time. Likes adventure, clearly. But I think he's glad to be home."

Nico clapped his visitor on both shoulders. "Signore, I say again, you are most *welcome* to Genova. If I were that way inclined, I would call it a miracle, but...," he paused, "can you bring the boy here, now?"

"Of course, he is with Master Winterhey. I can go to the ship and be back here in say... half an hour?"

"*Eccellente.*" Nico looked around and beckoned his junior clerk to his side. "Lorenzo, go at once to Casa Lercari. Ask for Signore Lercari to come to the Loggia. A matter of great importance. Say that Domenico Castello has requested it."

The boy nodded.

Nico shoved him. "Well, run then, *run*!"

Twenty minutes after Nico had dispatched young Lorenzo, Lercari arrived from his house, slightly out of breath. Ferrucio Lercari was a man in his middle years, and short in stature. When he stood next to Nico, there was a four-inch difference in height. But he was as powerfully built as Nico: almost as broad as he was long. His limbs looked as if they were fashioned out of forged iron. His familiar name 'Ferro' could scarcely be more appropriate.

Nico knew that Lercari would assume some urgent business matter was the cause of the summons. But when the banker asked him to explain, Nico demurred, telling Lercari to wait for 'something that will surprise you'. Initially the man was patient, but after a minute or two he started pacing up and down in the piazza, demanding Nico tell him more.

Nico held up a hand. "Just a few more minutes, Ferro."

Finally, over Lercari's shoulder, Nico caught sight of the returning Englishman, accompanied by an older man, a sailor by the look of him. And between the two of them, a skinny youth, his face tanned by sun and wind, his clothes threadbare. But it was the Lercari boy, no question.

Ferrucio Lercari noticed the direction of Nico's gaze and turned around. His eyes settled on the trio in front of him. He stared. And then, fell on his knees in the dust, overcome with the sight. As a crowd from the piazza gathered round the little group, Nico watched the joyous scene from the steps of the Loggia. There were surely few times in life, he told himself, when a father would publicly display his love for a grown-up son. A natural reticence, especially under the gaze of the crowd, made it the exception rather than the rule. But even more blessed for its rarity. The scenes that afternoon would be talked about in Piazza Banchi for many weeks, he predicted.

After ten minutes in the centre of the throng, Monty extracted himself and returned to Nico's *banca*. "I think my job is done here," he said.

Nico laughed. "Oh no, signore, *that's* not so. This story will bear much repeating. Signore Lercari for one will insist on that."

"Perhaps you're right. At least one Englishman will be welcome in some Genoa households," he added, referring to their earlier conversation. Nico sensed the Englishman's shyness.

Monty bowed farewell. "Well, until tomorrow then, signore."

"I look forward to it." They exchanged bows and Monty returned to the Lercaris, father and son, and the small crowd still clustered around them. Monty's back was being slapped so much he would surely have bruises tomorrow.

Chapter Fifteen

THE MERCHANTS' LOGGIA, PIAZZA
BANCHI: THE NEXT DAY

Monty entered the Loggia, making straight for the Castellos' *banca*. Nico welcomed him with a glass of fine Barbera, as befitted the man who'd returned Gino Lercari to the bosom of his family. They talked over the memorable events of the previous day. Eventually, Nico came to business: the banking of Monty's wool sales.

"I am curious, signore. That you approached *my* bank for this business? Since you have returned his long-lost son to him, Signore Lercari would no doubt be very happy to accommodate you."

"Well, in truth it was Master Winterhey, not I, that looked after Giovanni all that time. But yes, I'm sure I'll do business with Signore Lercari, in due course. But I believe we'll need more than one banker to support us. Thomas Sutton was quite clear – your bank was one I should approach."

"We would be pleased to bank the proceeds of your wool sales and remit the credits to our correspondents in London. You said that the Adventurers wanted to make purchases too?"

"Ah yes. The finest silk cloth. And spices: cloves, pepper, nutmeg."

"Well, as to spices, you should move cautiously. The prices are likely to fall as the summer progresses. And choose your suppliers wisely. Before you commit to any seller, let me advise you first."

"There's also the question of payment for these goods. It wasn't practicable to transport *all* the necessary funds here. We'll have the wool proceeds, of course, but they won't be sufficient on their own. So, we need to arrange credit for part of the trades."

"And the collateral?" Nico said. *No point in skirting around the issue.*

It seemed that Monty had anticipated his question. "I have with me notarised letters of credit from several London bankers. They will pay out to the final holder of these letters. And here," he handed over a single sheet of manuscript, "are the names of the bankers, and the credit they each stand good for."

Nico scanned the names on the list – and the pledged sums in each case. It was extraordinary. He read it again, just to be certain he had understood it correctly. In his head, he rapidly calculated the total: it was obvious that the deposits listed here would provide backing for one of the largest pieces of merchant business he had seen this, or for that matter, any other year.

But if Nico was surprised, he was certainly not going to show it. He handed the list back to Monty with a warning, "Most satisfactory, but I would advise caution before disclosing the size of your intended business here. Amounts such as these," he waived his hand at the document, "can cause the selling prices to move mysteriously upwards."

"Your point is well made, Signore Castello. But you can provide us with credit for these trades?"

Nico reached for the wine and refilled his visitor's glass again. *Saints, but this man had a thirst.*

"That would be my pleasure."

Nico sensed Monty's shoulders releasing their tension.

Sandro came by the Loggia, shortly after the Englishman had left.

"Perhaps we should be careful, Nico, before we advance him any credit? After all, what will happen next, after that assault on Cádiz? If Spain invades England, those letters of credit might be difficult to collect."

"I've told him there may be situations where we would decline further business. He understands that. But until that happens, I'm willing to accommodate him. The Merchant Adventurers are a solid credit, after all. These trades are fully backed by bullion. In London banks we already do business with."

"The English, they come, they go, like the tide. Good harvest, bad harvest. One year here, the next absent. Whereas the Spanish ..."

"I prefer the English business. They're not always here in Genova, that's true, but when they are here, they don't default on their promises."

"You're still set against lending to King Felipe?"

"If the Englishman defaults, we have the collateral, we can enforce it. And it's short-term. If war comes, we can withdraw from the business at a moment's notice. But not from the King's loan. What would we do if Felipe declares that he won't pay his creditors this year? We are powerless – and locked in."

FATHER GUIDO WALKED out of the brothel. He stood in the dismal forecourt of the crumbling house, contemplating the thanklessness of his task. Ministering to whores. Godless women, living in this pitiful alley. They didn't attend mass. They resented donating a few paltry *soldi* for the poor. Many of them verbally objected to his visiting at all, saying to his face that his presence deterred their customers and deprived them of their living. A comment from which he drew quiet satisfaction. Some would even speak disrespectfully, making lewd suggestions to him. He prided himself on the restraint with which he bore such taunts.

One or two of these slatterns at least had a care for their immortal souls and would regularly confess to him. But it was the identity of their customers that were Guido's principal concern, particularly if it was a man in whom Archbishop Sauli had expressed an interest. Before he gave them absolution, Guido would extract their little secrets concerning the sinners who had patronised them. Purely for evidential purposes, he was sometimes witness to a shameful coupling, listening on the other side of a threadbare curtain. The whores who provided him with this useful information were rewarded with small monetary doles, taken from the cathedral's fund for the relief of the poor. The Church's beneficence to these wretched women would no doubt encourage their sisters to follow their example.

From the dark unto the light. From the deep shadows at the bottom of Via San Luca, he stepped into a sun-bleached Piazza Banchi. After their Sunday of prayers and resting at home, the city's merchants were back, working hard at storing up riches on earth. He turned left in the direction of Campetto. When he reached the cathedral precincts some ten minutes later, a visitor was waiting for him. Ferrucio Lercari, the principal partner in Banco di Liguria, had just arrived.

Father Guido ushered Lercari into his room overlooking the cloisters. The banker took in his surroundings: the plain, rendered walls, the desk with its uncarved stool and the solitary chair for the rare visitor.

"I appreciate your coming here, Signore Lercari," Guido began, "rather than our meeting down at the Loggia, but the archbishop and I, we were anxious to hear news about the proposed loan to the Spanish king. How are your discussions with your partners progressing?"

Lercari had met with Balthasar de Zúñiga two weeks earlier. The discussions between the Spanish emissary and Lercari had ended on a more positive note than Zúñiga's discussions with Domenico Castello. Not that that would have been difficult, Guido reminded himself.

Lercari explained the assessment that was being undertaken within the bank. No doubt out of politeness to his host, he listed the pertinent factors but, at the same time, gave little of substance away.

"No doubt there are many factors to be considered. But I can tell the archbishop that an offer will be forthcoming shortly?"

A short pause. "You may say that. Although naturally, I can't say whether our terms will meet with Senor Zúñiga's favour."

Forcing a smile, Guido stood up to escort his visitor out. But as they were crossing the threshold, the banker apparently remembered something he had forgotten.

"Father, you could also convey a message to the archbishop for me?"

"By all means. And it is?"

"My younger son Giovanni is sixteen. He has been restored to us from the perils of the sea, by the grace of the Lord. I would like him to be considered for a novitiate, at the cathedral."

Guido noted the ease with which Lercari had managed to suggest a link between this request and his consideration of the Spanish credit, without saying so.

"Let me discuss it with the archbishop. I will let you know his decision as soon as possible."

"The impertinence!" Archbishop Sauli spluttered; his mouth full of the roast chicken he had been enjoying. A morsel flew out of his mouth and landed on the floor, just missing Guido's sandalled foot. "How dare he make such a request? That young runaway is utterly unsuitable for the priesthood."

"Your Grace, I merely said to Signore Lercari that I would ask you. I made no promises."

Sauli grunted. "Lercari's son is obviously full of lust and rebellion. You only need look at the father to see why. Their family may have a long lineage, but they are all driven by their appetites. Ferrucio Lercari openly keeps a mistress in a house near Porta Soprana, we hear."

Guido bowed. "Then, after a few days, I will tell Signore Lercari that regrettably..."

"You will do no such thing. We will have to accommodate his grubby little ambitions, otherwise I fear our Spanish friend will find his mission quite beyond him."

"Then should I indicate to Signore Lercari that his son's application will be looked upon favourably?"

Sauli stabbed another defenceless piece of chicken with his fork. "Though it irks me, we have little choice. Weeks have passed and Domenico Castello has still to confirm whether he will do any business with the king. So, yes, securing a loan from Lercari has become essential."

Guido hovered, expecting more. Sauli glared up at him. "Well, do you need to be told twice? Get to it."

When the priest had departed, Sauli considered what to do with these greedy bankers. He certainly didn't like the idea of being beholden to Lercari. And Castello was reluctant to be drawn. But with the Castellos at least, there were other influences that could be brought to bear.

Chapter Sixteen
CASA CASTELLO, STRADA NUOVA: TWO WEEKS LATER

Nico, standing by Sandro's side, glanced around the room. A gratifying sight: there were nearly a hundred guests in the *sala* and, he estimated, almost as many again in the gardens below. The credenzas along one wall were laden with platefuls of delicacies. The centrepiece was a wild boar on a majolica platter, his tusks still intact, the ferocity of his gaze somewhat undermined by the orange stuffed in his jaws.

The excuse for the *festa* was the completion of the formal gardens. Sandro, who had been the driving force behind their design, had enthusiastically supported Lisa's suggestion of such an event. Nico was impressed by the way the pair of them had thrown their energies into it. Even the Doge had graced the house with his attendance, if briefly. Genova's merchant community was fully represented, many of them customers of the bank. But Nico had also invited many of his fellow *cambisti*, even though they were Banco Castello's competitors. Important to show that the Castellos could stand above petty rivalries. Ferrucio Lercari and Battista Lomellino had come as he had expected, but most of the other *cambisti* had graciously accepted too.

Of course, as he had also anticipated, Nicolo Grimaldi had not made an appearance, even though they were near neighbours. The "Monarch" rarely fraternised with the rest of Genova's merchant class. But even the Grimaldis had been sensitive of the correct behaviour. Ansaldo, a younger member of their clan, was here to represent the family.

Nico had also extended invitations to Senor Zúñiga and Archbishop Sauli. They arrived more or less at the same moment, so while Sandro shepherded the cleric around the *sala*, Nico spoke with Zúñiga. The conversation with the Spaniard was awkward, not helped by Zúñiga's graceless manner, and the fact that Nico had no good news to convey. In the preceding days, he and Sandro had argued over the matter several times, without reaching agreement. Absent a major change in the circumstances, Nico's view would prevail. Not that he shared any of this with Zúñiga, of course. He talked in generalities about the loan size, the uncertain repayment date, and other technical factors without saying explicitly what he really felt - that he didn't like the king's poor credit record. Clearly frustrated, Zúñiga made his excuses and left early.

Returning to the *sala*, Nico tried to identify who had yet to arrive. He recalled sending an invitation to the English merchant, Signore Montague.

Given Lisa's obvious antipathy to Englishmen, Nico had broached with her the question of Monty's attendance beforehand. Lisa had for some time understood that her husband, in common with most of the *cambisti,* did business with every trading nation, whatever their allegiances - or their faiths. But it was still a step from that to inviting one of these merchants to their own home.

He recalled how her face had taken on a stony look.

"You never mentioned you were intending to invite that man."

"Well, I am doing it now."

"When it's too late to withdraw the invitation!"

"I only met him again this morning."

"And didn't consider my feelings."

"Just because he happens to be English? Surely you can see there is no connection between this man and that pirate, thousands of leagues away. No connection at all. They were born in the same country, that's all."

Her voice rose. "What difference does that make? Wherever they are, are the English not our enemy?"

"England may be Spain's enemy. But she is not mine. Kings can have the luxury of enemies, republics even, but not banks. I deal with borrowers, not nations."

Lisa ignored his comment. "And the English are the enemy of our church. Or do you hold yourself above religion too?"

Nico willed himself to keep his temper under control. "I am not here to judge their souls, just their credit."

"Their banker, not their confessor, is that it? And yet you often say you know how to judge a man. I thought only the Lord Our Father was our judge."

It was too much. "And I am *your* lord, Lisa. Remember that."

"And I suppose that means I must meekly stand by and watch as you, you ...." She did not finish.

Nico heard himself speaking with deliberate slowness. "My bank will lend to honest merchants, be they Catholic or Protestant, Mahommedan or Jew."

Lisa's face had high colour now. "Trade with whom you please," she spat out, "that doesn't mean I have to be *pleasant* to them."

He shut his eyes, remembering their argument. Fortunately, Lisa's temper was as quick to subside as it was to be aroused in the first place. She had grudgingly acknowledged that, as *donna di casa*, it was her responsibility to be the gracious hostess to all their guests even if, in a few cases, she might have to do it through gritted teeth.

Looking around the room, he wondered where his wife was. She had been with him when the *festa* commenced, greeting their guests as they arrived, but she had disappeared somewhere while Nico was talking with Zúñiga. Moments later, as if summoned by his thought, Lisa emerged through a narrow door beside the entrance to the *sala*, one which led directly to her bedroom via a private corridor. She was accompanied by Aunt Julia, who was helping Lisa with the voluminous skirts of her dress, so she could negotiate the passageway in safety. The dress itself was newly acquired. Layers of raw black silk, with slashed sleeves showing the ivory satin beneath. Lisa had fussed over its cost, her family instinct for parsimony coming to the fore, but Nico had been dismissive. What was money for? And now she was wearing it, he was pleased that he had encouraged the purchase. The tailor had indeed earned his fee. Judging by her expression, Aunt Julia was of the same view, even jealous, he suspected. And Lisa wore it as no other woman in the room could. He was a lucky man, if luck had anything to do with it.

Sandro brought Ansaldo Grimaldi across to meet them. Grimaldi was young, elegantly dressed and to Nico's mind, had a high opinion of himself. However, he complimented Lisa on her appearance, and then turned to Nico, congratulating him on having wed such a beautiful bride.

Grimaldi was running out of compliments when Nico caught sight of Monty Belltower. The Englishman was just arriving at the top of the main staircase. Nico took Lisa's arm. "If you will excuse us for a moment, Ansaldo, we must greet another arrival. We will return shortly, but Sandro can entertain you until then."

Monty was wearing a black velvet doublet, Nico noted, presumably one he reserved for major social occasions. He would never be an Apollo, with his oversized frame and unruly red hair, but he did not look undignified. Nico made the introductions. "*Signore, mia sposa, Lisa.* Lisa, this gentleman is from England. Signore Montague ...Belltover." He still struggled with the man's family name.

"Signora Castello, it is a great pleasure and honour to meet you," said Monty. Lisa curtsied in return, somewhat perfunctorily Nico thought.

Monty complimented her on the beauty of the house.

Lisa was dismissive. "Oh, it was my husband's house before our marriage, signore."

"Nevertheless, I am sure that it is you who deserves the plaudits for this wonderful evening."

"You are kind to say so. But among Genovese families, the *festa* is becoming a regular thing these days."

Monty's eyebrows rose a fraction. "Perhaps, signora. They are certainly not regular where I come from."

Nico cut in. "I understand you exactly, Signore Montague. Families in Bergamo didn't have them either, certainly not mine."

"Bergamo? I suppose I had assumed that the Castello family were from Genoa?" Monty looked questioningly at them both.

"Well, my father came here and set up as a silversmith many years ago, when I was a mere boy," Nico explained. "I suppose future generations of Castellos will regard Genova as our natural home. Whereas" his sideways glance directed the Englishman back towards Lisa, "my wife's family are Genovese, over many generations."

"I assume then, signora, your parents still live in Genoa?"

When the response did not come immediately, Nico glanced at his wife's face. It was as if the sun had gone behind a cloud. A large, black one.

"My parents are both deceased," she finally said. "And so," the inward breath was audible, "if you will excuse me, signore, I must check matters with the kitchen." Picking up the folds of her skirt, she turned on her heel.

She was striding at a fast pace down the corridor by the time Nico caught up with her. He grabbed her right elbow and spun her round. Her face had a distant look.

"Lisa, Lisa, listen to me. He was not to know."

"Maybe so. But unlike you, I cannot just close the door on my feelings."

"I do not ask for that. You feel what you feel. I merely say that you should try and think of him as a mere merchant. He has not come to our country to make war on us."

She took a deep breath. "My father, God rest his soul, would have said the same. But my heart is ... I cannot just dissemble and play the courtier."

Nico pulled her towards him. "God willing, time will heal that. You will see. Let us go back in."

Returning to the *sala* once Lisa was calmer, he walked her towards Sandro who, as always, managed to extract a smile from his sister-in-law. Monty was still where they had left him, having his glass refilled. Nico left his wife and brother together and went over to him. "Please excuse my wife, she was upset," he said.

"But I had no idea that the signora was an orphan, given her young age," protested Monty.

"Of course not." They had reached a corner of the room, out of earshot of other guests.

"I should probably explain. Lisa lost her mother to the plague when she was four years old. Thereafter, she was brought up by her father. An only child. They were close."

"Ah. And when did her father die?"

"It was a few months before we were betrothed. So, just over a year ago. Her aunt, Julia, was staying with her when the terrible news came."

"What news was that, if I may ask?"

"Cristoforo Della Volta died in New Spain. He was engaged on a survey of the Spanish silver trade. For the Banco di San Giorgio."

"Ah. What befell him there?"

Nico gave a grim laugh. "Your *countrymen* befell him. He was asleep in his bed when he was killed outright. By a cannonball from an English ship. I imagine you can guess the name of the captain of that ship, since you and I have talked of him before."

There was a brief pause. "You don't mean, Drake?"

Nico did a mock bow. "*Esatto*, signore."

Rather than leave Monty to dwell on the tale he had just imparted, Nico looked around for a suitable diversion. He gestured to Sandro, who came over with a pair of guests in tow. Sandro introduced Monty to Battista Lomellino and his wife, Caterina. They were near neighbours of the Castellos in Strada Nuova, he explained. Lomellino seemed surprised to meet an English visitor at his neighbour's house. He himself had visited London, on more than one occasion. But Nico inferred, from his description, that Lomellino was unimpressed by the city even if he appreciated its business opportunities. '*Cold and draughty houses, strange food*' seemed to sum up his assessment. Sandro berated him light-heartedly for failing to appreciate the benefits of travel.

A servant bearing a large flagon of wine hovered nearby and Monty took the chance to have his glass topped up again.

"So," said Nico, "have you seen the gardens?"

"Not yet. But I would be delighted to," he responded. Nico led Monty, who was now walking rather unsteadily, down the gallery staircase. They passed through an archway into the garden. Lit by dozens of lanterns among the marble nudes and potted shrubs, it was the perfect contrast to the merrymaking din upstairs in the *sala*. In the cloister adjoining it, a harpsichord player and a sextet of viols and recorders were making music. The fountain at the far end of the formal garden was lit by suspended lanterns and gave out a dappled, shimmering light.

"Never seen anythin' like it," Monty remarked. Truthfully, if his expression was any guide.

"No doubt it's a simple affair compared to the gardens where your Queen Elsabetta entertains her guests."

"Not so simple, I assure you," Monty replied. "In any case, there are few evenin's in England when we can entertain in the open air."

Nico shuddered at the thought. "That must be very confining..."

The sound of a cough came from the shadows behind them. Nico turned around as the bulky form of Archbishop Sauli stepped forward to greet him. To the prelate's left and half in shadow, was the figure of Father Guido, seemingly the author of the cough. Guiding them forward was Sandro, who had a concerned expression on his face.

"Your Grace, I trust we are entertaining you well...." Nico began.

"Indeed, Signore Castello, but regrettably we must now be leaving."

"Of course, of course," Nico responded sympathetically, "we are most honoured by your presence."

Sauli glanced beyond Nico, in Monty's direction. His eyes narrowed with barely disguised curiosity. Prompted by his glance, Nico said, "Before you leave, allow me to introduce to you a gentleman from England. Signore Montague Bell Tower."

He turned to Monty. "I have the honour to present His Grace the Archbishop, Cardinal Sauli." He swept his arm wider, indicating Sauli's companion, "And this gentleman is Father Guido."

Sauli moved a step closer. "An *English*man?" His tone of voice suggested he was talking about some unusual species of wild animal. "Well, I suppose we can tarry a little longer," continued the prelate, with a glance at Sandro.

"So, signore, what brings you to my city?" Sauli asked Monty.

Nico smiled inwardly at Sauli's use of "*my*".

"I come here as a wool merchant," said Monty, his voice slurred. "Genoa's reputation has reached the merchants of London, Your Grace."

"Genova, signore, Geno-Va," said Sauli, correcting the Englishman. "Those foreign merchants who deal honestly with us will find fair dealing here," Sauli continued, speaking to the group rather than just Monty. "For myself, I have not travelled as far as England." Sauli's tone suggested that Monty's homeland was somewhere off the edge of the map.

"But", added the archbishop, "I have had occasion to meet a few of your fellow-countrymen. When I was a young man, studying at Padova, there were one or two Englishmen attending the university."

"Do you recall any of them?" Monty asked.

"I do seem to remember one rather stern young man." Sauli touched his temple with the tip of his middle finger. "I believe he has since become quite elevated in your country. Val-si-nam, was that the name?" he added.

"Sir Francis Walsin'ham, I'd venture," said Monty.

Sauli's eyes glinted in recognition. "*Esatto*. Do you know him, by chance?"

Monty waved his right arm, apparently unaware that he had spilt some drops of wine on the archbishop's mantle. "Alas, I have not had that pleasure."

Sauli smirked. "Well, I've heard it said that a meeting with *that* gentleman is a pleasure that some of your fellow citizens would go a long way to avoid."

"Your Grace, I am a mere merchant. Matters of state do not concern me."

"Just so." Nico saw Sauli purse his lips, as if to say that matters of state were certainly *his* province. Then, touching Nico on the shoulder, the churchman steered his host away from the group, and out of earshot.

"My dear Castello," he began, keeping his voice low, "I wanted to have a brief word with you alone. Naturally, we were expecting that by now you would have responded positively to Senor Zúñiga's request. But I gather there are still difficulties." He glanced towards Sandro.

"We have been considering the matter, your grace, and at length. It is not an easy decision, but, as I have told Senor Zúñiga, we do not wish to send out false hopes. If I may suggest to you, you should encourage him to look elsewhere for credit."

The corners of Sauli's mouth turned downwards. "That will be a disappointment to him. And, I may say, to myself also. Is there no prospect of changing your mind?"

"I doubt my view will change."

Sauli's tone turned colder. "Well, you must proceed as you see fit. But I would advise you to reflect on it further. It is not for me to tell you your business, signore, but I would be sorry to learn that your bank is unwilling to help the allies of the church."

It's not a matter of will. It's a matter of arithmetic, Nico thought. He was about to say something emollient, when the sound of rhythmical music came from the house.

Guido came across and leant close to the archbishop's ear, making a private remark. Sauli nodded in agreement with his subordinate. "Signore Castello, as I said, we must be leaving," he announced. And after a curt bow to Nico and Sandro, and an even briefer one to Monty, he swept off. Sandro ran after the archbishop and the priest and escorted them to the lobby.

"Pompous old cleric," muttered Monty under his breath. The drink had obviously loosened his tongue, so Nico ignored the comment.

"Now the Church has left us, the party can properly get going," he said.

Seeing his guest's baffled expression, he explained. "Oh, it wouldn't be proper for our spiritual leader to be present at such revels. Or at least, that's Father Guido's viewpoint. But it's the tradition, for *festas* in Genova, that the host lead his guests in the *gagliarda*. So, if you follow me to the *sala*, you can witness my poor attempts at dancing."

"Ah, the galliard," observed Monty. "It is popular with us, also."

When they arrived, the room had been cleared by the servants. As the viols played a loud chord to tune themselves up, Lisa stepped into the middle of the room and clapped her hands loudly. The buzz of conversation died away and, as the troupe of musicians struck up the introduction, Nico stepped out to join her. Her left hand in his right, they faced the guests, bowed to them and then to each other. Nico walked around his partner in time to the music. In places, the dance was energetic; at times either he or Lisa would perform leaps in the air and on one occasion he raised her off her feet, his arms around her waist. What Nico lacked in elegance and style, he made up for with energy and strength, easily lifting his spouse. They were warmly applauded by the company.

After the *gagliarda*, the guests took to the floor. After a couple of dances, Nico noticed Monty standing around the edge. He was, of course, lacking a lady partner and probably fearful of the right etiquette in asking someone to dance. Nico considered whether he should suggest to Lisa that she dance with the Englishman but thought better of it. He motioned to Monty to join them. Just after he reached their side, a loud fanfare erupted from the musicians. A quartet of young women entered the room. They were dressed in their party finery but wearing masks.

"Why don't you describe to our English guest what is happening, Lisa?" Nico said. He hoped her obvious reluctance was not obvious to Monty.

"You will witness one of our Genovese customs, signore, *la comedia all'impriviso*," she said. It was a theatrical performance, but one where party guests were players for the night.

The lights were doused, and the assembled company fell quiet. Four young men entered the room. On top of their own clothes, they had donned servant's garb, simple cotton smocks and hats. One of the four 'servants' was soon to be married. He was spending the night before his wedding out drinking with his male friends. The four men proceeded to engage a group of masked ladies in conversation. Nico wondered if Monty would pick up much of their colloquial Italian, but judging by his amused reaction he had the essence of the story. The actors' stagecraft was sufficient to suggest the bawdy innuendo in their speech. At one point, the bridegroom made an aside to the audience in a loud whisper. He was hoping to get in some practice for his wedding night 'performance'. Soon, the audience were all laughing.

The four young women were playing wives whose husbands were away with the navy. They were lonely for male company and the male performers – as servants of the big house - provided it. There was more than a suggestion of illicit behaviour. Some of the performing couples were rather wooden in their acting, but one pair were clearly attracted to one another and became much engrossed in their parts: a convincing demonstration of the lure of forbidden pleasures. At the end of the comedy, there was enthusiastic applause: the lusty couple took several bows.

As the 'actors' departed the room, Monty commented to his hosts. "As good as anythin' I've seen."

"So, your theatres in London have plays like this?" Lisa asked.

"Ah well, they do, but...," he paused before continuing, "Her Majesty will not permit women actors. All the parts are played by men."

Lisa's face showed her surprise. "You mean: the men, they dress up as... *women*?"

"Exactly so, signora."

"But how could two men, however talented as actors, truthfully show relations between a man and a woman?"

"I must confess, this performance tends to support your argument."

"Perhaps you should propose a change in the law to your Queen," suggested Nico.

Monty laughed. "Sadly, I would have little prospect of getting such a change approved. But, if I ever have the chance, I will be sure to recommend it."

IT WAS PAST MIDNIGHT. Having escorted their last few guests to the lobby, the Castello brothers sat around the table in the *salotto*. Lisa had retired to bed – to her own apartment, Nico noted. He drained his glass. While the *festa* was in full swing, neither brother had drunk much. But now, they had finished a bottle of Chianti between them. Although Sandro had drunk most of it. His younger brother was not his usual talkative self, either.

"It was a fine *festa*, Sandro, was it not?"

Sandro didn't respond.

"And I should mention, I spoke to Senor Zúñiga earlier about the loan."

"I gathered that from the archbishop."

"I said I couldn't see a way for us to go ahead. No point in dragging this out."

"Suppose not."

"You're not happy about it."

"Should I be?"

"But with no collateral? Why in heaven's name are you still pushing for this?"

But Nico sensed that Sandro wasn't really listening. Sandro refilled his glass and then, as an afterthought, filled Nico's too. "There's more at stake here than just business," he muttered.

"There is?" Nico tried to catch Sandro's expression, but Sandro was staring hard at the tablecloth. What was he missing here?

"The archbishop said, as he was leaving, that I should persuade you to change your mind. I said I didn't think there was a chance you would do so. He became threatening. He said that if that was really the position...." Sandro paused, fiddling with the stem of his glass. ".... then he might be forced to make public what he knew."

"What he knew?" Nico began to feel that he was repeating Sandro's phrases back to him. "About what?"

Sandro's voice dropped to a low register. "Knew about me," he said.

"What's there to know?"

"Guido had found out that I'm part of Bernardo Pareto's circle."

Nico recalled the name. Pareto was a spendthrift nobleman and apparently close to the Governor's son, Prince Andrea. His influence on the young man was not universally approved.

"The archbishop said... the relationships between us men were an abomination, against God's teaching. And that if he informed the Governor, I and several others would be ruined, if not worse."

"You're saying he accused you of... sodomy?"

Sandro nodded slowly.

"You denied it, of course."

"Yes," said Sandro finally, "but he didn't believe me. He claimed he could produce a witness, an undoubted source."

For a while, Nico didn't respond. But it couldn't be left hanging. "And should he have believed you?" he said.

"I never admitted anything. Who knew where that would've led?"

"*Should* he have believed you?" Nico repeated.

"Well, no," Sandro spat out the words quickly, as if to be rid of them. To distance himself from his brother's questioning. So that was it, the rumours were true. And, worse than that, Sauli knew it. And had Sandro on the rack.

Sandro breathed out deeply. "So, I pleaded with him not to make it public. I said that although these were lies and slanders, I would still be ruined if they became known."

Sandro was talking freely now, his confession out of the way. Nico didn't interrupt.

"So, he said that there was only one way he could see to keeping it private. That was if .... we agreed to grant the Spanish loan. I knew I had to tell you, and quickly."

Nico had heard it said that among Pareto's circle, there were those who flouted Genova's laws on relations between males. But Sandro? How could he have missed this? Over the years, he had witnessed the effortless way his handsome brother could attract women. A few married ladies had made it obvious that they would be willing to break their vows in exchange for an afternoon in Sandro's bed. At least, that's what their eyes said. And, so far as Nico knew, some of them had gone beyond wishing. Nico didn't know whether he was more surprised by Sandro's confession itself - or the fact that he had missed the truth for so long.

"But I don't understand, Sandro. Remember how it was, back in the old days in Pre? And it isn't *that* long since you and I last visited the 'Paradiso'. Was that all play-acting on your part? All the while you really preferred, well...." His voice tailed off.

Sandro shook his head slightly. "No, that's not it. I *like* the company of women, probably as much as I do men. I realise I must be discreet about the latter, but..."

"Not discreet enough, obviously," muttered Nico.

Sandro looked sideways, clearly frustrated by his brother's tone.

Nico took a deep draught from his wine. Neither spoke for a time. Finally, Nico stretched his hand across the table, a gesture of conciliation. "You are right, Sandro. My first thought would have been to judge you, I admit. This news will take getting used to."

"You think I don't know that?"

Nico breathed in and out deeply. "You are my brother, and I am yours. Nothing changes that."

Nico pushed back his chair and walked around the table to his brother. As Sandro stood up, Nico grabbed him by the shoulders. He could feel the tension running through Sandro's limbs. He wondered if, having unburdened himself of his long-held secret, Sandro would now be tempted to tell others. That must not happen. The floodgates of gossip would open - and destroy them both.

Chapter Seventeen

CASA CASTELLO, STRADA NUOVA: THE NEXT DAY

It was near dawn when Nico finally drifted off to sleep. But soon after, the bells of San Siro jolted him awake again. Then he remembered; it was Saturday, he should visit his father. It was a fair way to Vittorio's house in Boccadasse, but he hauled himself out of bed. Being away for the day was almost a relief after the events of last night. And perhaps he could see things more clearly after a ride in the fresh air.

Some years back, after Nico's mother had died, Vittorio started to neglect his business affairs. Without his wife, he had simply lost heart. The dwindling goodwill of his silversmith trade and his specialist tools, he passed on to a colleague in the Guild. The reins of the bank he passed over to his sons. "You built it," he said to Nico, in a gruff voice, "you can have it."

Vittorio retired to a small seaside house, a few miles down the coast, where his needs were simple. Nico and Sandro would take it in turns to pay a Saturday visit to him. Sandro would usually entertain his father with the current gossip going around the city or describe his latest hunting trip with young Doria and his circle. Nico would bring his father up to date with the progress of the business and listen to Vittorio's opinions. He sensed that his father preferred Sandro's humorous chatter to his meatier conversation. Perhaps because Nico had taken Banco Castello far beyond anything that his father had been capable of, and Vittorio knew it. But Nico persisted in consulting him on banking matters, sitting patiently while his father propounded his traditional views. It was a simple matter of respect. After all, despite whatever misgivings he may have had, Vittorio had backed his son's first venture all those years ago.

Gildo, his groom, brought out Nico's favourite horse: Mimi, his childhood name for his late mother. The chestnut mare was indulged by Nico like no other creature, saving perhaps Lisa. Once in the saddle, Nico looked up to the window of Lisa's apartment. The curtains were still drawn. "Ask Maria tell the Signora where I have gone," he said to Gildo, as he nudged the horse into a trot.

AUNT JULIA PEERED at her niece over the sewing on her lap.

"You have my sympathies, Lisa. Your husband, I am sorry to say, is an insensitive man. But you cannot be surprised, surely. After all, *look* where he has come from, look at his family."

"But it is so.... galling, Aunt."

Julia paused with her needle. "My dear, you are in no position to require Nico to cease doing business with this Englishman. Business matters are *his* domain. He will do as he sees fit in such cases, and there is nothing you can do about it."

Julia gave Lisa a superior smile and renewed her sewing, as if that were the end of the discussion.

"And meekly accept that he will ignore my feelings?"

Julia put down her work again, with an air of mild irritation. "And pray tell me Lisa, what alternative do you have?"

Lisa began to pace the room like a caged animal. After a couple of turns, Julia stopped her in mid-stride, sat her in the opposite chair and held her by the shoulders. "It is the way of the world, Lisa. Our role is home and family, and the man's is the world outside. And you were best not to question him on his doings in it."

Lisa squirmed, trying to struggle out of Julia's bony grip.

"*Stupid* girl. Do you not see how fortunate you are? Married to one of the wealthiest men in the Republic, a fine house to live in, a houseful of servants to command as you please. No doubt you would have preferred the convent!"

The golden-brown eyes glowered back at Julia. Both women knew full well that her wedding to Nico had been a deliverance. She had been within a hair's breadth of ending up as a nun. Being confined in a convent would have been a living death. Shortly followed by her actual death. Lisa shut her eyes, unable to escape the plain truth of her aunt's assessment.

NICO SPENT much of his time in his *studiolo* over the next couple of days. All his instincts as a banker were at war with his feelings of loyalty to his family. His wife didn't want him to lend to the English. His brother was begging him to lend to the Spanish. How could he accede to either of them without risking the business on which they all depended?

Sandro, meanwhile, was in an agitated state, fearful of exposure by the archbishop. Nico tried to reassure him, when Lisa was out of earshot.

"Remember, the Church cannot prosecute you. Only the Council of the Republic can do that. The archbishop can threaten as much as he likes, but all he can really do is make a formal complaint."

Sandro looked unconvinced. "That's not his tactic. He said he would tell the Governor. I would be exiled from court."

"Maybe a threat he won't carry out."

"The only way we can be sure – is if we grant the Spanish credit."

"If we do what Sauli wants, he'll probably keep his allegations to himself. But think about that, Sandro. Can we really allow him to dictate who we lend to? Where would that end?"

"Well, once the Spanish loan was advanced, he would leave us alone, surely?"

Nico shook his head. "Until the *next* time the king needs money. Sauli would have power over us, power to make us lend to Felipe – on terms he'd set, not our own. Or to refuse credit to his enemies, real or perceived. How could a man like the cardinal resist exercising that power?"

Sandro didn't answer the question.

"No, Sandro. We must keep the bank free of his clutches. Otherwise, we're done for. If not by this loan, then at some point in the future. We must stick to our refusal, or close up and leave the city."

Easy for me to say, thought Nico, after he said it. Not so easy to put into practice.

A HOODED FIGURE emerged from a pew at the rear of San Lorenzo's nave. Draped in a full-length velvet cloak, she swept down the southern aisle of the church. Parted the faded maroon curtains of the confessional box. Entered, and drew them closed again. The grille opened in a sharp, single movement.

Since she had been of age, Lisa had been going to confession regularly. Her father had never adopted the practice, despite its having become customary in his youth. But Cristoforo had not actively discouraged his daughter from it.

"Have you anything to confess, my child?" said a voice she knew.

"I have been guilty of anger and pride, Father."

She recounted the details of her recent arguments with Nico.

"When it comes to the husband's calling, my child, it is not for the wife to question his decisions. Her role lies elsewhere."

"But if he does business with heretics?"

There was a pause before the response came from the other side of the grille.

"In such a case, it would be the wife's duty to guide her husband to find the right way."

"And if that conflicts with her duty to obey him?"

"Her duty to God comes first. By performing her Christian duty, the good wife will help her husband to perform his."

Minutes later, Lisa was praying in the John the Baptist Chapel, as the priest had instructed her, before giving his absolution. Focused on her penances, she did not notice Father Guido leave the confessional box, almost colliding with his next confessant, and stride towards the door that led to the archbishop's residence.

NICO WAS ADMITTED to the Doge's Chamber in Palazzo Ducale. It was an imposing room, fit for the city's leader, but the scale of the chamber belied the reality that the Doge held his position at the behest of his electors. It was with the Council, the *Gran Consiglio*, and the Governor, where the real power lay. There was a time when Nico would have been overawed by this room, and its occupant. But now he saw it was merely a perquisite of office, albeit one that men from each of the old families vied to occupy in turn, as a mark of their standing in the Republic.

Ambrogio Di Negro was seated in his ornate chair in the centre of the room. A notoriously short man, he did not rise when greeting Nico.

"Greetings, my Doge," said Nico, halting a few paces off and bowing suitably low. "And thank you for seeing me."

Di Negro waved his right hand dismissively. "And so," he said, moving in his seat and adjusting his robes, "what brings you to us?"

"It is a delicate matter, one for private discussion?" Nico glanced sideways at the Doge's secretary perched at a desk in the corner, scribbling away.

Di Negro ordered the stone-faced cleric out of the room. Along with his two guards, who exited via the doorway through which Nico had just entered. He motioned Nico to begin.

"It concerns a group of young men who keep regular company in our city. They include my younger brother, Alessandro. Their self-appointed leader is Bernardo Pareto."

There was no reaction on Di Negro's face. Ever the politician.

"Certain allegations have been made against them. Allegations that their association with one another involves behaviour which contradicts our Republic's laws. And God's law."

"Nothing like this has been brought to my attention," said Di Negro, frowning.

"The allegations have not been put to the magistrates. But my brother is concerned that they could be."

"I imagine he is. This is a serious matter. Who makes these allegations?"

Nico glanced out of the Doge's window, which afforded a view of the belltower of the cathedral. From that perch, an observer could probably see into this room.

"They come from San Lorenzo. I hesitate to say that they come from Cardinal Sauli himself – a member of his clergy apparently claims he has the evidence – but he no doubt has the archbishop's support."

Di Negro drummed his fingers on the arm of his chair.

"Well, Signore Castello, if the archbishop is of a mind to proceed with this, I can scarcely prevent him, can I?" He sounded irritated.

"Excellency, my intention was that you be forewarned of this matter, in case it becomes public. And to have the chance to consult the *Gran Consiglio*."

"Once a matter becomes a formal complaint, I am in some difficulty to intervene with the due process of law. You realise."

"I do. But if it *were* to come to that, the consequences would be unfortunate, to say the least."

"Consequences?"

"You see, this circle of young men includes Prince Andrea - and for that matter, the sons of several of your fellow councillors."

Di Negro raised his eyes heavenwards, no doubt thanking the Lord that he had raised only daughters.

"If a pebble is tossed in that pond, who can say where the ripples would end?" Nico concluded.

The fingers started drumming again, but more slowly. Nico calculated that Di Negro's principal concern would be to avoid disclosure. True, he did not have to survive a re-election. His two-year term of office would expire in November and a newly elected Doge would assume his place. But he would not wish the remaining months of his Dogate to be overshadowed by a distasteful - and very public - scandal. And neither would some of his fellow councillors, who had even more at stake, it seemed. Nico hoped that was enough. That, and the age–old rivalry between Church and Republic, for jurisdiction over Genova's citizens.

Di Negro patted the arm of his chair once.

"Who else knows of this, Signore Castello?"

"In my family, only myself and Alessandro. And I imagine, only a small number at the cathedral."

"Let us hope it stays that way."

"There are the others in Pareto's circle, of course. But perhaps I can impress on Signore Pareto the need for their discretion."

"Do so. If this becomes public knowledge, the Council will find its hands tied."

Nico felt he had been given his marching orders.

THEY WENT to Bernardo Pareto's house, which was in the old city, in sight of San Donato's tower. Sandro had been Pareto's guest several times, but for Nico it was a first visit. Sandro had described the man as a collector of art, but when Nico entered the *sala* it was clear that was an understatement. The sheer quantity of male and female flesh on display, either represented on canvas or carved in wood or marble, was something to behold. There was scarcely room left for furniture, and what there was, was cluttered with discarded wine glasses, bottles, crockery, abandoned clothes, footwear. Nico felt he had stumbled into the unorganised storehouse of a free-spending gentleman.

Pareto greeted Sandro and Nico with a distant air. He took them through the maze of artefacts to an adjoining room which had fine views over the harbour below and, more importantly, space for a daybed and two chairs. He spread himself across the bed and invited Nico and Sandro to take a chair each. Nico observed their host. So, this was the young man who held thrall over Prince Andrea and his fellow pleasure-seekers? He took in the flamboyant curls, the aquiline nose, the permanent half-smile. An appeal to common sense and caution didn't seem likely to endear itself to Pareto.

"Young Doria tells me that I must heed your advice, signori. Well, I was not aware that I needed any. But if my prince suggests it then I must listen, I suppose. Which of you will explain it to me?"

Nico and Sandro had had an audience with Prince Andrea a few days earlier, to ask him to use his influence on Pareto. Obviously, that intervention had had the desired effect.

Nico allowed Sandro to do the talking. Pareto's expression, slightly bored as if reluctantly indulging his guests, did not change. If he was surprised by Sandro's account, it did not show.

"And so," Sandro concluded, "it is vital that we are all discreet – that we give the archbishop no further excuse for his allegations."

Pareto raised an eyebrow. "And this is your opinion also, Signore Castello? That we should hide behind our doors, not daring to associate with our friends? And if challenged, we should merely... lie?"

Nico felt he was being toyed with. Pareto was as capable as anyone of dissembling, if first impressions were any judge.

"I merely say that it is for the accusers to prove their case. Why make it easy for them? Especially when the consequences could be so unpleasant."

"Well, I am surprised at you, Signore Castello. By your reputation, at least, I had you as a man who kept his own counsel, not heeding the prejudices of others."

"Perhaps. But I make sure that I can defend myself. Against those who might have the power to make me pay for my free opinions."

Pareto laughed. "A good answer. But what makes you think that our little band cannot defend itself?"

Nico glanced across at Sandro, who clearly had no inkling of Pareto's possible meaning.

"I know little about you, Signore Pareto," Nico responded, "or your friends, saving the prince, and my brother here. But how, exactly, would you defend yourselves against, let us say, the sworn testimony of a leading member of the Church?"

Pareto showed no apparent concern at the question. "I am not so stupid as to believe that we can rely on the scales of Genovese justice to weigh in our favour, signore. Of course, a few friends in the right places will do no harm."

"But Prince Andrea would not want his name bandied about town, merely to discourage the magistrates from doing their duty. He would be concerned if reports of it came to his father's ears. And the Doge is sympathetic, but his discretion only goes so far."

Pareto examined his fingernails. "No doubt you are right. Which is why I always believe in retaining some kind of surety."

"Surety? What would that be?"

"I feel confident that our esteemed clergy would not pursue their petty allegations if they believed that by doing so, they would only invite the same charges, and worse, upon their own heads. The Florentines, Signore Castello, they love their engines of war. But they have a saying about them, you may know it. *'Do not be hoist by your own petardo'*. It is just the same for the priests at the cathedral."

"But... that would be mere accusation? Charge and counter charge?"

Pareto leaned back on the daybed and glanced out of the window, as if he were checking the weather. "Not if one had verifiable proof."

"And you do," said Nico.

"Well, let us say that there are certain items one has received. Personal letters. Gifts, keepsakes and the like. Things beyond the means of a mere priest, suggesting they would have been paid for out of cathedral funds."

So, Pareto would casually betray a confidence, Nico thought, if that could save him from persecution. Well, I suppose our enemy's enemy can be our friend. There would come a time when he would advise Sandro to choose his companions more wisely. This wasn't it.

"And the archbishop. Does he know of this ...friendship, do you think?"

"Not so far as I know. He might suspect that some members of his clergy have broken their vows with other men. But that is probably as far as it has gone. It's hardly likely that anyone would have volunteered the information, is it?"

"Understood. But that leads us to another question. If your friends in San Lorenzo are discreet, then how is it that the archbishop is making these threats? What is his source of information?"

Pareto pursed his lips. "*Allora*, I hope – no, I believe – that none of *our* friends would betray us for forty pieces of silver – or whatever inducement the archbishop is offering. So, the source, as you put it, must be elsewhere. I'm sure that Cardinal Sauli didn't achieve his elevated position, without having a band of helpers. No doubt there are a few citizens willing to be his eyes and ears in the city."

Nico tended to agree with Pareto's judgment about the archbishop. But that made it difficult to gauge the danger Sandro and the others were in. Perhaps the archbishop's informers had no verifiable proof, they were just peddling rumours and suppositions. In which case, Sauli was bluffing, testing out Sandro to see if his insinuations would strike home. Either way, there seemed little choice but to wait upon events, to brazen it out.

"Can I offer you gentlemen something to drink?" said their host, looking around the room for the means to magically appear.

Chapter Eighteen
THE MOLO, GENOA HARBOUR: THE SAME DAY

M onty stared at her in wonder. Nothing short of a miracle. He glanced across at Master Winterhey.

"Considerin' what she's bin' through, she don't look too bad, eh?" was the sailor's assessment.

Monty shook his head. "I think she looks absolutely *beautiful*."

Winterhey's smile indicated he knew what Monty meant. The "*Kateryn*" had just limped into harbour, having by some God-given grace survived the storm. And when her master, Benedict, told them how, her arrival seemed even more remarkable. The "*Kateryn*" had lost her boatswain and a deckhand, both swept overboard in the middle of the night. Another two seamen had been killed stone dead by the foremast when part of it crashed down onto the deck. With her remaining sails furled and the course set for her by the storm, she had ridden the waves bearing her through the darkness.

Benedict was too modest to say so, but by a combination of good fortune and fine seamanship, he had managed to nurse her to within a few leagues of Madeira, without being driven on to the rocks. Unbeknown to him, the "*Mary Gale*" and the "*Clement*" had already quit their anchorage on the leeward side of the island. At dawn the next day, the "*Kateryn*" was spotted by local fishermen who guided her towards their home harbour. In that Portuguese port, where English ships were still made welcome, Benedict arranged repairs, strapping a new foremast to the broken stump of the old one. Three weeks or so behind her sisters, the "*Kateryn*" had set out for the Mediterranean, following the course already taken by Master Winterhey.

On arrival, Benedict had sought out Winterhey who, under his mask of gruffness, was overjoyed to see his fellow mariner. Winterhey had immediately marched him around to Monty's lodgings and the three of them had walked down to the Molo together, to see the ship with their own eyes: battered and broken, but her hull sound, her cargo unspoilt and her crew in good spirits, having finally reached their destination.

"A notable day. What say you to a drink, gentlemen?" proposed Monty.

"Well, I don' normally, but in this case..." the gap-toothed grin emerged on Winterhey's face and so, slapping Benedict and Winterhey on their backs, Monty marched them off to find the nearest hostelry.

Having said farewell to Winterhey and Benedict two hours later, Monty strolled westwards along Caricamento, rather unsteadily. Thinking of his good fortune in not losing a third of the Adventurers' cargo. He found himself opposite the Darsena, the naval yard that Winterhey had pointed out on the morning of their arrival. A crowd was gathered by the dockside. He threaded his way to the front for a better view.

A group of galleys, the Republic's red and white flags fluttering from their masts, were being loaded with stores. Their crews, accompanied by wives and sweethearts, stood by the gangways. The men looked tense, the women miserable. As one sailor stepped on board, the young woman he had left behind burst into tears. Monty caught the eye of his immediate neighbour - by the look and smell of him, a fisherman.

"I'm new in town," he said, "What's going on? Why are they all so unhappy?"

The fisherman gestured with his hands spread wide. "The men, they go to help the Spanish king, signore. The wives, they're afraid they'll soon be widows."

"How d'you mean?"

"Bound for Lisbon," explained the fisherman, "joining up with the Spanish fleet. And then, who knows?"

"Indeed," agreed Monty, though he said it more to himself.

As he made his way back, he recalled his earlier conversation with Nico Castello. So, why were the Spanish strengthening their naval forces? It couldn't be to garrison their harbours in New Spain. These

Genoese galleys weren't ocean-going. They were bound for a destination closer to home, surely?

NICO AND SANDRO walked through Piazza San Matteo, heading home after their visit to Bernardo Pareto. Nico was reflecting on what Pareto had told them, but Sandro wanted to talk.

"Do you think we convinced him – to be discreet?"

"Hard to say, only time I've met him. But he appears unconcerned by it all."

"That's just his manner. He makes a point of appearing untroubled, whether it be by the actions of men or the interventions of fate."

"Not a bad way to view things."

"He has a card up his sleeve, of course."

"Maybe, but the archbishop doesn't know that."

"It's not Bernardo who's being put on the rack. I'm the one he's pursuing," Sandro pointed out.

"Yes, he wants us to do business with Zúñiga. He believes that if he makes these threats, we will bend the knee. There's no benefit to him – or to the Spanish – if you're prosecuted. So, we must convince him that his threats are empty. That we won't change our decision because of them."

"Just brazen it out?"

"Yes. If he summons you again, make it clear that you're not intimidated and – well - just adopt Pareto's approach, "nothing touches me".

"Easy enough to say."

"Yes, I know. But don't see him alone. If the archbishop wants to talk, he can see us together."

They reached the house and turned into the courtyard. Above them, on the *piano nobile*, they could hear Lisa's voice, in conversation with one of the servants.

"Have you told Lisa?" asked Sandro, *sotto voce*.

"She knows nothing of this, brother. Frankly, I have put off telling her – she would find it hard to reconcile with her faith."

"She's already asking why I don't marry."

"I don't like secrets between husband and wife, Sandro, but this is not the right time."

"If it became public, she would find out anyway. Better to tell her first?"

Ascending the staircase, Nico didn't respond. But Sandro was surely right.

HIGH ABOVE THE CITY, Nico's party manoeuvred their mounts down the steep path that lead to Porta Carbonara. At a turn in the path, the rocky ground levelled out forming a projecting ledge. Nico drew his horse to a halt and gazed down on the slate-covered rooftops of the city far beneath. A patchwork of reflected light and contrasting shade. Monty pulled up alongside him, with Marco and Luca, their two escorts, close behind. Across to their right, the sun was sinking towards the mountains which formed Genova's western horizon, promising an end to the day's shimmering heat.

It had been a good day's work, one which compensated for the discomfort of riding under the unforgiving sun. Monty's Cotswold wool had found favour with the manufactories in the hill towns. The Englishman had taken Nico's advice and brought a sample bale along with them, borne by a pack horse. The customers became enthusiastic when they ran their fingers through the skein. By the end of a long, dusty day, Monty had sold nearly enough wool to empty the hold of the "*Mary Gale*".

Nico's presence had been instrumental, convincing the buyers of Monty's bona fides - and the credit that would be available to enable their purchases.

"How shall we celebrate your success, signore?" enquired Nico. The '*signore*' was said in jest. They were on familiar name terms by now, Nico and Monty.

"All I can think of, Nico, is a cool bath."

Monty added that he had grown to like the habit since coming to Genova, as he was slowly learning to call the city. Nico was surprised to hear that citizens in England did not bathe that frequently. Such curious people.

"I could drink your harbour dry, if it were wine instead of sea water," Monty added.

Nico laughed. "I have the answer to both your needs."

Half an hour later, they had ridden through Porta Carbonara and were getting close to Strada Nuova. But instead of stopping at his house, Nico continued into the old city, until he pulled up in a small piazza. In one corner, stood a public fountain. Its trickling waters speckled with gold, reflected the light from the house opposite. He dismounted and, handing the reins over to Luca, walked – a little stiffly after the long ride – across to the fountain. Sticking his head under the faucet, he let the cool water trickle over his face and hair. Suitably refreshed and shaking his locks as he walked back to Monty, he gestured at the brightly lit house. Monty dismounted and they walked up to the door. Nico exchanged a few words with the doorkeeper - and ushered his companion inside.

They were in a tiled courtyard, which was blissfully cool. The sound of a harpsichord being played *adagio* wafted down from a room somewhere on the floor above. In front of them, a double staircase in travertine marble curved elegantly upwards, its two flights meeting on a balcony on the next storey. Framed by its balustrades was a large piece of statuary – two lustful nymphs apparently enjoying each other's semi-naked charms.

Moments later, an extravagantly dressed woman appeared on the balcony above them. By her ample figure, she was in her middle years, but precision was impossible. She was heavily made up and wearing an enormous, powdered wig.

Descending the left-hand staircase at an imperiously slow pace, she greeted Nico as if she and he were ancient friends. Nico said, "Signora Luzzati, may I introduce Signore Montecchio? From England. He is a guest of mine."

Lina Luzzati took a step forward and proffered the back of her bejewelled hand for Monty to kiss.

"Signore Montecchio, *bienvenuto a mia casa*."

"Are you not joining us?" said Monty, looking back at Nico, who was heading for the door as La Luzzati ushered the Englishman towards the stairs.

"No. We will speak again tomorrow."

Half an hour later, Monty was lying in a marble bath large enough for several people to share, soaking his grateful limbs. The enormous bathroom was decorated with fine ceiling paintings. He recognised the central fresco as the tale of Diana and Actaeon. The golden-haired goddess was clearly furious with the young man for glimpsing her naked form, but at the same time teasing her other audience – Monty, on this occasion – with a pretence of coyness.

Two women of the household, dressed in flowing, sleeveless robes, ministered to his needs, pouring warm water into his bath from bronze ewers and serving him chilled white wine and candied fruits. Reluctantly, he towelled off and slipped into the bathrobe one of the girls provided. He was shown into a softly lit room adjoining the bathroom. Laying back on the large, canopied bed, he closed his eyes.

He was about to drift off when one of the maids brought in a tray – wine, two glasses and small plates of shellfish and chicken - which she placed on the credenza near the bed. She withdrew, not closing the door behind her. Moments later, a raven-haired young woman entered through the same doorway. In contrast to the simple robes of the maid, she was in an elegant silk dress the colour of lapis lazuli, which barely covered her shoulders, and a necklace of silver thread which dipped invitingly towards her bosom.

He stared, silenced by the young woman's beauty. She sat herself on the edge of the bed.

"Mi chiamo Bianca, signore, come si chiama?" she said.

"I am called Monty, signorina."

Bianca poured Chianti into the two glasses on the credenza and passed one to him. As they sipped at their wine, her dark eyes inspected him over the rim of her glass.

"Monte," she repeated.

"As in, Montecchio," he explained. Unable to think of anything conversational, he took a deep pull at his wine.

She shuffled along the side of the bed closer to him, the silk of her skirts rustling as she moved. The silence was intense, but he was too tongue-tied to break it.

Bianca's fingertips grazed his cheek, scarcely touching him. With the tip of her index finger, she lighted on his earlobe and inscribed faint circles there. He shut his eyes, relishing the sensation.

"Un poco de vino?" she asked, as her fingertips slid down his neck and along his arm.

"I don't want more wine, I want...." he muttered, feeling his Adam's apple swell in his throat.

"Come si volete? *Come si volete*?" she asked, as she took his trembling hand and guided it to her left breast.

Chapter Nineteen

THE ARCHBISHOP'S PALAZZO: TWO DAYS LATER

"These bankers, they have only one God – their sacred profit. They forget themselves!"

For once, Balthasar de Zúñiga's high-pitched squawk suited his splenetic mood. The words came spilling out at a furious pace. Archbishop Sauli stared at the Spaniard, momentarily captivated.

"...And that Signore Lercari? Oh, yes, Banco di Liguria is honoured to accommodate His Majesty's request, but at what cost?"

Sauli wasn't tempted to venture an opinion, but Zúñiga didn't pause for a response.

"I will tell you. *Twenty-five* per cent interest. Over four months. Twenty-five per cent. That's usury."

Sauli lifted a paw from the chair arm to comment, but Zúñiga still did not draw breath.

"And then there is Domenico Castello. Your Grace advised me that this Castello was well disposed toward His Majesty. Well, we still await his decision to accommodate us."

The courtier leapt out of his chair and started pacing up and down. Rather than wait for his visitor to settle, Sauli spoke to Father Guido.

"You were telling me something about Signore Castello, Father – before his Excellency's *unexpected* arrival?"

As two sets of eyes fell on him, Guido related what he had witnessed at the Loggia on the previous day: Banco Castello had announced a substantial credit exchange. It was with an English wool merchant. In fact, that same Englishman who had attended the Castello's *festa*, his Grace may recall? His Grace did indeed remember that drunken oaf, the Bell Tower, or whatever his accursed name was. A foundling, no doubt. He formed his fat fingers into a bridge, recalling the sunburnt, Protestant face.

Zúñiga seemed to latch on to the word '*Inglese*', registering the essential point of the priest's story. "What treachery! Trading with heretics. And, what's more, the King's enemies."

"Regretfully, the transaction of banking business with foreigners, be they heretics or no, is not unlawful in the Republic," Sauli observed.

Zúñiga's disgusted expression indicated that, in his view, this omission was a serious lapse of duty by Genova's legislators.

"But these same bankers are free to decline credit to His Majesty?"

"Free to exercise their flawed judgment, yes – but such judgments are human – and can be changed."

Zúñiga evidently saw no comfort in that. "Can Your Grace not condemn them under canon law, the laws against usury?"

The archbishop was momentarily amused by the thought of his denouncing some of Genova's most prominent citizens, and San Lorenzo's largest benefactors. Ejecting the merchants from the Temple, in Christ's name. Of course, it would never happen. What world did this Spaniard inhabit, not to see the situation for what it was?

"Your Excellency, I can hardly accuse Signore Castello of usurious lending - if in fact no loan were to take place. As for Signore Lercari's terms, those I could perhaps condemn, but I assume you do not intend to *accept* twenty-five percent interest?"

"His Majesty, naturally, has not authorised me to borrow at such an outrageous rate."

"Yes. And as regards the English merchant, he may pay Domenico Castello what he wishes for the bank's services, his heretic soul is not my concern. Signore Castello's soul *is* my concern, true. But as I understand it from Father Guido's report, the terms of his transaction with this Englishman were not unconscionable. So, I would be hard pressed to condemn them."

It seemed for a moment that Zúñiga wanted to challenge the archbishop's assessment, but instead his anger fizzled out. He slumped back in his chair.

Sauli turned to Father Guido. "Father, make Signore Lercari aware of our disappointment that His Excellency was offered such terms. And add that it would not be our *wish* to accuse him of usury, but if he could see a way to reduce his charges, the issue would fall away....?"

"Assuredly Your Grace, but during such a conversation he will no doubt raise the subject of his son."

Sauli was nonplussed for a moment, until he remembered their conversation on the subject. "What about his son? Is he not settling in well as a novice?"

"It appears the boy is an utter reprobate. He was seen, by another novice, in bed with two young nuns from Santa Maria. At the same time. So, in the circumstances, we will have to terminate his novitiate..."

"In the *circumstances*, Father, you can tell Signore Lercari that provided he agrees to reduce the rate of interest on his loan substantially, his son can remain with us *despite* his misdemeanours. The boy is innocent enough, no doubt. He was obviously seduced by those two she-devils. Have those godless young women tested until they confess. Then have them thrown out of the convent."

Guido bowed. As the priest made to leave on his appointed errand, Sauli raised a solitary, stubby finger to halt his subordinate's departure.

"And then we have Signore Castello," the archbishop pronounced.

A resigned shrug came from Zúñiga.

But Sauli was not deterred. "I caution you to have patience, Excellency. We have potential allies in Signore Castello's brother - and his wife. If we handle that lady and gentleman appropriately, I am confident Castello can be persuaded to see the error of his ways."

He turned back to Guido. "Ask Signore Alessandro to come and see me, as soon as is convenient."

Father Guido bowed again and left. Sauli turned back to his visitor. "Tell me, Excellency, can you offer Signore Castello any collateral for this loan?"

Zúñiga opened his mouth to protest, but Sauli waved him down before any rant could emerge. "I *appreciate* that His Majesty's word should normally be enough, but regretfully these are not normal times. If the Enterprise is to be undertaken with dispatch, then sacrifices must be made, I am sure you would agree."

"It is possible. You are aware, I imagine, that his Majesty receives regular shipments from the Orient. Cargoes from Cathay and the Spice Islands?"

Sauli nodded: any suggestion that he was *not* fully informed of all King Felipe's doings around the world was – naturally - unthinkable.

"There is a great ship, near the end of its long voyage from Manila as we speak. Her cargoes would be ample security for the loan."

"And the name of this splendid vessel?"

Zúñiga stuck out his chest. "The *"San Felipe"*, Your Grace."

NICO PRESSED HIS BROTHER. "Agreed *what*, exactly?"

"Nothing, without your approval."

But Sandro started talking faster.

"The archbishop indicated that if you were willing to reconsider the loan, Zúñiga will provide us with full security. Assign a portion of the King's property."

"And what property is that?"

Sandro leaned forward, putting his hands on the table. "The carrack *"San Felipe"* and her sister ship are returning from the Indies. Laden with spices and silks. A manifest of more than three *million* ducats, at current prices. Zúñiga holds the *asientos* signed by Felipe's own hand."

"And you indicated...?"

"Oh, I said that in *those* circumstances, I was confident you would be willing to offer substantial credits. Subject to being reimbursed appropriately, of course."

"Appropriately," Nico echoed.

"The archbishop also told me confidentially that Banco di Liguria had offered Zúñiga a loan. No collateral, but a proposed return of twenty per cent. For just a four months' term. *Twenty per cent.*"

"Has he accepted?"

Sandro inclined his head sideways. "Not yet, no. He rejected twenty-five per cent apparently, but he is considering this proposal. Sauli expects he will agree. And if you think about it, where else can he go? Not Grimaldi's syndicate, it seems. We are his only other option. And even if we get this collateral, we could charge a similar rate, say seventeen or eighteen percent. What do you think of *that*?"

"And you said as much to the archbishop?"

"I...indicated that these were the sort of terms we might offer. Sauli thought they would find favour with Zúñiga."

Nico shook his head, prompting Sandro to press his case. "Nico, that's nearly double what we're earning from the English business. It seems to me..."

"This ship, *"San Felipe"*. Has she reached Spanish waters? Or is she on the high seas?"

"She is refitting in the Azores. From there, it's only a matter of days to Cádiz, after all."

"Not exactly in our hands then. What if she is struck by a great storm? Where's our collateral then?"

"A storm? It's late June, the weather's set fair."

Nico grabbed Sandro's wrist. "And had you forgotten that English pirate is still abroad? Suppose he takes her as a prize? Then, we would be *unsecured*, waiting on the king's favour to repay us. When his next boat comes in."

Sandro wrested himself free of Nico's grasp. "Il Drago is nowhere near the Azores. Down at the San Giorgio, they say he has turned north and is proceeding up the Portuguese coast. Right into the jaws of the Spanish fleet at Lisbon."

"He could change his course."

"You're grasping at straws. But let's say that he does. What are the chances he will run into the "*San Felipe*"? Will he pick the one spot on the Western Ocean where she's passing? The chances are almost nil, brother. And even if he did, what of it? The "*San Felipe*" is a huge warship, a thousand tonner, royally protected. That English pirate has nothing that could match her."

"You should never have offered to take the bet." Nico said, standing up and walking away.

Sandro stood in Nico's pathway. "If you don't like the risk, ask for other collateral. The man is getting desperate."

Nico wondered at his brother's credulity. "And what treasure could Zúñiga offer us, exactly? A box of his fancy lace ruffs?" he yelled.

He pushed Sandro aside, storming along the corridor and down the main staircase. "Saddle my horse!" he thundered at Gildo. Not questioning his master, the groom brought out Mimi. Nico was up in the saddle and careering out of the courtyard into Strada Nuova before Gildo could fully tighten the girth.

As soon as he was free of the crowded streets and down on Caricamento, he kicked his heels into his horse's loins and galloped along the promenade. He was heedless of any obstacle, flicking the reins to urge more speed out of her. Sailors and fishermen on the quayside had to leap out of his path to save themselves.

He reached the western edge of the harbour before he felt the barbs of anger draining away. He pulled hard on the reins, slowing the mare to a trot and carried on westwards for several minutes. He patted Mimi's neck, both man and horse bathed in sweat. "Easy my girl, it's all right." Turning her around, he headed home at a slow walking pace. Now he had expunged his anger, he was free to think.

As he dismounted back at Casa Castello, Gildo took the reins. He knew better than to comment on the mare's condition, but Nico volunteered it anyway.

"Yes, we've been for a fair, fine gallop. Give her a good rub down and a brush. When she's rested, you can feed her. Not too much."

Chapter Twenty

THE MERCHANTS' LOGGIA, PIAZZA BANCHI: LATE MAY

Nico sat in his banker's chair, weighing up the arguments for and against lending to Spain.

For, was the status that came with being the king's banker. He had dismissed the notion when arguing with Sandro, but it was dishonest to pretend he was indifferent to the effect on the bank's reputation. And it would likely bring with it more Spanish business, into the bargain. For, also, were the terms that Sandro had negotiated. A short duration, a high rate of interest, and most importantly, collateral which should more than exceed the requested advance. That offset the risk that Felipe might be tempted to delay repayment.

Against, there was one critical issue. The risk of losing the collateral. Until the ship reached Cádiz, at least. But perhaps Sandro was right; the risk was small, and probably containable. And Nico could see a way to reduce it. If they permitted only a portion of the loan to be drawn before the ship reached harbour. Once berthed, Nico's agents in Cádiz would ensure the cargo remained subject to the *asiento*.

Another factor was the effect on their reputation of withdrawing the offer. They were not legally bound by the assurances Sandro had given to the archbishop, true, but Sauli would no doubt be highly critical – in public and in private - if they appeared to have changed their minds.

Finally, there were the consequences for Sandro himself. The archbishop's threat of exposure had not gone away, despite Pareto's scheming behind the scenes. Whatever Nico may have said about the danger of appeasing Sauli, he could not deny the risks. The damage from a scandal could be almost as costly as their losses if the '*San Felipe*' sank to the bottom of the Ocean Sea.

He had come to a decision, he realised, and headed home to tell Sandro. He found his brother in the garden.

"Sandro, I can't say I'm overjoyed about it but, on balance, I feel we should proceed with Senor Zúñiga."

Sandro embraced him. "Thank you, Nico. That is good to hear."

"Let's hope we don't live to regret it.".

"You won't. What's the next step? Can I tell the archbishop?"

"We'll go together. But first, I have a condition." Sandro's hand slipped from Nico's shoulder.

"We need partners to join us in this loan. To put in a decent share, say a fifth each? I'll speak to Spinola and Lomellino. It shouldn't be too hard to persuade them. But we retain over half the loan - and the casting vote, of course."

Sandro's smile returned. "Agreed. And the interest rate?"

Nico shrugged. "You're right. Why should we take less than eighteen per cent?"

BUT THERE WAS one further complication with the Spanish business, one which became apparent when Nico reviewed the bank's books. The loan would bring them close to the bank's capital limit, even after the contributions from Signori Spinola and Lomellino. And that in turn meant they would have to scale back commitments elsewhere, including to Monty Belltower. So be it, said Sandro. Nico felt an unease about disappointing Monty, but he had always emphasised they must not overstretch the bank's capital.

Spinola and Lomellino both agreed to become loan partners, subject to seeing the loan terms. Nico immersed himself in preparing the document. Ordinarily, it was his clerk Mazzini's responsibility to document the bank's trades, but this was different. Apart from the fact that he wanted to make sure, doubly sure, that the agreement was in clear terms, no ambiguities or evasions, this was a confidential transaction, off the ledger. After a couple of days' effort, it was done.

The brothers watched proudly as Zúñiga put his signature to the document at the Spanish ambassador's residence. As they returned homewards, the signed deeds in Nico's satchel, Sandro was in boisterous mood, calling to mind his earlier phrase, "*The Castellos, bankers to the king!*" And now indeed, it was so.

Despite his fierce arguments with Sandro, Nico had to acknowledge that this was a significant day. What would his father have said, all those years ago, if Nico had suggested that such a thing could happen? Vittorio would have scoffed at his dreamer of a son. And then given him some menial chore to bring him back down to earth. But now, his father would feel only pride.

Arriving home, they gave the momentous news to Lisa. Or rather Sandro did, his words spilling out before Nico had the chance. Her face lit up with pleasure. She inserted herself between the brothers and, arm in arm, the three of them walked into the garden to watch the sunset over a celebratory glass of wine.

ON THE FOLLOWING DAY, Nico and Sandro were in Nico's study, deep in the bank's ledgers, when an unexpected guest was announced.

"I wonder what he wants?" Sandro asked.

The archbishop didn't often make social calls, or at least, not on the Castellos.

"Go and entertain him in the *sala*," Nico replied, "while I rouse the kitchen staff to perform an instant miracle." Lisa and Aunt Julia were out on a round of visits to relatives.

The brothers were none the wiser half an hour later. By that time, Sauli had devoured all the *antipasti* the kitchen could produce at short notice. Now he was making his way through a plate of candied sweetmeats, washed down with generous gulps of sweet Malvasia. The archbishop did not seem all that interested in getting to the point. In between their guest's mouthfuls, they exhausted the gossip surrounding the candidates for the new Doge in the autumn elections. And no, Domenico Castello was *not* interested in taking up the political life, but Nico thanked the archbishop for suggesting it. Finally, they were reduced to speculating as to the likelihood of the present heatwave continuing.

Sauli cut the astrological speculation short. "Oh, signori, I almost forgot to mention another matter."

"I should have offered you my congratulations," he added, once the servants had withdrawn from their presence. Nico raised his eyebrows in enquiry.

"Regarding the loan you have arranged with His Majesty."

"We were pleased to accommodate Senor Zúñiga's request, Your Grace."

"Well, the affairs of mammon are hardly my province, of course, but that sounds most satisfactory. And of course, King Felipe's cause is our cause...."

Nico watched Sauli's face for clues as to where this line of talk was headed but he found none.

"....and at the same time, one is pleased to be of service to our merchant congregation when one can."

Sandro said, "We were of course grateful for Your Grace's introduction to Senor Zúñiga."

Sauli looked as if the point had not occurred to him. "Perhaps I should say that, after your initial reluctance to proceed, Senor Zúñiga was not so well disposed towards your bank. Indeed, he took some persuading that Banco Castello was the right choice for this... delicate matter."

This last comment revealed Sauli's intent to Nico. He leant towards the archbishop. "As my brother was saying, we are most appreciative of your support. If there was a way to express that in more solid form," he placed his left-hand palm downwards on the table next to him and tapped it once, "please do not hesitate to mention it."

Sauli gave Nico a paternal smile. "Ah well, not for oneself, of course." The archbishop raised his eyes to the ceiling. "But, that said, there are many worthwhile causes to be funded. Causes for which the Cathedral must seek the aid of its devoted flock. For example, it is to our city's shame that John the Baptist's Chapel remains incomplete, not to mention the portraits on our altar panelling."

"Could you suggest the sort of sum that would be sufficient for the chapel to be completed?"

"Oh Signore Castello, you will understand that I have not made a *precise* assessment of those costs prior to coming here. But shall we say, fifty thousand would make a very significant difference?"

"Fifty."

"Indeed. Naturally, in the interests of modesty, the donation would be anonymous."

"Well, rest assured, Your Grace, that on full repayment of the Spanish loan, I will arrange the disbursement of fifty thousand lire to the Cathedral Treasury."

Sauli clasped his hands together. "Splendid. Such generosity is its own reward, to be sure, but may the blessings of Our Lord fall on you - and your family. You will have the benefit of our regular prayers of intercession."

The archbishop emptied his wine glass and dabbed his lips with the napkin. "And now you must excuse me. One has so many errands."

As soon as Sauli had departed, Nico and Sandro stared at one another. It was Sandro who broke the silence.

"Am I dreaming, or did we just agree to pay the archbishop a commission for the Spanish business?"

"We did. He can call it a donation of course, but it's a fee for his services."

"A cool nerve, even if he did mask the request under the cloak of the building fund."

"He knew we had no choice but to agree. Supposing I'd declined? When the time came for Felipe to repay us, Sauli could easily dissuade the king from acting promptly."

"I suppose so."

Nico sensed that his brother felt the unspoken criticism, but he could not stop himself. "Now we are committed to this loan, we must ensure that nothing, not least our worthy archbishop, stands in the way of our getting repaid. Even if we never make a single ducat's income out of it."

"Don't be so negative," Sandro countered. "You could say that the archbishop's fee is a kind of surety."

"How's that?"

"Well, the prospect of fifty thousand lire should spur Sauli on, to encourage the king to fulfil his obligations."

"Let's hope so. But if Felipe does delay, the collateral in the "*San Felipe*" will soon get eaten up by the interest. Either way, Sauli will still expect his fifty thousand."

But Sandro was right, he realised. He would do whatever it took to protect the bank. Even if that meant bolstering the archbishop's coffers.

LISA WAS on her way to the cathedral for confession, escorted by Luca. Nearing her destination, she met a group of novices from Santa Maria, walking in the opposite direction. Eyes downward, moving silently, not engaging with their companions. She could have been one of them, she reminded herself, had her life taken the usual course for an orphan. Instead, she was mistress of her own household and, as for spiritual comfort, she had her trusted advisors at the cathedral. She recalled, with a sense of irritation, her recent conversation with Nico.

"You doubt me?" Nico had said to her. "Ask Sandro, he was there when the archbishop came calling."

"Of course I believe you. But what is so wrong about his soliciting funds for the cathedral in return for his services?"

"Nothing - if that was his true purpose. The joke around the Loggia is that the archbishop has raised the cost of restoring that chapel several times over."

Lisa shook her head. It was not possible. And how typical that the *cambisti* would instinctively believe the worst.

"But, my dear, our noble cardinal didn't achieve his exalted position, simply by devout humility. A humble priest he is not."

"I realise the archbishop lives a life with some privileges, but that he should *personally* benefit from donations to the church, that I cannot believe."

Nico shrugged. "He is a wealthy man, Lisa. And getting wealthier. He doesn't seem too concerned about getting his camel through the eye of that needle."

"He may have acquired wealth. But he supports many good causes."

She sensed that Nico had been merely amused, rather than appalled, at the notion that the archbishop would pretend to piety to mask a covetous nature. How could she make him understand that Cardinal Sauli - and Father Guido, of course - were not driven by the same temptations that many of their congregation succumbed to?

She reached the west door of the great church and, leaving Luca outside in the piazza, went inside. After a few minutes of silent prayer at the Chapel of Our Lady, she stepped into a small recess in the south aisle and closed the curtain.

"What is your confession, my child?" said a comforting voice.

"So, Don Balthasar, it seems that our efforts with Domenico Castello have finally borne fruit." There was a casual tone to Sauli's voice, as he addressed his Spanish guest.

"Indeed. The Minister will be most grateful to Your Grace."

Sauli, feeling the compliment no more than his due, reached for his wine.

"That said...," Zúñiga continued. Sauli's goblet halted halfway to his lips.

"....it has taken some considerable time. Had these moneylenders not been so reluctant to proceed at the outset, we should have achieved our aims long before now."

"This was never going to be simple, as I'm sure you realised. Anyway, I gather our successes are not confined to Banco Castello?"

"Indeed. I have had assurances from Senor Lercari and his partners that they will be provide credits in the region of three quarters of a million ducats. Their terms were initially too steep, as you recall, but they were willing to make a satisfactory adjustment. Thank you for your assistance – especially the offer of that noviate to Senor Lercari's son."

"No doubt that eased your path with Signore Lercari but as important, if I may say so, was the fact that we persuaded Domenico Castello and his brother to make their loan. One must remember that the bankers in this city watch one another. They hate to miss out on an opportunity that a competitor has taken."

Sauli looked at Zúñiga as if talking to a small child. "As I told you at the beginning, Castello was the key. He may be the son of an illiterate immigrant, but where the Alchemist goes, why, the others surely follow."

THROUGH THE OPEN shutters of his room, Monty looked out over the city, shimmering in the afternoon heat. There, still moored on the Molo, was the *"Kateryn"*, awaiting her refit. The *"Mary Gale"* and the *"Clement"* were both at sea, taken to Palermo by Master Winterhey to earn their keep. But the fine view did not quell his concern that he wasn't close to completing Uncle Sutton's commission.

His earlier meeting with Nico Castello had not gone as expected. Confident that Nico would readily agree to finance it, he had agreed purchase terms with various silk merchants.

Nico had, as usual, come straight to the point.

"For the present, Monty," he said, "Banco Castello will not be able to provide any further credits."

"There's no problem with our collateral, surely?"

"No, it's simply that we have written a large volume of business in recent days. Any more credits for the Adventurers would put us beyond our capital limit. So, regretfully, we must pause." Seeing Monty's expression, he had quickly added, "But once certain other commitments have matured, we will review the situation. I hope that within a month or two, the position will have changed."

Monty recalled Thomas Sutton had once said something about bankers' capital and the rules applicable in Genoa. He wished now he'd bothered to listen.

Nico continued. "Of course you may decide to do business elsewhere in the meantime. We would entirely understand."

Walking back across the piazza, Monty realised he would have to find alternative credit quickly, if he was going to conclude the Adventurers' business by the August Exchange Fair, now only a month away. Not that he was in any great rush to go home. Life in Genoa – Genova he reminded himself - was rather to his liking. But Uncle Sutton was no doubt expecting more progress than Monty could show to date. His uncle had insisted on regular reports, he reminded himself, thinking of his unfinished letter on his desk back at Casa Cavalli.

He reviewed his prospects with Genova's other *cambisti*. It all looked rather uncertain. But if he couldn't replace the Castello credits elsewhere, he would have to wait until Nico was ready to do business again. And what if Nico's withdrawal wasn't in fact as temporary as he had claimed? Suppose he was being diplomatic, disguising his loyalty to his wife, who clearly held anyone who was English accountable for her father's death? He must try and find out what was behind Castello's change of policy. Perhaps he could prise it out of Nico after a shared bottle or two.

Chapter Twenty-One

OFF THE COAST OF THE AZORES:
18TH JUNE

All was quiet aboard *San Felipe,* as dawn broke over her prow. In the state room high in the sterncastle of the carrack, Miguel de Oquendo stirred in his bunk. The captain's fitful, dream-filled slumber was penetrated by distant voices. A change of the watch on the main deck below. Reaching across to his window, he pushed the central shutter open and looked out over the stern. A sheaf of long, thin shadows stretched away from the vessel, across the bay towards São Miguel. An image of the ship's masts, which the sunrise had etched on the calm waters. To his left, due south, lay the open sea which had borne *San Felipe* to this peaceful anchorage. The high cloud on the southern horizon meant fair weather for their final stretch into port. He saw in his mind's eye the spires and towers of Cádiz. At long last, he would be home. But even with an accommodating south-westerly, that was still many leagues and several days' sail ahead.

He breathed out heavily and slumped back on his bed. Lord, it had been a long, hard passage from the Orient. First, their sister, the *San Lorenzo* had sprung a leak and withdrew from the voyage, returning to Manila. The *San Lorenzo's* passengers had to be doubled up in the *San Felipe.* She was loaded to her deck boards, with the stricken vessel's cargo atop her own. Even the gun decks were so full that many of her cannon couldn't be brought into action. Then their Portuguese pilot, God rest his soul, had succumbed to the flux. Armed with the pilot's maps, Oquendo had made his way through the islands of the Indies. Then Africa. At least they had managed to avoid skirmishes with

African pirates, as they ploughed their wide course around the Windward Coast. But, like the slow drip of a tap, one by one, crew members and passengers alike had fallen sick of the plague. He had lost count of the bodies they had consigned to the watery depths.

Stretching his arms out in front of him, he was unable to control the trembling of his own fingers. Cádiz could not come soon enough. He would sleep for a week, bathe for a week, eat his fill of fresh food and whore it until.... until called to his Imperial Majesty's next duty on this, his royal ship. But the cargo she was carrying was of such quality, the barrels of fine spices, the bales of luxurious silk, the gemstones, the thousands of golden ducats, that his own bounty for the trip should be substantial. Just to be sure that he would not be disappointed with King Felipe's generosity, Oquendo had placed a small casket of gems to one side. They nestled out of sight under his bunk, the rest of the gold and jewellery being stored prominently in two huge, locked chests on the opposite side of the state room. He shut his eyes and rolled over to snatch another half hour of sleep.

Moments later, there was an urgent-sounding knock at his door.

"*Buenos dias, mi capitan.*"

Oquendo groaned. It was Jose, his steward.

"*¿Qué hora es?*"

The voice dropped to an apologetic tone. "*Son las cinco menos cuarto...*"

Yelling through the door, Oquendo cursed his steward for rousing him at such an hour.

The voice continued, pleading. "*Ma ....es un barco, mi capitan...*"

"*¿Un barco?*"

Oquendo forced himself out of bed, pulled on his boots and jerkin, and opened the cabin door. Jose was shaking, fearful no doubt that his master was angry for being woken so early. Oquendo shoved him out of the way and strode along the passageway which led to the steps down to the bridge. When he arrived, First Mate Manolo was scanning the horizon. Oquendo followed the direction of his gaze, towards the rising sun, over the prow of the ship.

His eyes adjusted to the brightness. It was a sail, no question, coming over the horizon. A trading vessel from one of the other islands, Terceira perhaps. But the ship was giving the coastline of São Miguel a wide berth. A Terceira ship would likely arrive from the other side of the island, from the northwest.

Captain and mate waited for a closer look. She was coming on, her hull now visible, a darkish spot. But, even at this distance, it was obvious she was a relative minnow. He doubted that she was more than half the size of the *San Felipe*. As she edged closer, Oquendo ordered the ship's pennants run up. The red crosses that matched her foresail and for her mainmast, the flag of Portugal.

Light clouds crossed low on the horizon, momentarily putting the object of their attention in shadow. As the sun emerged again, its rays lit her sails from behind. Like the soft light of a lamp. Pure white, no markings on them. No flag raised either. She was certainly a galleon, judging by her rig. But from where?

One of the watchmen, positioned high on the foremast, called out. Oquendo looked in the direction he was pointing, to the left of the oncoming ship. And then he spotted them. The topsails of two more ships. They were following the same line. He turned to Manolo to give him an order, but the Bo'sun was already running down to the main deck, yelling to the crew to put on sail and raise the anchors.

SOME EIGHT HUNDRED miles to the north-east of *San Felipe's* position, Minister Idiáquez was already hard at work. Trying to keep pace with his sovereign's flow of instructions. But his study was stifling despite the early hour.

Frustrated, he paused to open the shutters wide. His apartment, in the Escorial, looked west towards the Sierra Guadarrama. Blasted by dry winds that came down from those barren peaks, the king's palace was a freezing prison in winter, a furnace in summer. God, how he hated the place.

As he walked away from the window, a strong gust blew most of the papers off his desk. Cursing, he rescued them from the tiled floor. Among them was the letter from Zúñiga which he had just decoded. It was the only piece of good news he could take to the king.

Tempers were on a knife's edge in the Consejo de Guerra as they grappled with the king's lack of funds. The Duke of Parma was complaining of the delay, as his army kicked their heels in the Netherlands. The Marquis de Santa Cruz was struggling in Lisbon, with the armada's suppliers refusing further trade without some show of payment. And when would His Holiness in Rome get around to putting his signature to the much-promised loan?

It scarcely helped that that criminal, El Draque, was still plundering the western coast, seemingly unafraid of the prospect of a full-blown engagement with Santa Cruz. Not that the Captain-General had shown much inclination to take the fleet out and challenge him.

Perhaps Don Balthasar would release them from the chains of this spider's web. If his assurances were to be believed, the Genovese bankers would soon provide enough hard cash to silence the bleating from Parma and Santa Cruz. The terms that the bankers were demanding were eye-watering, true, but such was the price of war.

One surprising point in Zúñiga's report was that English merchants were also in the city, taking up large amounts of credit from the banks. Making his own negotiations that much harder. And driving up the lenders' prices. The English? That was curious, he thought, considering the harvests in England had reportedly been poor again last year. For some years, their merchants had scarcely ventured to the European fairs and here they were now, spending like Croesus apparently. Or was Zúñiga exaggerating, just to cover his own slow progress?

Inserting the folded letter in his doublet, he headed down the corridor to the king's apartments.

Chapter Twenty-Two
CASA CAVALLI, GENOA: THE SAME DAY

Some nine hundred miles east of the Escorial's gloomy corridors, Nico was about to leave his residence when a letter arrived. It was from Lorenzo Cavalli: an invitation to dine with himself and with Monty, at Casa Cavalli, in a few nights' time. He was aware that, since he had put a hold on new business, Monty had approached several of the other cambisti for credit. But, judging by the sporadic outcry of new transactions in the Loggia, he had had little success in bridging the gap. No doubt Monty had encouraged Cavalli to make his invitation to give the Englishman an opportunity to change Nico's mind. That wouldn't happen, but he accepted the invitation, nevertheless.

At the dinner held later that week, Nico and Monty were entertained by some of Cavalli's tales of the wild, early days of the Republic. But when the candles ran down and their host could no longer stifle a yawn, Monty suggested to Nico that the pair of them head over to the 'Paradiso' where, the Englishman asserted, he was now a frequent customer. Somewhat reluctantly, Nico agreed.

Once a regular client of the 'Paradiso' himself, especially when entertaining merchants, Nico had much reduced his patronage since his marriage. It was not something that sat easily with him now, even if life with Lisa had scarcely been a peaceful bower of love and harmony. Far from it. He tried to justify his occasional visits to the 'Paradiso', as being in reaction to one of Lisa's outbursts or her occasional withdrawal behind the doors of her own apartment. If only he and she were more in tune with one another, it would be easier to be a better husband. But underneath, he knew that excuse would not stand. The reverse was more likely true. If he were a better husband, then perhaps she would be a more contented wife. He resolved to make this his last visit.

An hour later, he was distracted from his thoughts by Adriana, raising herself from the day bed and reaching out to fill Nico's cup. Well, now he was here, he may as well enjoy himself. He motioned for her to attend to Monty as well, but Adriana passed the silver jug across the low table to her 'sister', the raven-haired Bianca who unwrapped herself from Monty and took the flask. The two men were lounging in their robes, but Bianca and Adriana were as naked as Eve in the Garden of Eden, the feathered masks over their eyes, their jewellery and the zuccolis on their dainty feet, their only concessions to clothing. The teasing banter which ran back and forth between Bianca and Adriana was diverting. That, and a couple of generous measures of the house's finest red wine, helped him suppress his feelings of guilt.

Adriana and Bianca left the room in search of sweetmeats. Alone, Nico and Monty spoke a mixture of Latin, English, which Nico had recently tasked himself with trying to learn and Italian, at which the Englishman was becoming more adept. As Monty became steadily drunk, Nico realised that the Englishman would probably forget that there had been a purpose to his invitation. So, he raised it himself.

"A word on business matters, Monty," he began. "Once again, my regrets that we have been unable to provide further credit. But the situation is temporary."

Monty's voice was slurred. "Must confess - wasn't entirely clear as to your reasons. My misunderstanding, no doubt."

Nico reiterated his previous explanation.

"But surely," ventured Monty, "as the bank trades, your bullion is replenished by the conclusion of other transactions. It goes out, it comes in?"

"Yes, but we have recently made some large commitments."

"Well, they must be substantial merchants."

"*No merchant he*," Nico thought, but didn't say. He had had too much wine, but he was not that drunk. "So, if you can be patient for a while longer...."

Bianca and Adriana had returned, their arms around each other, whispering and giggling.

"Well," Monty observed, "I can think of less interestin' ways to while away the time."

THE JULY HEAT became a major irritant for Monty, as much as for Genova's citizens in general. The sun glared down at the shameless city, its dazzling rays bouncing off the sea and into squinting eyes. In the piazzas, it was hot and dusty. Like a bear-pit, but one bleached with light, rather than dark like a furnace. '*Scottato*', as the locals called it. Merchants snapped at one another, tempers were quick and courtesies in short supply.

Despite feeling that he had stumbled into an enormous oven, Monty carried on with his wool sales. Summer wouldn't last forever. The buyers might be short-tempered and sour, but slowly he won them over. Handshake by handshake. Bottle of wine by bottle. But save for small cash purchases, any ordering of silk, cloves or nutmeg would have to wait until the August Fair, by which time he hoped Nico and his other bankers would be more accommodating.

In the evenings, if there were no other invitations on offer, he spent his time with the ladies of the 'Paradiso'. Preferably, when she was free, with Bianca. He asked Nico to join him there on several occasions, but the banker always found some excuse. At first that concerned him, but he kept reminding himself that Nico had no hidden motive for suspending credit.

LISA WAS SITTING with Julia in a shaded area of the terrace, half-listening to her aunt complaining about one of the servants. Thankfully, Julia's harangue was drowned out by raised voices nearby. Men were shouting in the street below. "I didn't hear you," Lisa mouthed, shaking her head.

Julia stopped talking and Lisa suddenly realised that the voices were familiar. And they were coming from the lobby. Dropping her needlework, she ran to the top of the staircase. Down in the lobby below, Nico and Sandro were yelling at one another, words Lisa hadn't heard from either of them before. Ugly words. And they were trading punches. Marco and Luca were trying, ineffectually, to separate them.

Lisa screamed out above the din. "What are you *doing*?"

Sandro paused, glancing up at Lisa, at the same instant as Nico swung his right fist. It connected with Sandro's undefended chin. He staggered backwards, stunned by the blow.

Lisa called out to Marco, "For pity's sake, do something!"

Marco stepped in front of his master but was elbowed out of the way. Luca helped Sandro to his feet. He tried to break free and half-lunge at his brother at the same time.

"Signori, signori, per favore, per favore..." pleaded Marco.

Sandro shrugged off Luca's grip, dusted himself down and with a glare at his brother marched up the stairs and past Lisa. Moments later she heard the door to his apartment being slammed. Nico, shaking with anger, headed for the gateway out to the street. Lisa ran down the staircase, catching up with him as he was about to step across the threshold.

"What in heaven's name has happened?"

Nico stared back at her, still breathing hard.

"Why are you fighting?" she yelled.

"The "*San Felipe*", wife," he finally blurted out. "She is lost."

"Lost – what? A storm?"

"No, no storm. She is *taken*."

Lisa shook her head, still not comprehending.

"Il Drago. Il Drago has taken her." He drew his forefinger across his throat.

Chapter Twenty-Three
THE MERCHANTS' LOGGIA, PIAZZA BANCHI: MID-JULY

The high cloud over the hills behind Genova looked promising. It presaged a storm which would afford some blessed relief from the heat, Monty hoped. But the rain that followed that afternoon, though heavy, was only brief. When it stopped, the temperature had fallen, but the stickiness of the air took away any benefit.

He returned to Piazza Banchi, stepping over the muddy puddles. He was surprised to find that the banca where the Castellos conducted business was deserted. As were several other stations. Mostly, it was the small fry that were left. He spotted a familiar face, that of Battista Lomellino. He seemed to be packing up to leave. Monty greeted him and received a mere nod in return. The banker's face was unsmiling. When he tried to engage Lomellino in conversation, he was rebuffed.

"You must excuse me, Signore Montecchio, we are extremely busy."

Aside from a bored-looking assistant, the area around Lomellino's *banca* was empty. No sign of any customers.

He crossed the piazza to speak to a wool buyer he knew, who was conversing with another merchant. The buyer seemed pleased to see him, probably remembering the evenings they'd shared at the Paradiso. After introducing Monty to his colleague, the buyer nudged him on the arm.

"Ah, signore. That man of yours, Il Drago."

"He's not *my* man," Monty asserted, "but what's he done now?"

"So, you haven't heard the latest news?" he said, with a knowing look. Monty confessed he hadn't, which pleased the buyer even more. Spreading gossip was, after all, one of life's chief pleasures if you worked in Piazza Banchi.

"He's grabbed a huge prize. Only King Felipe's greatest ship, signore. And a treasure trove of cargo with it. What d'you think of that?"

Monty didn't know what to think. Obviously, it was good news from Drake's point of view. No doubt from Queen Elizabeth's also. But for himself and his venture? He had a strong sense of unease.

"What more do we know about it?"

No-one seemed very clear how Drake had managed this feat. After all, the *"San Felipe"* was a great carrack, a thousand-tonner. And a royal one into the bargain, with cannon and military guard to match. Obviously, the merchant suggested, the pirate had a sizeable squadron at his command, to be able to override her defences. The wool buyer tried to top this with the suggestion that, once again, Il Drago had not raised his colours until the last minute of his assault and that, yet again, the Spanish were taken by surprise. A Drake speciality, it seemed to Monty.

When the merchants had exhausted their store of gossip, speculation turned to more mercantile concerns.

"That was a large cargo, signore," said the wool buyer. "It must mean that silk prices will soon rise. Pepper too. You'd be best advised to step in and buy, at the earliest opportunity," he added.

Yes, I should, thought Monty, but with what?

As if reading Monty's thoughts, the merchant spoke about the *cambisti*. How would this loss reverberate among the bankers of Genova? Some of them would surely lose by it. The man's rueful smile proclaimed the wisdom of hindsight. After all, you can't be lucky forever, the smile said.

Monty parted company with the pair and wandered down to the Molo. Drawn to the waterfront, as if he expected Drake's flotilla to sail into harbour at any moment. This damned pirate was haunting him, like some vengeful ghost. Wherever he turned, Drake had played an unseen hand. First Cádiz, where fears of war had unsettled everyone in Genova - and Monty had felt almost an enemy in their midst. Then, that awful story about Signora Castello and her father, which could so easily have scuppered his relations with her husband. And now this. The loss of that ship could put silk prices beyond his grasp if he didn't move quickly. Damn Drake. Damn him to hell.

NICO STARED out of his apartment window, with its view of the city below. But he was not really registering what he saw.

Precisely what he had feared had come to pass. The bank was committed to lend a huge sum to King Felipe and the security for that loan had vanished over the horizon. If he had not been so keen to avoid loss of face, he could have overridden Sandro's offer to the Spanish. It would have been embarrassing, but it was better than this situation.

Nor could he really blame Sandro. His brother's fears of personal condemnation and scandal were real enough. But Nico should have stuck to his first instincts and stayed away from lending to princes. He and Sandro could have ridden it out. Instead, he had been seduced by greed - and by the distinction of being the equal of Nicolo Grimaldi. Bankers to the king, indeed. It was vanity and greed, plain and simple.

And now he was faced with a dilemma. The sums he was obliged to make advance to Zúñiga, on top of what had already been lent, were close to the bank's entire capital. Even if Zúñiga offered other collateral, Nico knew he couldn't sleep soundly until the loan was repaid. But if he refused to advance more, that would antagonise not only the Spanish themselves, but also the archbishop, not to mention the San Giorgio's treasurer. And his competitors would, no doubt, take full advantage of his embarrassment.

Later that day, Nico was with Lisa and his brother in the *salotto*, their evening meal over. He concentrated on his plate of fruit and cheese, not feeling it necessary to break the silence between them. Sandro was staring out of the window at the garden. With each clatter of cutlery or polite cough from one of the servants behind them, Lisa seemed to become more agitated. She motioned to the servants to clear away the plates and leave the room. Throwing her napkin on the table in front of her, she stood up and addressed them both. Her voice sounded shaky but determined.

"We cannot go on like this. You are brothers. For the love you owe one another, you must face your trials together. Divided, you will surely be beaten. Make peace, at least for your father's sake."

Nico noticed that she did not say *'for my sake'*. He knew it was his place to initiate a reconciliation. He held out his hand to his brother. "Sandro, I should not have blamed you. It was my decision to go ahead."

The handshake became an arm-lock, as the brothers embraced.

"You're right, Lisa: that's the first thing I should have done," Nico said, looking at her over Sandro's shoulder. "And the second thing I should have done is to find a decent lawyer."

THE OFFICES of the *avvocato* and notary, Leonardo Tasso, were located close to the waterfront. The rent he paid to Andrea De Marini, the nobleman who owned the house, was high but Tasso considered it worth the premium. Partly because its rear windows afforded him a fine view over the eastern harbour and partly because the location placed him close to his clients, the merchants, ship-owners and bankers trading in nearby Piazza Banchi. And Tasso could afford the rent because his clients regularly favoured him with their instructions above Genova's other lawyers. On the rare occasion he took on a new client, his decision was not driven by their ability to pay his not inconsiderable fees. He had put aside enough to ensure his declining years were comfortable. Rather, he would accept the engagement if he adjudged the case to be worthy. Even at this stage of his professional life, he delighted in mining for that essential truth that would advance his client's case.

He was about to close his office for the evening, the key in his hand, when a smartly dressed youth ran up the steps to his doorway. He thought he had seen the lad before but could not recall where.

"Avvocato Tasso?" the young visitor said breathlessly.

When the lawyer confirmed as much, Lorenzo handed him a letter. Opening it, Tasso read that he was invited to attend Casa Castello where Signori Domenico and Alessandro would be pleased to receive him for an urgent consultation.

"Would that be...right now?" he asked, intrigued.

The lad had apparently been instructed on no account to return to the house without bringing the gentleman. Tasso had been looking forward to his supper, but then the Castellos were serious men of business, after all. It could wait for once.

He laid his hand on Lorenzo's shoulder. "Well in that case, let us make our way there."

Fifteen minutes later, he was ushered into the sala of Casa Castello where he was greeted by Nico and Sandro. While antipasti and wine were served, the lawyer took in his expensively decorated surroundings. He commented on the quality of the paintings adorning the walls. It was sincere praise, not mere flattery of his prospective clients. A small Nativity scene by the great Cambiaso especially caught his eye.

But Nico was keen to get to the point.

"Signore Tasso, we are grateful for your prompt attendance. We have a particular problem which may benefit from your advice."

"If I can, I would be happy to help."

"Then let me ask you to read this."

Nico placed a manuscript on the table between them. Tasso unrolled the document. After scanning the first few lines, he stopped.

"It seems to be the text of an agreement, but there are no names here."

"Ah yes, it is a copy I have made. Because of certain sensitivities, I have omitted the name of the debtor, where it appears. And one or two other details, the amount of the loan and the like." Nico opened his palms towards the lawyer. "But otherwise, it is the exact and complete text of an existing agreement."

"And the lender, I assume, is your bank?"

"Indeed. We intended to bring co-lenders in with us, but that aspect has not been concluded. As for the omitted details, I trust you will pardon our reticence."

Tasso could have spoken of the importance of original documents and full facts, the need for complete trust between lawyer and client. But instinct told him that, in this case, such grand words would avail him little. It was this 'version' or nothing.

He read on. The bank had agreed to make a loan to an unnamed person, the loan amount and interest rate left blank, the repayment date the first day of November. And in return, the debtor had agreed to issue an *asiento* of the entirety of a cargo he owned, from a ship the name of which was also omitted, until the bank had recovered both loan and interest in full. Tasso read it through twice and placed it back on the table.

"What is it that you would like my opinion on?"

"As I said, this is a recently made agreement. We hold the debtor's signed *asiento* over the cargo in question. But now, we hear that the ship is lost."

"Lost? You mean, she has foundered?"

He sensed that Nico was a little irritated by the question.

"Foundered, captured, lost. You may choose. But whichever, she is forever lost to our customer. He cannot recover her, nor any of the cargo within her."

"But your customer still wants the bank to advance the loan money?" Tasso said, though more to himself than to Nico.

"He accepts that the cargo is lost but says that the collateral was at our risk from the moment we accepted the *asiento*. So yes, he still '*wants his money*'."

"So, the loan has not been advanced, as yet?"

Sandro coughed, causing the lawyer to divert his eyes from Nico to his brother. "We have advanced just over a quarter of the loan. But the debtor is pressing for the balance."

"And you want to know whether you are still obliged to advance it."

Nico formed his fingers into a bridge. "Yes. And, if we can, accelerate repayment of what has already been lent."

"This is an interesting problem, signori. I would be pleased to undertake it." He waved the document in his hand. "Will you allow me to take this away? I need some time to consider it."

"How much time?" said Nico.

Tasso thought rapidly. "Would next Monday be acceptable?"

"This week would be more acceptable."

Tasso shrugged. "Very well. On Friday, then."

LEONARDO TASSO RETURNED on the Friday afternoon, as arranged. Once seated, he placed the momentous document on the table between himself and the two brothers.

"The first thing to say is that there is a difference between a transfer of property between a buyer and seller and a transfer under a contract such as this *asiento*. It promises the cargo to you as security only. By the terms of this document, it takes effect only when you advance the loan to him."

"As you were told, we have made a partial advance," said Nico.

"Yes. That is a pity."

Nico's eyes narrowed. "Is it important?"

"Well, if the cargo was lost *before* any advance was made, we could argue that the entire basis of the contract had collapsed before it could be implemented. In my parlance, we would rescind the agreement."

Sandro looked at his brother. "They say that the "*San ....*" Sandro corrected himself, "that the ship was seized on June 18th, did they not? That was before our first advance."

"Signori," said Tasso with a smile, "I perfectly understand your reluctance to identify the debtor. We need not speak of him or his ship. But I did wonder if the vessel we are talking about could be a certain Spanish carrack?"

Nico raised his hand, but Tasso cut him off. "Be assured of my discretion, signore. This will go no further. If you prefer, I will not retain any notes of our discussions. You may keep them."

Tasso sipped his wine, taking his time. "As I was saying, your rights over the collateral -if you can get hold of it - are not those of a buyer. You may only exercise the power of sale, if he fails to repay you on the appointed date. The transfer is security only, in other words."

That was obvious enough, Nico didn't say.

"So then," Tasso continued, "the borrower comes to you now asking for a second instalment of the advance, but at this point both parties know that the bank cannot enforce its security over the cargo, if the debtor defaults."

"Does that make a difference?" asked Sandro, gripping the stem of his wine glass, the knuckles white.

"That depends. On where the parties have agreed the risk of loss should fall. Now in this case," Tasso said, putting on his spectacles and picking up the document, "there is no provision dealing explicitly with that point. It might have said that if the cargo were lost, all advances would cease unless the debtor offered you alternative security."

Nico cursed inwardly. Next time he needed a loan agreement, he would get Tasso to draft it. If there *was* a next time.

"And therefore, one looks to the document more widely to ascertain the intent of the parties," said Tasso, warming to his task. "And here, it says that the debtor promises to take care of the collateral. And to deliver it into your custody, if demanded, until the point he repays you."

"And so?" said Nico.

Tasso looked over his glasses at his new clients. "My *dear* signori, the debtor is in default. He *hasn't* taken care of the assets. He's allowed them to be taken from him, you tell me. So, even if you continue to perform *your* obligations by making further advances, he can never perform certain of *his* obligations, because he doesn't control the collateral anymore."

He put down the document, as if he had reached a conclusion. Nico raised an index finger in the air. "But does that mean we're released from the obligation to lend more?"

Tasso pursed his lips. "There are no other documents or accords governing the matter?"

Nico shook his head.

"Well, in my opinion then, it could be argued that you are indeed released...."

Sandro blew air out through his lips. Nico didn't move. "You are sure of that?" he said.

"Oh, as I said, it depends where the risk of loss was intended to fall. Regrettably, this document is not conclusive, in my opinion. The borrower might argue that the parties were aware, when the contract was signed, that the collateral was a ship on the high seas. An asset subject to the vicissitudes of fortune, the risks of storm, pirates or poor navigation.... Of course, he still owes you the money, signori. He may be unable to perform his promises regarding the collateral, but he still must discharge the primary one, namely, to repay you with interest on the date agreed. In..." he glanced at the document, "...some four months from now."

"Can we ask for repayment early?" asked Nico.

"Not, I think, if he offers you alternative collateral of equivalent value."

"Could you at least opine that we are discharged from further lending unless he does, could you put that in writing?"

Tasso looked down his nose at Nico.

"I think I could say that."

The lawyer leaned back in his chair. "Is there any more of this excellent wine?" he said. Apparently, he was done advising.

BALTHASAR DE ZÚÑIGA paced up and down the room. Sauli noticed that the Spaniard was stepping on the same tiles each time he crossed the floor. He tried to concentrate on what Zúñiga was saying.

"I have demanded that Castello honour his agreement. He is saying that with the *'San Felipe'* gone, he wants alternative collateral before he advances the remainder of the loan. I thought Genovese bankers were men of principle, but I see they are all cowards and liars."

"And how did he justify refusing you?" the archbishop said, trying to maintain a calm exterior. "Take him to the Doge's court. Force him to stump up."

"That means delay. His Majesty needs funds, not lengthy lawsuits."

"Then find a hungry lawyer, there are enough of their *wretched* tribe in this city."

Zúñiga looked down his long nose at the archbishop. "Since my arrival here, I have heard nothing from Your Grace but assurances that all will be well. More than two months have passed. And what is there to show, for all the talks we have had? I have secured but a fifth of the credit I was deputed to arrange."

Sauli did not appreciate the criticism. "Our work on King Felipe's behalf has been unrelenting. And we would have been entirely successful, had his naval forces done their duty. Instead, that criminal Il Drago has shown the world that he is free to plunder as he sees fit. That mistake has cost the king dear."

Zúñiga became red-faced. "His Majesty cannot be criticised for the crimes of others."

"Then perhaps he should execute a few captains and generals, to stiffen the resolve of the rest."

Zúñiga opened his mouth to speak, but Sauli continued, not brooking interruption.

"At all events, it is scarcely the Church's fault that such a combination of English criminality and Spanish military incompetence has interfered with your plans. But it is temporary. We will redouble our efforts."

"If you want my opinion, Your Grace..." Zúñiga began. Sauli raised his hands in a plea, since he didn't particularly. ".... that traitor Castello has scared the other bankers away. We are talking to shadows, not real men."

"They will return. Even bankers must eat, Don Balthasar."

After Zúñiga had departed, the archbishop summoned Father Guido to vent his feelings.

"That two-faced gutter-rat Castello is stalling on advancing his loan to Senor Zúñiga. He uses the excuse of '*San Felipe*'s capture."

"I see," said Guido, absorbing the news. "Would you wish for his brother to be brought to your presence? I can send a message immediately."

"That may be necessary - but let us hold that in reserve for the moment."

"Then perhaps Signora Castello can persuade her husband to change his mind?"

Sauli scowled. "Frankly, your efforts in that direction have been ineffective to date."

Guido knew better than to challenge the archbishop's accusation. "I will continue to exhort her, Your Grace."

A LETTER WRITTEN on behalf of Zúñiga, by a lawyer that Nico had nearly consulted for a second opinion, predictably demanded that Banco Castello continue its obligation to make further advances to the Spanish envoy. Nico responded to it, but without making any promises. He also delivered a sealed letter to the postal agency in Via dei Corrieri. A fast courier would deliver his letter to Banco Castello's agent in Augsburg, directing him not to disburse any further money to the suppliers of Felipe's weaponry. The bullion should be retained, pending Nico's further instructions.

But *not* doing business with Zúñiga didn't put food on the Castellos' table, as Nico commented to his brother. So, with Sandro's agreement, Nico decided to resume issuing merchant credits. However, these would be short term only, to ensure that the bank retained sufficient liquidity while the dispute with Zúñiga worked its way to a conclusion. Those credits would include ones for the Englishman, they agreed.

When Monty arrived at Nico's banca the next day, his expression was guarded until Nico put him out of his misery.

Monty's relief was patent. "I am most appreciative, Nico."

But Nico held up a qualifying index figure. "But I must advise you, in the present disturbed times, our prices will need to rise."

Seeing the change in his client's face, Nico paid Monty the courtesy of justifying the necessity for price rises, even though he felt that as an experienced merchant Monty should have seen it coming. The result was a rise in the bank's margin by half as much again. Nico pointed out that he was being fair to his customer, at least by the lights of some of his competitors. Some had doubled their margins, or more, after the news about the '*San Felipe*'.

Monty stuck out his hand to accept.

ARMED WITH FRESH CREDIT, Monty headed back into the piazza. As he feared and indeed, as that wool buyer had predicted, some merchants were seeking to raise their prices for any goods originating from the Orient. But Nico advised him that such prices would not hold. There might be shortages of certain goods in due course, but right now there was still plenty on display. What there *weren't*, Nico pointed out, was buyers or rather, bankers willing to offer credit to would-be buyers. The result was obvious. Prices would simply come back down again.

As Monty approached one table, the merchant stood up and rushed round to greet him, talking rapidly. But even before he could get Monty to sit down, two other traders approached the Englishman on either side, touching his arms and talking, quietly but insistently, in his ears.

"*Per favore, signore,* if silks are your object, do not commit until you have seen our quality."

"Our prices are the keenest in the city, I assure you, signore."

"Do not waste your time, signore, at *this* table. We can offer you a superior cloth at a lower price."

Patiently listening, Monty worked his way through the stalls. The urgency in the voices of the sellers was unmistakeable. Nico was right. He would be able to bargain hard. Other than his own, not a single *cambiale* was announced from the Loggia that morning. The more he thought about it, the less aggrieved he felt regarding Nico's interest rise.

Chapter Twenty-Four
SCYTHING LANE, CITY OF LONDON: MID-JULY

Forcing himself to block out the spasms of pain in his gut, Walsingham considered his celebrated visitor. The man sat opposite him was bubbling with annoyance. Anger suited him, thought Walsingham, with that reddish hair and beard of his and even ruddier complexion: "old apple-cheeks". That face betrayed the fact that its owner had only recently returned from three months at sea. But Walsingham sympathised with Drake's latest grievance. They were, after all, both casualties of the same war: their battle to persuade the Queen to take a more robust stance where Philip of Spain was concerned.

The timing was less than ideal. Just days before, and despite the risk of stoking Elizabeth's renewed anger, Walsingham had finally settled the arrangements for Mary Stuart's burial. It was to be in Peterborough Cathedral, but the Queen had decided she would not attend, nor had they invited any foreign ambassadors. That would seem like gloating over the corpse. He still had to work out how the body, now in a lead coffin, would be brought from Fotheringhay to Peterborough, without creating a tide of rumours.

Walsingham had to swallow his frustrations when reasoning with his monarch. Whereas Drake felt comfortable enough in Walsingham's company to freely bemoan his sovereign's ingratitude. His Devon burr became more pronounced.

"Her Majesty accused me of disobeyin' her orders. But I explained,

I had already sailed from Plymouth by the time her letter, countermanding her previous instructions, ever got there..."

Walsingham poured more wine into Drake's glass. "She realises that. The Lady is just venting her anger – as if we are supposed to have foreknowledge, each time she changes her mind."

Drake grumbled into his beard. "She was quite happy moments earlier, when I told her what her share of the spoils would amount to. A tidy sum it is, too." He obviously expected that the capture of a prize like the "*San Felipe*" would put him in good standing with Elizabeth, permanently.

Walsingham had seen this tactic before. The Queen was using Drake's fear of her wrath merely to extract from him a larger share of the prize money. Of course, he knew from old that Drake was just as fond of the rewards of his freebooting as was the Queen herself. And just as reluctant to give them up. He tried to reassure the sailor.

"She may seem to you ungrateful, but I venture that underneath she was happy for you to do exactly what you did."

Drake pushed out his lower lip. "Must be so. She even suggested that I could sail for the Indies. Intercept the Spanish silver fleet."

"We need you closer at hand. In any case, I expect the *Flota* has already sailed."

From the sailor's expression, Walsingham guessed that Drake was intending to take a well-earned rest in his Devon home and enjoy the spoils. Walsingham envied him momentarily. At this time of year, he too should be with his family, down at Barn Elms. But there was too much to do. In any case, Doctor Baily was here in London and right now, he needed him constantly, if only to provide the pain-relieving potions he was coming to depend on. Ursula had left for Putney with Frances a week earlier but had left part of the household behind, so her husband would not want for anything in her absence.

Drake changed the subject. "You know, since my return we haven't had a proper opportunity to discuss Cádiz, Sir Francis."

"I would appreciate that, indeed." Walsingham had received confidential reports of Drake's stunning success in Cádiz harbour from his agent there, but there was no substitute for an account from the man who had carried it out. Besides, Drake would be happy to boast of his own success: it was what the man liked to do. And Walsingham could do with some cheering news: latest reports from the Netherlands were that the Duke of Parma was about to take the seaport of Sluis.

He listened without interrupting, but in truth quite entertained, as

Drake gave a dramatic account of the sea battle. You could almost hear cannon exploding, smell the gunpowder wafting through the rigging. He wondered if Drake was exaggerating the number of Spanish ships that had caught fire, but there was no arguing with the ships he had seized and sailed home with. The proof was moored down at Plymouth.

But numbers were important. He needed to gauge how much Philip's war preparations had been disrupted. Drake was happy to talk all afternoon about the fight, but Walsingham noted his reference to quayside stores.

"How much would you say was destroyed?"

Drake looked up at the ceiling, as he calculated. "Oh, I would guess, not less than a thousand ton. Powder, boxes, provisions, feed for the horses. But looking back, I think we should be most pleased about the staves."

"Staves?"

"Yes, the barrel staves. There were whole mountains of 'em. It took a fair time to catch fire, but when it did, goodness, that were some inferno. You could feel the heat on my ship, a hundred paces off. Seasoned timber, d'you see?"

Walsingham didn't.

"But Sir Francis," Drake persisted, "these staves? In due course, they'd have been fashioned into thousands of barrels for the Armada's provisions. Where are they going to find that much seasoned oak in short order?"

"So, you're saying that they can't sail until they have made new barrels....," mused Walsingham, out loud.

Drake broke into a laugh. He had achieved something rarely done by anyone. He had made Walsingham smile.

MONTY WAS LOOKING FORWARD to an evening with Bianca at the 'Paradiso'. There would not be many more such occasions. It was now the end of July: soon the August Fair would begin. When that was over and, God willing, the remainder of his business concluded, there would be no excuse to linger in Genoa. It would be time to head home to England - and Jane.

Jane: it struck him that in all this time away he had not thought of her that often. His marriage was no affair of the heart, true, but did that excuse his straying? He knew his Seventh Commandment, but in front of his mirror, he could not summon up a sense of shame about the times that he and Bianca had shared a bed. Surely, a husband and wife should be so entwined that mere physical absence could not separate their souls from one another. To lose that feeling merely because of a dalliance with a courtesan? He persuaded himself that Bianca saw him as more than merely another customer. But did he feel more for the girl than simple lust?

When he set out from Casa Cavalli, the streets were darkening. But by now, he joked to himself, he could thread his way across the city if he were blindfolded. Soon, he was being ushered into the lobby of the 'Paradiso'. As usual on a Friday evening, the household was in *festa* mood, rooms filled with the sound of laughter. Moments later, the now familiar figure of Lina Luzzati appeared at the head of the curving staircase. "Signore Montecchio, bienvenuto," she purred, as she descended to greet him. From her tone of voice, you would infer that Monty had not visited her establishment for months.

As he entered Bianca's room, she was standing close to the window. Her dress, one he had not seen before, was a deep red silk edged with black lace. As the maid softly closed the door behind Monty, Bianca turned her head. "Is something wrong?" she said, when he did not move towards her.

"Why no, not at all, I was ...," he paused, "...thinking how beautiful you look."

Bianca laughed lightly, but her smile indicated her pleasure at the compliment. She drew the curtains closed, throwing the room into near darkness. Monty removed his sword belt and unbuttoned his doublet, as she lit a few candles. Then, once he was stretched out on the bed, she poured wine into two gold-etched glasses and offered one to him. But instead of joining Monty on the bed, she crossed to an armchair and picked up the lute propped against it. She began to pluck the strings, humming softly.

Her song over, Bianca put down the instrument and walked towards him. She paused a couple of paces from the bed and slowly untied the laces from the bodice of her dress. Slipping off her shoulders, the dress dropped on the floor with a soft hiss as the silk material puddled. Her lawn under-dress revealed the delightful curves of her body.

She ran the tips of her fingers across his upturned palm. Then, taking his wrist gently between her thumb and forefinger, she placed it across her breast. Underneath the soft skin, he could feel her heartbeat. With his other arm, he reached out and encircled her waist, pulling her towards him.

It was the middle of the night when he left her. He promised to return as often as he could, saying that sadly, his departure for England would come all too soon.

"You could take me with you, instead," Bianca whispered.

"I would desire nothing more," he said.

He realised, as he closed the door behind him, that it was in fact the truth.

As he descended the staircase, he stumbled in the low light. The last of the candles on the floor below him guttered and died, making the darkness total. Feeling his way by holding the balustrade, he reached the floor of the lobby. A door opened somewhere in a distant part of the house.

"Signora Luzzati?" he called. No reply.

"Ah, Marcello. Bring some light, can you?" he said, hoping the doorkeeper was still about.

Silence. The moon emerged from behind a cloud and cast its beams through the lunette. He headed for the front door and found it unbolted. As he descended the steps to the piazza, a faint sound came from somewhere behind him. After a few moments, he realised what it was. The sound of someone breathing.

"Who's there?" he called, half-turning.

Before he could draw his sword, he was grabbed by both arms. Someone stuffed a cloth in his mouth and a blanket was thrown over his head. Kicking out, his boot connected with a man's crotch. His assailants threw him to the floor, kicking him on the back and the belly. He struggled to his feet. Only to fall again, stunned by a heavy blow to the head.

NICO EXPECTED that the correspondence between lawyers regarding the Spanish loan would drag on for weeks: a delay which in the circumstances would be very useful. But instead, Zúñiga had taken the short route to resolution. Nico was summoned to appear at the Doge's court, where Banco Castello's obligation to advance the balance of the agreed loan would be adjudicated. Argued out in public between the respective attorneys for the bank and the borrower.

Nico and Sandro met Avvocato Tasso in the lobby of the Palazzo Ducale a few minutes before the appointed hour. Almost immediately, Nico had the uneasy feeling that things would not turn out as expected. Tasso seemed less confident in his bearing than he had been at their early meetings.

"Well, we will do all we can, Signore Castello," he observed with a smile, "but I always said that our position was arguable, at best."

That was not exactly how Nico remembered it, but there was little point in arguing with his own lawyer. What mattered was how the judge saw it.

"I have just been handed a note by his attorney. It seems they are willing to provide alternative security, after all. The royal carrack, '*San Lorenzo*'," he added, peering at the note with his spectacles. "Which, they point out, is the sister ship of the '*San Felipe*'."

"A little late for that, isn't it? At the courtroom door?"

"It is often the way with these things. No doubt they will make much of it – and we shall merely appear churlish if we say it's too little, too late."

Nico scowled but said nothing.

"Shall we go in?" said Tasso, pointing the way with the sleeve of his robe.

Zúñiga and his attorney were already in their places. Aside from the court functionaries, no one else was in the room. After an awkward few minutes, where nothing passed between the parties other than a bare acknowledgment of each other's presence, the judge entered. Nico was surprised by his relative youth, close to the age of Zúñiga's attorney he judged, whereas Tasso's silvery locks proclaimed his years of experience.

Invited to begin, Zúñiga's attorney began not with the terms of the contract itself but with a declamation of the lofty, almost saintly, status of the claimant, the king's representative, as compared with the base, mercenary motives of the defendant. He stressed the urgency of the matter; the imperative that matters of state (alluded to but left unspecified) be properly funded; and the outright reasonableness, in the face of intransigence on the part of the defendant, of Senor Zúñiga.

"This, despite His Majesty's horrendous and unforeseen loss of his vessel. And notwithstanding the absence of any express obligation on His Majesty to add further collateral, he has now offered the defendant alternative security. Even so, Signore Castello has failed to honour his side of the bargain, stated clearly in the document." The attorney waved his copy of the agreement in the air with a flourish, before continuing, "Clearly he prefers to hold onto his money."

By the time Zúñiga's counsel had sat down, you would have had the clear impression that Zúñiga was a paragon of virtue in the clutches of a barbarous adversary.

When Tasso got to his feet, his approach was so different you might have almost assumed he was talking about an entirely different case. His approach was technical, stressing the nature of the covenants that the borrower had apparently broken.

The judge seemed unimpressed. "Scarcely a deliberate breach, Signore Tasso? And one the claimant has honourably offered to remedy." It was one of his few interventions. Tasso seemed not to have an alternative argument to fall back on.

In less than another hour, it was all over. The judge deliberated for mere minutes before pronouncing that the borrower was entirely within his rights to draw down the balance of the loan, having offered to pledge the cargo arriving at Cádiz in the hold of the '*San Lorenzo*'. So, the defendant would be ordered to make the necessary advance to the claimant in full within thirty days, as well as reimbursing Senor Zúñiga's legal costs. The only crumb of comfort was the judge's acknowledgment of the claimant's obligation to keep interest payments up to date, the first of which would fall due shortly.

Outside the chamber, Tasso appeared angry, proposed an appeal, but Nico cut him short.

"We will just be seen as dragging our feet. I'm not prepared to risk further legal costs just to end up in the same spot we are now."

He turned on his heel and walked off, leaving Sandro to mollify the attorney as best he could.

WHEN HE CAME TO, Monty could see nothing around him. The darkness was absolute. And someone was hammering away at his skull. From the inside. He was lying on cold flagstones. He moved to sit up, and found his wrists were tied together. His ankles were strapped as well.

As his eyes adjusted to the gloom, murky shapes emerged from the background, columns of stone. Nothing he could identify.

Gradually, the light strengthened. Looking upwards, he saw its source. A shaft of sunlight had penetrated a slit window in the wall high above him. His surroundings emerged from the gloom. In front of him, a blank wall of stone. Over his shoulder, two rows of pillars took the weight of the ceiling, each column as wide as a man's armspan. The stone pillars led to another forbidding wall, which contained an arched entrance to the cellar. And beyond that, a door. Shuffling across the floor on his backside, he reached the door. With an effort, he manoeuvred himself upwards by leaning against the archway. Fumbling with his tied hands, he tried to turn the latch. It was locked. From the small, barred window in the doorway, he could see a dim corridor and beyond it a couple of other heavy wooden doors, also with barred windows in them. The cellar, if that's what it was, didn't have any stores of food or racks of wine. With that thought, he became aware of the dryness in his throat. *'Let's not think about food and drink, Monty, let's consider something else.'*

He studied the bindings on his wrists and ankles. He could just reach the knots around his ankles, but he didn't have sufficient leverage in his fingers to loosen them. And he couldn't turn his hands enough to untie his wrists. He looked for some kind of tool that would help him get free, but the floor around him was bare, the walls smooth. Nothing to do but wait. Whoever had imprisoned him here, would surely pay him a visit soon.

He tried to think, speculating about the identity of his captors. This was a substantial building in which he was imprisoned, no question. Perhaps he was in a public gaol. Finding no sensible answers from talking to himself, he kept drifting into near-sleep. Each time his head would fall back and hit the wall, jarring him awake. By the fourth time, he decided he had had enough. He would have to rouse his captors.

"Who's there?" he yelled out, "who hears me?"

The only answer was his own voice echoing around the cellar walls. He yelled louder, loud enough to make his head throb again. Footsteps far away suggested he had been heard. Then, the sound of keys jingling in someone's hand. A bolt springing back and hinges creaking as a door was opened. The footsteps came nearer, descending stone stairs to the archway at the corner of the cellar.

The owner of the footsteps came into his vision. He shuffled across the room, halting within three paces of Monty. The man sported several days' beard and an eye-patch over his left eye. His fat belly was enclosed in a grubby smock and breeches. At Monty's eye level was his wide leather belt, carrying a heavy key ring on one side, a sheathed dagger on the other. Just behind him was a young boy, a scruffy urchin in rags. Presumably there to run errands for the gaoler. Eye-patch looked at his prisoner but didn't speak.

"Where am I?" demanded Monty in Italian. "Who is holding me?"

A sullen stare was the only reply.

"I need a drink."

The man pushed out his lower lip, as if to imply that request was difficult to satisfy.

"Would money help?"

The man gave him a ghastly smile.

"Bring me water," said Monty, realising that his purse was gone. "I will pay you when I'm released."

Eye-patch turned on his heel, the boy following close behind. Soon, the lad returned carrying an earthenware jug and bowl. Monty motioned for his hands to be untied, but the boy shook his head. He poured water into the bowl and then placed it on Monty's outstretched palms. The water tasted foul, and he spat it out. The boy shrugged. Monty was left alone again.

He shuffled towards his prison door and looked out through the bars. He heard movement coming from the adjoining cell.

"Is anyone there?" he called out.

The sounds stopped briefly but then someone appeared behind the door. A face came into view. He could not believe it. It was a young woman's face.

HIS FELLOW PRISONER had no English and Monty, in his present state, found that he had forgotten much of his Italian. After a few halting exchanges, they turned to French to converse. He established her name, Nicoletta, and that she came from the convent. He introduced himself with his name and his country of birth. He was about to ask more, starting with where they were being held, when the woman suddenly retreated from the door. He heard heavy footsteps descending the stairs to the cellar. Eye-patch had returned accompanied this time, not by the boy, but by another corpulent guard. He motioned to Monty to get on his feet.

"*Avanti.*"

Hampered by the bindings on his ankles, he shuffled across the cellar after the guards. Eye-patch waited as he struggled up the steps, one tread at a time. When Monty pointed to his shackles, Eye-patch refused him with a shake of the head. Slowed down by Monty's laboured progress, the trio finally reached the next floor. They headed along a corridor past several doorways, all closed.

Reaching the end of the passageway, they entered a room. It was lit by narrow slits near the ceiling, like Monty's cellar, but there were a few guttering candles in wall niches. Monty halted, and the two guards shackled his arms to chains on the wall.

"*Aspetta*," was Eye-patch's one word response to Monty's look of enquiry.

As he waited, Monty's gaze wandered around the room. An oak chair bore closer examination. Across the backrest were rows of spikes, the length of a man's knuckles. The seat of the chair was a cushion of smaller spikes. Shackles attached to the arms and footrest to restrain the sitter. It was not a chair for taking your ease in.

He heard someone approaching, their tread softer than the guards. He turned, expecting to come face to face with his captor at last. But the person entering the room wore a simple robe of black over a white surplice. A priest, no less.

The visitor did not speak to him at first, but turned to the guards, who obliged by leaving the room, closing the door behind them.

Monty pleaded, hoping his Italian was understandable. "Father, help me. I have been thrown in this jail, but no-one has told me why I am here."

To Monty's surprise, the priest spoke in English, albeit heavily accented.

"Signore Belltover, do you not know why you are here?"

Something in the voice seemed familiar. Monty tried to discern the man's features under the hood. As if to oblige, the visitor extracted his skinny arms from the full sleeves of his robe and pulled the hood back from his head, revealing a skull-like profile. Monty knew that he had seen the man before but could not place him.

"There can be no reason for this outrage. Please speak to the Doge. Demand to know why I have been imprisoned."

The priest shook his head. "You are not in the Doge's custody."

"No?"

"No. You are my prisoner."

This was not going the way Monty expected. "And you are, who?"

"My name is Father Guido."

For a moment, he stared at the lantern-jawed face. The memory of where he had met the priest came back to him. It had been at Nico

Castello's *festa,* of course. The man was the archbishop's assistant. None other.

"But this is not to be borne. I am a visitor to this city. If the archbishop knew that you had imprisoned me..."

"He is not interested in your plight, signore."

Monty felt his anger rising. "I am a foreign merchant, going about my lawful business. You have no authority over me. I demand you release me."

The priest raised an eyebrow in an expression which indicated that Monty was in no position to demand anything.

"Let us begin. Since your arrival in Genova, you have made many credit exchanges with our leading bankers. Isn't that so...?"

"What of it?"

"But what huge sums you have borrowed!"

"I am an agent for the Merchant Adventurers in London."

"But you borrow our bankers' silver like a *prince*, signore. More than the Genova Fairs have seen these past five years. Perhaps one of your so-called Adventurers is Midas himself?"

"And why should it matter to you?"

Guido appeared to acknowledge Monty's argument. "Your greed and luxury are of no consequence to us, that's true enough."

"So, then?"

"Nevertheless," continued Guido, "we need you to tell us – who is your principal? And why are you raising so much credit here? Does London not have banks? Or moneylenders?"

"As I told you, my principals are the Adventurers. How they conduct their merchant business is of no concern to you. No concern to anyone, save themselves."

"On the contrary, it is very much our concern if the wealth of our city is being drained by *stranieri* like you, merely to further the desires of your heretical people."

Monty exploded. "This is not to be borne. You cannot keep me here chained up like a dog. I demand..."

Guido, instead of shouting back, stepped closer. He spoke into Monty's ear, almost in a whisper. "You can demand.... nothing."

He turned his back to Monty and stepped towards the door, his voice reverting to a measured, even tone. "It is we who make the demands. You will cease your business here. Conduct no further trades. Withdraw from the transactions you have bargained for."

"And why, in God's name, should I do that?"

"If you undertake what we require, you can take your English wool and leave Genova on the next ship bound for a northern port. But if you refuse, then you will remain here."

He paused, running a hand along the back of the gruesome-looking chair. "You can see that an indefinite stay would be... undesirable."

Monty looked at the chair, still angry. His anger seemed to bounce off Father Guido like a speck of grit off the walls of the cell.

The priest replaced his hood, ready to leave the cell. "Reflect on your position and make your choice. The guards will know where to reach me when you do."

Chapter Twenty-Five
CASA CASTELLO, STRADA NUOVA: A WEEK LATER

Nico watched from the gallery above as Lisa and Julia left the courtyard, with their mounted escorts. His wife and her aunt were visiting Julia's cousin, who lived half a day's ride away along the coast at Albaro. They would return in a couple of days. Nico was in one sense relieved that Lisa would be away from the house. For now, he had to put all his energies into business. In fifteen days, if Zúñiga had assigned the new collateral, he would have to make the next advance. Before then, there were admittedly some substantial payments to be collected from merchants, including several from Monty's wool buyers. But otherwise, the bank's free reserves would be insufficient to make the Spanish advance in full. Perhaps he could try again at persuading Lomellino and Spinola to participate, based on the newly offered collateral, the '*San Lorenzo*' cargo. Work to be done.

When the ladies and their escorts were out of sight, he went to collect Sandro, who was devouring the remnants of breakfast in the salotto. Together, the brothers headed down to Piazza Banchi.

When they arrived, the Loggia was quiet. Mazzini had little to report from the opening of the day's trading. Hardly surprising, Nico thought, with the news regarding the *San Felipe*. He could feel several pairs of eyes discreetly observing him. True, only his bank was directly at risk, but that mere fact made the other *cambisti* fretful and nervous. What would Il Drago do next? Could this happen again? And even if it didn't, would the loss push Banco Castello into a position where it couldn't meet its commitments – including to each of them? So, Nico realised, trading conditions would remain dire for some time. And Banco Castello itself would be frozen out.

A tedious hour followed. He was about to suggest to Sandro that they return to the house, when his brother tapped him on the arm and nodded in the direction of the piazza. Nico turned around, only to come face to face with a young woman, hovering close to their banca. Her dress was modest, its colours muted, but underneath her hood he recognised the dark fringe of raven hair and the chiselled cheekbones. Ignoring the sideways glances and the pointed whispers from the nearby merchants, he ushered Bianca into a chair.

"Well, Signorina Bianca, I don't suppose you're here to seek credit from me."

There was no acknowledgement of his quip. He took in the dark rings around the eyes and sensed that the girl from the 'Paradiso' had recently been crying.

"I'm sorry to bother you, Signore Castello, but I didn't know where to turn," she began.

"I'm not sure if I can help, but tell me what is troubling you?"

"Is there somewhere a little more private?"

Nico thought for a moment and then led her across the piazza and into San Pietro. At that time of the afternoon, there was no-one in the little church. They sat in the pews towards the back of the nave. Bianca pulled back her hood, revealing the long black tresses that framed her exquisite face.

"I came to you, signore because, well, because you are his friend I think, not just his banker."

"Whose friend?"

"Signore Montecchio, the Englishman."

"Ah. And?"

"And, I have not seen him for a week or more, so… I am worried about him."

"Why so?" As he said it, he realised that he had not seen Monty for some time either.

"He usually visits the Paradiso at least twice a week, and he always asks for me." She looked down modestly.

And why wouldn't he, thought Nico, almost beguiled himself.

"Well, perhaps he has left Genova on merchant business."

She shook her head. "He told me – the last time I saw him, that is - he would return in two days, three at the most."

"Surely there is a simple explanation?"

"I thought so, but three nights became four, and then a week. So, this morning I went to his lodgings, to Signore Cavalli's, if you know him?"

Nico nodded.

"But the old gentleman only made me more concerned. He said that the English signore had not slept there for a while. In fact, not since the night I last saw him. He said it was unlike his guest not to mention an extended absence. He suggested you might shed some light on the matter."

"Your concern does you credit, signorina." He motioned her towards the door. "Let me make some enquiries. I am sure we will get to the bottom of it."

Parting company with Bianca, he re-joined Sandro.

His brother was smiling. "You caused quite a stir, going into the church with that young woman. Tongues were wagging all around the Loggia."

Nico shrugged. "No doubt they had great fun, pretending to be shocked. I'd bet each one of them will have visited the 'Paradiso' at one time or another..."

Sandro laughed aloud, mostly for the benefit of their neighbours. Then lowered his voice. "But what did the signorina want?"

When Nico told him, the smile disappeared from Sandro's face. "But perhaps he's travelling up-country, talking to prospective customers?"

"I wouldn't expect him to go unaccompanied. Or to tell no-one about it if he did. In any case, we were due to meet later today to discuss his credit. He would surely make a point of keeping our appointment – or at least letting me know if he couldn't?"

"Fair enough. Why don't I call on old Cavalli, just to confirm Bianca's story. In the meantime, you could ask the merchants around the Loggia. If we meet at the San Giorgio in say, a couple of hours? The clerks there might know something."

But when Sandro arrived at Monty's lodgings, Lorenzo Cavalli merely confirmed what Bianca had said. The brothers caught up at the San Giorgio, Nico reporting that no one else in Piazza Banchi had seen the Englishman. It was strange, but Monty had simply disappeared.

On the way home, Nico called on Bianca's employer, at the "Paradiso". When he asked Lina Luzzati about Monty, she shook her head. Her voluminous wig trembled, almost in time with the movement.

"No, signore, he is not here, but I recall that he visited us, oh about a week ago?"

"Yes, I believe he was here then. But it seems he didn't return to his lodgings that night. Did anyone see him leave, after that visit I mean?"

"Well, certainly I did not. It must have been in the small hours."

"Then why not return to his lodgings, I wonder?"

Luzzati opened her palms. "Possibly he went on – to another establishment?" Her tone suggested that such a decision indicated a lack of taste, after the sophisticated pleasures of the 'Paradiso'.

"But it's curious he has not been seen since."

"No doubt this little mystery will be solved in another day or two, signore. Now, is there any other way in which we can assist you?"

Her underlying meaning was clear enough.

"Thank you no, I must press on."

Fearful now of what he might find, Nico headed for the city's hospital. But the clerk at the Pammatone shook his head regretfully. No straniero of any nation, English or otherwise, had been admitted since last Friday. The only new patients were members of a local family who had been injured in a house fire, earlier that morning. Of course, they would notify Signore Castello immediately, should the English signore be admitted.

Nico walked along Strada Nuova to his house, questioning. Where in the devil was the Englishman?

MONTY SCRAPED his wrists across the floor, feeling his way. His hands nudged against the near-empty water bowl. Salving his parched mouth with the droplets, he realised that his existence had been reduced to the barest sensations. Perpetual thirst, and the pain in his limbs.

Well, you can still use your wits Monty, he told himself.

But his assessment was not encouraging. He couldn't think of any reason why Father Guido would want to interfere with his affairs. But however irrational, the priest was clearly determined on that course. And within the confines of this prison, he could do with Monty what he liked. The more he thought about it, the less likely it seemed that Guido would free him, whatever promises Monty might make under duress. Why bother to release him on a promise, when by keeping him imprisoned, the priest could achieve the same result?

The cancellation of all that merchant business – with less risk of being exposed as Monty's gaoler. And Guido had made no effort to hide his own identity. It followed he had no intention of letting Monty go.

In the meantime, no-one on the outside knew that Monty was a prisoner. There was only one conclusion. He had to escape while he still had sufficient strength. It was that simple – and that difficult.

When the urchin brought him water that evening, Monty decided to test the boy's loyalty.

"Well paid," Monty emphasised. "No questions. If you get word out about me."

The boy's expression was guarded, but he lingered.

"What's your name?"

"Fabio," the lad mumbled.

"Fabio, do you know Giovanni Lercari?"

The boy shook his head.

"He is a novice at the cathedral. Can you get a message to him?"

The lad's expression said, perhaps.

"Tell him, *'Campanile is here'*. Campanile, hear that? Ask him to go to his father. His father will help me, get me released."

With an effort, Monty removed his signet ring. "This proves who I am. It isn't worth a large amount, but if it gets to his father, he will give you ten ducats." He held the ring out. The boy opened his palm.

After Fabio had left, the hours passed slowly. He had already accepted the impossibility of single-handed escape, quite apart from his enfeebled condition. His only chance now was Lercari.

Fabio didn't return the next day. Or the day after. But instead of being fearful, Monty was increasingly indifferent to his fate, his senses numbed. Being held in this private dungeon for the remainder of his days seemed inevitable. Death would be a release.

GINO LERCARI LOOKED at the ring that young Fabio had thrust in his palm. He couldn't recall seeing 'Campanile' wearing it when they were on board the *'Mary Gale'*, although that was months ago, he reminded himself. But the initials 'MB' on the ring corresponded to his name and from the boy's description - big man, pale skin, red hair - who else would it be? There weren't two people in Genova who'd answer to the name 'Campanile' surely. And yet, it made no sense. Why would the archbishop imprison him here? What could he have done to merit such treatment?

He felt the need to confide in someone, one of the priests perhaps. But what if they didn't believe him? Suppose they decided he had stolen the ring? And that he and Fabio were in league together? He put the ring in the pocket of his robe.

He turned a corner of the cloister and bumped straight into Paolo Brozzi. As they stepped back, his fellow novice stared at him, a curious expression on his face. Brozzi, a year older than Gino, had assumed the mantle of leader of the novices some time before Gino had arrived. Most of the younger boys had knuckled under and accepted his orders, but Gino wasn't keen to take orders from anyone: certainly not from someone who wasn't entitled to hand them out. He tried to march on, but Brozzi moved to bar his way. He was almost a head taller than Giovanni.

"What did that filth Fabio want with you, Lercari?" he said. "I saw you talking to him earlier."

"Oh ...I think he was just fishing for an opportunity," said Gino, "he suggested I could take him on as a servant." He forced a laugh. "Perhaps he thought I was wealthy, because my father's a *cambisto*."

"What else did he say? You were talking for a while."

"I ...think he wanted to get out of working down in the vaults. Running errands for the cathedral guards. And the inmates."

"Inmates?" queried Brozzi, not moving out of his way

"Oh, he said there were a few wretches being held in the cells down there. He had to fetch and carry for them. Sounds grim, doesn't it, Paolo?" Gino feared he had let his tongue run away with him.

Brozzi took a step closer. Close enough that Gino could feel Brozzi's sour breath on his face.

"If I were you," warned Brozzi, "I wouldn't pay any attention to such tales. He's soft in the head. Anyway, you shouldn't be talking to the likes of him. Just keep that in mind in future."

Gino gave a non-committal nod and stepped around Brozzi. As he sat in the refectory later, he looked at the priests at the top table. There was really no-one he knew sufficiently well to trust with the story, after only being in the cathedral a matter of weeks. And anyway, who would believe him? He should take the ring to his father, as Fabio had requested. Papa would know what to do. But to be allowed home, he would need permission from one of the priests. Perhaps his father would visit him soon.

Nico swallowed the last of his breakfast and put down his fork.

"Well, where can he be?"

His brother, assuming the question was rhetorical, didn't respond.

Eventually, Nico tapped his palm downward on the table. "We must start a search."

"But where, exactly?" said Sandro. "We've been to the places Monty might have gone. We've asked the merchants he's doing business with. And we notified the Doge's Guard. What else can we do?"

"I can't sit here and just do nothing. Remember, if he doesn't turn up soon, some of the credits we negotiated will mature, and then where are we?"

Sandro breathed in heavily, and out again. "Alright. Let's cast the net wider. Where shall we look?"

"I have an idea."

They left the salotto and headed down the staircase. Sandro followed Nico to the stables.

"Are we riding?" he asked.

"We aren't going that far."

In the tack room, as well as saddlery, were all manner of tools and weapons. He selected a sword and strapped it on, motioning to Sandro to do the same.

Heading north-west, the brothers skirted San Marcellino and walked along Via Del Campo. With each street they crossed they were stepping down a level, so far as the wealth and standing of the residents were concerned. Finally, crossing the line of Barbarossa's old walls and under the twin towers at the Porta Sottana, they entered Pre. The immigrants' quarter. The houses shrank down in size, as if ashamed. The cross-streets became mere *caruggi,* alleyways deprived of the sun, and no wider than the axle of a cart.

Nico didn't talk for a while and Sandro was left to his own thoughts. He had not been down these narrow, lawless streets for years. Respectable citizens, if they entered this impoverished district at all, would touch the hilt of their sword by instinct, easing it in the scabbard. And check that their purse was securely belted.

But then Sandro remembered that for Nico, this was like coming home. His mother had told Sandro the story that, when she was already expecting Nico's birth, she and Vittorio had left Bergamo and arrived in Genova. This area near to the Darsena was the only place they could afford to live. It was where Vittorio set up his first workshop. It was a hard beginning and when Nico was born, Emilia was fearful that he might not survive. But Nico was a strong child and somehow endured all that life, and Pre in particular, could throw at him. There was a gap of several years before Sandro was born, and by then, Vittorio's business was beginning to thrive. By the time Sandro started school, he'd moved the workshop to Vico Scudai and the family to a house nearby, just off Campetto. A couple of years later, he'd moved the workshop yet again, to premises underneath San Pietro in Banchi, but the family had stayed where they were.

For Sandro then, Pre was a distant country, something his father and elder brother talked about, but not something he could instinctively feel. Whereas for Nico, this would always be his childhood world. A land of many tribes, dark and secretive, but familiar and comfortable at the same time. Sailors and whores, craftsmen and shop-owners, criminals and pilgrims. Strangers might feel threatened, but he sensed that for his brother it felt like the safest place in Genova.

Sandro broke the silence. "But why here, Nico? Not the sort of place where Monty would have spent any time."

Nico lowered his voice. "Maybe, but all the town's secrets end up here, brother. *Someone* will have heard *something* about an Englishman adrift in the city."

Sandro watched his brother speaking to tavern and shopkeepers. No-one had heard of an English merchant. That didn't stop Nico from giving each one a small tip, as thanks for their time. Nico spoke to the residents of Pre in a language that Sandro could barely recall. An unfamiliar dialect, and words which wouldn't have been widely understood in the Loggia, a mere mile away.

Around midday, they paused for some focaccia and wine in a taverna that Nico knew. He explained to Sandro, "I come here sometimes, on my own."

Sandro could not hide his surprise. "To do what?"

"To remember where we came from. And why we should be grateful for our transformed lives."

Chapter Twenty-Six
CATTEDRALE SAN LORENZO: THE FOLLOWING NIGHT

The guards roused Monty from a disturbed sleep, full of nightmares. At first, with their torches flickering in his eyes, he did not recall where he was. Hauled to his feet, he hadn't the strength to walk. They dragged him up the steps and along the corridor. He tried to resist, but he was too feeble.

He could feel his resolve slipping away. If they put him in the chair again, he would tell Guido anything, just to stop the pain. Did he yell out, "I swear on my life"? It seemed as if he was talking in a dream, or rather a nightmare. He was begging, pleading. It was coming out of him like a flood.

They reached a barred iron gate, which he didn't remember from before. Beyond the gate was a broader passageway, braziers along its length lighting the way. An elderly sentry was posted at the gate.

The man glanced at Monty, taking in his wretched appearance, and shrugged. He fumbled with his heavy key chain. "Well, hurry man. Open it," one of the guards said.

Moments later the lock turned, and the sentry swung the gate open. Was he being released, he wondered?

The guards dragged Monty out into the cloister. The moon was high, dawn still a long way off. He shivered in the fresh air, at the same moment realising he had not got his doublet around his shoulders. They were heading towards a pair of solid wooden gates on the opposite side of the cloister. Higher than a man's head. The carriage entrance to the cathedral precincts, it seemed. Then he remembered his conversation with the urchin. Was Ferrucio Lercari waiting outside? He dared to hope.

HE STARED at the empty street outside the gates. Crushed that Lercari had not come to release him, he looked at his captors.

"Where are you taking me?" he shouted, although the words came out as a croak.

Before Monty could say any more, a hood was pulled over his head and he was pushed forward. He heard the rustle of harnesses. The stamp of a horse's foot. He was bundled into some sort of carriage or cart, thrown on its wooden floor.

They took off, at some speed it seemed, because Monty was thrown around as the carriage lurched along the cobbled streets. He tried to call for help, but the words were muffled by his hood. No-one was out in the streets at that time of night anyway. Finally, the carriage stopped. Without removing the hood, his captors hauled him to his feet. They dragged him across a roadway. He started to feel an indefinite fear.

Then they were traversing a stony area. The two men hauling him along were breathing heavily with the effort. He heard the hiss of waves on shingle. They must be on a stretch of beach down by the harbour. The arms that had been holding him released their grip and he fell forwards onto his knees. Footsteps came towards him. The hood was removed.

The shoreline was in front of him, the near-black waves lapping at his knees. As he looked around him, the shelving beach rose upwards, the line between it and the blackness of the sky indistinct. Then he registered a single light coming from high above ground level and moving across his line of sight and to his left. It must be the Lanterna, perched on its promontory jutting out from the harbour. By its glancing light, the outline of his captors slowly separated itself from the background. Two of the men were of average height and looked heavily built. They stood close by him, one man at his shoulder, the other at his feet. The third of the triumvirate was standing back, observing him. Monty could not see his face, the man seemed taller, but he was of slighter build than the other pair.

Monty tried to get up, but one of the heavyweights kicked him from behind, pitching him down again, face forward. He felt a trickle of blood run down from his temple and into the crease at the corner of his left eye.

Monty yelled at them. "What is it you want?" At this moment, he'd promise them anything.

The men made no answer, staring down at him as if he were a small animal crawling on the earth.

The third man came a little too close. Launching himself forward, Monty swung his shackled fists upward with all the remaining strength he could muster, into the man's groin. The man reeled away, screaming at the other two. Suddenly energised, Monty was scrambling to his feet, trading blow for blow. A boot connected with Monty's gut. He gasped with pain and sank to his knees again. Only to see a glint of light in one man's hand. Then a sudden explosion inside his gut as something cold entered his body under the ribs. He screamed – or was it the man screaming abuse at him? For a moment, he knelt there, shaking.

The Lanterna's powerful beam swung somewhere in front of him, pulsing brighter, then darker. Until everything was pure, blinding white.

ON THE FOLLOWING MORNING, Nico and Sandro resumed their search. They had covered barely half the warren of streets and alleys that made up Pre district on the previous day. But once again, there was nothing to show for their efforts. A shake of the head, a shrug of the shoulders, an offer to sell them some wares. By early afternoon they reached Porta San Tommaso and Sandro sensed that even Nico was beginning to lose heart.

Heading homewards along Via di Pre, they entered a shop that had been closed on the previous day. But the candlemaker gave them the same response as all the other traders. Then, as they were leaving, he called after them, "You could try the old infirmary, signori?"

"Infirmary?"

"Si, Sant'Antonio."

Nico raised an index finger, remembering. "*Grazie*, amico. Remind me what street that's in, I had forgotten."

But when they were in the street again, he muttered to Sandro, "I'm sure this will be a waste of time, but we're here anyway, so there's no harm in trying."

After several minutes' walk, turning left and then right until

Sandro was utterly disoriented, Nico pointed to a narrow alley. The Vico Inferiore del Roso.

"Here?" said Sandro.

"Should be," affirmed Nico.

Within thirty paces they came to a small gateway set in the crumbling wall. Alongside was a sign, reading "Sant'Antonio Abate". Entering through the gate and along a dingy passageway, they came to a surprisingly large, square courtyard. Around its sides were cloisters, columns of stone and slate supporting semi-circular arches. Underneath them, old men and women sat on the floor, staring out in front of them vacantly. It was as if the city had forgotten them. Which indeed, it had, Sandro told himself.

One old man, hobbling with the aid of a stick, was curious enough to approach them.

"Per favore, *vecchio*, where is the sister-in-charge?" asked Nico.

The old man smiled. He had hardly any teeth. "I will take you," he stated, as if this was his appointed duty, his prerogative alone.

Crossing the courtyard behind the old boy, they came to a door whose paint had long since faded to an indeterminate grey. In response to the old man's knock, a nun in her middle years appeared at the doorway. Sandro considered her face. A curious amalgam: careworn, yet serene at the same time.

Once introductions were made, Nico explained their quest to Sister Maria. Nodding, she asked Nico for a description of Monty.

"Well, sister, he is a large man, thirty years old or thereabouts. Pale skin. Red hair and a beard."

She gave Nico a tolerant smile. "Well ...why, don't you follow me? We can look together."

She led them to a large room on the opposite side of the cloister. In it were rows of beds, closely ranked, some occupied. A couple of novices were tending to their needs. As they walked towards the far end of the room, checking each patient, Sandro spotted the corner bed. It was also occupied, but with a sheet covering whoever was lying there. As Sister Maria led them up to it, he was silently praying that this was not Monty, it couldn't be, surely.

The nun pulled back the sheet from the body. Sandro glanced at the man's face. His prayers had not been answered.

Chapter Twenty-Seven

SANT' ANTONIO ABATE, PRE: THE SAME DAY

Nico heard a curse leave his brother's lips. Sister Maria appeared not to notice.

He looked down at Monty. The Englishman was on his back, arms by his sides. His shirtfront was covered in blood, dull brown smudges blurred by seawater. His hair was matted and streaked across his forehead. Under the sodden shirt, there was a deep wound to Monty's chest. Nico slumped down on an empty bed and put his head in his hands.

Sister Maria broke the silence. "My condolences, signori. It is a terrible thing." Sandro asked how Monty had come to Sant'Antonio. Her explanation took only a few words. He had been brought to the infirmary earlier that morning by fishermen, who hoped the nuns would be able to revive him. She had examined him, but he was already dead. He had clearly suffered terrible violence at the hands of others before his death, may the Good Lord preserve his soul. The leader of the fishermen, a man called Simon, had left his name with her and how he could be reached. Should the dead man's family, presuming he had one, wish to talk to him. Or if the Doge's men had any questions.

Nico stood up. He had to get out of this dismal room and breathe fresh air. "Thank you, sister. We shall go and talk to this Simon." He glanced at Sandro. "We'll return later."

Their quarry was not hard to track down. The first men they spoke to on the harbourfront pointed to a small group a hundred paces along the quay. The crew of the "*Righi*", Nico was told. As Nico and Sandro came up to them, one man spotted them and detached himself from the group. He was obviously expecting them. His complexion was darkened by the sun, making his watery blue eyes seem even paler.

Nico explained his connection with the dead man and Simon offered his condolences. But could he tell them more, how he had found Monty for instance? Simon looked around and, suggesting the two signori may wish to talk more privately, ushered them towards a small taverna set back from the quay.

Ensconced in a quiet corner, with Sandro pouring the wine, Simon launched into his story.

We were returnin' with our catch early this mornin', about to enter the 'arbour. We were movin' past the Lanterna, on the incomin' tide. One of my men, Marco it was, yelled out and pointed across the port bow. There was somethin' there on the shingle, waves lappin' over it. Couldn't be certain what it was, at that distance. And soon, it'd be covered by the tide.

Well, we put the rowboat over the side and went for a closer look. By the time the oars were scrapin' the bottom, we'd realised it was a man. I leapt out and splashed' through the water to reach 'im. Rolled 'im over.

Simon's watchful eyes darted between Nico and Sandro. He opened his palms outwards as he continued.

Well, the man was young and by 'is manner of dress, well-born. First, I thought, he were drowned and washed ashore by the tide. Then I saw the bloodstains. I said we'd better get him to Sant'Antonio. We hauled 'im up the beach – Lord, 'e were a weight, signori – and got him on a cart, as quick as we could. When us reached Sant'Antonio, Sister Maria examined 'im. But she confirmed 'e was gone for sure, may the Lord give 'im rest.

Sister Maria searched the man's clothes. No clue to who 'e was. Said she'd have to call the Doge's men. Well, I had me morning's catch to sell, so I left me name and where I could be found, with the nuns. That was it – until you turned up, signori.

Simon gulped the wine down and leant back in his chair. Nico sensed he was a worried man. Probably fearing he might be in trouble himself, bringing an unexplained dead body in. And a proper gentleman, what's worse. Probably wishing he'd left well alone.

"You didn't see anything on the shore, no one else around?" Nico asked.

Simon shook his head. "Well, the lighthouse guard came down to take a look, but when we said we were goin' to get the man to the nuns as quick as we could, he let us get on with it."

"Could you take us back there, to the spot?" asked Nico. He put a few coins on the table.

A quarter of an hour later, they stood on a small, shingle beach. Above them, the boulders of the headland on which the great lighthouse stood, pointing heavenward. A rocky footpath led up from the beach and joined the cart-track connecting the lighthouse with the coastal road.

The trio walked along the shoreline for a few yards, until Simon stopped. "This is where we brought the boat in," he said. "But the tide's come and gone since, it were a bit further back," he added, pointing to the shingle immediately behind them. They separated and combed the area surrounding the spot designated by Simon. Nico thought that if Monty's antagonists had left anything behind, it would have been washed away by the waves. But something not the colour of pebbles caught his eye. He crouched down. It was a green leather purse. It was empty.

After traversing the area, they gave up trying to find more. Nico gestured towards the Lanterna. "We should talk to the guard."

THEY FOUND the sergeant of the guard in a small hut at the foot of the Lanterna, his home when on duty. A man in late middle years, grizzled beard streaked with grey. Duty at Genova's lighthouse was a peaceful posting for the city's old soldiers before retirement.

Nico confirmed that the man found on the beach was indeed dead. Sergente Luca shook his head a little.

"I am afraid, signori, there is little I can tell you. We 'eard the commotion this mornin' down by the beach. Saw the fisherman in the shallows."

Simon, standing in the doorway, held up a hand in recognition. "After I'd been down and seen the body, naturally I went and spoke to the two guards that were on duty last night. But neither of 'em had seen nor 'eard anything. That's all we can say," he finished, putting the flat of his right hand down on the table, as if to emphasise his certainty.

Nico turned and stood at the hut door, scanning the waterside below them. The soldier stayed put at his small desk. "A curious thing, though, sergeant?" Nico said.

"How d'you mean?" Nico could feel the man regarding his back.

"Well, curious that nothing was heard or seen during the night, don't you think?"

"Body was spotted at first light. Dark afore that."

"But the Lanterna would cast some light on the beach, no?"

"Yes. Some. But our men would be watchin' seawards, not towards the beach."

"A man was murdered down there, and nothing was heard?"

"For all anyone knows, he was killed out at sea before they brought 'im 'ere. Wouldn't have heard anythin' then."

Nico turned to face the man.

"You could be right there, sergeant...."

Luca's crinkly mouth creased into a smile.

"... but, if I had a dead man on my hands, a hefty one at that, would I bring him all this way, only to leave him on the beach....?"

The smile disappeared.

"...no, I'd probably dump the body in the sea."

Luca shrugged. "P'raps that's it. Tide could've washed the body 'ere..." If his expression was any judge, he was glad that this was Nico's problem, not his.

"But surely, the tide would have taken him the other way," said Nico. He beckoned the sergeant, who took the few grudging steps to the doorway. Nico pointed to the spot where Monty had been found.

"Just suppose then, he *was* murdered right there. He's slashed and cut many times, he's crying out for help, perhaps he screams with pain."

Luca shrugged. "But no-one 'eard 'im. With the sound o' the waves, the noise of the lamp burnin'...."

"His cries would've carried, surely? If I went down there now and screamed out, you'd hear it, wouldn't you?"

"Depends on the wind. Or the guards might've mistook it for sea birds."

Nico fought the urge to raise his voice.

"Sea birds...at night?"

Luca didn't want to look at the view any longer and retreated to his desk.

"Well, signori, I'm afraid that's all we know, so if you'll excuse me, I have to inspect the burner now." He jerked his head upwards to the top of the great lighthouse.

By the time they arrived back at Sant'Antonio, the Doge's men were there, a captain with his pair of escorts. Nico passed on what Simon had told them and what the Lanterna sergeant had said. The captain said he would take a formal statement from the captain of the "*Righi*" in due course. Once he had delivered the body to the mortuary in the Pammatone. Nico said there was no next of kin in Genova, so he would be taking charge of the funeral arrangements.

Minutes later, the brothers watched as the captain's men carried Monty's body to their carriage. Sister Maria joined them.

"Since you will be burying the poor man, signori," she said, "there are a few personal effects."

"We hadn't realised there were any," said Nico. "We found an empty purse on the beach."

"When we examined him, trying to find out who he was, it looked as though a ring had been taken, from his third finger," she said, "but mercifully, they didn't take his crucifix."

"It would be proper to bury him with it," she continued. "Also, the rosary we found in his doublet." She handed them both over.

Nico looked at the rosary. Something stirred in his memory.

Conversation between the brothers came and went fitfully. Eventually Nico said, "So, what was Monty doing, all the way down here?"

"Perhaps whoever killed him, brought the body here from somewhere else. As the old boy suggested."

"Or perhaps, they brought him here *to* kill him. Out of earshot of the city."

"Well, either way. But then, he went missing over a week ago. If he was killed just last night, what happened in between? Or, if they killed him a week ago, why has his body only been found now?"

Nico shook his head, no explanation to offer.

On the following day, the brothers went to the Pammatone and spoke to the mortuary doctor who had received Monty's body from the Captain of the Guard. Dottor Vannone, a heavy-set man with a slight limp, seemed to be a man of few words.

"So, Dottore," Nico asked, "Can you tell us if he died of his injuries? Or did he drown?"

Vannone shook his head. "At first sight, one knife wound looks deep enough to have been fatal. But I can't be certain until we have made a full *post-mortem* examination."

"May we know the results, when you have completed it?"

"Ah well, signore, I suggest you take that up with the captain."

"The fishermen who found him suggested that he might not have been dead for long. But he'd been missing for about a week before he was found. Could you tell either way?"

"Well, if you're asking me, '*Did this man die a week ago or just yesterday?*' I would think, almost certainly the latter. The body hasn't started to decompose. But as I say, it'll have to wait until we've completed our examination. Now, if you'll excuse me." He shuffled away wearily.

Nico glanced at Sandro and shrugged. They left the hospital, each buried in his own thoughts. But once they were home, their discussion resumed. Nico mentioned the effect on their own business. The dramatic events of the previous day had temporarily driven this subject from his thoughts.

"First, there's the purchases he's made with our credit – all the silk and spices. We're committed to paying his sellers – and soon."

"But there's substantial proceeds from his wool sales coming our way, no?" asked Sandro. "We can cover the payments with that."

"Perhaps, but what about Monty's estate? Who's entitled to those funds now? We'll have to send a message to London, get some instructions from his backers."

"At least we have collateral, those bank deposits in London he pledged to us?"

"Yes, but their banks may hold things up, while his affairs are being sorted out. We could be waiting a long time for our money."

"You're right, Nico, it's not so simple."

"I'll go and see Treasurer Saluzzo at the *San Giorgio*. He may have dealt with a situation like this before. In any event, he needs to know. After all, several other *cambisti* had dealings with Monty."

"Ferrucio Lercari was one, wasn't he?"

"You're right. Let's go and speak to him."

But before they could leave, the sound of carriage wheels turning into the lobby announced that Lisa and Aunt Julia had returned from Albaro. As he headed down the staircase to greet his wife, Nico thought it was probably for the best that she'd been away while all this was happening.

Once the ladies were unpacked, they made their way to the *sala*, where their midday meal was being laid out. Lisa chatted away about her visit. It seemed that travel, a change of scene, had lightened her mood. Perhaps, Nico thought, they should take their own trip down the coast when the August Fair was concluded. But the complications of Monty's death could make leaving Genova difficult for a while.

Later, as their plates were being cleared, Lisa said, "But you haven't told us what happened while we were away. Is there any news?"

"Yes, but not good news. Remember that Englishman, Montague Belltower? I was worried because we hadn't seen him in the city for some while," said Nico.

"Yes, I remember."

"We finally found him yesterday. He's dead."

Lisa's eyes opened wide. "Dead, but ... how?"

"He'd been stabbed and dumped on the beach." Nico told her of their search in Pre. For several minutes, Lisa didn't interrupt. Just the occasional shake of the head.

"Have I left anything out, Sandro?" said Nico, looking at his brother.

"I don't think so, except perhaps that conversation with the guard at the Lanterna. Not that he told us anything useful."

Lisa rubbed her upper arms, as if she were suddenly chilled and missing a shawl.

"Nico, that is terrible. I am – I feel sorry that I wasn't more ... welcoming towards him. After all, no-one deserves such an ending." She made the sign of the cross, her fingertips lightly touching her breast. Aunt Julia followed her example.

NICO AND SANDRO found Ferrucio Lercari in the Loggia later that afternoon.

"Can we have a word with you, Ferrucio?" Nico said, taking his arm and drawing him into a quiet corner. "I am afraid we have bad news. Montague Belltower is dead."

Nico could feel the jolt through Lercari's arm. "Dead? But that's... how?"

"He was found on the beach, near the Lanterna. It seems he was attacked and robbed. The fishermen who found him took him to

Sant'Antonio, that old infirmary in Pre, but he was pronounced dead by the Sister there."

"Oh, Saints above...." Lercari was not looking at Nico, his eyes focussed on some distant point. "... that is terrible news."

"What is the world coming to, when law-abiding merchants are struck down and killed in the street? Are we animals?" said Sandro.

Lercari did not respond.

Nico continued. "Sandro and I, we regarded Montague as a friend, not just a customer. I expect you'd come to know him well, also?"

"Me? Why ...*certamente,* he was a likeable fellow...."

"*Allora*, it's probably not the best moment to mention it, but I assume that you have outstanding credits with Signore Belltower? We certainly do."

Lercari stared at Nico. "I do indeed. That will be a problem, will it not?"

"We're not yet certain how best to handle it. Why don't we go together to the San Giorgio? Treasurer Saluzzo will need to be advised anyway, and he may have some suggestions for us."

"Yes, that's sensible," agreed Lercari. "Sensible," he repeated needlessly.

"So then. Shall we go now, before the San Giorgio closes?" said Nico.

Lercari shook his head. "Perhaps I can leave that to you for today, Domenico. I must...I need to pay a visit first, if you'll excuse me."

"Of course. No difficulty."

"*Grazie*. No doubt we'll speak again tomorrow morning."

Lercari gave them a curt bow and stepped away from the Loggia in the direction of Campetto. Nico looked at Sandro, who shrugged questioningly.

Chapter Twenty-Eight
"LE PORTE DI PARADISO": THE SAME EVENING

Lina Luzzati took Bianca to her private apartment in the 'Paradiso'. When the two women entered, Nico was still wondering what he would say to the girl. It didn't help that Bianca had an air of eager anticipation.

Signora Luzzati sat the young woman on a chair opposite Nico's and then arranged herself on her day bed between them, waiting for him to speak. Nico had briefly contemplated asking to speak to the girl alone, but there was little to be gained by that and anyway, Bianca might need her employer to comfort her after he had left.

"I have news for you, regarding Signore Montecchio," he began.

The girl's hands rushed to her cheeks. "Oh, thank you, signore. When La Signora said you were here, I guessed that you might."

He touched her arm, his voice low. "But I am afraid it is not good news. You must prepare yourself."

The smile faded from Bianca's face.

"Has he gone back to England? Does he have another lady? What is it? Tell me."

"Worse than that, I am afraid. He is dead."

"He can't...," she stopped mid-thought and was shaking her head gently.

"He was found near the Lanterna. By some fishermen. They carried him to a local infirmary in Pre. But he was already dead. My brother Sandro and I were searching for him at the time. That is where we found his body, just yesterday."

Bianca was looking downwards, unable to respond. Lina Luzzati spoke. "We are *sorry* to hear such sad news, Signore Castello. He seemed like such a nice young man." A pause. "Tell me, had he drowned?"

"We're not sure yet. It's possible he died of his injuries before he was in the water."

"Injuries, you say?"

"He'd been attacked, probably by robbers. When exactly, that's not clear. By whom, we don't yet know...."

Suddenly, there was a loud noise. It was so disembodied, so strange, that momentarily, Nico thought it was coming from outside the room. But then he realised it was Bianca screaming, her body rigid with anguish. As if stunned by her own efforts, she slipped forward on to her knees, gasping for breath. He knelt, his hands resting on her shoulders.

"My child, my child," said Signora Luzzati, stroking Bianca's hair, "this will do no good. *No* good."

It took several minutes before they could get Bianca up from the floor. Signora Luzatti placed her on the day bed and sat next to her, her arm around the girl's shoulder. With Bianca leaning on the woman's breast, staring vacantly into the distance, her employer resumed the conversation with Nico.

"They were the basest thieves, no doubt. A disgrace on our city, signore." Lina Luzzati shuddered. "But what can the English signore have been doing out there, as far as the Lanterna?"

"For all we know, he could have been killed before he was taken there. The last time he was seen was over a week ago. When he left here in fact, late on that Friday night."

Luzzati pursed her lips in disapproval. Any suggestion that the environs of the 'Paradiso' were unsafe for its discerning clients was naturally, unwelcome.

At this point, Bianca wriggled free of her employer's clasp and rose, as if wanting to quit the room as soon as possible. Nico stood up as well.

"I should probably take my leave, signorina," he said, restraining Bianca's arm. "Is there anything you wish me to do?"

Bianca's dark eyebrows knitted in thought. "I would like to see him." The voice was choked, almost a whisper.

"Of course. He is in the mortuary at the Pammatone, until the funeral. I can take you there tomorrow if that would be...suitable?"

As soon as Nico arrived in the Loggia on the following morning, Ferrucio Lercari came up to his banca. It was not a casual visit, two neighbours saying '*Buongiorno*', Nico sensed. He had some purpose in mind, even if he was not looking Nico straight in the eye.

"That matter we were discussing yesterday, Domenico," he began.

"You mean, the English merchant."

Lercari winced as if the subject was painful, like a pulled muscle. "Mmm, so how did you fare, at the San Giorgio, with Treasurer Saluzzo, I mean?"

"The offices were closing, so I only saw him briefly. But he had nothing very useful to offer. We must carry on, meet our commitments and write to the English Merchant Adventurers for their advice about Montague's assets."

"Scarcely any help, is it?" Lercari leaned forward, lowering his voice. "But could you – and Signore Alessandro, of course – come to my house later this afternoon, say five o'clock? Something we need to discuss about the Englishman but," he glanced around at the adjacent bancas, "not here."

Nico's carriage was at the entrance to the 'Paradiso', its door opened in readiness for Bianca as she walked down the steps. She was wearing a summer cloak, the hood over her head. She murmured a greeting.

As they rattled along to the hospital, Nico could think of nothing comforting to say. He looked out of the carriage window, as if willing it to go faster.

When their carriage pulled up at the Pammatone, he escorted Bianca to a small anteroom off the courtyard and asked her to wait there for him. Finding a clerk, he was informed that Signore Montagu's body had been moved to the hospital's new chapel that morning. The post-mortem was obviously over. Nico asked for Dottor Vannone. As he waited for the doctor, Nico recalled that the chapel building, Monty's current resting place, had been completed with the help of a donation he'd made after that argument with Lisa, months earlier. Not the happiest of coincidences.

A few minutes later, the doctor shuffled towards him.

"May we see his body?" asked Nico, after the initial greetings.

"*Certamente*, I have completed my work."

"And is he.... you see, Dottore, I have a young woman with me who knew him, she is somewhat distressed. So, is he... fit to be seen?"

"Oh yes, we have done our best."

"Did you determine what killed him?"

"Well, he didn't drown, signore. The stab wounds must have done the job. He had lost much blood."

"And could you tell when?"

"Hard to be certain, but I would say no more than twenty-four hours before the body was discovered. Perhaps less than that."

Nico expressed his thanks and Vannone took his leave. Rejoining Bianca, he ushered her towards the chapel. When they reached it, he paused outside the door.

"Would you like me to go in with you, or would you prefer to be alone?"

"Thank you, signore. If I may see him by myself for a while?"

When he looked in some time later, Bianca was sat by the coffin, her head close to Monty's, the hood pulled back from her face. Her lips were moving, as if in prayer. He was about to leave again, when she raised her head and turned to face him.

"You can stay longer if you wish," he said.

"No, signore, this is enough. I have said to him what I needed to say."

THAT SAME EVENING, Nico and Sandro found themselves in the sala of Casa Lercari, waiting for their host to explain his invitation. The brothers had assumed, as they walked to the house, that this was merely about the trades that Ferrucio Lercari had outstanding with Monty. As he poured the wine, Lercari seemed reluctant to get to the point and idly chatted about their colleagues in the Loggia.

After a few minutes, Nico opened his palms outwards. "So, Ferrucio, there was something particular you wanted to discuss?"

Lercari placed the flask back on the side table. His hands were shaking slightly, Nico noticed. On a man with such a solidly built frame, the effect was rather disconcerting.

"It...it involves my son, Gino. You'll recall, he recently began his novitiate at San Lorenzo. He nearly wasn't accepted, there was some scandal about his being in bed with two novice nuns from Santa Maria," Lercari's eyebrows shot heavenwards, suggesting the man felt this was characteristic of his son, "but the archbishop was prepared to overlook it, mercifully. I started to feel unsure about my decision to place him there. Was it going to be the right thing for him? In the early days, he assured me that all was going well, but it was obviously not so…"

Nico exchanged glances with Sandro. What was this about, this confessional?

"Not so…?" he prompted.

"Well, eventually he summoned up the courage and confessed to me that he wasn't enamoured of his new surroundings, or the discipline of being a novice. I had already guessed as much, but I hadn't been to see him for some days, a week or more. I was rather preoccupied, having to deal with that Spanish envoy, Zúñiga and other matters. But I should have gone to see him earlier. I blame myself now."

"It's easy to be self-critical, looking back," commented Nico, trying to remain patient.

Lercari shrugged. "So, we agreed to give things another month at San Lorenzo and if he still felt the same, then I would bring him out. Well, in the end it was last week when I paid him another visit." Lercari took a sip of his wine. "Before I could say anything, he hugged me and whispered in my ear. Said he didn't want to be overheard. Because he was passing on a secret he'd been told." Lercari gave his guests a troubled look.

Nico leaned closer to his host. "Ferro, *per favore*, you can rely on our discretion. What exactly did Gino tell you?"

"Well then, *cambisto a cambisto.*" Lercari said, smiling hesitantly. "That's when it emerged, that's when he told me about the … prisoners."

"Prisoners? You mean, inside San Lorenzo?"

"Yes, but …he said that Signore Montague was one of them."

"He said *what?*"

Finally, the floodgates opened, and the story poured out from Lercari.

"He told me that on the day before my visit, a young urchin called Fabio had approached him in the novices' dormitory. Fabio was often seen around the precincts. He runs errands for the priests and the cathedral workmen. A young gypsy, no family it seems. Anyway, this Fabio says to him '*Are you Giovanni Lercari?*' '*I am, what do you want?*'

Gino replies, all bluster. The lout says, '*I have a message from someone who knows you. He's a foreign gentleman.*' Fabio turns his thumb downwards and points. '*He's being held down in the vaults below us.*'

Gino doesn't believe him at first. '*Even if that's true, what's it to me?*' says my son. "He was always ready with a quick retort," added Lercari, his tone disapproving.

"So, this Fabio says, '*He told me to find you. He told me to say that "Campanile is here." He asks for your help*'. Well, apparently the name 'Campanile' was something of a joke between Signore Montague and Gino, when they were on board that English ship. A literal translation of the Englishman's family name. So, anyway, he hauls Fabio into a corner and makes him tell all. Which he does. That the Englishman was locked in a filthy cellar below the cloister. That he wasn't the only prisoner down there. Even a disgraced nun had recently been incarcerated, Fabio claimed. The prisoners were guarded by a couple of ruffians who made Fabio do the running around between the cells, fetching food and water and so on. So, when Gino hears this, he can scarcely credit it. '*Can I see him, then?*' he says to the boy. Fabio says no, too many locks, too many guards. And down there, Gino would be conspicuous. '*How else can I know what you say is true?*' says my son. There's a pause and then the urchin says, '*He told me to give you this*' and with that, he reaches into his pocket and draws out a ring. '*The Englishman told me to tell you, 'Take this to your father, he will know what to do. He'll find a way to get me out of here'.*'

"Did this Fabio say how long the Englishman had been held there?" Sandro asked.

Lercari paused, "Well no, I expect Gino didn't think to ask. But wait, let me tell you the rest." He sipped his wine. "*Allora*, this Fabio goes back to his duties and my son starts to think about what he's been told. At first, he thinks about telling one of the priests. But then, he worries he can't trust any of them with Fabio's story. Most likely it can't be true, and then he'll get into trouble for spreading false rumours. But if in fact it were true, the clergy might already know about the prisoners and were keeping it secret, in which case he's in even worse trouble. So, he realises he must get word to me quickly, and without anyone knowing about it. The problem is: he needs permission to leave the cathedral precincts. Then, by coincidence, two days later I pay him a visit. We take a walk around the cloister, and he blurts out the whole thing. The story I've just told you."

"What did you think?"

Lercari shook his head. "I thought it was incredible. I told him he must be mistaken. But he stood his ground, I have to say. And then, there was the ring."

Lercari reached into his hip pocket and drew out a signet ring, which he placed on the table next to Nico's wine glass. "It could be Montague's. See, it has the initials, MB."

Nico examined the ring. He asked Lercari, "Do you have any papers here that were signed by Montague?"

Lercari, catching Nico's drift, rushed out of the room. Moments later, he returned bearing a document. Nico applied the ring to the seal next to Monty's signature. The monogrammed ring sat snugly in the hardened wax.

Nico put the ring down slowly, trying to make sense of its appearance. What was it that Sister Maria had said at the hospice? *It looks like a ring was taken from his finger.*

Lercari resumed the story. "So, Gino pleads with me, '*Papa, I know Campanile is locked up down there. We must get him out.*' I told him I needed time to think. Obviously, this couldn't be happening. This is San Lorenzo we're talking about. Even if it were true, why would Montague be there at all? What crime had he committed against our Church to merit this? It made no sense. I told Gino to be patient while I decided what to do. In the meantime, I told him to give Fabio a message for Signore Montague. I gave Gino a ten-ducat piece to pass on to the boy. I didn't expect to ever see it again, but there we are. Then I left him in the cloister and headed home to think. My first thought was to approach the Doge and get him to intercede...."

Lercari took another drink. "I'd already seen the notice the Doge had had posted, your suggestion I believe, about Montague being missing. But then I decided that he wasn't likely to intervene, based on this flimsy story."

"Well, we know he prefers to avoid confrontations," said Nico, glancing at his brother.

"I tried to find this urchin, Fabio. After Gino passed him that ten-ducat piece, no one seems to have seen him. But when I told Gino to forget it, he pleaded with me again. So, I decided to take the matter to Father Guido."

"Father Guido?" said Nico.

"Yes, he was Gino's supervisor. He was also the person at San Lorenzo who'd first introduced me to Senor Zúñiga. Why do you ask?"

Nico gave a muted laugh. "A small world, to be sure. He's my wife's confessor."

"And what did he say?" asked Sandro.

"I thought he would be outraged by the suggestion that the clergy had imprisoned a respectable merchant. But he didn't react that way - took it calmly. Grateful for my coming to him. Assured me there was no truth in the rumour. That it was a fairy tale this lad Fabio had dreamed up."

"You showed him the ring?" said Nico, turning it in his fingers.

"Yes. He seemed taken aback at first, but then he said that the truth was surely that Fabio was a thief and a pickpocket. That he'd stolen the ring somewhere in the city. So, I suggested that Fabio be summoned to answer to the charge. Confess to his manufacturing this tale about Signore Montague. Guido said he would have dearly liked to, but they'd dismissed the boy from his post the previous day. Thrown him out for stealing food from the refectory."

"Anyway, he offered to show me around the cathedral vaults. I said that that wouldn't be necessary, that I didn't doubt his word as a priest. But he insisted that I come with him, so that I could satisfy myself."

"Guido explained that there were a few cells down there. Not just for the occasional wayward member of the cathedral clergy, but because it was also the mother church to several orders of monks and nuns in the city. On occasion, regrettably, a member of these orders would be put in a solitary cell as chastisement for some offence or other. A former nun, now disgraced, had been there recently. Well, he showed me the place. It wasn't a pleasant sight. Dark, wretched." Lercari remembered. "But it was empty. The cell doors were open. All apart from one, which held a priest who was apparently being punished. I saw the man through the grille. Guido didn't say what he was being punished for - and I didn't ask."

Lercari breathed out slowly. "So, that was it really. I thanked the Father and left. I felt satisfied that the whole thing was an invention by this Fabio. Afterwards I saw Gino and related the events to him. I tried to persuade him there was no truth in the story and that eventually, Signore Montague would turn up. He was unconvinced. He felt certain that the Englishman had been there. I told him to forget about it and concentrate on his duties."

"And you spoke to no-one else about it?" asked Nico.

"Well, who was there? In any case, it didn't seem a good idea to spread these rumours around. As far as I could see, they were just that.

I assumed the Englishman would turn up at some point and all would be explained."

"But then, yesterday, we told you he'd been found dead on the beach."

"Goodness, yes. That was a blow. But on the other hand, it could explain things. Perhaps this Fabio was part of the gang of thieves, and he'd somehow scavenged the ring. Of course I didn't reveal to you my thoughts at the time, forgive me, but I was thinking what was best to do. And I decided I must tell Gino, first, before the rumours reached him. The news would hit him hard, I knew, but at least it would put an end to all those fantastic stories about Montague being imprisoned in the cathedral." Lercari poured himself another drink, forgetting to offer the wine to his guests.

"So, you went to see Gino," Sandro prompted.

"Yes. Of course, he was sorely upset. But he held to his belief that Montague had been a prisoner there, whatever I might say to the contrary. I told him that, even if Montague had *ever* been a prisoner in San Lorenzo, he wasn't there when he died. There wasn't any connection. But I couldn't persuade him. *'They've had him killed, padre,'* he kept saying."

No-one spoke for several moments. "Later, we talked about his continuing his novitiate, staying at the cathedral," Lercari continued. "But Gino would have none of it. He was still convinced of Fabio's story and more than that, he was afraid."

"Afraid?"

"Yes, he felt he was a prisoner too, in a way. He told me he was being watched all the time. And punished for the least misdemeanour. He was fearful that he was marked out as an enemy within. Well, I tried to reassure him that he was imagining things, but he was unmoveable. Said he would run away to sea again rather than stay at San Lorenzo."

"And what did you do?" asked Nico.

Lercari blew the air out of his cheeks. "Well, what else was there to do? I brought him home with me. I made some excuse to one of the priests – Father Guido was not there at the time – that the boy was unwell and that his mother should look after him for a few days. He's still here with us." He finished and took a long pull from his wine glass.

Nico, still trying to make sense of what he had been told, eventually said, "So, Ferro, what is to be done?"

"Well, I've failed to persuade Gino that what this urchin told him was an invention, that it never happened. But you were there, down at the Lanterna. You saw the Englishman's body. Perhaps *you* can persuade him."

"Maybe. At this moment I'm unsure what the truth is myself. But we can talk to Gino together. Perhaps hearing his own account will help me understand things better."

Lercari opened his hands. "I would be very grateful if you would." He exhaled heavily. "*Allora*, it's late, and right now I feel too tired to think about it anymore. You'll no doubt be wanting your beds, too. Perhaps we can meet tomorrow morning?"

"*Certamente*. But come to our house. Bring Gino with you."

IN THE POORER parts of the city, death was a constant companion. Whether it was infirmity, plague, violence or some chance accident, the undertakers there did a brisk business. Even if the families had the means only for the simplest of coffins. And the greatest demand was for small coffins. Most families had to bury at least one of their offspring. The neighbourhood was a threshing floor, winnowing out hundreds of souls who would never see adulthood.

It did not take an especially hard-hearted undertaker to shrug at yet another young body. The lad was found lying in the street, in a small turning off Caruggio Della Pace, the Alleyway of Peace. It was a rough area just behind the naval yards at Darsena.

The boy could not have been more than eleven, the undertaker guessed. No-one had claimed him. Presumably an orphan. The clothes were ragged, the feet filthy, the hair an unkempt thatch. And yet, the face and body did not suggest the lad had died of hunger or disease. No marks on his body either. Although, when the undertaker looked closer, there were marks around the neck which suggested an untimely ending at someone's hand. A thief perhaps. But then, who was there to make a case out of this lad's death, since he was obviously destitute and without a family? He would have to be buried as a pauper and the cost of the interment claimed from the Doge's Office.

He was routinely searching the dead boy's pockets, when the undertaker had a surprise. A shiny ten ducat piece nestling among the debris. Not quite as destitute as he seemed, then. In fact, probably the richest pauper the undertaker had ever buried.

Chapter Twenty-Nine
CASA CASTELLO, STRADA NUOVA: THE NEXT MORNING

Nico had last seen Giovanni Lercari all those weeks ago in Piazza Banchi, when he'd been reunited with his father. There was something different about him now. True, he was in his novice's robes rather than the sun-bleached rags of a cabin boy. And he looked thinner, underfed if anything. But that wasn't it: the real change was elsewhere. The eyes were guarded, not looking directly at you for any length of time. The smile of greeting disappeared from his face all too rapidly. He seemed to have grown older in the few short months since his return from the sea. Older and wiser, but not happier.

Nico didn't make small talk with the youth. No need to ask how he was finding life at the cathedral: it was etched on his face.

"Your father told Sandro and me what you'd told him, about Signore Montague I mean," Nico began. "But we'd like to hear it again, in your words."

Gino complied, stiffly at first, just the essentials recited in a monotone voice. The story Lercari had related to the Castellos the night before. But, after gentle prodding by Nico, he began to speak more freely. The background colour emerged, with the viewpoint of a youth of sixteen. It was the colour of loneliness – and of fear.

"So, after your father told you that Father Guido had shown him around the cathedral vaults and Signore Montague wasn't there. What happened after that?"

Gino glanced at the ceiling, remembering. "While I was at breakfast the next day, I was summoned to the Father. He said that I had been spreading false rumours, malicious lies, outside the cathedral. About a *straniero* being imprisoned by some criminal elements in the vaults of San Lorenzo."

"And you said?"

"That I'd been told of it by someone else. He said that was no excuse. Asked me if it was Fabio who'd told me."

"Did you admit it?"

"Yes. Well, not at first. I refused. Then he hit me. Said I was a liar. I thought, what was the point in denying it? That sneak, Paolo Brozzi – one of the older novices - had seen me talking with Fabio anyway. So, I admitted it. Probably shouldn't have."

"What did Father Guido do then?" asked Sandro.

"He sent me to a cell. I was left alone for the rest of the day with just water to drink. The Father said I should have some notion of what being in a prison was like. And if I dared continue with these falsehoods, I'd be given lashes and confined for a much longer time."

"Father Guido said this?" said Lercari, making a fist of each hand.

"Yes, padre."

"Why didn't you tell me this at the time?"

Gino didn't answer his father.

Not wishing the thread to be lost, Nico continued. "And since then? Until your father brought you out, I mean."

Gino didn't respond. He cast his eyes downward, staring at his lap.

"Well, I'm going to assume that you weren't being treated kindly, is that fair?" said Nico.

The youth nodded, still looking down.

"And can you think why?" said Sandro.

Gino shook his head.

Lercari shut his eyes, clearly not wanting to see the distress on his son's face anymore.

"We're sorry to hear it, Gino," said Nico. "Let's talk about something else for a moment. When you spoke to that boy, Fabio, he said that a few of the priests were seen down in the prison cells from time to time? Did he say who? You're among family and friends. You aren't being disloyal."

There was another pause before Gino spoke again. "The only name he mentioned was Father Lanfranco. But I was told a few days ago, by one of the novices, that Father Lanfranco has just left Genova, on a pilgrimage they said."

"And you haven't seen this Fabio since you gave him the ten ducats from your father?"

"No. But then, I was in the cell for part of the following day. When I got back to the dormitory, I did ask one or two of the other novices if they'd seen him. No-one had."

"Did this Fabio say anything else, when you gave him the money?"

Gino thought for a moment. "Oh, only that he would pass a message to 'Signore Campanile' as soon as he could, but that he had been given work in the archbishop's garden, so he wouldn't be able to go to the cellars until later."

Nico leaned back in his chair. "Well, thank you Gino, for telling us. I think you handled yourself well at San Lorenzo. It can't have been easy."

Gino looked relieved. After a few moments he said, "Father said you were going to tell me about how you...found Signore Montague?"

Nico described that day, although he spared Gino some of the more unpleasant details. When he had finished, Nico tried to lighten the load a little by telling him about the respectful way in which Monty's body had been cared for at the Sant'Antonio Abate and then at the hospital. Nico wasn't very comfortable discussing the soul or the afterlife, so he stuck to the facts he knew.

Gino's steadfast expression told Nico there was no point in seeking to change Gino's convictions as to what had happened to the Englishman. He saw Ferrucio catch his eye, but in response he merely shook his head very slightly.

"Gino, your father and us, we will try and figure out what happened to Signore Montague. But you'll have to be patient, it may take time." He looked at the lad's slight frame.

"I'm sure that if you go to the kitchen, Maria will find you something nice."

Gino stood up. He was about to leave the room, when Nico had a further thought.

"One other thing, Gino. This nickname you had for Signore Montague, *Campanile*, when you were on the '*Mary Gale*'? How was it that you, excuse me for saying so, then just a cabin boy - or claiming to be such, at least - and him being a well-to-do merchant ten years your senior, came to know one another so well?"

Gino looked sideways, as if the answer was on the wall. "Oh, that was after the storm."

Nico thought back to his first meeting with Monty. "Ah yes,

Signore Montague told me, on the day he arrived, that there'd been a big storm in the Biscay. One of the ships was nearly lost. But why were you friends after that?"

"That was when he rescued me from the sea."

Lercari looked in the direction of Gino's departing back. "He saved my son's life," he muttered, "and I never knew. I never knew."

Nico encouraged Lercari to drink some more wine. After a pause he said, "Ferro, you and I will have some difficult business matters to unravel, regarding our late client, but that can wait for the present. For now, let's consider Gino's story – and what it means."

Lercari forced himself to concentrate. "Well, you've heard him. What do you think now?"

"I'm still trying to make sense of it. But whatever the truth, one thing is obvious to me, that there's no purpose in seeking to change Gino's mind on this. His conviction that Monty was being held in San Lorenzo, that's firm, don't you agree?"

Lercari appeared to accept the inevitable. "Perhaps so."

"*Allora*, as I see it, there can only be two explanations. First: that Fabio made up the whole thing after Monty had been robbed – and he's a convincing liar. Or second; that Fabio was speaking the truth and Monty was indeed being held at San Lorenzo before he was murdered."

"Surely you can't think that that's a possibility?"

"I don't know what I think yet. But let's consider the first alternative. Let's say that Montague had been set upon by thieves somewhere in the city, probably at night, dragged down to the beach, robbed, murdered and left there. That this Fabio was part of the gang, a lookout perhaps? And that his share of the proceeds included Montague's signet ring."

"*Esatto*. It must be something like that."

"Very well. So, the imprisonment story was invented. But then, you must ask: why was it necessary? Why tell it at all? He approached Gino, remember, he had no reason to fabricate such a tale. He could have left well alone. And then, what does he do? He gives away part of his share of the spoils to Gino. Why? To a youth he doesn't know, has never spoken to before."

"Perhaps he's become afraid of being caught. So, he thinks of a way to get rid of the evidence," suggested Lercari.

"Possible, but quite elaborate. Wouldn't it be simpler to just throw the ring away if he didn't want to be caught with it?"

"Yes, it would, but young people don't always do the simple thing." *And not just young people*, thought Nico.

"I think you're missing the key point, both of you." It was Sandro who spoke. They both looked at him. "What I mean is," he continued, "you could see why Fabio would make up some story to save his neck, and even why he would give away the damning evidence. It's a possible explanation, although it seems a little unlikely. But there's one point for which there's only one explanation."

"Which point?" demanded Lercari.

"Monty's nickname. *Campanile*. Only two people knew it, Montague himself – and Gino. You can't explain to me how Fabio could have known it – unless Montague had told him."

There was a silence, only broken by Nico rhythmically tapping the rim of his wine glass. No-one voiced the apparent conclusion: that Fabio's story had to be true.

Eventually Lercari said, "I can't believe it. This is San Lorenzo we're talking about!"

Nico, unlike his fellow *cambisto*, felt that it was perfectly possible that some of the cathedral clergy were involved. What he couldn't imagine, couldn't immediately find an explanation for, was why. Why would they set themselves against a merchant like Monty. What, in their eyes, was his crime?

Sandro voiced his own thoughts. "I'm not sure I can believe it myself, even if what we know points to exactly that conclusion. But perhaps what the three of us believe or don't believe isn't the important point. The fact is we couldn't prove it anyway. Without a witness, all we have is a ring and Gino's account of a conversation. Not enough, surely?"

"*Allora* let's consider Gino, then," suggested Nico. "You said he was expected back at the cathedral later today, Ferro?"

"Well, that's what they are expecting, but after what I've heard, he's not going back."

"I agree the cathedral is not a safe place for him – or for others, it seems. So, do you have another plan for him?"

"I had thought about placing him with another church in the city, but I have to be honest," Lercari confessed. "I should have recognised that Gino isn't cut out for the clergy. He might be treated better somewhere else, but his heart wouldn't be in it. I suppose that leaves the merchant life for him. He can stay with me, and I'll get him a job in Banco Liguria, doing something or other."

"But what will Father Guido – and whoever else knows of this - do when they realise that Gino isn't going to continue his novitiate?"

"What do you mean?"

"Well, if they're trying to hide something, won't they be concerned that he's carrying around a big secret about them? Even if what he's claiming isn't in fact true, they won't want it to come out."

"But if ever Gino did tell anyone and word of it got to the authorities," said Sandro, "surely the Church would just deny it. And who would people believe? On the one hand, a young lad, former runaway, who's decided to leave a church novitiate, or on the other hand, a senior priest at San Lorenzo?"

"Yes, that's probably how it would turn out, Sandro, but Father Guido might not see it that way." He turned back to Lercari. "Ferro, it's a matter for you of course, but you might want to keep Gino out of the city for a while. You have a farm up in the hills, don't you?"

"You're right. I will." Lercari looked across to the window overlooking the harbour. After a pause, he added, "I suppose I could tell the Father that Gino's run away to sea again. He would believe *that*. After all, the boy's done it once before, hasn't he?"

AFTER THE LERCARIS, father and son, had left the house, Nico decided he needed some air. Time alone to think. He walked out onto Strada Nuova and headed eastwards away from the city centre.

In no time, seemingly, he had reached Porta Sottana and entered the streets of Pre again. There were, no question, people in the district he used to call home who could have murdered a foreigner and dumped his body on the beach. Desperate souls, whose only means of survival, as they saw it, was violence.

Had been so, was so, always would be so. He tried to persuade himself that this was the more likely reason for Monty's death than his own fantastic explanation. The thieves had emptied Monty's purse but had left everything else. Perhaps they were disturbed in the act? By Fabio, who then grabbed the ring? But what about the rest of Pre's community, the more honest folk? A local cutthroat couldn't have kept a robbery and murder like that a secret for long. And even if some Pre residents would prefer to look the other way, there'd always be someone who was even more desperate than the guilty men. Someone susceptible to the lure of easy money. Nico had suggested to several residents that there would be a reward on offer for valuable information. So why, after those two days that he and Sandro had spent combing these streets, had no-one approached him wanting to claim a fat purse from 'the Alchemist'?

But thanks to Gino Lercari, a completely different explanation had now revealed itself. It seemed incredible that the finger of blame should turn onto San Lorenzo, but in Nico's mind the idea was unstoppable, like a runaway horse.

What should he do now? Nothing, an easy voice whispered in his ear. Leave Lercari to protect his son, concentrate on sorting out the business affairs of your deceased client, and as for the rest, leave it well alone. Don't get entangled with dangerous men like Father Guido. It had been risky enough, when Cardinal Sauli was threatening to expose Sandro's private life all over the city. Don't pick another fight with the Church now.

He found himself wrestling with this soft-spoken voice. In the names of all the saints, a murder has been committed. The victim is your client and friend. Not only that, but you have good reason to believe that you can identify one of the persons responsible. Isn't it your duty to make this known?

But then, what was the evidence? The word of a missing pauper, an orphan. Told to a runaway youth with a chequered history. And a signet ring with some initials on it. For all that he felt in his gut that Father Guido was somehow involved in Monty's death, especially when he considered that the priest had gone out of his way to show Lercari that the Englishman *wasn't* being held at San Lorenzo, that wasn't the same thing as proving it. Sandro was right. He didn't need to consult Avvocato Tasso to be aware that the case was as thin as paper. If Nico went to the authorities, would Doge Ambrogio even agree to investigate the claim? And if he did, what would be the outcome? Cardinal Sauli could easily talk his way around it, dismiss the accusations as the fantasies of an embittered youth, who had failed as a novice. Someone who had a grudge against his supervisor, Father Guido. A troublemaker who had suborned an orphan to tell malicious lies: that a man who was of impeccable, even austere, reputation was in fact, corrupt and violent. It would never get to a court. And all Nico would have achieved would be to make Cardinal Sauli his mortal enemy, and to embarrass the Doge and the Council. And put Gino in even greater danger.

No, there was nothing to be done, he told himself. Doge Ambrogio would have the murder investigated for a while, but that would merely lead to the conclusion that Monty was set upon and killed by incompetent thieves. Thieves who would likely never be caught.

He breathed out heavily, realising that he had decided nothing, and turned to head back home. Home. Lisa, he suddenly thought: what on earth should I tell her? He remembered their argument about the donation in support of the Netherlands missionaries. Her childhood experiences of Mother Church were so different from his. She would never give his explanation credence. If someone like Ferrucio Lercari struggles to believe what has happened, how much harder would it be for Lisa? It would surely drive a wedge between them.

Chapter Thirty

THE MERCHANTS' LOGGIA, PIAZZA BANCHI: A FEW DAYS LATER

The August Fair was nearing its close. A pale imitation of its recent predecessors. The usual crowds milled around the hot, dusty piazza, pushing and shoving between traders' stalls. The goods of the world on display - and for sale. But only to those with ready coin. For at this fair, and almost for the first time that Nico could remember, all the *cambisti* kept their ledgers tightly closed. And if a buyer was lucky enough to extract credit from one of them, it had better be from a banker whose reputation was undoubted. People would watch as, with slow deliberation, a *cambisto* counted out silver coins into the seller's waiting palm. You would think he was handing over his children, Nico observed to himself. And sellers were struggling too, caught between two imperatives. If you sold too cheaply for ready money, where was the profit? But if you were tempted by a higher offer, and then the buyer couldn't get credit, even worse. Not too many people were smiling in Piazza Banchi.

It was not surprising. After all, the *cambisti* hated uncertainty and in this year of all years, they had had plenty of that. Prices for goods from overseas were fluctuating wildly, making credit risky. War was in the air, and, despite the odds against them, it seemed that England's cockerel was quite willing to go into the cockpit and take on a much-fancied opponent. Not content with helping the Dutch rebels and then executing Mary of Scotland, the English had raided Cádiz. And then there was the capture of the '*San Felipe*'. Nico was not the only banker embarrassed by her loss.

There was little to stay for, so he walked down to the eastern quay, in the direction of Porta Siberia. There, deep in its cellars, was the remaining store of wool from the "*Kateryn*". Wool that Monty had been planning to sell at the Fair. Nico needed to get it released to unlock payments which had been pledged by the buyers. Without this money, he was exposed to crippling liabilities to Monty's bankers in London. Not to mention his obligation to make the next advance to Zúñiga, as required by the court judgment.

Passing through the arch between its barbican walls, he entered the port office. Behind a high desk stood one of the clerks, studying the day ledger in front of him.

"And signore, you would be....?" the clerk enquired in a bored tone.

Nico introduced himself and presented his papers. The clerk's body stiffened, as he registered that he was talking to a *cambisto*. He quickly reached for another ledger on a nearby shelf. He ticked off the particulars on Nico's dockets against the entries in his ledger.

It all matched, save in one respect. "It says here, to release the cargo to a Signore.... Montague?" he said.

"That's right, Montague Belltover, of London."

"And where is he?"

"He died - just days ago. But the cargo still needs to be released. I have a list of buyers to whom the Signore was contracted. I am his banker."

"You have proof?"

Nico reached into his satchel and produced a parchment bearing Monty's seal. A document Monty had signed some weeks before. "My authority."

The man looked doubtful. "But there's no mention of this in our ledgers. I'm not sure we can proceed. You'll appreciate our need for caution, Signore Castello."

"I most certainly do not," he said, his voice raised so that a group of merchants in the office looked around at the source of the commotion. "I am a respected *cambisto*, I don't expect to be kept waiting like this. You have seen my documents, let's get on with it."

The clerk's face coloured. "Excuse me a moment." He crossed the room and passed through a side door. A few minutes later, he was back accompanied by a heavier set man who was, no doubt, his superior.

The manager was emollient. "I am sorry, signore, but there are procedures to be followed."

Nico tried to restrain his temper. "Look here, I understand that you are in some difficulty. But the clerk who made the entries clearly misheard my client's instructions about his using our bank as his representative. You see, Signore Montague's Italian was probably not good enough to convey the precise details."

The manager's face conveyed his sympathy with Nico's predicament. "Of course, but you understand that it isn't just a matter of our ledgers. We need to be satisfied that, with your client being deceased, your authority remains valid."

"Isn't that what it says?"

"Signore, I am not an avvocato...."

"Then I'll be back. With *my* lawyer," yelled Nico, as he stormed out.

But he was, he knew, making an idle threat. The chances were that, since he couldn't provide proof of his authority over Monty's assets, the Englishman's cargo was going nowhere for the time being. And just like those wool bales, Nico was in limbo too. With financial embarrassment, if not far worse, staring him in the face.

GENOVA'S SILK MERCHANTS WERE, as Nico well knew, not accustomed to waiting for their money. Nico had assured Treasurer Saluzzo at the Banco di San Giorgio that payments would be made in full and on time. But with the proceeds of wool sales still to be unlocked, he had had to use up his remaining free capital to do so.

As for the imminent loan advance to Zúñiga, the Spaniard had finally delivered an *asiento* for the cargo of the "*San Lorenzo*" and demanded that he be paid the entire balance of the agreed loan in one drawing, as contemplated by the court judgment. Nico had incurred his wrath by saying that for now, due to capital constraints, the bank would only advance one third of that amount, bringing the monies lent thus far up to just half the agreed total commitment. Nico calculated that he would have to use his personal funds for this advance. Banco Castello was now trading on thin air.

The occasion of Monty's funeral was almost a welcome distraction. Seated in the front pew in San Pietro Della Porta, he could hear the shuffle of feet as Monty's coffin was brought into the church. The elderly priest walked ahead, chanting the opening prayers. As the pallbearers made their stately progress, Nico took in the congregation row by row from the back of the church. The merchants, whose trade was conducted outside this church, had turned out for their brother merchant from London. Many of the *cambisti* were there too, perhaps as much out of respect for Nico, as for any dealings they had had with the Englishman. It was no small crowd, considering Monty had been in Genova less than three months.

In the row behind him, Battista Lomellino and the younger Pallavicino. And there was Cavalli, Monty's landlord. In the front row, to Nico's left, was Ferrucio Lercari, his expression grim. On either side of him, his two sons, Luca and Gino, both a head taller than their father. Gino was no longer wearing his novice's habit, he noted. At Nico's right side was Lisa, dressed beguilingly in black lace, her head slightly bowed. Beyond her was Sandro and then Aunt Julia, gazing up at the high altar. Never one to miss a ceremonial occasion.

The priest in charge at San Pietro had agreed to officiate, despite his initial concern that the deceased was English and probably heretic. It had helped, no doubt, that both the Castellos and the Lercaris had recently made generous donations to San Pietro's fund for the orphans of sailors and fishermen.

The liturgy seemed endless, but the priest was making the most of his opportunity to impress a larger congregation than was usual in his small church. Finally, the Dismissal was given, and the mourners filed out onto the steps. Nico gathered up the select group who would accompany Monty to his grave, in the city's cemetery. Carriages took them up the steeply winding road that led from the city outskirts into the hills.

Half an hour later, he stood by the recently dug ground, half-listening to the familiar phrases uttered by the priest. It was a worthy resting place for the Englishman, he decided. A fine view over the city and the harbour beyond. Bordered by orange groves, which scented the air in spring. Today though, the place was hot, despite the offshore breeze. Mercifully, the priest was brief with the interment.

The small crowd slowly dispersed through the cemetery gates. Nico was about to climb into his own carriage, following his wife and brother, when he noticed a solitary figure outside the cemetery walls. Someone sheltering from the fierce sun under the canopy of an old olive tree. Removing his foot from the step, he told Sandro to proceed to Casa Castello and then send the carriage back for him. Lisa and Julia were seated opposite Sandro; both sent him a querying glance which he ignored.

He walked across the roadway. The young woman was wearing a full veil, but he knew who it would be.

"So, Bianca?"

She curtsied. "Signore Domenico. Thank you for letting me know about the funeral. It is a lovely setting here. I would have liked to attend the service, of course, but some of the congregation might have found my presence, well..." she tailed off.

"I am sure that Signore Montague would have been happy for you to be there. As would I. But I understand your delicacy."

"It is enough to know where he is buried. You won't mind if I come here sometimes, to lay some flowers?" She was holding a small bunch of white roses.

"Of course you may. Why don't you come with me now?"

The Castellos had placed a large wreath of red and white blooms at the foot of the grave. She laid her posy next to it and stood back.

They were silent for a while. A breeze caught the olive branches, setting their silver leaves rustling. When the wind from the sea subsided, the silence was punctuated by the tinkle of goat bells wafting down from the hills above.

He watched her remove the veil from her face, as if her own private funeral had just ended. "Monterosso, I called him," she said. "Like the village, if you know it. 'Monte' because he was such a big man - and 'Rosso' for his red hair."

Nico heard the catch in her voice.

"He said he wanted to take me to England," she continued, looking towards the sea. "He was married, but they had no children. Apparently, it was not a love match. He said he could get an annulment."

She turned back to face him. She looked as she had on her visit to the Pammatone a few days before, but there was something else, an underlying resolve in her expression.

"I know you think me foolish, signore, but he was being sincere. He made jokes all the time, about himself especially, but about this he did not joke. Men tell me pretty lies all the time: I *can* tell the difference."

"Doubtless you would have made each other happy. That is not to say it would have been an easy road to choose."

"So, signore, are the authorities going to find out who was responsible for this... crime? It is hard to carry on, without knowing how he met his fate."

"I have of course pressed the Doge to act. I'm sure he will search for the perpetrators with vigour. But try not to worry, signorina. Some things are perhaps best left as they are. After all, it won't bring him back to you."

Watching her expression, Nico told himself there are things that we know to be true, but that doesn't make them true in our hearts.

Chapter Thirty-One
THE ESCORIAL PALACE, OUTSIDE
MADRID: MID-AUGUST

Removing his shirt, Juan de Idiáquez wiped the sweat from his neck. By rights, he should have escaped this sweltering prison of a palace and headed for cooler climes. But the king, as he got older and more infirm, was less inclined to move his Court around the country. And more wedded to staying put in the place where he would finally be buried.

Idiáquez promoted the idea of a summer tour of the northern provinces, but Felipe was against their moving out of Castile arguing that, with their sovereign many days' ride away, all the *Consejos* in Madrid would simply down tools; nothing would be achieved. There was some justice in that view, Idiáquez had to acknowledge, but he suspected that in truth the king dreaded more the lengthy carriage journeys over stony roads which would aggravate the pain of his gout. And perhaps Idiáquez' promotion of a royal visit to Bilbao had been seen by the king for what it was, in part at least, a chance for Idiáquez to visit his wife and young son at home. Since his appointment as Foreign Minister a year ago, he had scarcely seen them. Things had been so much happier when he had been ambassador to Genova. Mencia had loved their life in Italy. They were always together then, save for the rare occasions when he was summoned to Spain. Young Alonso was nearly a man now, but at least Idiáquez had been there for his early years.

Shaking his head, as if to bring himself to concentrate on the issues at hand, the minister completed his formal attire for the meeting. As he attached a ruff around his collar, he pondered how this recent period, normally a quiet season for the affairs of state, had been anything but. The dreadful news of *San Felipe's* capture had pushed the king into a frenzy. Santa Cruz had been forced, much against his judgment, to take the fleet out from Lisbon and head for the Azores to recapture her and kill that pirate, El Draque. The fleet hadn't found the pirate and, in the end, when they ran out of stores, had been forced to head back to port. It scarcely gave one confidence in the success of the English Enterprise.

A more positive achievement, one in which he took personal pride, was that at long last Pope Sixtus had put his signature to the loan agreement. Completed at the end of July, a copy of the historic document had been couriered from Rome to Madrid and arrived several days earlier. Three *million* ducats. It would offset a significant part of the costs of the Enterprise, Felipe had noted with pleasure. But Idiáquez had had to temper Felipe's expectations, lest the monarch be carried away in his enthusiasm. After all, they had been unable to budge Sixtus from his insistence that the loan would only be advanced when Spanish troops had landed on English soil. His promise was valuable, but it didn't pay the bills now. Without bullion to pay the victuallers and to keep their troops with the fleet, the armada would languish in harbour for another season.

Ushered into the royal apartments by the ever-loyal Sebastian, Idiáquez found the king in his customary place, at his desk and surrounded by bundles of documents. But in readiness to receive his minister, Felipe had removed the tell-tale spectacles which lay part-obscured by the paper he had been studying.

"So, Don Juan," said Felipe, rising stiffly from his chair, "what is the news from Lisbon? Is the Marquis ready to prepare for sailing?"

Idiáquez disguised his frustration with the king's unrealistic expectations. "I have of course advised Don Alvaro, as soon as we had confirmation of His Holiness' signing of the loan, that the funds have been promised. But the Marquis has only had the report for a few days, so there is still much for him to do. In his reply, he points out that he can obtain some stores on credit, but that in most cases suppliers expect to be paid in coin, not *asientos*."

The king cleared his throat, clearly unhappy with this situation. "While I realise that Pope Sixtus' loan cannot be drawn until we have landed, you assured me that this would not delay matters. I thought that your fellow Zúñiga was getting short-term credits in Genova. What is happening there?"

Idiáquez had expected that this question would be asked, but he had no placatory answer. "Don Balthasar reports that our account with the Banco di San Giorgio has received some funds, senor, but nothing approaching the five million ducats we were seeking. The House of Lomellino has put up less than half a million and Banco di Liguria – the Lercari family, that is – a little more. A smaller sum has come from Banco Castello, who promised much, but has failed to deliver. You were aware that Senor Grimaldi was unwilling to participate while their loan of last year remains outstanding...."

"Yes, yes," said Felipe, flicking his right hand as if shooing away a fly. Relations with Nicolo Grimaldi, normally solid, were currently an embarrassment to the king. "But this is hardly satisfactory, no?"

"Agreed, senor – extremely unsatisfactory. Nor does our emissary expect a significant increase in the sums he can borrow this season. He blames tensions in the market there and suggests that the criminal activities of El Draque have scared the bankers away."

"Well, it seems that the Genovese bankers are not so scared that they're unwilling to finance Protestant merchants, Don Juan."

Idiáquez was caught off guard. One of his earlier reports to the *Consejo de Finanza* had referred to the large credits being offered to the Dutch and English – especially the English – by the same bankers who were now baulking at lending to Spain. Felipe had obviously read his minister's *consulta* carefully.

"That is especially frustrating. I am sorry to say that Don Balthasar de Zúñiga has disappointed me. I fear that his mission has proved to be well beyond his capabilities. I take the blame for selecting him, of course, senor."

Idiáquez cursed inwardly at having to apologise. Perhaps he should have gone to Genova himself, not trusted this vital mission to a less experienced ambassador. After all, from his five years there, he knew the city well and many of its bankers. But then, to do that he would have had to leave Felipe to his fellow ministers for several months. A year into his post as head of the Junta, Idiáquez was careful to ensure that he was the gateway through which others had to pass to reach the king.

AFTER A WEEK at the Escorial in which little transpired, other than the heat becoming even more intense, an urgent courier came to

Idiáquez with an uncoded message from Cádiz. Idiáquez read it and yelled out loud with relief.

"Senor, senor, great news," he announced, bursting in on Felipe before Sebastian could restrain him. "From Cádiz. The *Flota* has at last arrived. All of them, safely home."

Felipe hobbled, as fast as his gout would permit, around his desk and shook Idiáquez by the hands. "The Almighty has answered my prayers," he said, his voice trembling with emotion. "Now we can *begin*, Don Juan."

Idiáquez bowed low, relishing the moment.

"Indeed senor, I will arrange for bullion to be shipped to Lisbon, once we have made a proper accounting of it. In the meantime, I will advise the Marquis de Santa Cruz that the funds will be on their way shortly."

But Idiáquez knew that even transporting the money needed would be no small operation. At thirty thousand ducats a day to maintain the fleet in readiness, Santa Cruz would need a huge – and secure - shipment.

"Excellent, excellent. But there is so much to do," the king added, "I gather the Cádiz squadron still lacks barrels for their stores."

As usual, Felipe had homed in on the detail, rather than stay with the wider picture. "True, senor, I understand that they were struggling to find enough seasoned oak. But now we have new funds, I'm sure that it can be sourced."

Felipe put his hands together, as if in prayer. But he was directing, not pleading. "I don't care if they chop down all the forests of Aracena. Just get it done."

Idiáquez bowed again. "As you command, senor." This was not a day for doubts, but even so, it was already the second half of August. Could the armada be made ready before the winter closed in?

Chapter Thirty-Two

BANCO DI SAN GIORGIO, GENOA
HARBOUR: LATE AUGUST

Nico entered the boardroom and was ushered to a seat at the foot of the long table. At the opposite end sat Benedetto Saluzzo, the bank's Chief Treasurer, looking grim-faced. On either side of him, a group of Nico's fellow bankers. To Saluzzo's left, Leonardo Di Castro and Franco Caffaro. On his right: Giovanni Spazio, a worried-looking Ferrucio Lercari and Nico's syndicate partner, Battista Lomellino. No sign of Spinola. Young Ansaldo Grimaldi sat slightly apart from the others, his face a picture of boredom. None of these men would normally be working on a Saturday morning. More often, they would have been out hunting with friends or enjoying the company of their, or perhaps other men's, wives. But not today it seemed. Each of these men were shareholders in the Banco di San Giorgio. A position Nico had yet to acquire, despite his prominence among the *cambisti*. Perhaps in the past, some of them had resisted awarding Nico that privilege out of sheer jealousy. Whereas Saluzzo, he suspected, considered that Nico's lowly parentage barred him from such a rank.

Saluzzo had summoned Nico to the bank at short notice. He had expected a severe reprimand or maybe worse, from the treasurer. He had not expected to be presented with his entire committee. There was no buzz of conversation, the room was hushed, expectant. Just like a court when the accused is brought to the dock. Which of course, Nico told himself, was exactly what it was.

Saluzzo drew the meeting to order. "Signori, I am grateful for your attendance at short notice."

Nico had the feeling that the treasurer was addressing the Bank's shareholders, but not Nico himself.

"As you know," Saluzzo continued, "the August Fair has recently concluded. As Consul of the Fair, it is my duty to ensure that all members' accounts are reconciled, and their liabilities discharged. In the course of discharging that duty, it has emerged that one of our members, Signore Castello here, has failed to meet certain of his commitments."

Low mutterings around the table. A slight shake of his head by Ansaldo Grimaldi. Saluzzo raised one index finger to silence the murmurings.

"But first, I will ask Signore Colombo to summarize the ledger positions." Immediately behind Saluzzo and close enough to whisper in his ear was Saluzzo's principal secretary, young Giuseppe Colombo, scion of the great explorer's family.

Nico guessed that, for all Saluzzo's self-important delivery, it would have been Colombo who had kept the candles burning at the Bank last night, preparing for this meeting. The young man opened the heavy, leather-bound volume in front of him, a ledger book thicker than the span of a man's hand. The room fell quiet. The sound of seagulls in the harbour, with their mocking cries, pierced the silence.

Colombo cleared his throat. "These figures were taken from the schedule of accounts submitted by Signore Castello. But we have since confirmed the figures with each creditor. Giulio Castagna, twenty-five thousand *scudi*; Luigi Foscolo, thirty thousand *scudi*; Domenico De Franchi, ninety-five thousand *scudi*..." Nico knew the list by heart. "The total of unresolved accounts, two hundred and twenty-eight thousand *scudi di marco*." Or a quarter of a million lire in real money, thought Nico.

Colombo finished reading. The silence was finally broken by Leonardo Di Castro. "How is this possible, signore? None of us should have a deficiency of this size."

Nico was about to respond, but Saluzzo raised a paw. "If you'll be patient, Signore Di Castro, we shall hear from Signore Castello shortly. In any case, I gather this is not the end of the matter. I have also received a communication from a Spanish gentleman currently residing in the city, one Don Balthasar de Zúñiga. He states that he submitted a request to draw funds from Signore Castello, pursuant to a notarised deed, but has not received them. I gather," he looked over the top of the document in his hands and towards Nico, "that the arrangement was recently the subject of court proceedings, and the judge had found in Senor Zúñiga's favour."

Lomellino, Nico's syndicate partner, looked at his hands at the mention of Zúñiga's name, but one or two of the others glanced towards Ansaldo Grimaldi. They all knew, Nico realised, who the Spaniard was – and the august personage he represented, even if that royal name wasn't to be mentioned. And they also knew that the Grimaldi family had until recently been the main provider of credit to that gentleman. But Ansaldo Grimaldi didn't react, his expression unreadable.

"Presumably, Signore Castello, you can confirm whether this Spanish gentleman is correct in his assertions. That despite the court judgment you have not permitted him to draw down?" asked Saluzzo.

Nico cleared his throat. "We made a first advance some weeks ago but yes, we have not implemented the second drawdown request that he has submitted. Or at least, not in full."

"And the reason?"

"My lawyer is recommending an appeal against the court's judgment - but that is not the issue fundamentally. The reality is that we currently have insufficient free capital to allow further drawdowns. And although there are some cash reserves, I am not willing to trade beyond the bank's capital limit."

"And this lack of capital has also prevented you from honouring these several merchant commitments, as enumerated by Signore Colombo?"

"Yes."

"How do you, an experienced *cambisto*, account for this lapse?"

"The means to settle all these claims is just a short walk from here, Signore Saluzzo. It lies deep in the vaults of the Siberia. Shiploads of English wool. The sale proceeds are owing to my bank. But I cannot collect payment from the wool buyers, because I cannot deliver the wool to them. The English merchant who agreed to sell the goods has died – and until his affairs are settled, it seems that the wool must stay there, underground. So, if you will, my liabilities are free to oppress me, but my assets are beyond my reach."

Lomellino's fists were clenched on the table, his knuckles standing out white. The knuckles told Nico that, aside from Ferrucio Lercari,

Lomellino was perhaps his only supporter on the committee. But how far would that support go?

"Are you saying, signore," queried Saluzzo, "that, absent receipt of these wool proceeds, you have no means to satisfy these claims?"

"I am endeavouring to raise the capital elsewhere, but that will take time."

"Totally unacceptable," muttered Di Castro.

"This default, signore, may be your personal misfortune," Saluzzo addressed Nico in that smooth tone of his, "but it has placed several other members in temporary difficulty. Members, that is, who also have dealings with your merchant counterparties."

He paused, perhaps waiting for an apology. Nico was not going to oblige him.

"And aside from that," Saluzzo continued, after a glance around the table, "there is the risk that if these matters are not resolved quickly the contagion could spread. Credit would contract across the market. That would be very unwelcome for the Republic. Our reputation, so hard won, would be compromised. That we cannot tolerate; it calls for decisive measures."

Saluzzo paused again. Several heads were nodding in agreement with his schoolmasterly tone. *How easy to be wise after the event*, thought Nico. *Especially if you are not at risk yourself.*

"If the bank could see its way to help," Nico heard himself saying, "with regard to payments to the spice and silk merchants on your list, that would give me time to sort out the Englishman's affairs."

"You mean," said Saluzzo, "a loan from the San Giorgio?"

There were disapproving murmurs around the table. "Yes," said Nico, raising his voice above the chatter, "once I have got the wool released, I can pay the Bank back. With interest of course."

Saluzzo merely raised an eyebrow. "I think," he said, glancing at his colleagues, "that we should discuss the options *in camera*. So, if you will excuse us, Signore Castello, please take a seat in the anteroom for the time being."

Nico sat outside the boardroom for what seemed like an interminable length of time. From time to time, he could hear voices raised, the meeting was obviously getting heated. Eventually, he was summoned back inside.

Initially, Saluzzo stated that the dispute between Banco Castello and Senor Zúñiga was entirely a private question, and the *San Giorgio* would not involve itself, unless that dispute compromised Signore

Castello's ability to discharge his mercantile obligations. He would have to resolve the matter as best he could. Nico had no problem with that; he expected nothing less. But he also knew that, within the next few weeks, Zúñiga would go back to the court, claiming that the judgment in his favour had not been satisfied by the defendant. The next step would inevitably be a possession order for Nico's goods, which would then be sold by the bailiffs to pay the claimant. And since they wouldn't be sufficient to cover the judgment in full, the next step was bankruptcy – and prison.

The treasurer surprised Nico when, in his next utterance, he asked Ansaldo Grimaldi to speak on behalf of the committee.

"In relation to the various merchant claims, the shareholders have considered your request, Signore Castello, but we are afraid that a loan is quite impossible, especially given the risk of default if you can't resolve things satisfactorily with Senor Zúñiga. However, we would be prepared to take an assignment of your rights to the wool proceeds. We would pay you for them – and that payment would be sufficient to enable you to discharge your obligations to these spice and silk merchants who are currently out of pocket."

"So, what is your proposed discount?" Nico said, although he was afraid that he already knew the answer.

Grimaldi pretended to look surprised. "Discount? Well, we see this as a straight exchange. Your wool claims in exchange for our settling your merchant liabilities."

"But my wool claims are worth at least double the merchant liabilities. So that amounts to just ten soldi to the lira. Are you trying to rob me?" As soon as he said it, Nico knew that "rob" was not the best way of expressing himself. But his temper was rising.

Di Castro sat back in his chair. "Of course, we are sorry for your predicament, Signore Castello, but the San Giorgio is not a charitable institution - and neither is my own bank."

Nico could no longer contain himself. His palms slammed down on the table, and he stood up, stepping towards Di Castro. "You are taking advantage of my difficulties. I am asking for a loan, not charity. I will pay you all back, with interest, over the next three Fairs."

Di Castro stood up too, yelling back at Nico. Moments later, several of the other *cambisti* were waving their fists and shouting. Young Colombo stepped around the table and stood between Di Castro and Nico; his hands raised in a plea for calm.

When everyone had finally sat down, Saluzzo spoke again. "I think,

Signore Castello, you should appreciate – indeed, we should *all* appreciate - that the reputation of Genova will suffer if those who are in difficulties cannot reconcile their bills promptly. The remedy may be costly, but our standing abroad counts for far more."

"That's easy for you to say, it isn't your money we're talking about," muttered Nico. He realised he was doing himself no good, but the floodgates had now opened. All the frustrations and pressures of recent weeks had finally come to the surface, and he was powerless to stop them.

Saluzzo did not respond, but his face coloured.

After another half hour of heated argument around the table a proposal was hammered out. Nico would have forty-five days' grace to raise the capital to settle his debts to the unpaid silk and spice merchants. If by that date he had not done so, then he would immediately assign to the San Giorgio his wool claims in full, at a price equivalent to twelve soldi to the lira. By way of payment for the assignment, the bank would then discharge the merchants' claims directly. It was sheer robbery, but Nico could see that he had no choice. Besides, it would all be irrelevant if by the time it was implemented, Zúñiga had used his court judgment to push Nico into bankruptcy.

Nico stood up, about to quit the room, but Saluzzo had one further announcement to make. In view of Nico's failure to meet his obligations as a *cambisto*, his licence to operate in the Loggia was revoked with immediate effect. He would have liberty to reapply in a year's time. It was calculating of Saluzzo, Nico felt, to keep this cruellest of blows back until the end of the meeting. After all, if he couldn't trade, how would he be able to crawl his way back from the abyss?

NICO RETURNED HOME from consulting Avvocato Tasso, in the late afternoon. The sun was finally losing its power. But it was not the day's oppressive heat that had engendered a feeling of weariness in him. Rather, his fear that the forces of chaos were descending on his bank, and through it, the rest of his world. How could he negotiate a safe passage through this storm?

Monty's wool, the sale of which would provide the means to honour his other commitments, was still locked in the vaults at Porta Siberia and it seemed no legal power on earth could unlock it. Short of the miraculous resurrection of its owner or the almost as unlikely arrival of Monty's colleagues, the Merchant Adventurers, in Genova to unravel the property tangle and complete the sales. The other side of the bank's balance sheet was just as problematic. He was committed to large loan advances to Zúñiga, not to mention payment to the silk merchants for their bales of cloth. Even if he could be allowed to re-sell the silk, for which poor Monty no longer had a use, it would likely be at a significant loss in the local market.

After supper with Sandro, Julia and Lisa in which he'd conversed little, Nico retired to his apartment early. Taking a flask of Chianti with him.

Lisa followed him through the door. He sat on the day bed pouring himself a glass. He offered it to her, but Lisa declined. "You seem to be drinking more wine lately, Nico," she said. It was an observation, a gesture of concern, not a complaint, he noted.

"I've been struggling to work out how to resolve Monty's affairs." He said eventually.

"You'll find a way."

"Not so easy. We can't conclude any of his transactions without his widow being involved, which will slow things up enormously. And in the meantime, we have large liabilities we can't extract ourselves from." Lisa did not respond, and for a while they sat in silence.

"I have decided we have to sell this house," he suddenly said.

"*Sell*?" Lisa responded, those amber eyes opening wide. "Has it come to that?"

"Well, I first thought of mortgaging it, to provide the respite we need. But the *cambisti* I approached weren't willing to advance anywhere near enough on that security."

Lisa touched his arm.

"Then I thought of selling the contents and dismissing some of the staff. But the paintings and the plate aside, we wouldn't get much from selling the fittings. Besides, what would be the point of a big house with no servants and no furniture?"

"But suppose you can get Montague's goods released?"

"And suppose I can't? Better to sell the house before we are forced to by creditors. In that circumstance, any buyer would take full advantage of us."

"At least we have my father's house. We could live there, while you rebuild the bank's fortunes. Or we could sell Casa Della Volta instead?"

Nico had considered that approach but had calculated that the value of it was nowhere near enough to cover his liabilities. He didn't want to say that to Lisa.

"Would you really want to sell your old house, with all its memories?"

She shrugged. "I have my memories. They don't depend on owning the building. Sell it, if it becomes necessary."

Chapter Thirty-Three

CASA DELLA VOLTA, CARICAMENTO:
EARLY SEPTEMBER 1587

Lisa stepped across the threshold. For the first time since her wedding, she was back in her childhood bedroom. She pulled back the shutters and the early morning light draped itself over the undressed bed. On the opposite wall, her old *canterali*, with its carved drawer fronts, greeted her. Laid over it was a protective cloth edged with lace. The sunlight caught the weave: she could see on it the mark of a heavy object. Then she remembered. It was the illustrated copy of "*The Golden Legend*" that the archbishop had given to her at the time of her engagement to Nico. A mark of his favour. She had brought the volume back with her from her bedroom at Casa Castello.

She could hear grunts and groans from the porters as they tried to manoeuvre some heavy furniture into place in the sala. Everything that had come from Casa Castello – she wondered momentarily what the new owners would call it – was too big for its new, more modest home. When a corner of the credenza hit one of the walls with a bang, Maria berated the porters for their clumsiness. When her maid's prattle subsided, Lisa realised that Nico had not followed her into the room. She returned to the principal bedroom which overlooked the harbour. The room that had been her parents' bedroom and would now be hers and Nico's.

Her husband was sat on the side of the bed, staring out of the window. He did not look round. She sat down beside him.

"This will suit us well enough," she said, with more confidence than she felt.

"Hmm, it will have to."

"It was good enough for my parents. It will be good enough for us."

He put his hand on hers. "Of course it will. For a moment I had forgotten. In any case it's not the house itself that's to blame, it's me."

"You did all you could."

"To try and rescue us from a situation which I shouldn't have put us in in the first place."

She stood up. "I must go and help Maria with organising the kitchen."

"Can't you let Paola do that?"

"I had to let her go, Nico. We can function well enough without her."

The domestic servants were her responsibility. But Nico's expression said it was yet another reminder of their fall from the dizzy heights of life on Strada Nuova.

Left alone, he walked over to the window and gazed down at the scene below. The long road which flanked the great harbour. To his far left the jutting presence of the Banco di San Giorgio. Below him, Piazza Darsena and beyond the naval harbour, looking emptier of galleys than was usual. And to his right, past Porta Sottana, he could see the low, crowded roofs of Pre district. That he was now back, almost within a stone's throw of the area where he had grown up, struck him forcibly. He had begun in that humble tenement in Pre, had clawed his way up the hill to the elegance of Strada Nuova and now, it seemed, he was sliding back down to the anonymous life where he had started.

And who was to say if that wouldn't be his ultimate destination? His only prospect of financial safety, never mind the chance of recovering his licence as a *cambisto*, would be to discharge, in full and promptly, his merchant liabilities. The offer that the shareholders of the San Giorgio had made, no doubt engineered by the Grimaldi clan, would have been a deadly bargain, losing him most of his capital in one blow. So, within the bare six weeks that the shareholders had allowed him to pay off the silk and pepper merchants, he had sold Casa Castello, and all his plate and the paintings, to a member of Spinola's family (they owned the house next door) and transferred the proceeds to those same creditors. It took everything he had, but at least it meant that, as and when Monty's estate was finally unravelled, he could still sell the wool and keep the funds it generated. Selling his house to the first bidder meant that he had sold at a loss, but that was a better outcome than holding out for its true worth and losing the wool in the process.

He glanced around the room. He and Lisa would sleep in here, brother Sandro in Lisa's old room. There was no suite of apartments to accommodate Aunt Julia or her maid and no money for the manner of living she aspired to. So it was, with some relief to them both, that Julia had decided to return to Livorno and her rented villa there. The Castellos now had only Maria, and a novice kitchen maid as domestic staff and Nico had retained from his team at the Loggia dei Mercanti, only young Lorenzo and his former treasury guard, Luca. Mazzini, his manager, had gone: Nico had persuaded Ferrucio Lercari, who was expanding the Banco di Liguria, to take him on, along with Marco, Nico's other guard. And Gildo, the groom, had gone too along with the carriage and horses, which had been sold, saving only the mare, Mimi. For now, at least, he could not contemplate parting with her.

These measures would help keep their heads above water for a while. What was currently unclear though, was how he and Sandro would earn any income, what indeed they would do, if not allowed to trade as moneychangers. For the moment, they would have to live on air.

IT HIT Nico hard to remember when he woke each morning that there was no point in heading down to Piazza Banchi. Saluzzo had ordered that the *banca* at which he conducted business be removed from the Loggia. A ritual death.

It was not a Saturday, the usual day for riding out to Boccadasse, but Nico decided that he would have to tell his father the depressing news. Vittorio was sitting on the balcony of his simple cottage, looking out towards the fishing boats. He looked well enough, but age was slowing him up, Nico noticed. After the preliminary chatter, Nico related the most recent developments of these eventful few weeks. His father listened, his expression sanguine.

"My son, this is a brief episode of misfortune. After all, you have your health, your marriage, and your wits for business. In God's good time, things will change. The Almighty didn't give you your talent as a *cambisto* for nothing. He will see you through. You will recover your former strength. Have faith in Him."

"But our *name*, padre. The reputation we struggled to build; what price does that command now?"

Vittorio smiled indulgently at his son. "Do you worry that people will say that the 'Alchemist' has lost his touch? I thought you weren't concerned with what people think?" Nico didn't reply, but felt the words strike home.

"Hear me, Nico. The opinion of the crowd is nothing to be concerned with. They like to build you up and then knock you down. Think instead of your peers, those at least whose good opinion is worth having. They will judge you, not by your successes, but by how you deal with adversity. And when you are reinstated, they will think all the more of you."

Vittorio finished his homily. His gaze wandered across the terrace of the villa, out to sea. For a while all that could be heard was the lapping of waves on the shore below.

"I have a little saved up," he continued cautiously, not wanting to tread on Nico's pride. "If that would help."

"*Padre mio*, you are kind to offer, but no. I don't want to worry about you being short of money, on top of everything else."

"As I say, all will be well in time. You were never destined to be a silversmith like me."

"Clearly not. I'd have made a bad one."

Vittorio didn't laugh. Finally, he said, "I worry about Sandro, though. His path is not so clear."

Six months ago, Nico's first thought would have been that, as ever, Sandro was his father's favourite. Indulged, whereas Nico was expected to fight his own battles. But he suddenly realised that those old feelings of resentment, that tinge of jealousy of his brother, this was all gone now. And without knowing it, his father had found the nub of it. Nico and the bank had lost their money. Sandro stood to lose much more.

Vittorio added, musing, "How will he fare, I wonder, without all his fine friends?"

"He will adjust, we both will."

"But then, he has a strong brother to look out for him. I am proud of you, son."

On his way back to the city, Nico reflected on his father's comments. Neither he nor Sandro had felt able to tell Vittorio about the accusations made against Sandro by the archbishop. Nico doubted his father would ever understand. What then did Vittorio mean by Sandro's path being more difficult? Not just an observation about

Sandro's relentless pursuit of life's pleasures, which some might call licentious? Did their father in fact see what the brothers had assumed he was blind to?

A FEW MORNINGS LATER, Lorenzo Cavalli knocked on the front door. He explained to Maria, who opened it, that he had just called at Strada Nuova, only to be told that Signore Castello had moved house. With him was Thomas Winterhey, master of the "*Mary Gale*", recently back in Genova. Winterhey had gone to Cavalli's house to speak to Signore Montague, in anticipation of their homeward journey to London. Cavalli had broken the news to the sailor that Montague was dead and then, unable to answer Winterhey's inevitable questions, had brought him to meet the English signore's banker.

Sat with Nico in the sala, Winterhey began. "Can you tell me, Signore, 'ow young Master Belltorr died? Signore Cavalli says I should ask *you*."

"I'm sorry to tell you that he was found dead on the beach."

"Oh, my lord. My lord."

"About a month ago. It appears he was attacked at night in the street, badly beaten and left to die."

"Terrible, that is, terrible," said Winterhey. He looked across at Cavalli. "Were they thieves, then?"

Cavalli raised his hands in a helpless-looking gesture and directed his questioner back to Nico.

"That is what the Doge's officers believe," said Nico.

Winterhey scratched his chin, grizzled with stubble. "I s'ppose that must be it."

"Well, maybe so. I don't know what other reason someone could have had for killing him."

Winterhey shook his head but made no response.

"I'm afraid that I can't help you much further, Master Winterhey. There's a cargo of silk and spice which should really be heading for London, but unless we can resolve Master Montague's affairs, it will have to languish here for the time being."

Winterhey nodded. "Well, here's hopin' you can get it sorted."

"If not, I may even have to go to England myself. Perhaps you could accommodate a passenger?"

"Certainly. An honour. I'm awaitin' another small consignment bound for England at present. So, the *Mary Gale* will be here for a short while, if that's any use to you."

"That may suit. I will let you know as soon as I can. But I doubt I will be able to pay for my passage until we get to London, and I can sort things out with Montague's family."

Winterhey shrugged his shoulders. "That's of no consequence, signore. I know you'll settle with me as soon as you can."

ONE EVENING around the supper table, Lisa having already retired to bed, Sandro voiced his continuing fears of exposure by Cardinal Sauli.

The last few weeks had flown by, it seemed to Nico, with all that had happened. It was only now that he registered the fact that the archbishop had made no public move against Sandro. He suggested to his brother that this was some reassurance.

Sandro looked doubtful. "Maybe, but I still feel vulnerable. The same for Bernardo and the others, to some extent. We've all been disinvited from the Governor's Palazzo."

"You had a falling out with Prince Andrea?"

"Not really. The Governor found out about his son's relationship with Bernardo and the rest of us – how, I don't know, perhaps the archbishop told him – and he was incensed. Threatened Andrea with all kinds of consequences if it didn't stop."

"Perhaps it will blow over in time."

"I doubt it. Bernardo has decided to leave Genova. Go to Firenze. He says that life will be easier there, he won't be hounded by prejudiced old men."

"But didn't Pareto have a card up his sleeve? At least, so far as the archbishop's concerned. That story about the priest and those incriminating letters?"

"He told me the other day that the archbishop had several of his priests tested and, in the process, at least one of them had confessed to a shaming relationship. He's been dismissed from the cathedral. So, Bernardo's trump is now a discard."

"Well, Sauli may have no constraints anymore, but at the same time, what would he gain by denouncing you? He knows we can't make good the loan anyway, whatever he does, so what purpose would it serve?"

Sandro's mouth creased into a half-smile. "Just out of spite, because we've failed his client."

Nico wondered if his brother was right. Cardinal Sauli took care, it seemed, to cultivate a reputation for unwavering principle. Nico distrusted such certainty.

Sandro continued, "Perhaps I should follow Bernardo's example and go to Firenze. Safer there. I think. If I stay here, I could end up in jail."

Nico had to admit that all things considered, the sooner Sandro was out of Genova the better. But surely not Firenze, and not with Pareto.

"But where else would I go?" asked Sandro.

Nico tapped his fingers on the table, thinking. "Well, wherever you live, you will need something to live *on*. Perhaps we could set you up as a *cambisto* somewhere else."

"But where would that be?"

"Well, Venezia has a market for finance, but given the rivalry between the two republics, I suspect we'd find it hard to make headway there. And there's nowhere else in Italy which handles foreign business at the same level as Genova."

Sandro shook his head in agreement.

"No," continued Nico, "I think you'd have to go north. Bruges perhaps? Or Antwerp. After all, we already know many of the leading merchants there. And their bankers."

"But what would I do for capital?"

"Start small, just like we did down at the Loggia all those years ago. You can build it in the same way, given time."

ARCHBISHOP SAULI WATCHED the departing figure of Zúñiga, relieved that his meeting with this quarrelsome man was over. As before in their regular sessions, Balthasar de Zúñiga had berated the merchant community of Genova and almost anyone else, save for his native countrymen. Naturally, the archbishop had countered that at least the English merchant, God perish his soul, was no longer active in the market for credit.

This was scant comfort for Zúñiga, however. He informed the archbishop that the legal case that he had won against Banco Castello was just so much paper. The plain fact was that the bank was no longer able to fund the king's loan. Zúñiga's lawyer had recently verified the fact that the bank's capital was exhausted. Yes, he could pursue the Castellos into personal bankruptcy, but that wouldn't raise a single additional ducat: in fact, he would be expending more funds just keeping his lawyer busy, for no practical purpose. So, he had told them to down tools. The lawyer's final act, he told Sauli with some relish, was to inform Signore Castello's lawyer that, in the light of the bank's failure to meet its obligations, the *asiento* for the cargo of the "*San Lorenzo*" was considered null and void. And Zúñiga would withhold all future interest payments on the earlier advances, in compensation.

And then there was Banco di Liguria: though this bank was clearly not in the same difficulties as the Castellos' bank, Signore Lercari was indicating that no further credits would be offered this season. And the remainder of that godless community of usurers in the Loggia had also shied away, scared by the latest rumours, whether they be about that pirate, Il Drago, or the troubles afflicting their fellow banker, Castello, or the random murder of a foreign merchant. Whichever way you looked at it, Senor Zúñiga's mission had scarcely advanced a step in weeks.

After Zúñiga left, the archbishop wondered how the Spaniard's self-justifying missives to Minister Idiáquez would be received. Would Zúñiga try to deflect blame onto him? He scowled at Father Guido, who had also been present at the meeting.

"Well, that is that. We have tried our best. But these bankers, Father, they are a pestilence, a stain on the honour of the city. They have no sense of their duty to God - or to the Republic. I wish we could eradicate them all – and their vile trade."

"Your Grace, you are right. The world would no doubt be a better place without these moneylenders."

"*They that get riches, not by right, shall leave them in the midst of their days.*" Sauli quoted, determined that Father Guido should not have the last word.

The prelate, satisfied now that he had vented his spleen, glanced at a wine bottle on his side table. The wine was part of a recent gift from Signore Lercari. He summoned a page to bring him a single glass. Father Guido would not partake, of course.

As he sipped his wine, Sauli mused about the coming weeks and days. "But let us move on to other matters, Father, I trust there is no chance of the cathedral being somehow entangled in this grubby business with that Englishman. I gather that his untimely demise is still the subject of idle gossip in the city. Or so my dinner guests yesterday informed me."

"I think not, Your Grace. I imagine that the original source of that gossip has now dried up. Perhaps I should also mention that Signore Lercari's son has not returned to continue his novitiate. No doubt he'll be whispering poison about us in his father's ear, but I doubt that the Lercaris would be so indiscreet as to make their views public."

"I always maintained that the boy was totally unsuited for the priesthood. Licentious, credulous, utterly unreliable. Yet you insisted on accepting him. We must be more careful about who we allow to enter these precincts."

Suppressing his strong sense of injustice at the archbishop's blame-shifting, Guido kept his face expressionless. The irony that the archbishop was indulging himself with wine from the same Lercari family helped him to deflect those unworthy feelings.

IN THE STUDY of his London residence, Thomas Sutton was engaged in the daily ritual of his correspondence. A fire crackled in the grate, the first of the autumn. He had seen the mist hovering over the Thames that morning and decided that summer was over.

It had been a poor season for business and the harvests threatened to be as poor as they had been for the past two years. He made a mental note to review his credits for his customers with large farm estates.

The only thing that would redeem the season would have been good news from Genoa. But he had not heard from Monty for many weeks now. His nephew wasn't the most diligent correspondent, true, but even so. The last missive had reported positive progress on the wool sales. Monty had arranged substantial credits from Banco Castello and Banco di Liguria. But since then, nothing. He had sent Monty a letter, care of Signore Cavalli, demanding a further report. That had been four weeks ago, so he should hear back soon.

He half-regretted that he had not travelled with Monty. The boy was inclined to spend too much time in the taverns. And had I gone, I would have been warmer than here in London, he sighed, throwing another log on the fire.

But in Genova, the summer's heat had not yet left, even if the days were now shorter. An enervating blanket seemed to have settled over the city, and the lethargy infected all mercantile affairs. Or so it seemed to Nico. His continued efforts to get Monty's wool released or unwind his merchant purchases were to no avail. In the light of Tasso's pessimistic advice, he was beginning to believe that his business would still be in limbo when the last of his money had run out. Vittorio had assured him that in the end all would be well, but he was increasingly doubtful as to the route to salvation.

The only thing that was measurably growing was his indebtedness. His reserves had dwindled to a few weeks' money. He could no longer expect any further interest payments from Zúñiga - and there was every chance that King Felipe would never repay the loans which had been advanced. He had already paid the costs incurred in the court proceedings to Zúñiga's lawyer – given he had lost the case – otherwise the bailiffs could have seized what little remained of their household effects. And Tasso was asking, deferentially it was true, for at least a down payment on his own fees.

Lisa surprised him by remaining sanguine about their financial state, but as she pointed out, before her marriage she had been used to a life of modest means. The brief year at Casa Castello had been the exception, in her life's experience. When he questioned her, it emerged that she had even pawned some of her jewellery. Though not any of his engagement presents, she stressed. She seemed to be coping remarkably with their much-reduced income, but it did not alter his own feelings: that a way out of their predicament was desperately overdue. And it was for him to navigate it.

They were sat around the supper table in their small *sala* with Sandro one evening when his brother asked, in an offhand tone, if he could go over the bank's ledgers with Nico. The brothers excused themselves from the sala and went into the box room that Nico had adapted for his *studiolo*. Lisa headed for bed.

"I can't imagine what there is to review, Sandro, so little has changed these last weeks after all..."

"Oh, that was just an excuse. I didn't want to talk about it in front of Lisa."

"Ah." Nico sat down.

Sandro took the other chair.

"So then?"

"I've been thinking about your idea of my moving to the Netherlands. And you're right, it's the best thing to do. Probably the only thing."

"I'm glad you agree. The way things are going here, I'm beginning to wonder if I shouldn't go with you." Sensing the irony, Nico laughed.

"So, why *don't* you come? You and Lisa, I mean. It would be better if we were all together, wouldn't it?"

"Yes, but there's Father to think of. And the money for a permanent move has to come from somewhere. Besides, I've got to get those wool trades completed first."

"But you could both join me later. Bring Father too, if he'll come. In the meantime, I can live there very simply. I'll need a little money for the journey of course, but we can stretch to that."

Nico suppressed a smile. The thought that Sandro would find it easy to 'live simply' would have been laughable a few short months ago.

"If you're going to Antwerp, our friends there will have to help you, until you're properly established. I'll write to Huysmans in the morning."

But when Nico thought about the practicalities of Sandro's journey and how his brother would fare in a foreign country, he felt contrasting emotions. On the one hand, it had come very suddenly and now he was faced with the reality that he would not see Sandro for some time. On the other hand, it was energising. At last, there was some action to be taken, rather than passively awaiting their fate. He had his hand on the door handle when a comment from Sandro made him pause.

"Lisa still doesn't know - about me - does she?"

Nico turned around.

"No, I've delayed telling her. There hasn't been the right moment."

Chapter Thirty-Four
BANCO DI SAN GIORGIO: MID-SEPTEMBER

Nico's discussion with Treasurer Saluzzo was not going well. The director of the San Giorgio had accepted, grudgingly it seemed to Nico, that a line had been drawn under the Spanish loan, but he was not going to reverse the bank's prior ruling as regards merchant business.

"But unless I can have the merchandise in the Porta Siberia released to me, I won't have the capital to restart the business."

"I understand that, Signore Castello," said Saluzzo, in that patronising tone of his. "But the most important thing is that you have met your commitments to the merchant sellers. That after all, is the basis of our profession. We stand by our word."

"I had to sell my house and effects to do it," said Nico with some feeling. "But that's done and over with. As regards the wool, I have written to the Merchant Adventurers in London, but there's no response yet. For my part, I have done all I can, but it's a one-sided arrangement if the Bank can't help me."

"I'm afraid that due process must be observed in these cases, hard though it may be on the *cambisto* involved. We have taken advice on the matter and the shareholders have decided that if no-one comes forward to claim the goods on behalf of the Englishman's principals by, say, the Easter Fair then it may be released, under the supervision of the Bank of course. The terms of any onward sale must also be approved by the Bank and a portion of the proceeds lodged here, as surety."

"But the Easter Fair's more than six months away."

"Several shareholders considered even that to be a risk. They were arguing for the August Fair, but I managed to persuade them to be more flexible."

Nico could sense time dripping away and with it his remaining resources. No income coming in, no licence to trade and only the dwindling funds from the house sale to support the family.

"If I travelled to England, I could bring back the necessary documentary evidence?"

"No doubt, although when you consider the likely duration of a return journey and the time spent over there, it may not be that much quicker?"

Nico knew that assessment was right, even if his preference was to act rather than wait upon others to act. But if he wasn't back in funds by the year's end, it would be largely irrelevant anyway. Bankruptcy – and prison - would be unavoidable.

"We recognise," said Saluzzo, as if reading his thoughts, "that your present difficulties arise out of the most regrettable death of the English merchant. The San Giorgio cannot make exceptions, you understand, but we will temper our sanctions in that light. As I say, once the goods have been released after the Easter Fair, and your solvency is assured, you can apply for a renewal of your licence. I am hopeful that reinstatement will follow."

Saluzzo closed the ledger book in front of him with a heavy finality. The interview was over.

LOOKING EAST FROM CARICAMENTO, the red glow of dawn put the four-square profile of the Banco di San Giorgio into sharp silhouette. Sandro stood in the street outside Casa Della Volta pacifying the two horses they had hired, as Luca checked the fastenings on the baggage mules for the fourth time. The front door opened quietly, and Nico and Lisa stepped outside. No need to disturb the neighbours.

Nico had told Lisa something of a half-truth to justify the secrecy: Sandro's departure for Antwerp was justified by the need to find an alternative base for business if things didn't work out in Genova. He hadn't waited for a reply from Jan Huysmans to his letter but, since the merchant was one of Nico's most loyal customers, he would surely make Sandro welcome when he arrived. Sandro's leaving would not be made public for the time being, lest it give the impression that the partners in Banco Castello were contemplating flight from their responsibilities. When bidding farewell to his father, Sandro had been similarly discreet.

He planned to ride northwards and cross the mountain pass into Savoy, escorted by Luca. Once they were through the pass, Luca would turn around and return to Genova. Sandro would descend to the Rhone valley and take a boat northward up that mighty waterway. Reaching its navigable limits, he would continue on horseback, out of France and into the Hapsburg lands. The final leg would be by boat down the Scheldt to his destination. It would be a long, tiresome journey with few comforts on hand.

Anxious to be off before the city awoke, Sandro went to Lisa and opened his arms. When they broke off from their embrace, she pressed something into his hand. It was an image of San Cristoforo on a slim gold chain.

"My father gave it to me when I was little. I should have given it back to him when he left for the other side of the Western Ocean – it might have kept him safe. But now, I am giving it to you, and I pray it will keep you from harm."

Sandro turned to his brother, clasping his shoulders. "I'll do my best to get things going in Antwerp, I swear."

Nico put his hands over his brother's. "We need a solid start, especially if things don't improve here."

Nico glanced across at Luca, who nodded to his master. All was as ready as it could be. He released his brother. "Very well, then. A safe journey."

Sandro put his foot into his stirrup and hauled himself into the saddle. Luca followed suit. With a last look at his native city, Sandro urged his mount forward.

Nico followed his wife back inside the house. As he closed their door, he could hear the shutters being opened in the next-door property. The working day was beginning.

Bianca Bastone passed through the front door of the "Paradiso". She had not been there since the funeral, having put off her return to work as long as possible. Her dream of a different life, as the loving companion – she had never assumed marriage – of her funny, shy Englishman, had shattered with his death. She had some savings, courtesy of the generous clients of the "Paradiso". But sooner or later the bills would have to be paid, she told her bedroom mirror. No doubt Signora Luzzati would be content for her to continue as one of her favoured hostesses for several years. Perhaps even make Bianca her junior partner. Time spent smiling at wayward husbands, laughing at unfunny stories, flattering men of limited talent. But what else was she equipped to do? Playing the lute with the musicians at court, acting in plays and masques. That would scarcely cover her rent. Become the mistress of a well-to-do gentleman? While she was still young and pleasing in looks, she could catch the eye of someone who was willing to keep her in discreet comfort. But would a Genovese man see her in the way that Monterosso had? And how long would such a relationship last anyway?

At the top of the stairs was her friend Adriana.

"Where have you *been*, Merlo? We all missed you." Bianca's blackbird nickname referenced her raven locks.

"I told Signora Luzzati that I was too upset to come in. But I'm fine now," said Bianca, feeling anything but. "Was she angry with me?"

Adriana laughed. "She was furious at first. But I dare say it's worn off by now."

"I had better make my peace with her. Is she in her apartment?"

"Yes, although I think she has someone with her."

Bianca stepped along the corridor. She was about to knock on her employer's door when she realised that it was ajar, and she could hear voices within.

Moving closer, she heard Lina Luzzati speaking. "But I feel *so* uncomfortable. They keep asking me about Signore Montague – what time he left the 'Paradiso' that night, and so on?"

When the visitor replied, Bianca realised she knew his voice. She looked around to check she was not being observed and carried on listening.

BALTHASAR DE ZÚÑIGA dined alone at the ambassador's residence. He faced the unpalatable truth: his mission had been a failure. Genova's bankers were effectively closed for business and there was little prospect of change. Even Grimaldi himself had expressed his regrets but in these conditions, *senor*, further advances were quite impossible. On any terms.

Zúñiga drafted a final missive to Minister Idiáquez. He hoped that Don Juan would read it in a spirit of fairness, but he had no illusions that this would excuse him from responsibility. The personal risk to the Minister, if the Consejo de Finanza was inclined to attribute this failure to his own policy rather than to Zúñiga's implementation of it, was too great. No, however honourably Zúñiga had discharged his duties, the blame would be laid squarely at his feet. His career as an emissary was no doubt over for the present, but he could at least return to his estates and await better times. When the Enterprise was finally launched, he would volunteer to serve with the Marquis de Santa Cruz. Death or glory. That would be the honourable way to redeem his name.

On the following morning, the archbishop gave him an audience. The courtier morosely announced his imminent return to Spain. Sauli was, on most occasions when his sympathy might be called for, a stranger to any feelings for the misfortunes of his fellow men. He resisted the temptation to make an exception for the Spaniard.

But if Zúñiga was headed for oblivion, he himself was headed for Rome, as the Church's newest cardinal. To the heart of things. The Vatican Office had, a few weeks before, confirmed to him that his Eminence had at long last signed the loan agreement with King Felipe. And he, Sauli, was to be Pope Sixtus' agent in administering the papal loan. He would be the pivot around which relations between Rome and Madrid would turn. And much depended on that pivot. The Vatican informed him that not a ducat would be advanced to Felipe until the Spanish set foot on English soil. The secrets that would find their way to *his* desk - it was intoxicating.

He could afford to smile benevolently at his guest.

MORE FROM HABIT than any expectation of a change in his fortunes, Nico found himself walking through Piazza Banchi, with no destination in mind. Even the pretence of some sort of purpose was preferable to moping around the house. Lisa had kept a certain distance from him, following his revelation of the Lercari story. Perhaps she was unwilling to be continuously reminded, by his presence, of the awful accusations made against her beloved Church. He glanced inside the Loggia, where the *cambisti,* were busy at their trade. How he envied their industry!

He was contemplating moving on, perhaps down to the port, when his young page, Lorenzo, ran up to him carrying a note.

"A message was left for you at the Loggia, signore," said Lorenzo slightly out of breath, "One of the other gentlemen had this sent to your house."

The message inside only took moments to read. "Very well, go back home and tell Signora Castello that I have to meet someone here and will be home for supper."

After ten minutes' uphill walk, he caught sight of the tower of San Donato, his destination, breaching the skyline of the old city. More beautiful than the cathedral's bell tower, he had always thought. He was perspiring freely by the time he reached the church. Stepping inside, it was delightfully cool and dark in the nave. Not seeing the author of the message in the pews, he moved down the right-hand aisle. There in the southern apse, below the Madonna's portrait, sat a woman. Her head turned as she heard his approaching footstep.

"Ah, Signore Domenico," Bianca began, "Thank you for coming. I hope you did not mind the message, but I thought it better to meet here than embarrass you a second time in the Piazza Banchi."

Nico smiled, remembering. "Your note was lucky to find me. I don't have a *banca* anymore, and I've moved house as well. We're living on Caricamento, in that row of houses in front of San Luca."

Bianca merely nodded; no doubt too discreet to question the change in his circumstances.

"So, what is it that you must tell me?"

Bianca exhaled deeply. "*Allora,* yesterday, I returned to Signora Luzzati's house for the first time since the funeral. Intending to tell her I was going to leave the "Paradiso" and make a new life, away from Genova. But when I reached her apartment, it turned out she already had a visitor. The door was slightly ajar, so I could hear voices although I couldn't see in. Then I realised she was talking about Signore Montague. I shouldn't have done, but I was so surprised I carried on listening."

"She was saying what, exactly?"

"Oh, that the Doge's Guard were questioning her about the English signore, when he had last been seen at the 'Paradiso' and so on. Her visitor, it was Father Vacchero, was trying to calm her down."

"She was talking to a priest?"

"Oh yes, I recognised his voice, signore. But then, he said something quite strange. That she should say the Englishman left here during the time of the August Fair. When in fact it was *before* the Fair started that I last saw him – as I told you."

"Who is this Father Vacchero?"

"He is a senior cleric at San Lorenzo, close to the archbishop they say. But no-one at the "Paradiso" likes Guido Vacchero, save for Signora Luzzati, perhaps."

"Ah, Guido. I never knew his *family* name," muttered Nico, but almost to himself.

"You know him too?"

"N-yes. Not important. But why was he at the "Paradiso"? Scarcely a place for a priest to be seen, is it?"

She laughed, scorn in her voice. "Oh, he is a regular visitor. He comes to preach to us girls about the wickedness of men's urges. Calls on us to renounce the sins of the flesh. He asks for doles for the poor 'in expiation of our guilt'. But we suspect that in truth, he finds the idea of all that 'sin' going on around him, exciting. We only give him money to be rid of him, so that he isn't around when our clients arrive."

"But if he is so uncharitable towards you all, why would Signora Luzzati admit him to the house?"

"Oh, she has little choice. He's conducting the archbishop's business after all."

"How's that?"

"The archbishop owns the property. Lina Luzzati is his tenant."

"How do you know that?"

"She confided in me once, after too much wine. I've seen Father Guido in her apartment several times. He visits each Friday. To collect the rent no doubt, as well as give the girls a lecture."

Nico didn't respond, digesting the strange news.

"So, I carried on listening at the door," she continued. "Signora Luzzati said it wasn't worth her while to lie. At that point, Father Guido got rather threatening, raised his voice. Said that if she didn't cooperate, he would make things difficult for her. Wouldn't renew the lease. So, after a while, she changed her tone. Said she would do what he asked. Then she changed the subject, talked about something to do with building repairs."

"So then, did you go in?"

"I didn't want to knock. I was fearful they'd suspect I'd been eavesdropping. So, I crept away and spoke to her later in the day." She paused. "But signore, why would it matter to Father Guido what day my Montague left here?"

Nico glanced behind them, to check they were still alone. "I can perhaps guess it, signorina."

"What do you mean?"

Nico hesitated. "No... I could put you in needless danger."

She put her hands together, as if begging for alms. "Trust me, signore, I will *never* betray your confidence."

Well, Nico thought, *I do trust her somehow. And she has confided in me.* "Who else have you talked to about what you overheard?"

"Oh no-one, signore, not even Adriana. Although I would trust her with my life."

"Alright then. But *don't* tell Adriana – or anyone - what I am about to tell *you*." Bianca agreed, swearing to secrecy on her patron saint.

"Well, I believe that this priest ... was somehow involved in Montague's death."

Bianca stared at him.

Nico related a version of Gino Lercari's story, or as much as he felt it safe to tell her.

Bianca was silent for a long while after he was done. "I almost wish I hadn't overheard them," she said finally. "Until now, I had a sort of peace. After what you tell me, I am angry, heartsore, that he should have suffered so."

"At least he isn't suffering anymore."

"But what can I do about it?"

"Do? Bianca, knowing what we know is one thing. In a just world, Father Guido, and whoever else was in with him, would be brought to trial. But I doubt if he ever will. And even then, what magistrate would find him guilty?"

"You're saying I should just...let it be?"

"I'm saying that it would take more than your testimony - and Gino Lercari's - to ever get Guido Vacchero convicted. Much more."

BIANCA GLANCED AROUND HER ROOM, checking if there was anything she had forgotten. The packing cases containing her wardrobe stood by the door, waiting for the *portiere* to take them to the harbour. She had booked passage on a boat heading down the coast to Livorno.

She hoped to find kindred spirits among its canals and piazzas. It was also said there were several English gentlemen in residence there. Not that she expected anyone to replace 'Monterosso' in her affections. Those feelings she had placed in a sealed casket among her dearest memories.

As dusk settled on the street outside, she stood up. Time to go to the "Paradiso" for a last visit: a duty call. She took a deep breath.

NICO REALISED that he was tired. Not in a bodily sense, but a desperate need for a sense of order and proportion in his life. There seemed to be no time just to breathe in and out. After their evening meal, he went with Lisa into the small courtyard behind the house. Sitting on one of the stone benches, they gazed at the stars in the square of sky between their roof and the house behind them. The heavenly bodies seemed to respond to his unvoiced need. We are here in the sky, they said, and we will be here tomorrow. And when you are gone, we will still be here.

They were about to go upstairs for the night when they heard a commotion in the lobby. Nico ran to the bottom of the staircase, to find Luca struggling to restrain a younger man. As they wrestled, he recognised Marcello, the doorkeeper from the 'Paradiso'.

Marcello wriggled out of Luca's grasp and ran towards him. "Per favore, signore," he pleaded, "If you don't come now, we fear she will kill herself. Or someone."

Chapter Thirty-Five
"LE PORTE DI PARADISO": THE SAME DAY

Nico stared at Marcello. "Who will? Bianca?"

"Yes. Adriana says she has a knife."

Luca caught up with the youth and was about to drag him away, but Nico ordered him to stand back.

Catching his breath, Marcello said, "I've never seen her distressed like this. *Please* hurry, Signore."

Nico told Luca to bring his horse, just as Lisa reached the base of the stairs.

"What's happening?"

"I won't be long."

"You're going? Where?"

"There's no time. I'll explain all when I get back," he said to her, while Luca helped him into the saddle.

"Luca, go to the Palazzo Ducale. Bring someone from the Guard Office to the 'Paradiso'. I'll meet you there."

He rode off at a fast pace, leaving Marcello trailing behind him. When he reached the 'Paradiso' several minutes later, the front door was ajar, probably left that way by Marcello in his haste. Inside, all the lamps were alight.

He was halfway down the entrance hall when he heard a loud crash coming from the upper floor. Furniture being upended and then a woman's piercing scream. He ran up the stairs, two at a time. A group of the Paradiso's girls, some half-dressed, emerged onto the landing. They looked terrified.

"Where's Bianca?" he yelled.

One of the girls pointed a trembling hand down the high-ceilinged corridor, to the double doors at the end.

He ran full tilt down the passage. The double doors at the far end were closed but he kept on, bracing his shoulder for the impact. The doors flew open with a screech of splitting wood. He came to a halt in the middle of the room. On his right was Lina Luzzati. Seeing Nico, breathing hard, his doublet half-unbuttoned and his sword unsheathed, she inched backwards.

He dropped the sword point.

"Signora, I mean you no harm."

"Oh, Signore Castello," she said, "Please. She will kill us all."

His eyes followed the direction of her terrified glance. On his left side, was a deep alcove, incorporating a day bed. On it, Father Guido lay sprawled, his left arm raised in defence, fist clenched. There was a gash near his right ear, blood pouring from it. Standing over him, Bianca. In her right hand a dagger, poised to strike again. She seemed not to notice Nico's arrival.

In three strides, Nico was at her side. At the last moment, she realised his intent and tried to fend him off with the dagger. Nico grabbed her wrist with his left hand. She struggled to get free, fighting with unnatural strength. Finding his left arm forced downwards, Nico dropped his sword at his feet, grabbed her wrist with both hands and jerked it backwards. Bianca squealed with pain and the dagger spun out of her grasp onto the floor behind her. Then grabbing both her wrists, he dragged her across to the other side of the room and forced her into a chair. For a few moments she continued resisting, but finally seemed to accept the inevitable and slumped, beaten.

He turned around. Signora Luzzati had fainted during his struggle with Bianca and her ample body was stretched across her day bed. Moments later, her eyes fluttered open, "Where am I?" she wailed softly. Nico ignored her. Keeping one eye on Bianca and another on the priest, he moved swiftly across the room and picked up his sword. He thrust Bianca's dagger into his belt. Breathing out with relief, Father Guido moved to rise from the daybed. But Nico raised the point of his sword a fraction. "I suggest you stay where you are, Father."

He returned to the immobile figure of Bianca.

"What is this, Bianca?"

"The whore tried to kill me," snarled Guido, from across the room. He was holding his neck, trying to stem the flow of blood.

"It's true, Signore Castello," said Signora Luzzati, suddenly recovered, "she was clearly deranged."

Nico looked at the priest. "And why would she want to kill *you*, Father?"

Guido keeping his hand pressed on the wound, said, "She is in the grip of the Devil, no doubt."

Nico could feel the urge rising to strike the priest himself. It was as much as he could do not to accuse Guido of Monty's murder. Then he registered that, behind him, Bianca had started talking, in a low voice. Her eyes were shut. "What are you saying, Bianca?" he asked. But after a moment he realised that she was not talking to him, she was talking to God. "*Pater Noster, qui in caelo es....*"

For several moments, no one else spoke. Then he heard raised voices coming from downstairs. Moments later, a sergeant of the Doge's Guard and a couple of guardsmen entered the room, followed by Luca. Nico, realising the matter was now out of his hands, thanked his patron saint that he had not succumbed to the desire to kill Guido moments before. He sheathed his sword.

The sergeant was a man in his middle years, Nico guessed. Two young guardsmen took up position either side of the doorway. The sergeant, unsure to whom he should first speak, ranged over the room. Bianca had apparently finished her prayer, the eyes were open, but she sat immobile, staring into some imagined distance.

"I am Sergente Spazio. Who can tell me what happened here?" He had a rough, country accent.

Released from his temporary detention, Guido limped across to the sergeant.

"I am Father Guido Vacchero. Look here," he said pointing to his wound, "this whore attacked me. Tried to kill me in fact."

"And can you think," the sergeant asked, looking at Bianca, "why she should take it into her head to attack you?"

"Of course not," said Guido, sounding affronted by the very idea. He slumped back on the bed.

The sergeant turned to Lina Luzzati. "Are you responsible for this girl, signora?"

Luzzati bowed her head in acknowledgment. "This is my house, Sergente. The young girl, tormented soul that she is, worked for me." A momentary pause. "Helping to serve our guests."

The sergeant nodded, apparently aware of what Bianca's services were likely to include.

"But Father Guido is right. She attacked him most violently. Most extraordinary, completely unprovoked."

"And her name, signora?"

Luzzati told him.

The sergeant turned to Nico. "Signore Castello, isn't it?" This said with an ironical tone of regret, as if he was sorry to find the respected Domenico Castello in this building. "And did you witness the assault, signore?"

"No. When I came in, Father Guido was there on the bed. And Signorina Bianca was standing near him, holding this." He handed the weapon to the sergeant.

"And you just happened to arrive at that moment?" The sergeant coughed, conscious that he was straying into potentially delicate territory.

"Exactly. I'm a client here," Nico said, calculating that was easier than explaining his connection with Bianca. "I was along the corridor when I heard screaming, furniture being turned over. I quickly sent my man," he pointed at Luca, "to raise the Guard and I came in here, as I said."

The sergeant turned finally to Bianca, leaning over her chair. "Signorina, can you hear me?"

Bianca was staring into the middle of the room, not looking at the sergeant. She gave a slight nod.

"Very well. You attacked Father Guido. With this dagger. Do you confess?"

Bianca stared at the weapon, as if it were foreign to her. She didn't respond.

The sergeant tried again. "Did you assault the priest? Yes, or no?"

Again, there was silence. It was as if she had just surfaced from sleep. A nightmare probably. Nico willed her not to answer, lest she say anything utterly damning.

But Bianca kept silent. Eventually, Spazio admitted defeat and turned to the assembled company. "I am taking this young woman into the Doge's custody. Given the late hour, I will take formal statements from each of you tomorrow. After that, the Doge's Office will determine the charges to be laid against her."

Nico calculated that any decision about Bianca Bastone's fate would not be taken by this officer, but by higher authority, so there was little point in attempting to influence matters at this moment, and especially not in front of Father Guido. When Nico's statement was taken, he would do what he could to save Bianca's neck. He gave the sergeant his house address and took his leave, collecting Luca on the way out. As he passed the seated Bianca, who was still mute, he touched her lightly on the shoulder.

WHEN NICO GOT BACK to the house, it was two o'clock in the morning, but Lisa was waiting in the sala. She was drowsy, but she shook herself awake and got off the daybed to greet him.

"No need to have stayed up for me," he said as they separated from their embrace.

"I was worried, of course; I didn't understand why you had to go like that."

"Well, I'm back now. Nothing to worry over. Let's get to bed," he said, turning for the stairs.

"But aren't you going to explain it? What am I supposed to think?"

He held his hand up. "You will hear it all, I promise. But not now, Lisa; it's very late and I need sleep. I'll tell you the story in the morning."

THE SUN WAS THROWING its glancing light on his pillow when Nico opened his eyes. Lisa was still in bed beside him but sitting up, fully awake. He could hear Maria downstairs, bustling to get breakfast ready. That could wait: his wife deserved an explanation. He had already decided that Lisa would hear the whole story: the Lercaris, Monty, everything. She would not be happy to hear it, but there was no postponing this any longer.

"Well?" she said. He could hear the doubt in her voice.

"It's a long tale, Lisa. I need to begin a few weeks back. The morning that you and Julia left for Albaro?"

Lisa nodded.

"Later that morning, Sandro and I were down at our *banca*. Business was slow. But we did receive one visitor. A young woman. Bianca Bastone."

"And she is....?"

"A friend of Signore Montague. Or rather, was."

"What do you mean, a friend?"

"An intimate friend, let us say. A courtesan from a house called 'Le Porte di Paradiso'."

Lisa's lips parted in surprise, but she made no comment.

"You remember Monty's funeral?' he continued. "*Allora*, at the interment, there was a woman waiting outside the cemetery. You and Sandro went home in the carriage, and I spoke to her."

"Oh yes, I recall. You never explained how you knew her though." Nico returned her gaze steadily. Those golden eyes.

"Well, this was the same woman, Bianca. She had stayed away from the funeral itself. Just wanted permission to lay some flowers on his grave. It was then that she told me about their relationship. It seems that, despite her station, this Bianca had fallen in love with him."

"But you were saying that before that, she had come to see *you* in the Loggia. Why?"

"Monty had told her I was one of the few people he knew in Genoa more than just as a business acquaintance. She was worried because Monty hadn't been seen, hadn't visited her, for some days. She feared he might be in danger and thought, with my connection, I was the best person to help."

Lisa didn't comment.

"So, Sandro and I, we asked Monty's landlord, Lorenzo Cavalli. The old man said that Monty hadn't slept at the house for nearly two weeks. We made enquiries around the Loggia and at the San Giorgio. No-one had seen or heard of him. Then, on the following day – you were still in Albaro, with Julia – Sandro and I went down to Pre district, as you know."

"That's when you ...found Montague's body."

"After a couple of days, yes. And so, I thought that was it. Monty had been killed by thieves in Pre. We would never catch those responsible, unless someone turned informant."

"But then, a couple of days later," he continued, "Sandro and I were approached by Ferrucio Lercari. Well, eventually he got around to what it was about – his son Gino. You remember that he'd become a novice at San Lorenzo?"

"Yes, but what's that got to do with last night?"

"Bear with me. Gino had told his father a secret, just a few days before Monty's body was found. The boy had heard rumours of a prisoner being held in the cellars of the cathedral - an English merchant."

Lisa frowned. "And Signore Lercari thought that this person could be ...Signore Montague?"

"Well, it would explain why Monty had been missing for so long before we found his body. Admittedly, Gino's story didn't seem at all likely until we heard the next part. It was about a young orphan working at the cathedral, called Fabio. He'd approached Gino in the cloisters."

NICO REACHED for a crumpled sheet of parchment on the table on his side of the bed. He uncovered the small object wrapped in it and put it between them. "This ring," he said quietly. "You might recognise it as the one he wore."

Instinctively, her fingertips went to her lips.

"And" he continued, "if you impress it on something, like so, it makes his initials, M B. Montague Belltower."

Lisa shook her head. "But it can't have been Montague. You found his body miles away down by the Lanterna. Why would he end up there if he was being held in San Lorenzo? If there *was* a prisoner there, it obviously wasn't Montague. Perhaps it was someone who'd stolen his ring?"

"I don't think so. Father Guido suggested to Lercari that Fabio might have been the thief, but that still doesn't explain one thing."

"Which was?"

"The message that Fabio had passed onto Gino Lercari. *'Campanile needs your help'*. Only Montague himself would have known the nickname that Gino had given him. And that it was the *one thing* that would convince him of the truth. Convince him enough to go to his father."

"But Nico, if it was him, there must have been some reason for Montague being a prisoner? What if he wasn't the merchant he appeared to be? If he was an agent of the English queen, bent on, bent on..." She ran out of words.

"On what, exactly? I doubt he was capable of any such dissembling. This man was a gentle giant, if ever there was one. He drank too much, I grant you. A jester, yes. Indiscreet, certainly. But an agent, a conspirator? A man full of treachery? Surely not."

"But did we know the man underneath all that?"

"Let me tell you a story that Gino told me. On *Mary Gale's* voyage to Genoa, there was a great storm. The lad fell from the rigging. Would have drowned. But for the fact that Monty saved his life. Risked his own neck in the raging waters to drag the boy to safety. I remember when I first met Monty, he mentioned a bad storm. But he *never* mentioned that he'd rescued someone. To Gino, this man was a knight in shining armour. Young people aren't so easily deceived by their elders, Lisa. They tend to know a good man when they meet him, it's an instinct."

"Alright, Nico, alright. He was a brave - and modest - man. But obviously something hidden as well. Or else why would this happen?"

"What is that something?" demanded Nico, spreading his hands. "What threat could he pose to the Church, or the Republic? Just one man, a foreigner in a strange city. What was he here to do? Assassinate the archbishop? Or the Doge? No, I give that no credence, Lisa."

"But suppose it *were* true? Not a subtle agent perhaps, but a fierce Protestant, out to avenge himself on our clergy?"

"Ferrucio Lercari suggested that too. But Montague was no zealot. Did he *ever* talk to you about religion?"

"No, but he would hardly parade his beliefs in front of us, would he?"

"Agreed. And, as it turns out, they were well hidden."

Lisa frowned. "What do you mean?"

"Because he's one of us, Lisa. A true Catholic. He comes from a Yorkshire family, in the North of England. Most of them have stayed with our religion rather than accept Queen Elisabetta's dictates."

"Did he tell you this?"

"The last time I saw him, he told me in confidence of his private faith. Something not many of his acquaintances would know, I'll wager. The English Council, they suspect all English Catholics of disloyalty to their Queen. So, he's bound to be discreet about it. He swore me to secrecy. But I suppose I'm discharged from that, now he's dead."

Lisa shook her head but did not respond.

"And anyway, I saw the proof on his body in Sant'Antonio."

"Proof?"

"The crucifix around his neck, the one that his so-called robbers had seen fit not to steal. Along with the rosary in his pocket."

Lisa was clearly struggling to make sense of the story. "But Nico," she said, putting her hand on his chest as she moved closer, "you can't expect me to believe that someone in the clergy had the man *murdered*? For what reason?"

Nico put his hand over hers. "That's just it. *I don't* know why. All I know is, the finger is pointing at *them*. And not just at San Lorenzo in general."

"What do you mean?"

"I told you what happened when Ferrucio Lercari spoke to Father Guido?"

"But that doesn't prove he is involved!"

"Not on its own perhaps, but there is more." He related to her the conversation that Bianca had overheard in Lina Luzzati's apartment.

"And the end result was," he concluded, "that Bianca Bastone decided on a vendetta against Father Guido. She might have succeeded too, if I hadn't stopped her. She was convinced that he'd murdered Monty."

She pulled her hand free. "She may have believed that. But I can't accept it. I *won't*."

There was silence for a while. Instinctively, he reached out for her, but Lisa hugged her knees, making herself into a tight ball on the far side of the bed.

"I'm only telling you what I've discovered, Lisa. I'd rather it *wasn't* true. But wishing it not so, doesn't make it go away. The evidence is there. I didn't share it with you because I expected you to believe it unquestioningly. I'm sharing it with you because, well, because we shouldn't have any secrets between us."

As soon as he said it, he remembered his reticence about Sandro. And, for that matter, that he'd not acknowledged having been a client of the "Paradiso" himself at one time. Some things had to stay secret, perhaps.

After a while Lisa unclasped her knees and lay back against her pillow. He reached for her hand and this time she did not pull back. Eventually she said, "I know you are being honest with me," she said, "but I can't believe that the Father has done such a terrible thing. Montague was a good man, no doubt. An honourable one, too. But he's gone. And we can't be *certain* who killed him. Can't we let him rest in peace?"

Chapter Thirty-Six
PALAZZO DUCALE, GENOA: EARLY SEPTEMBER

Two days later, Nico was in the Office of the Doge's Guard, across the desk from Sergente Spazio. The man was not in a hurry. But then, this was probably the most newsworthy case he had been involved in for many years. You could say it had everything from the sergeant's point of view: a young courtesan, a priest, a voluptuous madam and a formerly wealthy banker. Like one of those fanciful plays put on for a *festa*.

"Can we get on with this, Sergente?"

Spazio did not look up from his paperwork. "All in good time, signore, we have our procedures, you understand."

Nico drummed his fingers on the desk. "Signorina Bastone, is she still in custody?"

Spazio stopped scribbling. "Oh, yes."

"Is it possible to see her?"

The sergeant looked up at Nico. "Impossible, I'm afraid."

"Who is allowed to see her, then?"

"Well, a lawyer, but she has yet to appoint one."

"I could send Avvocato Tasso. He may be willing to represent her."

The sergeant's eyebrows went up a fraction. "It's more a question of what Signorina Bastone herself is willing to do."

Nico inferred that Bianca was still refusing to speak about the incident. Spazio leant forward across the desk, lowering his voice to Nico. "Signore, if you'll permit me to say, I think you're best advised to consider your own position, rather than worry about the young woman."

My own position? What was that? Nico wondered.

Spazio was passed a note by one of the guards. He stood up. "So, if you'll be kind enough to follow me, signore."

He led Nico into the rear office. There, behind another desk was a younger member of the Guard, but one senior in rank to Spazio. He stood up, extending his hand towards a chair.

"Please have a seat, Signore Castello. I am Capitano Merello."

Merello was, Nico estimated, in his early thirties. Heavy-set, but imposing in his uniform. A broad, well-fed face, given definition by his well-trimmed beard. The eyes were steady, not averting his gaze from his visitor.

The captain glanced at the note in front of him, the evidence taken by Spazio at the 'Paradiso' Nico guessed. He asked Nico to repeat his story, if he'd be so kind. The sergeant, seated in the corner of the room, promptly started taking another note.

When Nico concluded, he merely said, "So that's all you can tell us, Signore Castello?" The tone was one of regret.

"Of course, I was only at the scene briefly."

"Didn't it strike you as being strange? That a young woman would assault a defenceless priest. With a deadly weapon?"

"The more I see of this city, the less I am surprised by what goes on in it."

"Signore Castello, you must allow that the circumstances are … far from ordinary? Did you not wonder why Signorina Bastone should have done such a thing?"

"What does she say about it?"

"I have asked her."

Nico couldn't tell from Merello's expression whether he had got no satisfactory answer or, if he had, that he wasn't going to tell Nico about it.

"And Father Guido has no possible explanation?"

"I am still talking to him. And Signora Luzzati."

There was a pause, the only sound in the room being Spazio scratching away with his quill. Nico started to feel frustrated at the time this was all taking. Merello's next question relieved Nico of that feeling.

"Before two nights ago, did you know Bianca Bastone?"

"I had met her once at the 'Paradiso', I recall."

"But no other times?"

Nico thought rapidly. He had talked to Bianca at the Loggia, he realised, where anyone could have seen them.

"Well, now that I think about it, our paths may have crossed once or twice, out in the city. We conversed briefly."

"About what, signore?"

"*About?* What do you mean?"

"I mean it appears that you have *some* sort of relationship with her. One you are understandably keen to dismiss as insignificant. You happen to be in the building when she attacks Father Guido. You say nothing to Sergente Spazio about the fact that the girl was already known to you."

"But Signora Luzzati can support my testimony. That I merely prevented the fight from going any further. Ask her."

"I'm asking *you*. What do you say about your relationship with Bianca Bastone?"

"I've told you. There *is* no relationship."

Nico could scarcely credit how this interview was going. What had the captain been told? Lina Luzzati would hardly have suggested to him that Nico and Bianca were connected. After all, she was aware of Bianca's attachment to Monty and her reaction to his death. And Bianca, well, she was probably still refusing to explain herself. Which left Guido Vacchero. Had he tried to implicate Nico in some way? Or was this all just a wild theory being pursued by the captain?

"I am an innocent bystander. I intervened to stop a fight between a man and a woman. And all I have got for my pains are your insinuations."

He stood up. "I assume I am free to go."

"Of course, signore. Please understand that we are merely trying to establish what happened, how to explain this crime. At present things are far from clear." The smile looked insincere.

When Nico arrived home, Lisa rushed to greet him. After a few moments, she released him from their tense embrace.

"You had been *so* long, Nico. I was about to come to the Palazzo myself when you returned. What was the delay?"

"I can't be sure. The Captain of the Guard is trying to find out why Bianca Bastone attacked Father Guido. Perhaps he wonders if I'm involved in some way."

"Why would he think that?"

"There's no reason. I've asked Avvocato Tasso if he can find out more."

In the intervening days, Nico and Lisa had not spoken again regarding Monty's death and Nico's explanation of it. He sensed his wife was still turning all these facts over in her mind, adding new information, trying to reach her own conclusions. Better that, he told himself, than a futile attempt to persuade her to his point of view.

On the following day, Tasso called on the Castellos. Husband and wife sat together to hear his report.

"This Signorina Bastone is likely to be charged with grievous assault, but it seems that the captain is deferring that decision pending further investigation. I haven't been told what the girl has said. But I assume that she's not talking: if she'd confessed to an attempt on the priest's life, things would be proceeding rather differently."

"What about the testimony of Father Guido? Or Signora Luzzati?" asked Nico.

Tasso opened his palms. "I am not permitted to know the details of any statements. After all, I merely represent you, a witness."

"Would you be willing to represent Signorina Bianca? I don't suppose she has any money to speak of, but I could take responsibility for her fee. I don't have it presently, as you know, but ..."

The lawyer shook his head. "No, it's not the money, signore."

"What then?"

Tasso breathed in and out, slowly. "I don't see your interests and hers as being aligned, let's say. In court, she will no doubt be described to the Examining Magistrates as a reckless and immoral woman. In the presence of witnesses, including I may say yourself, she has attacked an unarmed member of the clergy and threatened to kill him. There's no obvious justification such as self-defence, is there? If she were my client, all I could do would be to make a speech on her behalf, pleading for leniency, suggesting that she was not in clear possession of her mind at the crucial moment, something of that sort."

"But supposing," Nico began slowly, "that there was something else that could be said on Bianca's behalf. Suppose it were to come out that this was her vendetta against the priest?"

Tasso pulled a face. "Revenge? For what?"

"For killing her lover."

The lawyer closed his eyes momentarily. "Signore Domenico, you told me your involvement in this incident was pure happenstance. The wrong place at the right time. Are you now telling me your knowledge of it goes deeper?"

"I'm afraid it does." Nico noticed Tasso's sideways glance at Lisa. "The Signora has heard everything I'm about to tell you, by the way."

Lisa withdrew her hand from Nico's. "But Nico, you can't prove *any* of this. Father Guido may well be innocent. We mustn't slander his name to the lawyer."

Tasso held up his hand, palm outwards. "Do not be concerned, signora. Anything your husband tells me about the case is a confidential client matter. Better that I hear it all, than operate with partial knowledge."

"You may think otherwise when you've heard it."

Tasso, his face impassive, motioned for Nico to proceed.

"Very well. The events of that evening unfolded exactly as I told the Captain of the Guard. I had no prior knowledge that Bianca was planning to assault, much less try and kill, Father Guido. That I was able to stop her that night was pure good fortune, perhaps. But true though that all is, it is not all the truth."

Tasso's eyebrows rose a fraction, but he said nothing.

"*Allora*, to start at the beginning, Bianca Bastone was in love with a foreign merchant, an Englishman. He was a regular client of hers at the 'Paradiso', but the relationship had grown to something deeper, on her side at least, perhaps his as well. This same merchant was also a customer of mine."

"So, you tell me, Signore Leonardo," Nico concluded, "that the law will probably conclude that Bianca is guilty of grievous assault. And that's my fault," he added. "The only reason she's in this position is because of something I told her. Something I knew - but can't prove."

After a few moments pause, Tasso responded.

"Well, I suppose the first question for me to consider is: what legal difference this makes to the case. I'd have to say not a great deal. Or at least, not that's helpful from her point of view."

"The point is," Tasso continued, "if it were believed, it would provide the prosecuting officer with his motive. It would be a perfectly plausible reason for her to want to kill him. The lesser charge of grievous assault would then be replaced with a more serious one. Attempted murder. Of course, it might help in the sense that the court will have sympathy for the accused. But that only goes to the sentence to be imposed on her. It doesn't make her innocent, quite the opposite."

Nico shook his head, wondering how it had got to this. "You're saying she'd be better advised to plead an aberration of the mind, a moment's insanity?"

"Almost certainly. Of course, if you were asked a direct question in court, no doubt you'd have to answer truthfully and reveal what you know. But, if you're not asked...well, you're not obliged to take mere suspicions to Capitano Merello. That would merely deepen your involvement for no benefit to the young woman I can see. And of course, if they *disbelieved* your story - which seems quite likely - what would you have gained? After all, most people would be inclined to doubt that this priest could be guilty." He glanced at Lisa as he spoke.

"So, you're saying that I can do nothing?"

"Well, if you had conclusive proof that Father Guido had the Englishman done away with, we could take that to the Doge's Office."

"Proof? How can I prove his guilt without a witness – or a confession?"

"*Proprio così*. You can't. Whatever this Signorina Bastone says in court will be discounted. She is the accused, after all, so it will be assumed that she will say anything to save herself. I agree that Giovanni Lercari's evidence is disturbing – and there's also that signet ring – but we don't have any witnesses who saw the Englishman being held in the cells below San Lorenzo – much less anyone who saw him being killed. As for Father Guido, if he was guilty, he wouldn't confess it, would he? At least, not to any earthly power."

"So much for the law," said Nico, once Tasso had left the house.

"But he's right, Nico, you have no real proof. You heard his advice. Making these allegations won't benefit anyone, the reverse in fact, you'll make it worse for the Bastone girl. And... for the three of us."

"*Three* of us? What's this to do with Sandro?"

"Nothing, actually. I mean You. And Me." She came and stood

next to him, a serious expression on her face. "And... the baby I'm carrying."

He stood up and took her in his arms. She was shaking. "That's wonderful - how long have you known?" was all he could manage to blurt out.

"A little while. But things have been difficult for us recently, and now there's this case. I put off telling you, but I decided today I couldn't wait any longer. You would start to notice soon, anyway."

"It's marvellous news." They embraced again.

Nico went off to find a bottle to celebrate with. On returning suitably equipped, he opened the shutters of the window facing Caricamento and they looked out over the moonlit harbour, sipping their Barolo.

A small glass of wine – Lisa seldom drank much – loosened her tongue.

"I worry that we were struggling before, Nico, and now there's a child to consider. Will you *please* take the lawyer's advice and leave this story about Montague well alone? Don't entangle yourself with this woman's fate."

Nico bit his lower lip. He could see that in the end, Lisa was right, but the situation irked him, nonetheless.

"I swear to you, Lisa, on my blessed mother's grave, that our child will be my prime concern. All else comes second."

She touched his arm. "Thank you."

"But if I *could* bring Monty's killers to justice without endangering us in any way, I would still do it. You understand that don't you?"

"Yes, I see that. I am not asking you to forgo your honour, Nico. But you must promise me not to put yourself, or us, in harm's way."

"You mean, don't make an enemy of Father Guido?"

Her eyebrows knitted in a frown. "No, I don't mean that. I mean you should think twice, and accept Signore Tasso's counsel, before you make any accusations. And if – which I can't believe – Father Guido is somehow involved in the case, then remember that there must have been a good reason for it. Maybe a reason you can't see, but a reason nonetheless."

Chapter Thirty-Seven
CRIMINAL COURTS, PALAZZO DUCALE:
LATE SEPTEMBER

Two days later, the Doge's Office announced by public proclamation that the trial of Bianca Bastone for her deadly assault on Father Guido would commence in the following week. The fact that a courtesan was the accused, was more than enough to send word flying down the steps of the palazzo and around the city like a demented insect. The revelation that the Bastone girl was, *well, a woman from the 'Paradiso', if you know what I'm referring to, signore,* stoked the anticipation of Genova's citizens. The fact that her intended victim was a priest from the cathedral, and that the scene of the crime was a bordello, just added to the spice. What on earth was one of God's foot soldiers doing in such a house? What was his connection to the accused? By the day of the trial, the queue for public seats stretched all around the courthouse.

The Doge had given Chief Examiner Frugone clear instructions: keep the furore to the minimum. Privately, Doge Ambrogio was not *too* distressed that the scandal had reached all the way to the pulpit of San Lorenzo. Archbishop Sauli needed cutting down to size, in his opinion. Just so long as the Republic did not appear in a bad light.

The restive spectators were finally quieted when the Chief Examiner and the two other justices took their seats behind the *banca*. Below them, was an army of scribes. In the front row sat Capitano Merello, who had assembled the evidence and briefed the Chief Examiner. Along the row from Merello sat Bianca Bastone's counsel, Avvocato Cusani, who had been recommended to her by Avvocato Tasso. Tasso himself was a couple of rows back, sat next to Nico and Lisa. On the other side of the room, flanked by junior members of the San Lorenzo clergy, was Father Guido. He looked distinctly uncomfortable, as though his priest's habit irritated him. But then he always did, Nico recalled.

After what seemed an age, Bianca Bastone was brought into the room. The crowd behind Nico gasped, stunned by her beauty. Exquisitely dressed in an emerald gown, her hair braided and falling down to the nape of her neck, a pearl choker under her chin. Tasso whispered that her advocate would have advised her to look her finest, both to impress the judges and to dispel any suggestion of guilt or remorse that more humble attire might create.

She was directed to a chair on a raised platform to the left of the judges. As she sat down and arranged herself, Nico wondered if she had emerged from that dazed state of mind that had afflicted her on the fateful night. She seemed calmer to his eye but still had an air of otherworldliness about her.

The two charges against the accused, attempted murder and in the alternative, unlawful wounding, were read out by a clerk. Prompted by Capitano Merello, the clerk referred to the items to be presented in evidence. There were not many, but the dagger, its blade glinting in the slanting morning light, drew the biggest response from the crowd.

Lina Luzzati was called as the first witness. As she entered the room, it was obvious that she relished her hour of fame, her moment to shine. An elderly court clerk almost choked on the sight as she floated towards the witness' chair, in a sea of peacock blue silk, with her hair a delicate shade of orange and set off with an array of birds' feathers.

But that was nothing compared to her actual testimony. The prosecutor presumably intended that her function, as first witness, was to establish a clear picture of what had taken place on that fateful night. But Luzzati's testimony was as colourful as her attire. She gave her occupation as the proprietor of the "Paradiso", a fine dining and drinking establishment. When asked by the Chief Examiner, she stated that if any of her girls illicitly offered their favours to her gentlemen customers, it was not something she condoned or took any part in. As regards her relationship with the accused, she portrayed herself as a generous and matronly protector. But Bianca was unappreciative of her care: a monster of ingratitude, from time to time she had accused Signora Luzzati of imagined crimes and indignities. More than once had physically threatened her employer, to the point where she was fearful for her own life, *your worships*. The girl was clearly unbalanced in her opinion.

Finally, the Chief Examiner arrived at the fateful night in question. Asked when, on that evening, she had first seen the accused, Luzzati seized her moment.

"She burst into my private apartment, signori, like a mad woman. Her hair was in complete disarray, her clothes half unbuttoned. She had a wicked expression about her like…"

Frugone sighed. "What were her actual words, signora?"

"Insanity. The ravings of a broken mind. '*You have murdered my lover. The two of you are in it together*' says she. I can assure you, signori, that this wretched girl had no lover. A few gentlemen visitors, perhaps," she added, leering at the spectators. "I tried to reason with her, but then she produced a dagger."

The Examiner had the offending instrument displayed again, which produced another chorus of sighs and exclamations from the spectators. He resumed once the mutterings in the crowd had subsided.

"Is this the cruel blade?"

Lina Luzzati did not even look at it. "That's the one," she cried, as if about to faint.

"Tell us what happened next," Frugone said, his voice rising.

"I thought my hour had come, that I would meet my maker," she crossed herself as she spoke. "Bianca advanced towards me, brandishing the blade. I tried to reason with her, but to no avail. I was helpless, terrified. It was only by sheer good fortune that Father Guido, my loyal confessor, was in my apartment at the same moment."

The Examiner declined to ask *why* Father Guido was there, leaving the impression that Lina Luzzati would have been engaged in her devotions.

She paused in her narrative, to dab her cheek with a lace napkin.

"Continue, signora," pressed the Examiner.

"Well, Father Guido bravely wrestled Bianca away from me. But the demented girl turned on him, lunging out with that *wicked-looking* knife. They struggled, Bianca having the strength of an enraged animal and the good Father being, as you may see, signori, a slightly built person. And of course, unarmed. She stabbed him viciously."

Gasps from the crowd.

"You saw the blade pierce Father Guido's neck?"

"Oh, oh, the blood." Lina Luzzati began to weep into her napkin. The crowd maintained a respectful silence.

Composed again but in a sniffly voice, she said that she couldn't tell whether the wicked girl had stabbed Father Guido more than once, as he tried to fend her off. She claimed she was unsure because precisely at that moment, another gentleman burst into the apartment. Having heard Luzzati's cries for help, no doubt.

"And that would have been Signore Castello, sat *here*?" said the Examiner, pointing at Nico.

Signora Luzzati affirmed it.

"And what happened after Signore Castello arrived?"

Lina Luzzati shook her head, the bird feathers threatening to take flight. "By then I was so distressed. And fearful that the good Father might be mortally wounded. But I seem to recall that Signore Castello threatened Bianca - the accused, I mean – with his own weapon and finally he got the dagger away from her. Then the Guard arrived, and it was all over, thank the Lord."

At this point Frugone thanked the Signora for her testimony and asked her to step down. Lina Luzzati sailed down the aisle in triumph, the tears of a moment before miraculously replaced by smiles towards her audience.

Following her, Sergente Spazio gave his testimony, the circumstance in which he arrested Signorina Bastone. By comparison with the Signora, his evidence was dull, mechanical even. Then, the Examiner took evidence from several of the "Paradiso" girls. As each of them arrived at the witness chair, bedecked in their finery, there was an explosion of cheers and whistles from the public gallery. The girls shamelessly milked the adulation, blowing kisses to the crowd. Red-faced, the Examiner hammered on his *banca* to try and restore order. But the girls' evidence was of limited value, confirming merely that the accused left their company wearing a dagger around her hips, after which they heard an argument taking place in Signora Luzzati's apartment. They recognised Bianca's voice as she screamed accusations and they heard Father Guido shout back, his voice also being familiar to them. Adriana, who was the last girl to be called, started to blurt out that Bianca was not the monster that had been portrayed, and tried to suggest she was the victim of a great wrong, before she was cut short by Frugone.

Then the Examiner announced he would question Father Guido Vacchero. To say the priest was taciturn in his replies, was like saying that King Felipe was Spanish. After the entertainment provided by the previous witnesses, his responses were dull stuff. The crowd started to become restless.

In a flat monotone he confirmed that the dagger produced in court was the same one with which the accused attacked him. He confirmed the extent of his wounds, being one knife stab between neck and shoulder.

"Did you consider, when the deceased turned on you with this dagger, the one the clerk is holding, that she intended your death?" asked the Examiner.

"My life is for the Lord to dispose of as He sees fit. I place no importance on it," came the response. "I tried to wrest the weapon from her but in the struggle, the blade penetrated my shoulder, here." Guido touched his cassock, just above the collar bone.

"Yes, yes, but do you believe she intended to kill you?"

Guido looked hard at Frugone. "I believed my life to be in danger, yes. But Almighty God strengthened my arm with His avenging sword."

The Examiner was apparently satisfied. He decided that further questioning of Father Guido was unnecessary. He briefly consulted with his two colleagues on the *banca* and then announced that there would be one further witness.

Nico sat in the witness chair and looked up at the Examiner. Frugone began by asking Nico to describe the scene upon his entry to Signora Luzzati's apartment.

"And you grabbed the accused's arm? The one holding this dagger?"

"Yes. Then I took the weapon from her."

"And before you took hold of the dagger, where was she pointing it? Poised above Father Guido, as if to strike?"

"I couldn't say her intent."

"Just say where she was pointing it."

"Yes, at his chest."

"What did you do once you had control of the weapon?"

"I put some distance between her and Father Guido. I asked her what had happened. But she didn't seem to hear me. Moments later I heard her uttering the Lord's Prayer."

The Examiner smirked. "Praying for forgiveness, no doubt, for her wicked deed."

Nico shook his head. "Well, I had the impression that she was not really aware...."

The Examiner cut him off. "We don't need your speculation as to her state of mind, Signore. You are excused."

Nico sat down, his feelings torn between relief and anger. Relief given his promise to Lisa, who briefly squeezed his hand, but at the same time anger that there was no prospect of the magistrates pursuing the obvious question why this assault had happened at all.

There was then a recess for midday refreshments, after which Frugone announced that the accused would be questioned. For the gallery, restless after the tedium of unexciting, repetitive witness statements, this was the moment they'd been anticipating. The murmur of conversation died down when Bianca Bastone stood up to give her answers.

"Signorina, you have heard the testimony of the witnesses. It has been stated by several persons that you entered the apartment of Signora Luzzati, bearing the dagger presented in evidence. Then without warning, you attacked Father Guido Vacchero, a defenceless priest, stabbing him in the neck. You were poised to strike again when Signore Castello entered the room and dispossessed you of the weapon." Frugone paused for effect. "So, do you accept or deny the testimony of all these witnesses?"

Bianca did not respond immediately. When she did speak, it seemed to Nico that she was forming her words as she went, unsure where it would lead. "I can do neither. I don't remember it."

"Don't *remember*? Come now, signorina, you cannot recollect the events of that evening at all?"

"I remember leaving my apartment to go to the 'Paradiso', but then I can't remember anything until I was in a cell in Palazzo Ducale."

Nico thought at first that Bianca was answering in the manner advised by her lawyer, but as she continued in this vein, he began to believe that her lapse of memory was genuine.

Frustrated, the Chief Examiner changed tack.

"This dagger," he signalled to a clerk to show it to the court again, "do you recognise it?"

Bianca stared at the weapon, held just ten feet away from her. As if she were looking at a strange animal.

"Yes, it's mine," she said, as though that were a surprise.

"How do you own such a weapon?"

"A client gave it to me."

"A client? You mean, a guest of the 'Paradiso'?"

"He said I should keep it with me, that the streets of Genova were not safe."

Frugone coughed, ignoring the slight on the ability of the justices to maintain public safety. "Did you have it with you on the evening Father Guido was attacked?"

There was no answer. Frugone ordered the priest to stand. "Let the accused see the wound."

Guido loosened the cowl of his habit and pulled the cloak to one side. There was the gash, still angry looking but healing, nonetheless. "Do you deny that you caused this injury. It's time for the truth," asserted the Examiner.

Bianca stared at Guido's neck and collarbone. Again, she didn't answer.

"Why attack this man? What was your reason?"

Her blank stare had changed to a more emotional expression, one which seemed to have pain etched in it. Nico caught sight of her lawyer putting his hands together, praying apparently.

"I don't remember *attacking* him. But now," she added, "I remember that I hate him."

"Hate? How's that?"

"He stole something from me."

"Stole? Stole what, exactly?"

"He stole ...my lover's life."

Before Frugone could ask his next question, Bianca collapsed on the floor in a faint. The gallery went wild, cries from the 'Paradiso' girls, shouts and whistles from the public.

BIANCA REVIVED and the examination resumed. She was asked the reason for her belief that Father Guido had killed someone dear to her. She merely reasserted her accusation. Asked to name her lover, she declined. Forced to describe their relationship, she admitted her lover had been a client of the 'Paradiso'. Asked what evidence she had for such a monstrous charge, she did not reply. At this moment, Lisa squeezed Nico's hand hard enough to make his fingers numb. Pressed further by Frugone, Bianca recounted the overheard conversation between Signora Luzzati and the priest, claiming that eavesdropping as her evidence. But as Bianca told her story, it sounded to Nico barely credible. What possible reason, the Examiner thundered at Bianca, would Signora Luzzati have, for betraying her customer? And why would her confessor be involved? There was no answer from the accused.

The Chief Examiner, accepting that he had extracted all that he could from Bianca, called on her lawyer to present her defence. Avvocato Cusani duly brought forward witnesses, both from the 'Paradiso' and from outside, who all attested to Bianca Bastone's gentle nature and good character. He presented no evidence as to the attack itself but noted that the alleged actions of the accused were so opposite in nature from the person that his witnesses had described, as to invite doubt in any right-thinking person. Cusani acknowledged that the magistrates might conclude that events had unfolded in the way various witnesses had testified. But he invited them to consider the state of mind of the accused on the night in question. The accused herself had no memory of the events, and no-one else could testify as to her intentions.

Cusani acknowledged that the accused had admitted to her animosity to the victim, indeed her belief that he had wronged her dreadfully, but that was not determinative. In the absence of any relevant evidence being brought forward by the prosecutor, he did not propose to speculate whether there was any basis in fact for the accused's beliefs. A vendetta, if that's what it had been, was of course no defence to a criminal charge, he said, his index finger raised. But he put it to their honours on the bench that all the witness testimony, indeed the demeanour and responses of the accused herself, led to one conclusion: that the accused was not, on the night in question, in a state of mind to be responsible for her actions. Her subsequent loss of memory also suggested some affliction of the mind, which remained with her.

Reaching his conclusion, Cusani averred that if the magistrates believed Bianca Bastone to be in full possession of her faculties on that night, they may convict her of deliberate assault and wounding. Whereas if they accepted the defence's assertion that she was not in her right mind, they must acquit and send her to a medical institution like the Pammatone. He sat down, to cheers from the 'Paradiso' girls and most of the crowd in the public gallery.

There was a second recess for the magistrates to consider the evidence and determine their verdict. Nico and Lisa whispered their impressions to each other. She was convinced that Bianca had intended to kill Father Guido but acknowledged the arguments put forward by

Bianca's advocate had been persuasive. Nico doubted that, however elegant Cusani's advocacy, it would count for much with the judges.

Upon resumption, Chief Examiner Frugone announced that each member of the bench would stand to give their individual judgments in turn. The first judge said that attempted murder was a serious matter, and without reliable evidence that the accused intended to kill, such a charge could not, in his view, hold. While he respected the honestly held belief of Father Guido that that was indeed Bianca Bastone's intention, the fact was that the Doge's Guard had failed to produce any other evidence as to the accused's purpose. When he said this, Capitano Merello, sitting in the front row, looked angry. As to the secondary assault charge, the judge said that was a different matter. Clearly there had been an attack and a consequent injury, and Avvocato Cusani, eloquent though he was, could not expect the court to discharge the accused on the supposed grounds that she was not in her right mind at the time. It was also telling, he felt, that Bastone - whatever her state of memory - was not sorry she had inflicted the wound. Guilty of assault and wounding. He sat down, as murmuring spread through the public gallery.

The second judge was briefer. Disagreeing with his colleague, he said that the accused's intent could be discerned by considering evidence of her character. In his view Signora Luzzati's assessment of the accused was to be preferred to that of the shameless trollops who had given evidence subsequently. Moreover, out of her own mouth, the accused had admitted her antipathy towards her victim. That indicated that she had struck Father Guido with malice. The judge believed Father Guido's testimony that he was protecting himself against a deadly assault. Guilty of the primary charge of attempted murder. A louder reaction, some gasps from Bianca's supporters, but here and there, some yells of support for the judge's hard line.

Finally, Chief Examiner Frugone stood up to give his judgment. He exuded the assurance of a man who holds the casting vote over his two colleagues. He said it was clear that the accused had stabbed Father Guido with malicious intent. Given factors such as the type of weapon, where on the body the wound was sustained, the way the accused was prevented from continuing her assault, and her obvious antipathy to her victim, it was hard to conceive what *other* purpose Bianca Bastone could have had, if not to kill. It was the Examiner's view that the charge of attempted murder had been proven.

The crowd in the gallery began shouting after this declaration, until the Examiner summoned the guards to stand next to those responsible, intimidating them into silence. By a majority therefore, he continued, the court had found the accused guilty of the primary charge. The magistrates retired from the courtroom to consider what would be Bianca Bastone's punishment.

After half an hour, which for Nico dragged interminably, the three judges returned to the courtroom. Chief Examiner Frugone announced that they were agreed as to the proper penalty. Ordinarily the punishment for attempted murder would be imprisonment for up to ten years, he said with some relish. The crowd cooed. But in this case, he continued, they had decided to temper mercy with justice. They took account not only of the sex and youth of the accused but also the indications that, whatever her state of mind on the night in question, she was now seriously disturbed. Accordingly, the judges had considered alternative approaches. They had dismissed a sentence of exile from the Republic: hardly a sufficient penalty, and in any case, there was the risk of her reoffending somewhere else. Some form of custodial arrangement would be necessary, where the girl could be properly supervised.

At this point, he paused, having been given a brief note by his clerk. Frugone scanned it quickly and then continued. He was pleased to confirm that a custodial cell could be found for Bastone at the Convent of Santa Maria. For this solution, Frugone expressed his gratitude to Father Guido, whose Christian forbearance towards his attacker was an example to everyone. With confirming nods from his two fellow judges, he declared that Bianca Bastone would therefore be confined in Santa Maria for five years. At the end of that term, she would be interviewed to assess her state of mind and if appropriate, she could be released. He sat down, to a mixture of cheers and yells from the divided audience.

The crowd continued noisily until the three judges left the room, when there was a stampede for the exit. Nico and Lisa waited until the courtroom was thinning out, before making their way out of the building and into the piazza.

"Well, she may have intended to kill," said Lisa, after they had walked for a while in silence, "but I don't envy her being sentenced to a small cell at the convent."

Nico didn't respond. When Bianca's conviction had been confirmed, he had felt the burden of his own guilt. Trusting Bianca with what he knew about Guido Vacchero had led to this. But something else struck him, as they walked home: that Father Guido had hardly been convincing in court as a master conspirator. While there could be little doubt now, that he had been instrumental in the abduction and murder of Monty Belltower, was he the kind of man to initiate such a scheme? It seemed doubtful. That meant that Father Guido was following orders: someone else was pulling the strings that moved this puppet.

There were no indications that anyone outside San Lorenzo had been involved. And above Father Guido there was only one man. The archbishop himself. Was he the puppet-master? Having seen Cardinal Sauli at close hand, Nico told himself that here was a man without scruple. The archbishop's dealings with Sandro alone told him that. If it suited his plans, Sauli was more than capable of putting in motion any criminal action, even murder, provided someone else was the actual perpetrator. Would Father Guido have done what he did without authority from above? Nico knew the answer as soon as he posed the question.

But if Sauli was as much involved in the death of Monty as his priest, that left the question Nico couldn't answer. What was their purpose?

Lisa touched his arm. They were outside their own front door, not that he had realised. He remembered his promise to his expectant wife. Even if he could prove what he suspected – and he knew he could not – for the sake of his new family he would have to leave Monty to sleep unavenged at the cemetery.

Chapter Thirty-Eight

CONVENT OF SANTA MARIA; EARLY OCTOBER

Adriana was escorted by two nuns down the corridors of Santa Maria. The convent was chilly, the nuns' demeanour the same: they were only too aware of her profession. She hated coming here, but she had promised Bianca not to abandon her to a solitary fate. Although incarcerated at the convent by the order of the magistrates, Bianca was permitted a weekly visitor and Adriana was, in truth, her only family.

"Hello, Merlo," she said cheerfully as she entered Bianca's cell. Bianca was barely recognisable as her former bosom companion at the 'Paradiso'. In a plain grey shift from collar to toe, her face devoid of make-up and beneath her headscarf, those tumbling raven locks shorn so that they merely framed her face. The first time she had visited, shortly after the trial, Bianca was listless and melancholy. But on this her third visit, Adriana noticed a spark of hope in her friend's eyes.

They embraced, and after the usual enquiries after health and well-being, sat down close to one another so they could talk *sotto voce*. Adriana was ready to pass on the 'Paradiso' gossip, which usually lightened Bianca's mood. But this time, Bianca had something else on her mind, something she had to impart first.

A young novice, Nicoletta, had been ejected from the convent, she told her visitor. Prior to her disgrace, and as a punishment, she had apparently been taken to San Lorenzo to languish in a cell there for several days. But before being thrown out, she had described her prison experience to a fellow nun. And this nun happened to be one of the sisters assigned to look after Bianca, who passed it on. But the intriguing part, from Bianca's viewpoint, was that this Nicoletta had been put in a cell next to a foreign merchant.

"Really? You don't think he was your Englishman?"

The words spilled out of Bianca. "This novice only saw the man's head and shoulders through the door grille. But he was tall, had to stoop to look through the grille, with a beard and reddish hair. And he said he was English and his name was Montecchio. So, who else can it be?"

"Goodness, what you've been saying all this time, it was true!"

A pained expression crossed Bianca's face. "Did you ever doubt me?"

"I knew you were sincere, but I'll be honest, it seemed so incredible."

There was a pause and neither spoke.

"Very well," said Adriana finally, "it's true, but what can you do about it? And besides, digging this all up won't bring your *amore* back, will it?"

"Yes, but don't you see? It could get me out of this awful place."

"How, exactly?"

Bianca gripped her visitor's upper arms. "You've got to find this Nicoletta and speak to her yourself."

"Alright, I can do that," said Adriana patiently. "But what do we know about her?"

"She comes from a good family. The De Marinis."

"Why was she thrown out of the convent?"

"Oh, the archbishop ordered it: she was accused of sleeping with a novice priest."

Adrian giggled, despite herself. Bianca frowned at her friend. "But it wasn't true. That's what the nun believes anyway - and she knew Nicoletta."

Adrian raised a hand in appeasement. "I will try and speak to her, Blackbird, I promise. But after I've got the story from her own lips, what should I do?"

"Go to Signore Castello. They say he can tell a bird's feathers just by looking at the shell. He'll know what to do."

Lisa heard a commotion at the front door. Soft female voices gave way to Maria's sterner tones, denying the callers whatever was being requested. She went to investigate. There in the lobby were two young women. She recognised one as Adriana, a witness at Bianca Bastone's trial. The other young woman Lisa didn't know. In contrast to Adriana, who was dressed as befitted her scandalous profession, her companion was plainly attired.

"Signora, I explained that you were not receiving visitors," said Maria, her voice still raised, "but the... signorinas want to speak to Signore Castello. Shall I fetch Luca? Make them leave?"

Lisa shook her head. In days past, she wouldn't have expected to be in the same room as Adriana, but with all that had happened in recent weeks, the old certainties seemed to have evaporated. "That won't be necessary, Maria."

She turned to Adriana. "But you must be brief. My husband is very busy."

"Signora Castello, my apologies for the intrusion. I would not have troubled you, but...well it was important." She tailed off.

"And you are, signorina?" Lisa said to the other girl.

"Nicoletta De Marini, signora," the young girl said, making a deep curtsey. Her manner was that of a gentlewoman. The De Marinis were an ancient family, Lisa knew, as distinguished perhaps as the Della Voltas. She wondered what such a person was doing in the company of Adriana.

"Very well then." The two women were shown into the *sala*. "I will bring him to you, but no more than a few minutes, mind."

She fetched Nico from his *studiolo*. In truth, there was very little paperwork to do currently, but these days he often retreated there. Once introductions were made, Lisa sat next to her husband on the cushioned bench and the two visitors were offered chairs. Adriana apologised again for the intrusion. Nico spread his hands in enquiry.

"Well, I should explain that Signorina Nicoletta here," began Adriana, "is a former resident of Santa Maria."

"You are a nun?" Nico asked the young stranger.

Until that moment he had not paid her much attention, largely focussing on Adriana, the person he knew. Despite the way she was wearing her hair, under a scarf, and her plain dress, this girl had a serene sort of beauty.

Nicoletta's smile in response was tinged with sadness. "A novice, Signore Castello. Or rather, I was."

"You'll remember, signore," interjected Adriana, "that Santa Maria is where my friend Bianca Bastone is presently confined. After the trial."

"Yes, I realise. But your purpose in coming to me....?" Nico asked.

"Perhaps I can let Nicoletta tell the story?" asked Adriana.

Nicoletta cleared her throat. "Well, it was my father's choice that I should become a nun, but I took my vows seriously."

Despite her youth, Nico could see the underlying assurance in the way she addressed him, her gaze steady and unaffected.

"However," she continued, "rumours started circulating at San Lorenzo. It was said that I and another nun had broken our vows of chastity with a young man, a novice at the cathedral."

"And that wasn't true?"

"Not true at all," she replied firmly, "never. Oh, he was good-looking, perhaps, but I'd only seen him from afar in San Lorenzo. No conversation had even taken place, although I noticed that he was... looking at me across the Choir. I went to the abbess to get her advice. I acknowledged I felt a certain attraction and asked her help to quell those feelings. She gave me a lecture about entrapping young males – and a scourge to use on myself."

Nico smiled grimly.

"This novice, his name, if I can ask?" he said.

"It was a lad from the Lercari family, Giovanni Lercari."

Nico sensed Lisa shooting him a sideways glance.

"Well, it seemed that this Lercari was a braggart. I was told he had boasted to the other novices that he'd had intimacy with me and Sister Angelica. Together." She blushed deeply.

"It wasn't true, of course, but it was believed. The story got to the archbishop, and he ordered that I be taken from the convent to San Lorenzo. I was locked in a filthy cell under the cloisters for several days with just bread and water."

Lisa shook her head but said nothing.

Nicoletta continued, "My only visitors were the gaoler, a brute with an eyepatch, and a young scrap of a boy, who did all his fetching and carrying."

She took a deep breath. "But mine wasn't the only cell down there. There were probably a number, but I could only see the doors of two cells on either side of mine - through the barred window in my door. One of them was empty...."

"And the other one became occupied?" urged Nico, anticipating the conclusion.

"After two days perhaps, I'm not exactly sure, I heard the guards bringing someone into the next cell. It was dark - they were bearing torches. The door slammed, they left, and it was quiet. An hour or two later, a man started yelling for help. From that cell. Eventually, he came to his cell door. We started communicating, this 'neighbour' and me. When the gaoler wasn't in earshot, of course. I thought he might be a member of San Lorenzo's clergy, being chastised. But it turned out – conversing was difficult, but he spoke a little Italian and some French – that he was a merchant, an Englishman, no less. He had no idea why he was being held there."

"And this man...he told you his name?"

"He said his given name was Montecchio. I forget, though, how he said it in English."

"Montague," Nico said. He glimpsed Lisa shutting her eyes, momentarily. "And then you were released?"

"Yes. I was taken back to Santa Maria. At first, I thought the affair was over until the Abbess said I could no longer be a nun, in view of my sin. I protested my innocence, but she said I had confessed, at San Lorenzo. I don't remember, but it's possible I might have said it, to put an end to..." Nicoletta didn't finish the sentence.

"And what happened then?"

"Well, on the next day, I was thrown out with my few possessions and sent home in disgrace. My father has hardly spoken to me since. And then Adriana came to the house and asked to see me. Father was out - I'm not sure he would have let me meet Adriana – and I had little to occupy me, so I spoke with her. She told me how she had heard that this Montecchio had been held inside San Lorenzo and afterward killed. And that her friend, Bianca, had been enamoured of this Englishman. She pleaded for my help, wanting to know if I could confirm the story. Which of course, I did. I'm not sure what it signifies, though."

"I think it signifies that Giovanni Lercari is a truthful young man," responded Nico, glancing at his wife. "But thank you for bringing your story to me. I'm sure that you'd rather not have re-lived it."

Nico turned to her companion. "And so, Adriana, what is it you want from me?"

"Signore, hopefully you can see that this young gentlewoman has been grossly wronged, just as Bianca has been. I do not know what is to be done about it, but Bianca felt that the information about poor Signore Montecchio could be as important to you as it is to her. She said you would know what best to do. Please counsel us."

"Did you tell Signora Luzzati about this?"

Adriana's face darkened. "I am no longer with the Signora. The 'Paradiso' is in the past. I have left that life behind me forever. And after all the things that she said about Bianca, things that were quite untrue, I don't want to speak to her again." Nicoletta, by her expression, appeared to understand what Adriana was talking about. She had the decency to blush again.

He leant back against the cushion, saying nothing for a moment. Nicoletta's story was of course vital evidence. While claims would doubtless be made in some quarters as to her character - that she was not as innocent as she claimed – she was surely being truthful. But he recalled his promise to Lisa, not to further embroil the family in a deadly feud with the Church. He tapped the arm of the bench.

"Well, this is an important story, one that the Guard should know of, *certamente*. But I am probably not the best person to take it to them."

Adriana's face showed her disappointment.

"Right now, signorina, my position in the city is," he opened his palms, "well, a shadow of what it once was."

"Then you cannot help us?"

"I did not say that, just that I am not the right mouthpiece. Is there not someone in your family who could stand up with you at Palazzo Ducale?"

Nicoletta shook her head. "My father still credits the story about that novice."

"He'd rather believe the word of a stranger over that of his own daughter?" Nico said. "In that case, I suspect there's only one thing to be done."

FERRUCIO LERCARI FIDGETED in his chair as though there was something on the seat underneath him.

"Didn't you question Gino about these allegations?" Nico asked.

"Well, not immediately. Father Guido promised me he would not make a public example of the lad. He was willing to keep him on as a novice despite the accusations, for which I was grateful – at the time. I didn't see Gino for a while after that, because he was confined to San Lorenzo. When I finally saw him, he said he'd merely been speaking with another novice, one youth to another, about one of the novice nuns. Innocent stuff: that she was very attractive, a shame such a beauty would become a nun, that sort of thing. But this novice didn't keep it to himself, it got passed on and with each telling it got elaborated. By the time it got to Father Guido, the story was that Gino had been in her bed, that they'd been spied… fornicating."

Nico briefly wondered if the source of the invented story was Paolo Brozzi. But in the grand scheme of things, that wasn't so important. "And then?" he asked.

"Well, then the whole thing seemed to blow over, Gino carried on at San Lorenzo, so I suppose I thought no more about it."

"It didn't exactly blow over for one of the nuns involved."

"How so?"

Nico related Nicoletta's story. Lercari looked chastened by the time Nico had finished.

"It never occurred to me that anything like that would happen to her," he pleaded. "After all, if Father Guido had been disposed to be tolerant as far as Gino was concerned, why would a novice nun be punished?"

"Looking at it another way, why do you think that Father Guido was lenient towards Gino, if he believed the accusation to be true? Doesn't seem to be in his character."

Lercari's face coloured. "Well, now that I think about it, he and I were talking about the bank's loan to Senor Zúñiga, the Spanish envoy. I suppose he was suggesting that if I could soften the bank's terms a little, that would be greatly appreciated at San Lorenzo. It wasn't exactly explicit, you understand…."

Nico understood. There was a brief silence.

"Look, Ferrucio," said Nico, "he's your son so it's not for me to say, but perhaps Gino could see his way to telling the truth about what really happened. To Nicoletta De Marini's father. After all, she's been ejected from the convent, and her father probably still thinks of her as sinful. All for something she didn't do. Once her father has been persuaded otherwise, he might be willing to present her testimony about Montague to the Guard?"

Lercari touched his temple with an index finger. The man was working himself up to doing the right thing.

INITIALLY, Gino was pleased that his father had brought him back to Genova after being up at the family farm for over a month. But then his father told him the purpose behind his return, which quickly tempered his happiness.

The De Marini family had their grand residence not far from the waterfront, behind the Banco di San Giorgio. It was an easy walk along Luccoli and then Soziglia, but to Gino it felt like torture. Initially he had resisted going, saying it would bring shame on him and what good would it serve anyway? But Ferrucio Lercari was unmoved. Gino's idle gossip had

helped to place Nicoletta De Marini at odds with her family. He had an obligation, at the very least, to protect her reputation. An obligation he must face up to like a man. Accepted it was not him who had told those wicked lies about her, but his loose tongue had triggered their invention. How would he feel if she were cut off by her father without a lira?

Gino was scared – his father could tell – but he could raise no plausible case for shirking this embarrassment.

"Suppose her father demands his revenge? How would I defend myself?"

Lercari raised his hand to his son's shoulder. "I will be there with you. To see that this is carried off in a seemly manner. Between gentlemen. Just tell the truth."

Lercari wondered privately if De Marini would explode with anger on seeing the boy. He would be entitled, for sure. Had it been his daughter.... well, he would have done. But he had spoken privately to the man, the day beforehand, to prepare the ground.

They reached the De Marini residence. Lercari rapped the knocker firmly, which prompted Gino into holding himself stiff and erect. A servant opened the door to admit them.

GINO WAS BROUGHT in to tell his story.

Andrea De Marini, patrician to his fingertips, sat in the elegant surroundings of his *sala* and surveyed the forlorn young man standing in front of him. Gino kept his eyes on the marble floor beneath his feet. Ferrucio sat on the opposite side of the fireplace from De Marini observing the engagement.

De Marini's voice was stern. "Your father tells me that you have something to say to me. So, speak, you have the floor."

Gino laboured through his admission. He ended with an apology which, though heartfelt, was scarcely eloquent. Lercari suspected that style was as important to their host as substance.

"This is a serious matter, young man. You have allowed the honour of my daughter to be traduced. She has lost her place in the novitiate, suffered undeserved indignities. And all because of your loose tongue – and even looser morals."

Lercari winced inwardly at their host's last remark. An observation which implied poor parenting. But he kept his peace, knowing there was some truth in the implication.

Gino kept his eyes downwards.

"By rights, I ought to have you whipped in Piazza Banchi, in front of the whole city."

At this, Gino recovered his spirit and started to defend himself. "But I never did or even said anything to dishonour her name. That was all invented by others. All I ever said was that your daughter was a beautiful young woman and that it was a shame …that she was to become a nun."

De Marini seemed to choke but recovered his poise.

"Look at me, young man. You're telling me that you've never touched my daughter?"

"Sir, I've only ever seen her across the Choir in San Lorenzo. I've never even spoken to her. I would have liked the chance to do so, but…"

Lercari raised his eyes heavenwards.

"Why would someone else claim that you had? That you'd done far more than just talk to her, in fact?"

Gino hesitated.

"Why are you the one in trouble, rather than these fabricators?"

"I don't know exactly, sir, all I can say is that their story, false though it is, was believed in preference to mine. Some people prefer to believe the worst of others."

"You're talking about members of the clergy!"

"I can't account for it, but more than one novice has been treated harshly for things they didn't do. Just, if I may say so, like your daughter."

"You may not. That's no business of yours." De Marini took a deep breath. "Now, go and wait in the lobby. Your father and I will decide what is to be done about you." He spoke as if he were talking about a lame horse.

When Gino was out of earshot, Lercari reiterated his plea. "Andrea, please believe my son. He may be unsuited for the clergy, but underneath he is honourable. He doesn't lie, I assure you."

De Marini put his hands together. "Well, Ferrucio, I find that I believe your boy's story. I had a lengthy talk with my daughter last night, after your visit. She has sworn to me, on her blessed mother's grave," he looked up at the portrait of an elegant matron hanging above the fireplace, "that she is pure. Originally, I had assumed that what was being said at San Lorenzo was nothing less than the truth. But now I'm convinced it's my daughter that's being truthful. And your son."

"A relief to you, I'm sure."

"You'll forgive me if I questioned Giovanni severely, but I wanted to hear it from his lips. So, it seems that all your lad is guilty of, is a loose tongue when discussing the fair sex. And perhaps, a tendency to trust others when he should be more cautious."

"These young people, Andrea, they don't have our discretion," suggested Lercari.

"Indeed. But the thing which exercises my mind is, why the clergy would not only believe idle gossip, but act on it. Punish my daughter without proper process?"

"I agree, that is disturbing, but I don't have any explanation. I wasn't happy either, I mean, with the way my son was treated at San Lorenzo. It appears there are a few rotten apples in that barrel. I expect you've also heard about the investigation by the Ducal Guard into the death of some foreign merchant. They say that even one of the priests there was caught up in it."

Lercari was saying far less than he knew, but he calculated that there was no benefit and some risk in embroiling De Marini in the bigger story.

"Yes, news of that has come to my ears. What a stain on our church!" De Marini stood up. "Well, signore, let us go and put your boy out of his misery."

They walked out to the lobby. Gino was standing at the base of the staircase and looking upwards with a soulful expression. From the gallery above, a young woman was looking down at him, coolly, but with a hint of a smile

"Hmm. Seems we're too late for that, Ferrucio," muttered De Marini under his breath.

Chapter Thirty-Nine
CASA DELLA VOLTA, CARICAMENTO: MID-
OCTOBER

Nico sat in their *sala,* reviewing his financial position. It did not take long. He had already reduced their household spending to the minimum. Any credit the Castello name could buy with local tradesmen had long since expired. He had retained only old Maria, Luca and the boy Lorenzo to make up the household. On a couple of occasions Nico had suggested to Luca that he look for other employment – after all, he wasn't currently able to pay him - but Luca had stoutly refused.

The problem, simple enough to state, was that his capital had shrunk to nothing, and no income was coming in. His father's small savings wouldn't cover even their present modest obligations for more than a few months and in any case, he was too proud to ask. Ferrucio Lercari had generously made him a small loan, one *cambisto* to another, but it was unthinkable to ask him for more help. And in under six months from now there would be another mouth to feed.

He couldn't understand why there was still no word from London, until he calculated that for his couriered letter to reach Thomas Sutton, for the Merchant Adventurers to address his request for documentation and for their response to get back to him in Genova, would take eight weeks at the least. Probably more. It had been two months since Monty's body had been discovered, so perhaps something would be heard soon. Or so he assured Lisa, but without much conviction. In truth, he was merely doing so to lighten her mood: the early weeks of her pregnancy were proving difficult, and she was often confined to bed.

They had not spoken much about the trial since the day itself: the subject of Father Guido was, in any case, out of bounds so far as his wife was concerned. But that did not stop the feeling gnawing away at him, the realisation that the court case had done nothing to reveal the true events of that summer: it had merely buried them.

FERRUCIO LERCARI WAS THINKING of sending his son back to the safety of his estate up in the hills. But when he recalled Gino's having run away to sea and then his long months as a persecuted novice at San Lorenzo, Lercari felt a rush of paternal sentiment.

Surely, he told himself, I can ensure that Gino is protected when going about in the city. In any case, with the Bastone trial now past and gone, and no sign of any investigation being launched against Father Guido, the position is much safer than it was.

But as it turned out, Gino was just as restless in Genova as he had been in the country. Lercari mentioned his predicament to Nico who, conscious that he was indebted to Lercari, felt an obligation to listen sympathetically – and if possible, assist him.

"He just doesn't seem to settle on anything. It reminds me of the weeks before he ran away to sea. I'm trying to teach him about business, but I wonder if he'll ever have the patience to learn it."

"Well, if you were willing, I could give the lad some coaching. You know, sometimes young men take instructions easier from an outsider than from their parents," suggested Nico.

And so, it was agreed. For both master and pupil, the arrangement seemed to be beneficial. Remembering his own father's impatience at Nico's limited aptitude as a silversmith, Nico taught Gino how he might become a *cambisto*, not by rote instruction on things like the rules of the business, the use of the abacus or accounting arithmetic, as by explaining real examples from past transactions. Conscious that the lad found it wearying to be sat still and indoors for any length of time, they walked through the Merchants' Loggia in Piazza Banchi and down to Porta Siberia, as Nico described the trading activity that was going on all around them.

As for Gino, once you engaged his curiosity, he was an apt pupil.

Not one to be sat down with a page of numbers, but if you discoursed on how an astute merchant would set his prices, what unexpected setbacks might throw him off course, then the boy began asking questions, tentatively at first, but as he became more confident, in a torrent.

After a couple of weeks, Lercari Senior noticed the change in his son's mood. He mentioned it Nico, who already knew he had succeeded in igniting Gino's interest. Nico reflected that, while he could not yet repay Lercari for the credit he'd provided, this at least was some form of down-payment.

Gino did not walk alone to attend these lessons. Ferrucio Lercari, if he did not accompany the lad himself, would send a manservant along and, on the return journey, Nico would return his charge to Casa Lercari in time for supper.

The days were growing shorter, and the evenings were noticeably cooler. The sun had just sunk over the western hills when Nico and Gino left the house on Caricamento one evening and turned eastward. By the time they had passed the north flank of Saint Mary of the Vine and entered Piazza Soziglia, lamps were being lit outside the tradesmen's workshops. A low mist wafted into the city from the harbour and smothered the light even more. They turned left into Vicolo Macelli. Casa Lercari stood at the far end of Via Luccoli, close to the fountain, but this alleyway was a shorter route which cut off the corner. It was maybe two hundred paces along the winding alley, crossing one deserted side street after another. Vicolo Macelli was well-lit at either end but half-way along it, the lamps were few and far between.

Gino must have noticed Nico pulling his cloak tighter around his shoulders.

"We're nearly there, Signore Domenico, just fifty yards. Why don't you head back for Caricamento?"

Nico shook his head. "No, I said to your father I would see you home."

The firmness in Nico's voice was somewhat offset by his tripping over a loose flagstone in the semi-dark at the same moment. The dewfall was making the pavement slippery.

"Please don't trouble yourself," said Gino, striding ahead at pace.

The confidence of youth, Nico mused, remembering his own adventurous spirit at Gino's age. He looked along Macelli, but Gino must have turned south, along a small *caruggio* towards Via Luccoli.

He could hear fading footsteps from that direction. Spotting the entrance to a footpath on the right-hand side, he jogged down it. He had gone perhaps fifteen paces when he caught the sound of low voices and then, unmistakably, a shout from Gino. He realised it was coming not from ahead of him, but from an adjacent alley to his left. He had taken the wrong path.

Doubling back to Caruggio Macelli, he ran around the corner and down the parallel alleyway. This wasn't familiar, but Nico's instinct told him it was right. Hearing a scuffle ahead he broke into a run, yelling out as he went, "Gino, we're right behind you." He prayed it was enough to unsettle whoever was there.

Coming around a dogleg in the alley, he made out two silhouettes: Gino was one, low to the ground with an arm raised to fend off his attacker. The other figure stood over him, heavy-set, a weapon in his right hand. Seeing Nico, Gino yelled out to him. There was no time to draw his sword, so Nico flung himself at the standing man, full tilt. They crashed onto the paving slabs with Nico on top, his weight and speed winding the man. His blade clattered onto the ground and slid away from him. The man tried to rise and throw Nico off him. As his head rose, Nico made a fist and punched with all his strength into the man's temple. The man's head banged into the ground inches below. He was stunned, immobile. Rising to his haunches, Nico stretched out an arm to Gino, to help him to his feet.

The sound of steel gliding from a scabbard caused Nico to glance to his right. A tall, hooded figure was coming straight at him, from the doorway behind Gino. The tip of the attacker's blade slid past his left shoulder, slicing through his doublet, and clanged on the low stonework at Nico's back. Nico felt a sharp pain in his left shoulder. Twisting to put all his weight behind his right arm, Nico grabbed the man's wrist and forced him to release his weapon. Catching his underweight opponent slightly off balance, he grabbed him around the neck with his right arm and locked him in a hold, punching him with his left at the same time. The man kicked out furiously, but into thin air. Nico kept his grip tight until he gave up the struggle. Rolling the man onto his left side, he released his arm and sprang to his feet, drawing his sword in the same movement. He stood over his attacker and pointed his blade at the man's throat. With a deft stroke of the tip, Nico pushed back the man's hood. The face revealed was that of a youth, hollow-cheeked with spiky, straw-coloured hair.

To his left, Nico heard the other thug stir from the ground. He readied himself to repel another attack, but the man had apparently had enough and slunk away down the alley towards Via Luccoli. Nico thought he had seen an eyepatch strapped across the man's face, but it was too dark to be certain.

Gino was on his feet now but breathing hard. "Are you hurt?" Nico asked.

"No, they knocked me about a bit - but you got there just in time. Are you alright?" he added looking at Nico's ripped doublet.

"I'm fine," he said. But as he sheathed his sword, a sharp pain came from his left collarbone. He felt inside his doublet. His shirt was wet, and when he removed his hand, his fingertips were bloody. "Well, one scratch perhaps."

He looked down at the youth beneath their feet. "Any notion who this rogue is?" he asked.

Gino stared down at the sullen face. "That's my fellow novice, Paolo Brozzi."

THEY LED BROZZI, each holding an arm, the short distance to Casa Lercari. As they walked, Nico kept alert for the possibility that Brozzi's accomplice might spring out from the shadows at any moment. But he had obviously not stayed around for a second bout.

"What on earth has happened?" said Ferrucio Lercari when they were admitted to the house. "And who is this?"

Giovanni told his father, producing Brozzi's weapon which he'd collected from the alleyway.

"You cur!" Lercari yelled at their attacker, still pinioned between Nico and Giovanni. He struck the youth in the face and would have carried on beating him, but Nico intervened to hold him back. He yelled in Lercari's ear, "Steady, Ferro. Is there somewhere we can put him?"

Lercari ceased struggling with Nico and relaxed his arms. Took a deep breath. "Follow me," he said grimly. They descended to the cellars of the house and there, between the dry goods and wine casks, Brozzi was deposited, roped to a heavy bench. Lercari clearly enjoyed making the rope fast.

"There," he said aloud, so the youth could hear, "he can rot for a while."

Brozzi's eyes narrowed, but he said nothing.

"What do you think should we do, Nico?" Lercari asked, when they and Gino were back in the *sala*.

"I say - try and get the truth out of Brozzi if we can. He has no personal reason to attack Gino – or me – so what was his purpose? We should hand him over to the Guard, of course, but they'll treat it as a simple attempted robbery or something of that kind. First, I'd like to find out what he can tell us about Signore Montague."

"After all," Nico added after a pause, "we surely know that a certain priest at San Lorenzo must be behind all this. Don't we?"

"Was it Father Guido with him?" asked Lercari.

"No, the man was heavily built. Probably just a hired bully. What do you think, Gino?"

"No, Signore, it wasn't the Father. The man who attacked me had an eyepatch and I remember now that Fabio - the boy who worked at San Lorenzo – described such a man to me."

"That was the gaoler who had charge of Signore Montague, yes? Well, perhaps Brozzi will tell us."

"Shall we wait until the morning? A night chained in a cellar might loosen his tongue," said Lercari senior. Besides, it's getting late," Lercari added, "your wife will be wondering where you have got to." He laid a hand on Nico's shoulder, making him wince. "You should get that bandaged, Nico."

"Yes. Until morning then."

"And what have you to say to Signore Domenico, Gino?"

"Thank you, signore, for…"

Nico held up his hand, feeling suddenly tired. "No need, Gino, no need. But next time, let's keep to the main streets."

FERRUCIO LERCARI WAS RIGHT. Lisa was pacing around the *sala*, waiting for his return. The half hour that Nico had anticipated when he'd left for Casa Lercari had turned into nearly three. She ran to embrace him.

Suddenly, she withdrew her hand from his shoulder. "Dear God, you're injured!" she said, seeing the blood on her right palm. She called out to Maria to bring water, towels and alcohol. Helping him off with his doublet, she saw the blood-soaked shirt. That, she removed more gingerly and then dabbed alcohol around the wound. All the while

Nico was telling her not to make such a fuss. But he drank a full tumbler of Malvasia to dull the pain.

For a while husband and wife affectionately berated one another, Maria brought needles and silk thread, realising that it would need a stitch or three. Finally, Nico was bandaged up from neck to armpit and they could all pause for breath. He took another gulp of wine: the rest of the bottle went into his glass.

"You were attacked on the way back with Gino? How did that happen?"

He told her. Her eyes grew wider.

"This novice, Brozzi? And the other man. They were trying... to *kill* you?" was all she could manage. She stole a mouthful of wine from his glass.

"Yes. But probably because I was in the way. I'm sure their real target was Gino."

"But why, he's just a...." But she paused mid-sentence, sensing the likely answer.

"A lad, yes. But remember, Gino knew about Signore Montague being imprisoned at San Lorenzo. And Brozzi knew that he knew. That's dangerous knowledge. Dangerous to the people who get Brozzi to do their bidding."

"And dangerous for us too, Nico."

"I haven't forgotten that, Lisa. Look, I'm not going around accusing the clergy of wickedness. But if the evidence were presented to the Doge's men, it's up to him what he does with it."

Lisa shut her eyes, a slight shake of the head.

Nico picked up his empty wine glass and examined the lack of contents. "Well, I need another drink." He went off to fetch it.

"And tomorrow," he said on his return, "we'll find out what else Paolo Brozzi knows."

BUT INITIALLY, Brozzi maintained his defiance the following morning. After an hour of getting next to nothing out of him, the two bankers conferred in Lercari's sala.

"Where's Gino today?" asked Nico, as they sat down.

"Sleeping it off. Nursing his bruises. I've decided to send him back to the country once Master Brozzi is off our hands. I'll tell him it's for a few days' recuperation, but in truth I was wrong to bring him back, he's safer there. But I should have asked - how's the shoulder?"

"Sore. But if we can get Brozzi to talk, the pain will disappear."

"He's been stubborn so far."

"He believes that Father Guido can protect him. If we show him otherwise, we can get him to talk."

"Agreed," said Lercari, nodding. He slammed his large fist into the palm of his other hand. "I'll get the truth out of him. Make him more afraid of *us* than he is of Guido Vacchero."

"Yes and no," countered Nico, "Surely, we need to convince him that he'll be *safer* on our side than theirs. Then he'll cooperate."

"How would we do that?"

"By telling him that the Doge's Court will treat him leniently - *if* he provides us with information that leads us to the real culprits."

"But Nico, we can't make good on such a promise! Only the magistrates have that discretion."

"Maybe. But let's face it, he's not that bright. I'll tell him I've spoken to the Doge already. Make it clear that we have some influence there. He knows that his assault on us last night is enough to get him arrested – and incarcerated, on its own. So, what has he to lose? Nothing, provided he believes there's the *chance* of leniency."

Lercari's broad face creased into a smile. "I often wondered how you became a successful *cambisto*."

"Was, Ferro, was."

The smile faded a little. "Let's say that the Doge was willing to let Brozzi off lightly in exchange for information: wouldn't Brozzi be afraid of what Father Guido might do to him?"

"Not if the priest is apprehended quickly."

NICO DID THE TALKING. Lercari sat on the other side of the cellar, saying nothing but staring at Brozzi. And jangling the cellar keys in his hand as if to intimidate him. A night in the cellar had obviously weakened the youth's resolve to brazen it out.

"So, we'll take you to the Ducal Guard. They'll put you in the gaol. Attempted murder of two respectable citizens. Father Guido won't lift a finger to help you…"

"Father Guido…," Brozzi began.

"And even if he wanted to," Nico continued, "he has no civil power to stop your prosecution. You'll be in prison for many years. Even the archbishop himself couldn't stop it."

He paused.

"I can see only one way for you to avoid such a fate, Brozzi…"

Nico let the sentence hang, but Brozzi didn't respond. Nico looked across at Lercari. "Well, I guess that's it, Signore Lercari, let's take him in." He picked up his hat.

Lercari stood up and followed Nico to the cellar door.

"What way?" muttered Brozzi, barely audible.

Nico motioned to Lercari to unlock the door, ignoring their prisoner. Lercari turned the lock.

"I said, what way?" said Brozzi, a little louder.

Nico continued not to look at him. "It's no matter."

"No harm in telling him," Lercari suggested, his hand still on the key.

Nico sighed, as if he found the conversation tedious. Slowly, he walked across and sat down facing Brozzi.

"We know that you – and Signore Eyepatch – weren't doing what you did last night for your own benefit. Someone else – and we know who that someone is – ordered you to do away with Giovanni Lercari. And now, this person has left you to take the consequences."

Brozzi scowled. "You said there was a way out of it."

Nico ignored his comment. "And we also know why this person wanted Giovanni out of the way. After all, Giovanni was the only person with evidence of what happened to that English merchant. Wasn't he?"

"You can't prove it."

"What? About the Englishman you stabbed – and left for dead on the beach? The Englishmen who uttered his dying words to the lighthouse guard, describing his killers? The Englishman who was held in the bowels of San Lorenzo? Who took his signet ring and gave it to Giovanni?"

Nico reached into his pocket. "This one?" he said, turning the ring slowly between thumb and forefinger.

Brozzi swallowed. He started talking, rapidly and in a higher pitch. "I didn't kill him; it wasn't me that did it…"

Nico held up a hand. "Brozzi, listen to me. The only way out of this for you, a charge of murdering the Englishman – and attempting to kill Giovanni Lercari – is to tell us all you know. The Doge knows that you're just the errand boy. He's prepared to look leniently on you - if you help to get those truly responsible brought to justice."

Brozzi was wide-eyed, his gaze alternating between Nico and Lercari, his mouth slack.

"... But if you don't cooperate, then you - and only you - will pay the full price. And for the rest of your life. What's it to be?"

Chapter Forty
PALAZZO DUCALE: MID-OCTOBER

Gino Lercari, who'd never been inside the Office of the Doge's Guard, looked around the large room, fascinated by his surroundings. The uniformed men rushing on their various errands, the assorted weapons on display, wall charts of the Genova coastline, shelves of ledgers and scrolls. Whereas his father and Nico were focussed, waiting for Sergente Spazio's summary. And impatient with the officer's even-paced manner.

The sergeant lay his quill down with a deliberate air and scanned the note he had made. "So, signori, let's see if I have got this correctly," he said, looking at his visitors in turn, "To begin with the events of last night. You, Signore Castello and young Master Lercari here, were attacked, close to Via Luccoli, by two men, one who's escaped – you've given me a bare description of him – and the other being the youth who you've brought into us, Paolo Brozzi." Spazio gestured in the direction of the Guardroom where Brozzi was now being held.

"These men were armed, *serioso*. They were in the process of rendering Master Lercari insensible when you, Signore Castello, fought one of them to the ground and stunned him, only to be attacked by the other, this Paolo Brozzi. You sustained an injury to your shoulder when deflecting his sword thrust, which otherwise could have been fatal to you. The other man slipped away while this was taking place. You managed to overpower Brozzi and take him to Signore Lercari's residence. The hour being late, you held him there overnight and brought him to us this morning. Am I correct thus far?"

Nico nodded. "*Essato.*"

Spazio picked up his quill and made a mark against his notes. "Before er ...bringing him to us, you questioned Brozzi as to why he and this other man had attacked you. His answer was that he had been ordered to do so by Father Guido Vacchero." Spazio raised his eyebrows inquiringly.

The morning dragged on as Nico and Lercari senior confirmed the confession that Paolo Brozzi had made and Sergente Spazio dutifully noted it all down: Brozzi's part in taking Monty prisoner, the subsequent events at San Lorenzo, how Monty was removed from the cathedral and finally how his end came, at the hands of the same priest.

Spazio breathed out heavily, puffing his cheeks. "Did Brozzi say why he did Father Guido's bidding in these ...matters?"

Nico shook his head. "Not really. I expect that for the gaoler Orso, it was largely a matter of money. But as regards Brozzi, no doubt Father Guido had power over him. His calling as a novice, his chances for advancement, his future life really, Guido could decide it all: whether his fortunes would flourish - or wither and die."

Spazio paused to review his note. Then he asked Gino, "And this orphan who worked at San Lorenzo, Fabio was it? Is he still there?"

"I didn't see him around the cathedral in the days before I left. And I haven't heard of him since."

"We've tried to find him," put in Nico, "but no one seems to know his whereabouts."

"You still have the foreigner's ring, Giovanni?" Spazio added, without looking up.

"Here it is," said Nico, placing it on the desk next to Spazio's inkwell. The sergeant put down his quill and picked up the ring, turning it between thumb and forefinger. Eventually he said, "I think that is enough for the present. Capitano Merello will need to consider this report carefully. So please make yourselves available, if he should have further questions."

"Shouldn't you apprehend Guido?" asked Nico. "He will no doubt be speculating why Brozzi didn't return last night."

"That is a matter for the Capitano. I expect he will need to question Brozzi first, to verify your testimonies. You will appreciate that your accounts in themselves do not amount to a formal confession. That can only be given by the prisoner himself, to an officer of the Guard."

"We indicated to Brozzi that things would go better for him if he made a full confession. Perhaps I could discuss that with Capitano Merello?"

Spazio stood up, sheaf of notes in hand. "I will mention it to him. I expect he will want to speak to you shortly, in any case."

It was late afternoon when the Lercaris and Nico emerged from Palazzo Ducale and went their separate ways, each to their home. By the time Nico reached Caricamento, he felt exhausted, and his shoulder was throbbing.

Lisa took Nico to their bedroom and painstakingly removed his bandages, reanointing the wound.

"I will be fine, there's no need to nursemaid me," he said, his voice slurred by tiredness.

"Let me be the judge of that," she responded. As she applied fresh bandages, Nico related the day's events, Paolo Brozzi's confession being the core of his account. A couple of times, when Nico mentioned the role of Father Guido especially, she paused; he could feel the tension in her through her bandaging. Once finished, she positioned the pillows behind Nico and inserted herself into the hollow of his uninjured left shoulder. Holding him as if he had been absent for a month, not a day.

For a while they lay there, hardly speaking, as the light outside faded. The room shrank in the increasing darkness. Nico felt an unfamiliar sense of union with her.

Finally, she spoke. "Nico, there's something I must tell you."

"I'm sure it can wait until morning."

"It can't."

She extracted herself from his left arm and faced him, leaning on her pillow. "You know what a struggle it was for me, believing what Gino had said about Father Guido and Signore Montague?"

"Yes, I know."

"But now I see it clearly. I can see many things more clearly."

"Hard to change what you were brought up to believe."

"Monty was a good man, not the treacherous enemy that Father Guido claimed. Yet Guido imprisoned him. And killed him. Condemned him because of his country, and his assumed heresy."

"He did."

"Was I any better? I reproached you for having anything to do with him, just because he was English." She sat up in bed, hugging her knees. "But I had tied myself to a false prophet. Not even a prophet, a demon."

"That was understandable: your grief at losing your father overrode any other consideration. Just try and remember - good and bad live inside us all. There are good Englishmen, just as there are bad Genovese. As my father would say, we are all of us an amalgam, like silver and lead. Some parts good, some parts bad."

"*My* father, God rest his soul, would have agreed. Papa always told me to judge each person on their merits, not by their reputation. He was true to his own beliefs, but he did not judge a man as wrong-headed for not sharing them. I believed it then, or at least I thought I did. But, when that pirate killed him in Cartagena, my heart was full of hate. I wanted revenge. Il Drago had taken from me everything I cared for. And I allowed myself to forget Papa's advice."

Nico stroked her hair, letting her talk.

"And of course, all the time I was in the convent, Father Guido was counselling me, telling me that my vengeful feelings were true and honourable. That Il Drago was the very Devil, and so were his Queen Elisabetta and all her subjects. That I must be a soldier for the True Faith. That together, the Church and its people, we would defeat these heretics, send them to damnation."

"I can see why that would have been a salve to you. A way to get back at fate."

"I suppose that, when we were married, I was still grieving for Papa. And wanting to punish his killer. And there was Father Guido, taking my confessions, still uttering that same vengeful sermon of his." She touched his forearm. "In such a frame of mind, I didn't devote myself to our marriage. I was devoted to something else, something much darker. I lost my way."

"And I failed to see it. I could have helped you. Instead, I just argued with you."

Lisa shook her head. "I'm not sure it would have made much difference. When you defended your right to do business with Protestants, when you said that Il Drago may be wicked, but that didn't condemn the rest of the English, I couldn't see that. And when you started doing business with Montague, an Englishman, I somehow felt you had betrayed me. All I could see was that you were willing to ignore my grief and do so merely for the sake of money."

Nico felt her words as if he had been stung.

She looked across at him, questioning. "Will *you* be my confessor, then?"

"Of course. We can be each other's."

"Yes, but it's I who must begin."

"Begin?"

She took a deep breath, as if steeling herself to speak.

"Please listen, Nico. When you have heard what I have to say, I pray you will forgive me."

He shook his head, as if to say that wasn't necessary, but she raised her hand to his chin, stopping him.

"When I was going to confession with Father Guido, he would ask me about your business. I told him that you were granting credit to the Englishman. That Sandro and I had argued against your decision. He encouraged me to keep up the fight with you, he said it was my Christian duty, as your wife, to help you find the true path. And, blinded as I was, I believed that it *was* my duty to God. And that duty was greater than my duty to my husband. To you."

Nico felt an instant pang, dismay at her disloyalty. But he fought it down, knowing that she had to finish her 'confession'. Her hand was clenched in a tight fist. He tried to unfurl her fingers, but she resisted putting his knuckles in her mouth and biting down hard.

"It's alright. It's alright," he repeated softly.

A tear left the corner of her eye. "But it's not right. It's *not*. I betrayed you. Kept on betraying you to a priest who shouldn't be...." Her voice cracked with emotion.

"You didn't know that's what you were doing."

"But I told him *everything*."

"Really? You told him that I was doing business with Monty Belltower. He didn't need that information from you. He knew it already. What he really wanted was to use you, to persuade me not to lend to Monty."

"Well, maybe. I suppose so, yes. That was why he was asking me all those questions during confession. It should have been obvious to me. Father Guido had no care for your soul or mine, whether you were lending to a so-called heretic or not. He had just been using me as his informant, and his mouthpiece. Not just for some holy cause, but to stop Montague doing business. And thereby somehow further the interests of the Church, as he saw it. And no doubt, his own personal advancement with the archbishop." She paused again, her breathing coming faster.

"Nothing you did, or could have done differently, made any real difference to the outcome. Remember, it was Lina Luzzati who must have told Guido that Monty was at the 'Paradiso'. You could say she betrayed her customer. If anyone was Guido's accomplice, apart from Brozzi and Orso, it was her. Not you."

Her voice rose, in anguish. "But don't you *see*? However small my part, in some way I am involved in his death. I helped a man be killed, just for going about his affairs."

"Guido would have found out about Monty anyway. And killed him just the same, without your being involved..."

Lisa cut across him. "And that would be bad enough. But it's not just that. I still think that Father Guido was acting alone - at least, I pray that's true - but what if he was doing Archbishop Sauli's bidding? Perhaps the archbishop was using me for his own purposes, all the time? Even at the beginning, when I was orphaned. Even when he proposed that," her words were suddenly halting, as if she was choking on them, ".... that you and I should be married, Nico. Even our... union was part of their plan. As a way of reaching *you*, tying *you* to them."

She burst into sobs. He pulled her towards him, trying to stop the tremors.

"I didn't marry you because the archbishop proposed it. I married you because I wanted to be married, and to *you*. I still do," he said.

But she was not listening. "You should divorce me. I'm a faithless wife!"

She wriggled in his grasp, but he held her with his left arm, not allowing her to escape. He kept telling her that it made no difference to his feelings, that they would stay together and ride the storm. She kept blocking his words out, fighting the notion that he *could* love her, even though she had betrayed him. Exhausted by resisting him and, he guessed, by the release she felt in facing up to the truth, the convulsions ended, and she went limp in his arms, still sobbing quietly. Finally, her anguish subsided, and she drifted into sleep.

Nico slept fitfully, her words repeating themselves in his mind and the pain in his shoulder returning whenever he moved. By the time he gave up trying to sleep, it was close to dawn. Leaving Lisa sleeping, he dressed and walked down to the harbour to try and clear his mind.

The thought of Lisa's betrayal of his business confidences was, yes, he had to admit, a shock. A blow to his pride. Perhaps he expected her loyalty simply as his due, as her husband. Had he failed to recognise that it had, in some sense, to be earned? At the beginning, had he ridden roughshod over her feelings about the Englishman? He, who prided himself on his ability to read into the hearts and minds of his customers, to judge their honesty and steadfastness. Careful so far as the bank's affairs were concerned, he had failed to consider the heart and mind of his own wife. To recognise her pain, the emotions fighting within her.

And then, that the church had engineered her betrayal, he had been blind to that possibility also. Even though it was something he would have always considered Sauli capable of. Too close to home, perhaps. There seemed every chance that Lisa had hit upon one reason why their marriage had been arranged, that Sauli had furthered their union merely to influence him. Well, so be it. He and Lisa would prove Sauli wrong. Make this a marriage of two loving souls, not one of mere convenience. Her heartfelt confession was a first step, one he must respond to. Show her that this was a new beginning for them.

Turning for home as the sun rose over Porta Siberia, he found himself breaking into laughter. Here he was, the Alchemist, with his reputation for never being bested in business: a man whose marriage was based on a falsehood, whose fortune so hard won, had now all gone, who had no prospect of gainful employment, debts all over the city, no friends at Court, and who was ensnared in a deadly struggle with the archbishop and his minions. Well, at least things were as bad as they could get. He strode westwards along Caricamento, determined to face it all.

IN THE GUARD OFFICE, Capitano Merello reread Sergente Spazio's report with increasing alarm. On two counts: first, as regards his own reputation with the Doge and the Gran Consiglio. His earlier investigation into the unlawful death of that English merchant had not found the guilty parties. That was perhaps excusable, but then, there was that business with the courtesan Bastone's trial, where the magistrates had presumed to criticise him for the paucity of the evidence, and where the accused had made unexpected allegations against her victim. And now, he had in front of him a confession from a cathedral novice which not only identified the merchant's killer but even established a link between that murder and La Bastone's wild accusations against the priest, this Father

Guido Vacchero. Accusations which amazingly, now appeared to be true.

And second, and more important from the Republic's point of view, was the fact that the orchestrator of all this mayhem, and possibly the murderer of that Englishman, was a priest. And not just any priest, but a senior member of the clergy at San Lorenzo. Nor was the Brozzi confession the only evidence that the clergy had been involved in the Englishman's death. A few days ago, Andrea De Marini no less, had come to the Palazzo with his daughter, and she had testified to the same Englishman being held captive in the cellars of San Lorenzo. With this sort of evidence of abduction and murder, it was arguably his duty to arrest Guido Vacchero as soon as possible and question him. And, depending on the answers, to charge him and bring him to trial along with his accomplices. If ever a case called for the file to mysteriously go missing, it was this one.

Just to add extra complication, that Domenico Castello, the man who had brought this unwelcome offering to Merello's table, had proposed that the novice, Brozzi, who clearly deserved to be thrown in the deepest dungeon in the Republic, should instead be treated with leniency, in recognition of the testimony he had volunteered against his prestigious employers.

Tempted though he was to put the report under a pile of other, equally urgent matters, Merello knew it would emerge eventually. In any case, Signori Lercari and Castello would be pressing for action soon enough.

There was, he realised, only one course of action to take. Go higher. He would have to put the whole matter in Doge Ambrogio's lap. He went to find Ambrogio's secretary to arrange a meeting.

LISA RETURNED to her bed in the late morning, complaining of feelings of sickness. Nico was at a loose end. Capitano Merello seemed to be taking an age to act against Father Guido, despite the clear evidence.

It relieved the tedium a little when a courier arrived at the house, bearing a letter from Sandro. He had arrived safely in Antwerp, he reported. Jan Huysmans, who had a fine house close to the River Scheldt, had insisted Sandro stay as his guest for as long as he needed. The port was large, with all manner of goods being imported. But the locals were complaining, firstly, that the Sea Beggars were blockading the port, and the Spanish didn't seem able to stop them. And second, and most importantly, that residents were being taxed to the hilt to pay for the war against the rebels. He was managing with the limited funds that they had put aside and so did not need to ask for an additional remittance. Nico smiled at Sandro's assumption that he had any money to send. There was no mention of any business being done, but to be fair to Sandro, it was early days.

He had reached the penultimate paragraph, mostly gossip which he had skimmed over, when he heard an agonising scream. Followed by two more, less loud but still pained. He rushed upstairs to find Lisa in bed, looking distraught, and Maria by her side with something wrapped in a towel. There was blood on the bed sheets.

Lisa cried again, incoherently, as he rushed to her side. Until he deciphered the words, "My baby, my baby!" He buried her face in his chest, trying vainly to quell the storm that racked her body. Her forehead pressed against his sword wound, and he flinched at the sharp sting of pain. But he let her push again and again; he wanted to feel the pain more.

He had been mistaken before: things had not been as bad as they would get.

Chapter Forty-One
THE ARCHBISHOP'S PALAZZO: MID-OCTOBER

Archbishop Sauli was well attuned to Father Guido's demeanour when in his presence. Usually, it fell somewhere between piety and smugness. But today, as the priest stood before him in the library, he noticed something else. A look, not of defeat exactly, but as if Guido feared that a demon was waiting to pounce on him from behind each bookcase. But it was hardly surprising if the man felt hounded by evil forces, perhaps by something more readily identifiable than Satan. The information imparted to him by the archbishop had scarcely been comforting.

The evening before, Doge Ambrogio had requested a private audience with the archbishop, alone. He had summarised the information laid by Giovanni Lercari and Domenico Castello. And, more crucially, the confession extracted by the Guard from Brozzi. The novice had been initially close-mouthed but, encouraged by a few days' solitary confinement, relieved only by brief episodes strapped to an interrogation chair, he had repeated exactly what he had previously admitted to Signori Castello and Lercari, embellished it even, with more damning details of his dirty work for Guido Vacchero.

Assessing the situation rapidly, the archbishop had expressed horror at these revelations. What an abomination, that a member of his own clergy could carry out such criminality! The Doge's assumption that Sauli couldn't possibly be aware of the priest's nefarious activities was left unsaid, hardly needed to be stated. Ambrogio merely asked that the archbishop deliver the accused to the civil authorities. He would send round the Ducal Guard to make the arrest in the morning.

Sauli responded, not missing a beat. Why of course, he would afford the Doge's men every facility. The priest, Guido, would be confined to the cathedral precincts in the meantime. But, come to think of it, he had not seen that priest since at least Matins on the previous day. He assured the Doge that a search would be made tonight, if by any remote chance this Guido did not appear for Vespers. As regards Orso, the supposed gaoler, the archbishop had, of course, no knowledge of him. He presumed that the ruffian had been hired by Guido without reference to anyone.

Immediately the Doge had departed, Sauli summoned Father Guido to his chambers. Paolo Brozzi's disappearance had obviously worried the priest for some days, but Guido had assumed, based on Orso's account, that he was probably dead, cut through by Castello. He had informed the archbishop accordingly. The stark fact that the youth was now incarcerated and worse, was implicating him in his crimes, momentarily robbed him of speech.

"Obviously, there is no question of your remaining here," continued Sauli. "The prospect of your undergoing a public trial is of course unthinkable. You must leave immediately, go to the monastery up at Santa Chiara for a few days," instructed the archbishop. "And take that degenerate, Orso, with you. That's until I decide where you should go permanently. Reconcile yourself to being exiled from Genova for the forseeable future."

Guido bowed, apparently accepting the inevitable. But then a thought occurred to him. "But it was Your Grace who expressed the wish that we be rid of Castello and the Lercari boy. I was merely the instrument of that wish. Is there no way to quash this prosecution?"

Sauli's eyes narrowed. Guido was obviously now so desperate to cling on to his privileged place that he was willing to threaten the archbishop himself. This would not be borne.

"What I said to you, Father Guido, was that you should leave Castello and the Lercaris well alone. What could they prove? All they had were suspicions. A signet ring. And the testimony of a child beggar who now, it seems, cannot be traced. The Englishman was dead; his whore is confined at Santa Maria and assumed out of her wits. But now, thanks to your incompetence, the position has changed. That traitor Brozzi has landed you in it. Perhaps the prosecuting officer may think Brozzi's evidence unreliable, but it seems they're going ahead despite it."

"But ..."

"I may at one time," interrupted Sauli, "have expressed the view that Castello was a thorn in my side, a friend to heretics, but that was then – and hardly the same thing. Now we face a very different problem."

Guido paused. "Then I shall await your word, Your Grace, and naturally, I will say nothing of our various conversations."

"You will keep your mouth closed, indefinitely. I could throw you to the Doge's wolves, Father Guido. That you're hanging on to your liberty at all is entirely within my gift. Don't forget that. And as for Orso, I leave you to decide what's best for *him*."

Watching Guido's back as he departed the room, the archbishop could feel his blood seething. This was insupportable: one way or another, Guido must be out of the way. No betrayal so deep, so cutting as that of a most trusted servant. He tried to focus on the immediate task. The Doge's Guard would be here in the morning, to arrest Guido. It might appear to them that Guido had been forewarned, but that was easily deflected. He was gratified that he'd had the presence of mind to say that Guido had not been seen for a couple of days. Come to think of it, it was more than two days ago. He could suggest to the Guard that Guido – and his accomplice, Orso - had probably taken fright because of Brozzi's failure to return from his criminal assignment. That would be it.

Once Guido was gone from Genova, the archbishop could put this messy interlude behind him. He would soon be called to the Vatican in any case. That thought gave him some relief from his anger.

In view of his extended absences in Rome, it was necessary to appoint a Coadjutor Bishop in Genova. A role he himself had held during Archbishop Pallavicino's final illness. At one time, that was a position which Father Guido had clearly coveted; indeed, Sauli had earmarked him for the very job. Now, that was obviously out of the question. He decided that Father Bernadino would be awarded the office. He would announce it in the Chapter House in the morning. Guido would get to hear of it soon enough: that would put him in his place. He could still be useful, wherever the archbishop was pleased to send him. Perhaps the Spanish Netherlands.

As for Castello, if what Doge Ambrogio had told him was true, the merchant had lost all his wealth, his only source of power. The time was surely approaching when he could be brought down. Anything he might say afterwards, any wild accusations against the Church, would be seen for what they were, the desperate throw of a desperate man.

JUST AFTER DAWN, Capitano Merello went to San Lorenzo, taking an armed escort with him as befitted the Captain of the Watch. It was not every day that you were called upon to arrest a senior member of the clergy. But his precautions proved to be unavailing. The bird had flown its nest. Father Bernardino, who admitted Merello and his men to the Archbishop's Palazzo, was apparently shocked to report the news to him.

"We have searched the precincts high and low, Capitano, but Father Guido has not been found. I regret to say that it appears he has absconded. His meagre possessions are no longer in his cell. And there is no sign of that fellow Orso, either."

Merello ground his teeth. As he had suspected, with a troublesome case like this, San Lorenzo had closed its ranks against the civil power.

"Is the archbishop aware of it?" he finally managed.

Father Bernadino bowed his head gravely, as if to say he was fully cognizant of his responsibilities. "I have informed His Grace. However, he is preparing to depart for Rome. To assume his duties as cardinal. So, he is somewhat engaged at present. However, he has seen fit to appoint me as Coadjutor-Bishop during his absence. If I can assist you in any way..."

"I would like to see Father Guido's cell."

"But of course. Although as I say, it is empty, so I doubt it would assist you much."

"And I would like to talk to the clergy generally. To ask if anyone knows anything about his departure."

Bernadino bowed again. *Much good it may do me*, thought Merello. He dismissed his now redundant escort, save for one guardsman, and followed the priest across the cloister to the dormitory. They arrived at the door to Father Guido's 'cell', which took up one corner of the building.

"I am sure you have many duties to attend to, Father Bernadino," Merello said, wanting to be left alone.

"Of course, let me know when you wish to address the clergy. I shall be in the lobby of the archbishop's residence, meantime."

Positioning his guardsman outside, Merello shut the door and looked around the room. It was simply furnished, but spacious enough for a man who proclaimed self-denial. The instruments of mortification hung on the walls but did not appear well-used. The bed was soft and covered with fresh linen. Perhaps it was only his skeletal appearance which gave Guido his austere reputation.

There was a desk in one corner. It had some books and a few document boxes on the shelves above. Half an hour spent reading through the contents of the boxes revealed little of import. He stripped the bed of its sheets and pillows, moved the furniture to see if anything was hidden behind, and examined the wardrobe, although few of Guido's clothes remained there. Nothing. Resigned, he started to replace everything. As he moved the wardrobe back into its allotted place, it juddered as it hit the corner of a flagstone.

He stared downwards absently. The flagstone had an iron ring. He reached down, and slipping his fingers through it, pulled upwards. The stone shifted under his hand.

Bringing a candle down to the floor, he looked down into the cavity that he'd revealed. It was not deep, but deep enough to contain a document box. He lifted it out. Locked. He peered into the cavity again and there, jammed in a crease of the mortar, was the glint of metal, a small key.

He opened the box. It was empty save for a slim bundle of papers. Moving nearer to the window to catch the light, he scanned them. A smile spread across his lips. The bundle appeared to relate to the "Paradiso", that dubious establishment where Guido had been attacked by that crazed courtesan. There was correspondence from Signora Luzzati. There was even an interesting ledger, one entry noting that the week's rent had been reduced in exchange for certain unspecified services. He put the bundle to one side, imagining Doge Ambrogio's expression when he described his find. But there was no document indicating any connection between Guido and that English merchant. But if any had existed, Guido would have taken them or – more likely - burned them before his sudden departure.

Following the loss of her baby, Nico and Lisa made it clear to friends and family alike that they were not 'at home' to visitors, at least not for the time being. Nico had no merchant business to transact, so their only callers were the porters who delivered food and other staples. Or the occasional process server, with papers relating to some debt or other of Nico's that remained unpaid. Fortunately, the wheels of debt collection ran slow in Genova, a fact which Nico knew very well from the days when he had been on the other side of the credit bargain. Aside from taking their *passeggiata* along the waterfront, to stretch their legs and relieve the monotony, the couple largely confined themselves to their sala and the principal bedroom.

But as Lisa's grief slowly subsided, with Nico continually reassuring her that they would try again soon, they found themselves in the unfamiliar position of each being the rock upon which the other could rest. Their sense of the common enterprise of just surviving, and the proximity in which they now existed, had taken the place of other feelings. They went to Mass on Sundays, but Lisa had noticeably absented herself from confession in recent weeks.

Their lives acquired a certain routine. Nico saw a bit more of his father than had been the case when he had the bank to run, but otherwise they were quite solitary. Nico realised that he missed his brother. Sandro had been a thorn in his side sometimes, but his easy manner and youthful humour had enlivened the household. Nico started writing a letter to Sandro, to pass on the news that Father Guido was now being sought by the authorities for Monty's murder and that Paolo Brozzi was in custody. He imagined how Sandro's jaw would drop on receiving it.

But Nico was not an assiduous correspondent. The letter lay on his desk in his *studiolo,* the small storage room in the back of the house that he had adopted for the purpose, barely begun. For once, he seemed to lack energy. And there was always some other distraction to take his attention away. He had started again late one drizzly afternoon when Lisa came into the room. She was carrying a glass of wine for them both. As they chatted about Sandro, he decided that now was as good a time as any to tell Lisa about the real reason for his brother's sudden departure from Genova. She sipped her wine, thinking.

"Why didn't you tell me this before?" she said eventually.

"I'd always intended to," he began, "but there never seemed to be the right time. And Sandro was always fearful of your good opinion."

"You hoped that the risk of his being disclosed would disappear before you needed to tell me, was that it?"

"Not really, Lisa.... in truth, I felt you would struggle to accept

Sandro's admission, given the Church's teaching on these things. Was I wrong in that?"

Lisa didn't respond. Nico waited for the outburst – whether that was her anger at not being trusted or her condemnation of Sandro's illicit behaviour - but none came. Her words, when she did speak, surprised him.

"What did you *think,* Nico? That I would betray your brother? I would never do that. No, I should rather say he is *my* brother. The only one I have, after all. Nothing changes that, whichever of God's laws he might have broken."

"Sandro is what he is, Lisa. As God made him, laws or not."

Lisa laid her hand on top of his. "As are we all, I know. It's a pity that you – or Sandro - didn't confide in me earlier. But I can understand why you were ... wary. You're right, had you told me this a few months ago, I would probably have struggled to accept it. It will still take me time to come to terms with, but..." she reached out to him with both arms, "my family, whatever they are, come first."

Over supper that evening, Lisa was in a lighter humour. "You know, I often wondered why there seemed no prospect of Sandro's marrying. After all, he is such a handsome fellow."

Nico smiled inwardly at the implied comparison with himself.

"In fact," she continued after a pause, "I think he should take a wife. A wealthy widow perhaps?"

"Marry?" Nico puckered his lips. "Well, I suppose that would stop the rumours. But it would be an unusual woman who would willingly accept the other side to his life. Most ladies would find that hard, surely?"

Lisa leaned over and kissed her husband on the cheek, as if he were a small child. "Nico, how little you know about women!"

Nico would have been the first to acknowledge his limitations in that respect.

"If women's gossip is to be credited, there were enough eligible ladies in Genova who would have considered it their dream to be on Sandro's arm," she continued. "They might still feel that way even if it came with certain... complications."

"Well perhaps. We shall see when the time comes for him to return. That may be some months away, though, if not longer. For the present, he will have to make Antwerp his home. I would like to visit him, but we simply don't have the funds for that."

THE CAPTAIN of the Watch passed the single sheet of paper to one of his men, with a curt instruction. "Nail that on the palazzo gates." The guard glanced at the text and, with a slight bow to his commander, stepped outside.

Finding a suitable spot at head height, he fixed it to the woodwork and then stepped back a couple of paces to read it at his leisure.

"PROCLAMATION

Be it known that the Ducal Guard seeks Fra. Guido Vacchero, formerly of Cattedrale San Lorenzo, in connection with the recent death of a foreign merchant, one Montecchio Bell'Tover, and a later assault on one Giovanni Lercari and regarding diverse other matters. Also sought in the same case is Gennaro Orso, late of Pre, who may be in the company of Fra. Guido.

All citizens are hereby called upon, if they know the whereabouts of Fra. Guido, or Gennaro Orso to inform the Guard by presenting themselves at Palazzo Ducale without delay. All information provided will be treated in strict confidence. A reward is offered for information which leads to the apprehension of these men.

By Order of the Doge, in his justice and power, this fifteenth day of October in the year of Our Lord 1587

Sealed by Ambrogio Di Negro."

Satisfied, the guard turned on his heel, as a couple of curious citizens shuffled forwards into the space he had occupied and began to read the notice.

Chapter Forty-Two

THE MOLO, GENOA HARBOUR; MID-OCTOBER

Master Winterhey followed the line of Bo'sun Verney's arm pointing towards the horizon. They were standing on the bridge of the *"Mary Gale"*.

"I see 'er. You're right, she ain't a Spanish rig. Could be an English ship, I s'ppose, but...." He continued watching the unknown vessel until she rounded the end of the Molo and headed towards a vacant berth. At this distance, you couldn't really tell if her flag was Genoa's or England's, it was just a red and white blur. And the lettering on her prow was too small and weather-encrusted, to be able to read her name.

A few of her company disembarked and started heading down the Molo towards them. There was no doubt of her provenance now, as Winterhey caught the familiar West Country lilt in the sailors' calls to one another. After a while, a solitary gentleman emerged from the ship. At least, a gentleman by his clothes and English too, if Winterhey was any judge. He started walking along the Molo, no doubt headed for Porta Siberia. But when he reached the quay alongside the *"Mary Gale"*, he stopped and looked up, directly at Winterhey.

"Be you the Master?" he enquired.

Winterhey didn't recognise the speaker, but after all those years bringing coal down to London from the Humber, he knew a Yorkshire accent when he heard one.

THERE WAS a knock at the studiolo door, and the ever-faithful Luca stepped inside.

"Excuse me, Signore Domenico, but there are two gentlemen wishing to see you urgently. I have placed them in the sala."

Nico steeled himself to enter the room, wondering if it was a creditor come to press him, accompanied by some grasping lawyer. The man standing by the fireplace was neither. It was Winterhey, master of the "*Mary Gale*". As Nico greeted the English sailor, his unsmiling companion, obviously not waiting to be introduced, stepped forward.

"Signore Castello, I presume?"

Nico returned the bow. "Of course. And, your name, signore...?"

"Thomas Sutton, from London."

Momentarily, Nico chastised himself for his unpreparedness: there had been a time when he knew all the comings and goings at the port. And this was Thomas Sutton himself, the man he had written to after Monty's funeral, but had begun to think he would never hear from. Putting aside his annoyance at himself, he considered the visitor. He was middle-aged, slim and compact in build, with close-cropped silver hair and a neat, pointed beard. His lightly embroidered doublet and soft leather boots told of his discreet wealth. His expression purposeful, his eyes observant.

When all three were seated, the initial conversation was stilted. Sutton spoke in Italian, his usage of the tongue hardly fluent but perfectly adequate. As the Englishman was speaking, Nico attuned himself to Sutton's accent. It reminded him a little of Monty. He recalled that both uncle and nephew came from the same region of England. Yorkshire, that was it. But this Sutton seemed a very different character from Monty, more polished, but also more reserved.

"So, you have come here to Genova because of my letter," said Nico after a few minutes. A statement of fact.

"Indeed. And thank you for writing to me."

"I understood that as well as your agent here, Signore Montague was your nephew. My condolences, signore. He was a fine young man."

Sutton inclined his head slightly by way of acknowledgment. His emotions were obviously well below the surface, which Nico had understood was a characteristic of many English people. Not including Monty though, he recalled.

"Although, when your letter arrived, I had already decided I would come here," Sutton said. "You see, it was part of the arrangement between Montague and me, that he would send me regular reports of his progress. I had become concerned because for several weeks no reports had arrived. And then your letter explained why. So, I decided to take the next available sailing. As it happened, we – the Merchant Adventurers that is – had always planned that if the first trades were successful – and it seemed from Monty's early reports that they were – we would ship more cargoes of wool. So, I have also brought a second shipment with me. But that aside, I apprehended from your letter that Montague's death has left several trades in which your bank was involved, incomplete."

"That's true enough."

"When my ship berthed this morning, I saw Master Winterhey at the quayside here, aboard our "*Mary Gale*". I mentioned my purpose – you had already informed him of Montague's death, I understand – and he told me that you had moved house in recent weeks. I insisted we come here immediately. My apologies for our arriving unannounced."

"Do not concern yourself, my house is open to you, Signore Sutton." His guest looked around the modest room. Obviously not quite what he was expecting.

Master Winterhey stood up. He looked uncomfortable, as if he preferred to be on board in a storm rather than navigate perilous waters on land. "I think I should be a-leavin' you gen'lemen to discuss your affairs in private."

Sutton nodded. "Thank you for escorting me here, Winterhey."

Winterhey inclined his head. "You're welcome, sir, I'm sure. If ye need me, ye knows where to find me."

Once the sailor had left, Sutton made a few general remarks on business matters. Nico was surprised that Sutton should be so matter of fact until he reflected that the Englishman had already had several weeks to come to terms with his nephew's premature death. But Sutton's next comment showed his assessment was in any case mistaken.

Sutton spread his hands wide. "Your letter, Signore Castello. That was terrible news. But it only gave me the barest details. I'm hoping that there will be more you can impart."

"Obviously, I will tell you what I can, signore," said Nico, "but I fear it will be scant consolation to you." *More to tell?* Nico wondered. *Should he reveal everything he knew?*

"I'm sure that whatever you may know will be helpful." The Englishman leaned back in his chair, looking suddenly weary.

Nico saw Maria lingering just outside the doorway. "But how

thoughtless of me. Would you take some refreshment? I imagine you are thirsty having come directly from your ship."

As they waited for the maid to return, Nico began, starting with Monty's disappearance - though he made no mention of Bianca's involvement or of Monty's incarceration at San Lorenzo – continuing with the discovery of Monty's body and ending with the funeral itself. Nico told the story as he had experienced it, day by day. He tried to avoid inserting into his narrative information which had become known to him after the event. Sutton listened intently, not interrupting. "At that time, the Doge's Guard believed Montague had been set upon by thieves while walking in the city and that his body was then taken to the beach. And left there." Nico concluded.

Sutton shook his head. "What baffles me about that is, how Monty came to be alone and so vulnerable. He was a big, strong fellow, Signore Castello. Not the swiftest sword perhaps, but certainly able to look after himself in a fight."

"Perhaps, but it was dark, the streets were unfamiliar to him but not to his assailants, there were probably several of them."

Maria arrived with some wine and bread, which interrupted the flow of conversation for a few moments. Sutton ate and drank a little – he seemed quite fastidious compared to Monty – and then leaned back in his chair. His eyes narrowed in a frown. "A moment ago - what was it you said – that it was the Guard's opinion *at the time*? Has that changed?"

Nico had already decided to be forthcoming with more of the story, even if the part about Bianca should be omitted to spare Sutton's embarrassment. He would have to reveal the role of Guido Vacchero. But since the priest was now a wanted criminal so far as the Ducal Guard was concerned, that was not so problematic.

"It has."

"What do they think now?"

"Something very different. But then, I always had my doubts about the likelihood of it being a simple robbery...."

"But in your letter," said Sutton, interrupting, "you told me otherwise."

"Well, what I *wrote*, Signore Sutton, was that this was what the authorities believed. I admit I had a very different theory."

Sutton's expression showed his unhappiness that he'd been kept in ignorance.

"I withheld my theory because at that time I only had my suspicions, there was no evidence to back them up and, in any case, it wasn't the sort of thing that was safe to put in a letter. So please forgive my reticence, but that will all become clearer as I tell you what has been uncovered since then."

Sutton's face softened. "I understand. Please continue."

"I suppose my doubts began with Dottor Vannone, the physician who'd conducted the *postmortem* examination. He confirmed that Montague had died only hours before his body was discovered. Whereas by that time, Montague had already been missing from his lodgings for about two weeks. So, to me that was suspicious."

Nico moved on to relate the intervention of the Lercari family and Gino's nickname for Monty. The story of the signet ring. Again, he skipped over Bianca's involvement and her subsequent trial, moving straight to Paolo Brozzi's assault on Gino and his subsequent confession. The authorities had accepted that the evidence was sufficient and had attempted – but failed - to arrest Guido Vacchero. Nico finally added, without naming her, Nicoletta De Marini's recent confirmation that Monty had been locked in a cell at San Lorenzo.

Sutton didn't interrupt during this second stage of Nico's story, but his expression became more pained as the narrative unfolded. Rather than attempt to state any grand conclusions, Nico left it to Sutton to draw his own.

"So, Signore Castello..."

"Please, signore, you may call me Nico."

"Nico then, you're telling me that my nephew was murdered," said Sutton, slowly and deliberately, "not by penniless rogues, but by this priest?" He almost spat the last word out. "And not just any priest, but a senior member of the clergy at Genoa cathedral?"

"Either Guido did the deed himself, or he arranged for it to be done by hired killers. That isn't certain - but yes, that's exactly what I'm saying."

Sutton stared at his wine glass and took a quick drink from it.

"This is hard to credit," he said. "Why would a priest arrange such an act? And why incarcerate a foreign visitor for such a length of time? What on earth was his purpose?"

"That I've always struggled with. What benefit could accrue from it? That's presuming, of course, that it was *his* purpose."

"What do you mean?"

"For myself, I doubt that Father Guido, however senior he was, conceived and carried out these crimes, on his own. Something so heinous as murdering a foreign merchant would surely call for higher authority than that."

"But that authority could only be – those senior to him in the cathedral?"

"*Esattamente.*"

"Lord in Heaven," muttered Sutton.

There was a long silence. Eventually Sutton raised himself to his feet. It seemed to be a struggle.

"Of course, that still doesn't explain the reason for Montague being selected," said Nico, "but perhaps Guido was intent on blocking Monty's business affairs. An antipathy to foreign merchants?"

"Why would the Church care about such matters?"

Nico shrugged. "England's path, Queen Elisabetta's insistence on pursuing religious reform. Not popular with our clergy."

"I suppose so," said Sutton, but as if he were saying it to himself.

"You must be weary after a long journey and now this to contend with," suggested Nico.

"What, oh yes, I am staying with Signore Cavalli. Montague lodged with him, of course."

"Yes, I recall."

Making his farewells for the time being, Sutton added, "No doubt you and I have business matters to discuss, Nico."

"I'm sure it can wait until you're ready to do so."

Two mornings later, Sutton called again at the Caricamento house. A couple of good nights' rest in a bed which didn't roll with every wave combined with Signore Cavalli's hospitality had obviously restored some of his energy, if not his mood.

"I went to the Palazzo Ducale yesterday," he announced. "Just to see how things stood and in case they needed any personal information about Montague. The captain, Merello was the name, explained it all. It's exactly as you said, signore..." he corrected himself, "er, Nico. They are still searching for this Father Guido, but they don't seem very hopeful at present."

Nico invited the Englishman to stay for some refreshment but instead Sutton proposed they walk together down to the harbour. Apparently, he was ready for business.

"Had you come to know my nephew well?" he asked, as the pair walked in the direction of the Banco di San Giorgio.

"Yes, I think so. We did a substantial amount of business together. And Signore Montague – Monty, he allowed me to call him - was a regular visitor at my old house. I came to think of him as a friend."

"Judging by Monty's letters, I should also meet with the officers of Banco di Liguria."

"Surely. Monty did business with my fellow *cambisto*, Ferrucio Lercari, who is their chief manager. I can of course introduce you to him too – just say when it would be convenient."

"Yes, I should do so soon. For that matter, it would be good to talk to his son. Especially in the light of what you told me yesterday."

Nico wondered whether he should return to a subject which would clearly be painful to the Englishman. "I am sure that Ferrucio would be happy to arrange that."

They turned to the right, keeping close to the waterfront, and the mass of Porta Siberia came into view. Nico mentioned that much of the wool from Monty's ships was still in store there. Nico had financed trades on the back of these cargoes but still could not get them released.

"They're registered in your nephew's name," he explained. "The managers of the Siberia need proof of the owner's consent to release. The signature of a dead man. Or that of his executors. The Siberia also holds bales of silk that he purchased, much of it financed by me. I can't step in and resell it for the same reason."

Sutton halted in his tracks. "But we are talking about very large sums. Speaking frankly, Nico, that must have put a considerable strain on your capital?"

Nico laughed ironically. "You might put it that way. The truth is that the freezing of these goods came at just the wrong moment for me. Everything in business is a matter of timing of course, but as things stand, I have no capital to trade with, even if the San Giorgio hadn't taken away my licence."

"Then we must untangle this web just as soon as possible."

"I fear that it will take time. Time that I don't really have. After all, it will need Montague's estate to be settled, will it not? I did mention that in my letter to you."

Sutton shook his head. "These things need not stand in our way, Nico. We don't need Monty's will to be proved to get them resolved. Oh, Monty had power of sale and purchase, that's true, but he was merely our agent. He wasn't the owner of the wool, nor the silk either. I and my fellow Adventurers are."

"But the authorities here will need to be convinced of that to release the goods."

"No doubt they will. But I have the documents here with me. And a set of notary's translations in Italian. They are at Signore Cavalli's house. I can be back with them in the hour."

Later that afternoon, with Nico providing explanations where needed, Sutton presented his documents to the senior manager of the Siberia. First, a copy of the deed he had signed, empowering Monty as agent. Which provided that full right and authority would always remain with the Adventurers and that all of Monty's powers would revert to the owners in the event of his death or the relinquishing of his office. Then, the records of wool purchased by the Adventurers in England, showing tag numbers that corresponded with those on the bales in the Siberia's cellars. Finally, the charter for the "*Mary Gale*" and her two sister ships. The manager seemed impressed, if cautious.

"You will understand, signori, that it will take us a little time to consider these documents. My clerks will need to confirm that all is as it should be. But if it is as you have just explained, I see no great difficulty."

Sutton raised a warning index finger. "There has been a significant delay in releasing these cargoes already. Any further delay will not be welcome to the Merchant Adventurers – and I dare say the officers of the San Giorgio will be none too impressed either. So, I suggest you make your review a speedy one."

The manager smiled nervously. "I am sure we can, Signore Sutton. I will contact you as soon as it is completed."

"Mmm. We will return in say, three days' time. You'd better be ready by then."

As the pair left the Siberia and walked further along the quayside, Nico felt that at least a part of his present burden had been raised off his shoulders.

"To*mas*, if I can call you that – in Genova we say 'Tommaso' - I must thank you. I was beginning to wonder if I would ever see the end of this nightmare."

Sutton grunted. "Such thanks are quite unnecessary. I have done no more than discharge the Adventurers' obligations to you. And that, very belatedly. It is I who should apologise to you."

"Well, to be frank, I'm also concerned about the collateral I hold.

Montague assigned to my bank the rights to certain deposits in London banks. As security for his purchases. Can these be released to us?"

"Don't be concerned. If the London bankers raise any questions about reimbursing you, they will answer to me. But, just to put your mind at rest, I will put my seal to any confirmation you require."

They walked on down the Molo, Nico with a lighter step. Within ten minutes they had reached the vessel that had brought the Englishman to Genova. Standing up close, the "*George Bonaventure*" impressed Nico. Her lines were sleek, unlike the Spanish carracks that regularly arrived in the port.

"London built. A hundred and forty tons," explained Sutton.

Nico spotted the guns mounted on the forecastle and along the half-deck. Almost equal to a warship's armoury, he commented.

"Enough to ward off those who might be tempted to seize her," said Sutton. "Mostly four-pounders and minions, but there's two demi-culverins up there on the forecastle, as you see. Given the risks of piracy, the Adventurers insisted on the stoutest boat we could find."

"Best to be prepared," agreed Nico. "An expensive charter?"

Sutton pursed his lips. "Not cheap. But then again, compared to the value of the wool she's brought here, a good investment."

As he was speaking the dockside crane lifted a bale of fleece over the ship's rail. It hovered, swaying slightly until the foreman ashore judged it safely clear, and it descended slowly to the quay, coming to rest just yards from where they were standing. Behind them, the caravani were already trundling their carts down the Molo to the Siberia, bearing the bales already landed.

Nico glanced at the dappled sky above them. "Autumn is already upon us and soon people will start to think of their winter warmth. You should do well with these."

"I had hoped that you would be able to handle it for us."

"Alas, as I explained, without a licence – and the capital – I am for the present unable to help you. But if I could suggest, Signore Lercari's bank would no doubt be happy to take on the trades. Otherwise, you may have to find buyers with ready money."

"You're right about that. I went to the Loggia di Banchi this morning. Hardly the same as on my last visit two years ago. Where *are* all the bankers?"

"The *cambisti* have gone to their estates in the hills, to wait for better times."

"The merchants I spoke to said there was very little credit available currently. It had disappeared like snow in springtime, one said. There's clearly been a large contraction of capital, wouldn't you say? Or" Sutton's eyebrows raised, "did your present difficulties scare the others off?"

"Well, in all modesty, I suppose that the suspension of Banco Castello gave *some* of them pause for thought. But there was a whole chain of events over a short period, which changed people's attitudes. The seas are full of pirates. The Ottomans are threatening again. We especially began to worry about the situation between Spain and England. Was it peace - or war? The *cambisti* want to know which, before they open their books to foreign merchants again. Even Spain herself is challenged to raise new credit."

"Is that so? Mind you, this is the same fear that concerned the Merchant Adventurers too. No doubt you've heard of Drake, Sir Francis Drake?"

Nico gave a sardonic laugh. "Ah, Il Drago, signore. Well, I think every merchant or ship's master in Europe has heard of *him*. Especially after the assault on Cádiz."

"Well, in early July I think it was, Drake arrived back in England from the Western Ocean. Bringing with him the "*San Felipe*", a royal ship. I saw her at anchor on the way out from Plymouth."

So, Drake sailed home with his prize intact, thought Nico. *The Spanish must be smarting, if they'd been unable to stop him.* "Yes, we heard of her capture," he merely said.

"After hearing *that*," continued Sutton, "I did wonder how things would be going for Monty. Another reason I decided to come here myself."

Nico felt an impulse to tell Sutton that the capture of the "*San Felipe*" was more than just part of the 'chain of events' he'd referred to. But he resisted it.

Chapter Forty-Three
CASA DELLA VOLTA, CARICAMENTO: LATE OCTOBER

As Sutton had requested, the officials at Porta Siberia finally confirmed that his documents of title were in order. So, the wool that Monty had brought to Genova in the "*Kateryn*" and her sister ships was duly released and delivered to its buyers. The purchase payments that Nico had financed were reimbursed to him. He could also now be confident of receiving the Merchant Adventurer's bank deposits in London, which covered Monty's purchases of silk and spices. True to his word, Sutton had sent urgent instructions to the London bankers to release the funds to the order of Banco Castello. Once these transactions were discharged, Nico's accounts would at last be squared off. The ever-present threat of bankruptcy would be lifted.

And, miracle of miracles, he found himself in overall profit on the trades. His first response was to apply that surplus to pay off his personal debts: first, the loan from Ferrucio Lercari; then his patient lawyer, Tasso, for his unpaid fees; and finally, the bills of his not so patient household creditors. Luca, Maria and young Lorenzo got their back wages and each a bonus for their loyalty. Once all that was cleared off, Nico went to see Treasurer Saluzzo at the San Giorgio, to discuss his licence. Saluzzo was in his office attended by his principal secretary, Giuseppe Colombo.

"I congratulate you, Signore Castello. Quite a relief no doubt," said the direttore. His tone made Nico feel that his recent trials were small matters, of no great consequence to the San Giorgio. "So, we look forward to renewing your permits - at the All-Saints' Fair."

"Do we need to wait until then? I have met all the bank's conditions," said Nico.

"The Fair is merely a few weeks away, now. And it would be highly irregular for the board to consider such matters between Fairs."

"But there are so few transactions being done in the Loggia right now," Nico argued. "If I can write substantial new business with Signore Sutton's Merchant Adventurers, for example, it would encourage the other *cambisti* to get going again."

The treasurer gave Nico a long look. "Perhaps so. I will speak to my committee."

Saluzzo glanced across at Secretary Colombo, who duly made a note in his ledger.

OVER THE COURSE of the following weeks, Sutton was invited to dinner at Casa Castello several times. Nico was in a mood to celebrate his having cheated bankruptcy and, while the setting wasn't as grand as it would once have been at the house on Strada Nuova, the food and wine were of the best. Over the dinner table, Lisa was charm itself towards their guest: the fact of his being English didn't appear to appear to concern her anymore, Nico noted. The meal over, Lisa excused herself, leaving banker and merchant to their business talk. And their wine.

Sutton leaned towards his host. "I congratulate you, signore, excuse me, Nico, you are most fortunate in your marriage," he said. "I recall Monty mentioning the Signora in one of his letters to me. He was struck by her great beauty - and her intelligence."

"When she came to know his true character, my wife admired your nephew also. But, if you don't mind my saying, he...he might also have told you that initially she was, well to be frank with you, a little reluctant to regard him as a welcome house guest. Or any Englishman, for that matter."

"Yes, you remind me. In one of his letters Monty related that terrible business about her father. Made quite an impression on him. And myself, I have to say. I have taken the opportunity to express my sympathies to Signora Castello."

"Yes, she mentioned it. No doubt as time passes, that pain will ease for her."

"But that does not make good her loss, does it? In my judgment, she is owed an apology from Drake, some recompense even. He's my fellow-countryman, but I tell you, Nico, merchant to merchant, that man needs to be stopped. Or at least, curbed." He reached for his wine, after that little speech.

"Well, you are gracious to say so. But would he not claim that he is merely doing his sovereign's business?"

Sutton's wine glass was mid-way to his lips, but he paused and put it down. "Perhaps he would. And perhaps for *some*, his freebooter ways suit the times. But I believe that peaceful trade with other nations will gain us more, much more in the long run, than his kind of...plundering. Of course, King Philip would need to see it that way as well. Until he does, we English must defend ourselves. So, I suppose that for now, a man like Drake is a kind of necessary evil."

Nico didn't comment.

"You see, Nico," continued Sutton, "for a long time now, relations between my country and Spain have been broken. Skewered somewhere between peace and war. And we've also known for several years that, given the opportunity, Philip would seize our kingdom and replace Elizabeth, our prince, with someone more acceptable to Spain. I'm not saying anything to you, Nico, that isn't freely talked about, across the courts of Europe. Not openly perhaps, but as the subject of whispers in the corridors and anterooms."

"The *'Enterprise of England'*, I believe they call it," confirmed Nico.

"Exactly so. But these days, it is not just gossip among Europe's courtiers. It has become real – and imminent. And as you also know, Drake – and others – have been doing their best to reduce Philip's ability to invade us. His taking of prizes and burning of stores was part of that strategy, no doubt. I said before that I don't approve of Drake's freebooting methods – speaking as a merchant – but his piracy is merely the consequence of his being expected to fight for his Sovereign, without being paid for it."

"And so far, the strategy as you call it, seems to have worked."

Sutton shrugged. "It has delayed Philip, no doubt, but it has not altered his resolve one jot. If anything, it has made him more determined. And remember, we may have the Queen's navy as well as Drake's ships and those of the other privateers, but Philip has a huge standing army, the most feared in Europe. And his navy is getting larger all the time. At this rate, he will soon be able to crush us like an insect."

"All this is no doubt true, Tomas, but there's not a lot you and I can do about it, is there? Like you said, we're just private merchants." He refilled Sutton's glass.

He sensed that Sutton wanted to continue the topic but had then thought better of it. Instead, Sutton changed the subject to the following day's business.

AFTER AN ANXIOUS WAIT, Nico's licence was restored to him by the San Giorgio, although only temporarily, until the Easter Fair. He discovered some time later that he largely had Giuseppe Colombo, the Secretary, to thank for the expedition with which this was handled, although both Ferrucio Lercari and Battista Lomellino were vocally supportive of his case. It enabled him to complete new trades for Sutton's sales of wool from the "*George Buonaventure*", generating his first real income for many weeks. As he had predicted, the cooler weather had provided the necessary prod to the manufactories to increase their purchases of English wool. The sales were quickly agreed. By the third week of October, all Sutton's wool was accounted for and the silks and spices that Monty had originally purchased were being stowed aboard ship, ready for Sutton's homeward voyage.

On one of these fine autumn days, Sutton accepted an invitation from Nico to go hunting. To Nico, the fact that it could happen at all was a sign of his restoration. He had been forced to sell all his horses back in the summer, saving beloved Mimi, but Luca had found a couple of mounts to hire for the day.

It was one of the first hunts of the new season. Just after dawn on a mist-cloaked morning, Nico and Sutton joined the assembled riders at Porta San Tommaso. Astride the hunter, the Englishman looked even smaller than usual, but he showed himself to be a confident horseman as they made their way up the rough pathways to the Polcevera valley.

Later that afternoon, the Doge's hounds flushed out a stag, but despite a gallant chase their quarry escaped into deep woodland. As Nico and Sutton pulled up, their mounts breathing hard in the cool air, the Englishman was elated.

"Well, no prizes for us today I think," he said between gulps of air, "but that was great sport, Nico."

The sun was setting by the time the two men returned to the city. A change of clothes and a last evening meal at Nico's house would follow, but first, Sutton had an errand in mind. "A visit to San Luca, I think, before I head for my lodgings. That is if you don't mind, Nico."

It was full dusk when they reached the simple church, but even so its stone and marble shone proudly in the fading light. They walked down the aisle, and the Englishman dropped some coins in a box, placing a couple of candles beneath the Virgin. Then, walking across to a side chapel, he went through his prayers. Nico studied his guest as he performed his observances. As Nico had supposed, Sutton like his nephew had kept to the old religion.

After sitting back in his pew and contemplating for a few moments, Sutton stood up and re-joined Nico.

"You're ready?"

"Oh yes, thank you." They walked to the door. "I asked the saint if it were possible to have calm seas and an uneventful journey homewards," he added, as Nico held the door open for him to pass through.

"That is my wish also, Tomas."

NICO LOOKED at the writing on a letter which Maria handed to him. He recognised Sandro's hand and felt a pang of guilt that he had only recently responded to his brother's first letter. It was evident from Sandro's opening words that Nico's letter had not yet arrived when it was written. Sandro was hoping to conclude his first transaction, for an alum merchant, but he cautioned that Antwerp's trade, especially that across the North Sea, with England, Sweden and the League ports, was still being hampered by the river blockade by the Northern rebels. That might not last, but more seriously, there was a steady exodus from the city going on. The Duke of Parma had decreed that all Protestants in the city would be required, if they wished to stay, to renounce their heresy and return to the True Faith. Some had done so, but many people, including merchants and tradesmen, had decided to move north to the rebel provinces. Even Huysmans had hinted to Sandro that he was contemplating moving his business and his family to Amsterdam.

Being Sandro, his brother could not resist incorporating some local gossip in his missive, most of which Nico skimmed over. The names meant little to him, until he came to a section near the end which made him blink.

"As you can imagine, there are quite a few Italian merchants based

here, from Venezia and Napoli as well as Genova. Consequently, I am in much demand for social engagements. The other day, I was at one of these when I was told that another Genovese had just arrived in the city. You won't believe it, brother, but apparently it is Guido Vacchero. Did you know of his departure? Has he been banished? I said nothing of what we know, of course. How strange that he should be here, of all places."

Nico folded up the letter. He must follow up his recent letter to Sandro immediately. And warn him to be on his guard. That the priest had journeyed that far suggested that he had gone with the assistance and protection of the archbishop. He was not in hiding, either. But then, why would he need to? The writ of Genova's ducal authorities did not run in Antwerp. He was effectively immune from prosecution, unless he ever returned, which seemed unlikely. Nico could pass the information on to Capitano Merello, but in truth that would merely provide the captain with a reason to close his files. *The suspect has fled the country, nothing further to be done.*

He left the studiolo and took the letter with him. Lisa was in their bedroom, with the shutters open looking out from the balcony. The sun was sinking behind the hills, the ships' masts making long lines of shadow across the harbour.

"We have a letter from Sandro."

"Oh, let me see it. Is he well?" she asked, taking the letter at the same time.

"Oh yes, he's fine. I'll write back and tell him that we now have our licence restored and the wool cargo is sold. But read the paragraph near the end. He says that Guido Vacchero has been seen there."

She skimmed the relevant page. Still holding the letter, her arm dropped to her side, almost in resignation.

"To think, supposedly, a man of God. And he can't even bring himself to admit his crime, face his punishment. It is ...despicable."

To Nico, Guido's actions were entirely in character. But he realised that Lisa, even after all that had happened, still didn't see it that way. Probably never would. She expected the Lord's representatives, even those who've broken his most sacred laws, to show their penitence, to set a higher example.

Chapter Forty-Four
THE MERCHANTS' LOGGIA, PIAZZA BANCHI: EARLY NOVEMBER

Nico was making up for lost time. A licensed *cambisto* once again, he set about the steady grind of building up his book and thereby restoring the family's fortunes. Each morning, he duly took his place in the Loggia in Piazza Banchi and mingled with the merchants. He did not have his old corner position sadly, but he had a banca, that was the main thing. Banco Castello was open for business and the word soon got around the merchant stalls out in the piazza: the 'Alchemist' is back.

Luca was with him, taking up the role of guard once again. You could feel the lift in the man's mood as he fussed around the *banca*, checking the locks on the currency chest for the seventh time, moving on the timewasters and smiling at the genuine prospects. Young Lorenzo was there too, ready to run errands and take messages, itching to stand on the Loggia steps and announce their trades. Making people's heads turn, their ears prick up. His declaration that the cargo of the "*George Bonaventure*", Sutton's ship, was duly placed with several buyers, was a particular pleasure. It was good to be part of this great marketplace once more.

Nico had to bear the whole burden of managing the book, of course. There was no Sandro to take a turn in the chair, although he'd never been the most regular attendee in any case. And there was no Mazzini either. His former manager was still happily employed by the Lercaris at Banco di Liguria across the way. He would often drop by and make conversation. Nico wondered if Mazzini would be willing to return to his former employer, but he made no move to offer it. That time might come, but for now Nico was content to build slowly, not overextending his obligations until the bank was more solidly re-established.

He recalled it had taken him the best part of fifteen years to grow the bank from virtually nothing to its leading position, and just a few months to nearly lose it all. Second time around, it would not take fifteen years, with the benefit of experience. Even his past mistakes, or rather especially them, would serve him well this time.

So immersed was he in the business of the day that it was only when he finally walked out of Piazza Banchi and turned right onto Caricamento, that he remembered that Thomas Sutton was due to dine with them that evening. It was to be the last such occasion. Sutton's ship was ready, his trades completed, and the man itself was no doubt itching to get home. Or at least, to get the sailing over and done with before the winter storms set in.

Maria was in the kitchen, preparing the meal. Lisa was busy arranging the furniture and plate in the sala, assisted by young Lorenzo. On a couple of previous occasions when Sutton had dined with them, they had invited a few friends to make a small *festa*, but on this occasion at his request, it was just the Englishman.

"What time is our guest expected?" he asked, as he greeted his wife.

"Oh, in about an hour. He has gone back to Casa Cavalli to change."

"Gone back?"

"Yes, he was passing the house earlier and called to say he wanted to visit the cemetery. He was checking if he had enough time to do so. So, I said I would go with him, because he wasn't too sure of the way."

"He was visiting Monty's grave?"

"Yes, he wanted to go there before leaving for England. I think he was quite affected by seeing it."

Reaching over, Nico stole a grape from the majolica platter in the middle of the dining table. Lisa slapped his hand playfully.

"No more, Nico. That's for tonight. Oh, and I should tell you before he arrives, as we were heading back down from the cemetery, he brought up the subject of Guido Vacchero. Naturally, he wants his *vendetta*. And, well, we got to talking and I mentioned that I had felt betrayed by that man too. That he had used me to get to you, to persuade you to do business with the Spanish envoy. I'm sorry – I probably shouldn't have mentioned that – but it felt strange knowing what I knew, at the same time as he was so bitter about it all."

Nico shrugged. "Well, I don't make a practice of talking to one customer about another customer, it's true, but this case is a bit different. Besides, I don't expect the Spanish will be asking me for a loan in the future. And even if they did, I'd refuse."

"So, you're not cross with me? It just jumped out of my mouth, Nico. We were both roused to anger by seeing Monty's grave. Who said that cemeteries were havens of calm?"

When Sutton arrived, he was as ever the courteous and charming guest, but Nico had the feeling that he was preoccupied. He was looking vacantly into the middle distance from time to time and he was drinking rather more heavily than had been his practice on previous occasions.

Maria cleared away the plates from the main course and brought in a platter of nuts and cheeses. Lisa told her that she would not be needed any further that evening. Maria bobbed a curtsey and shut the sala door behind her. Nico opened another bottle and filled his guest's glass and then his wife's.

Sutton took a sip, placed his glass carefully down and glanced at them both. "Signora Lisa mentioned to me today that, before I came here, you had had some dealings with the Spanish envoy."

"That's true," said Nico, "although, strictly between us, the transaction never came to full fruition. The relationship broke down when I was having difficulties on other fronts."

"I can imagine. Rest assured, Nico, I can keep a confidence. We are, after all, in the same business."

"I never doubted that."

"I'd heard from some of the other *cambisti* that this Senor Zúñiga - was that it? – had been here in Genoa, trying to raise funds for King Philip. I expect that after your difficulties with lending to him, he tried to look elsewhere. Do you think he succeeded? You don't need to reveal anything you shouldn't."

While Sutton reached for the cheese board, Nico recalled the gossip that had surrounded Zúñiga's departure. The courtier had, so Nico was told by his source, departed the port with the minimum of ceremony. He was clearly out of sorts, short-tempered with all those around him. At one point, there being a shortage of sea-going traffic heading in the direction of Cádiz, one port official had suggested to Zúñiga that he might seek a berth on the "*Mary Gale*", Master Winterhey's ship, that was expected to leave harbour shortly to head through the Straits. Zúñiga had replied that he would rather swim to Seville, than share part of the voyage with those English pirates. He guessed that would amuse the Englishman.

"Well of course, this type of business the *cambisti* keep close to their chests," Nico began, "but with the shrinking of credit we have seen these last weeks and months, and the absence of certain players from the field, I would hazard quite a bit of money that Senor Zúñiga returned to Spain a disappointed man."

Nico saw a trace of a smile on Sutton's lips. It broadened into full laughter when Nico related the joke about the "*Mary Gale.*"

"NICO, my dear Lisa, you have both been honest with me, which I greatly appreciate, more than you know. And I will of course respect your confidence. Now it's my turn to be frank with you."

Nico wondered what Sutton could possibly have to confess, as the Englishman sipped his wine.

"Of course, I could have anticipated that this Senor Zúñiga – or another like him – would have been here in Genoa. It's surely no secret that the Spanish crown raises funds here."

Nico spread his hands outwards by way of concurring with his guest.

"But what I hadn't expected, what came as a surprise was when Signora Lisa told me that it was the archbishop and his priest who had been the intermediaries in this loan business. Archbishop Sauli and this …Guido Vacchero." He seemed to say the name with difficulty. "It's only now that I see their intent behind it all, that I realise why they – why they had my poor nephew killed."

Nico had always thought – had suggested to Sutton – that Monty was "in their way" because he was like them, on the hunt for large amounts of credit. But this sounded different. "You *know* why?" he said.

Sutton put both hands on the dining table, palms downward. "What I'm about to tell you both is a most delicate matter. I cannot emphasise enough that it cannot, must never, go beyond these walls. It seems to me that we are bound to each other by our mutual interests and therefore we can have confidence in one another's trust. I acknowledge that you might inform your brother of what I'm about to impart, since he already knows much of the same story, but I can accept that. It will be for you to decide when and whether it is prudent to do so."

Nico gestured his assent.

"Well then, I suppose this all began a few months ago, when I was summoned to the home of a Privy Councillor. Sir Francis Walsingham. You might know the name?"

Nico recalled it. That gentleman's name had come up when Monty and the archbishop had crossed swords verbally at the Castello's grand *festa*.

"He is the Queen's Principal Secretary and is I suppose known for being – well, not so well known. For handling all sorts of delicate and confidential matters for Her Majesty, at home and overseas. Imagine my surprise when he began our meeting by asking me questions about the banking trade. How was trade financed? Who were the leading players? Where did Philip borrow money to build his navy? How was it that Genoa's bankers continued to support Philip, despite his previous loan defaults? I answered them as best I could. Eventually I asked him straight out. *Why these questions?* Before he would answer, he first made me sign the Oath of Allegiance. Then he told me he wanted to find a way to stop Philip's bankers from lending to him. Walsingham felt, strongly, that England was unprepared to rebuff a Spanish invasion. He needed time to prepare her defences. If he could somehow delay Philip from receiving new loans, that time could be bought. I recall his next question, *"What would deter a banker from granting credit to an established customer?"*

"What was your answer?" said Nico.

"I said that there were only two reasons really: *one*, the risk of the borrower's default had become too high or *two*, the banker had been offered more attractive business elsewhere, and had taken it, thereby exhausting his capital."

Nico nodded approvingly, one banker to another.

"So, then he says to me: '*So, Master Sutton, if we were to offer the bankers in Genoa so much attractive business that it absorbed all their capital over a period of months, how would that be?*'."

Nico suddenly realised where this could be heading.

Sutton continued. "I thought about what Walsingham had said for a few days and then I met him again. I told him I thought it could be done. If the Council bought up England's surplus of premier quality wool and we took it to Genoa. We'd sell it mainly to weavers who didn't have ready funds, those who needed credit from their bankers, in other words. That way, we could absorb the bullion the Genoese bankers provided. He liked the proposal, but then we calculated how much that would amount to, in silver. He, Sir Francis, decides that isn't enough money to be certain of our goal. So, then I say to him, *"We can nearly double the effect if we are also buyers in the same market. If we buy up large cargoes of silk, pepper, cloves, nutmeg and we use loans from the local bankers to pay for it."* He asks how we could be sure that the bankers would lend to us. I said that if we offered them, as collateral, deposits of equivalent value, deposited in London banks that the Genoese trusted, that would give them the security they needed. It would be hard to resist."

How right Sutton was, thought Nico, remembering the list of deposit accounts that Monty had shown him on their first meeting. *The largest piece of merchant business this year, or any year,* he had said to himself at the time. And now he knew why. He could feel his heart beating faster. "And he agreed to all this?" he said, his voice husky with anticipation.

"He did. So, we put it in motion. No-one knew, apart from Walsingham and me. As far as I knew, he didn't tell any of his fellow Privy Councillors. Certainly not the Queen, even though it was her Exchequer he was spending. We agreed that the plan was only likely to succeed if *everyone* believed it was ordinary merchant business."

"So, those deposits, the ones assigned to me as part of the *cambio secco*, what you're telling me is that in truth that money came from the English Privy Council, not the Merchant Adventurers?"

"You have got there before me. It was from the Exchequer. Every penny. And indeed, it was the Exchequer's money which paid for the wool we purchased to bring here. Although, all this money went through the Merchant Adventurers' ledgers, so that it looked like ordinary mercantile business."

Nico shook his head. He recalled how Monty had tended to prefer the weavers who wanted to borrow from the *cambisti,* not the buyers with ready money. But he had never thought it suspicious. "Ingenious, Tomas, ingenious," he said, but inside he was furiously searching for the clues that he might have missed at the time.

Sutton breathed out heavily. "Perhaps so. All the same, I wish now I'd never thought of it."

Lisa heard the despair in her guest's voice. "Because of Monty," she said quietly.

"Yes of course, signora, because of Monty. Oh, I'd worried about the sea voyage here, but I assumed that once he was in Genoa, he would be safe. After all, who would be suspicious of a young merchant like him? No-one."

"Well, you didn't know that the Spanish were here at exactly the same time - and that they were aided by ...by *some* of our churchmen," she said.

"Oh, we assumed that *someone* would be here from Madrid trying to raise funds. That was the whole point of the stratagem, after all. If Walsingham knew about Zúñiga being here or even what Archbishop Sauli's role was and didn't want to tell me, I have no idea. The rumour in London is that Secretary Walsingham has agents in every capital in Europe. No doubt that includes Genoa."

"Did Monty know he was playing an actor's role?" Lisa asked.

Sutton shook his head. "Walsingham persuaded me that I mustn't tell him. Said he would be safer not knowing. Against my better judgment, I agreed."

"From what I saw of Monty, I wonder if Sir Francis wasn't in the right," said Nico. "As much as I came to think of him as a friend, he wasn't always the most tight-lipped person. How could he have kept such a big secret to himself?"

"Perhaps that's true. But he had a right to know the risk he was taking. No?"

"You can say that now, Tomas, but as I said, how would you ever have known beforehand that people like Guido Vacchero would go to any lengths, even murder, to assist the Spanish? And after all, we don't know that they killed Montague *because* of your scheme of make-believe. It's possible, likely even given the secrecy that surrounded it, that they weren't even aware of your plan. They could have murdered him simply because he was in their way, a large borrower soaking up "their" capital as they saw it."

"You try to temper my guilt, Nico, but the penny plain fact is I devised the plan, I drew my nephew into it and I didn't tell him the whole truth."

"Is it presumptuous of me to suggest that, had he died on the beach at the hands of common thieves, that would have been an even greater waste? At least he died being part of something important," he added. But even as he tried to reassure Sutton, Nico's mind was still swimming with the implications of what he'd just been told.

Sutton's voice sounded choked. "Yes, but not even knowing that he *had* succeeded. At the time of his last letter to me he feared he'd been a failure. Whereas in truth, I now know that the plan had worked, had succeeded beyond my expectations. Not all our trades had been concluded, true, but when I came here it appeared that we had locked up the capital in Genoa to the point where the Spanish went home empty-handed. As you confirmed earlier. And Monty didn't even know - that was what he was here for."

Sutton's expression was wretched, the enormity of it overwhelming him. Nico looked at the empty glass. Lisa stood up. "If you'd prefer to be alone for a moment, signore, Nico and I can leave you here," she said, glancing at her husband.

"Oh no. Please excuse me. I should be going in any case."

"As you wish, of course. But we insist that Luca escort you home," said Nico.

SUTTON WAS NOT the only one wishing to be alone. Having said goodnight to their guest, Lisa retired for the night. But Nico went straight to his studiolo and shut the door. For a long time, he sat at his desk staring at the walls. The rows of bank ledgers stared back at him. The documentary evidence of the transactions arranged by the 'Alchemist'. The proof of his supreme skill as a banker and his so-called prescience in matters of business.

The times he had argued with Sandro, saying that merchant business was vastly to be preferred to dealing with princes. How the English merchants could be trusted to meet their commitments, whereas the bank would be taking a huge risk dealing with King Felipe. And here he was, having imposed that policy, finding that he had been transacting business with a prince all the time, even if Queen Elsabetta was unaware of it herself. It would be funny were it not a bitter irony.

And then his arguments with Lisa. His insistence that bankers should ignore matters of state or religion and focus only on credit. On how much trust they could place in a client. How his words came back to haunt him!

What vanity it had been, Nico! What was it you used to claim? "We are open to borrowers of all faiths. We have but one creed. We believe that our customers will pay us back." *You fondly imagined you could judge honesty and transparency better than your fellow man or woman. You had come to believe in your own reputation, as if that were the same thing as the truth.*

He tried to console himself with the thought that key judgments on people hadn't been mistaken. Monty had been just as decent as he'd believed, an honourable citizen, one who never knew his unwitting role as Walsingham's agent. Even Sutton, though he was privy to the scheme, was driven to admit it by his sense of honour. And Nico's mistrust of Father Guido and the archbishop had been entirely vindicated. He'd known what they were, even if he hadn't anticipated the depravities of which they were capable.

But he'd also been taken in by Walsingham's game, along with everyone else. He recalled saying to Sandro, "*Don't underestimate that English wasp, Sandro, if it stings hard enough the Spanish bull will run off.*" Nico vowed not to underestimate the English again.

THE MORNING CAME TOO EARLY at Casa Castello and over a largely conversation-free breakfast Nico and Lisa kept mostly to their own thoughts. Then Nico remembered he was going across to Sutton's lodgings at Signore Cavalli to escort his client to the harbour. Sutton's embarkation on the "*George Bonaventure*" was now just hours away. He arranged that Lisa would meet them both on the quayside.

Signore Cavalli was in a jovial mood that morning and Nico and Sutton passed a pleasant hour until Sutton started thinking about the tide and fretting to leave. They headed off down the hill, with one of the porters from the *caravani* following behind, struggling to prevent Sutton's baggage from rolling away with the cart.

They had reached the San Giorgio when Nico said, "Tomas, I've been reflecting about last night, about what you told us. A compelling story. But I am wondering one thing: why tell us at all? You could have returned to England without saying a word about it. I wouldn't have been any the wiser."

"Yes, I could have done that but...it didn't sit right with me. I realised that I had withheld the truth from Monty, and that still troubles me. How could I make my peace with my poor nephew, while at the same time, keeping the story hidden from the man he trusted? Through your dealings with Monty and now with me, I felt I was safe to confide in you."

"Rest assured, you are."

"In telling you of Walsingham's plan, I also said to myself," Sutton continued, "that it had achieved its purpose. To be frank, the risk of its becoming known about by those loyal to Spain was no longer critical. And I knew we would never essay this game a *second* time. It would only ever work the once. One day soon, Philip will complete his invasion fleet and when he does, England will have to fight him with more than just our credit exchanges."

"But you have your own navy?"

"Yes, but our ships will be outnumbered - and heavily I suspect."

"It isn't the ships that make a navy, it's the captains who command them," Nico observed.

THE "*GEORGE BONAVENTURE*" was more than ready by the look of her. Pennants flying from the main and mizzen masts. Just two ropes, fore and aft, to be released. And a single gangway waiting for Sutton to cross. She looked like a hunting dog, tugging at the leash.

Sutton embraced Lisa and thanked her for her hospitality. "And for the gift. It will have pride of place on my sideboard." Lisa had, unprompted by Nico, given the Englishman a beautifully carved majolica plate bearing on its design the oranges of Genova and the wine grapes of its hillside vines. And on its rim the legend of Banco Castello.

"I have something for you also," he said. Lisa opened the small parcel. Inside was a brooch, studded with small pearls. And in the centre a small emerald. Her lips parted in a sign of her pleasure at the gift. "I noticed that you have other jewellery with these stones, so hopefully it is to your taste," he said casually.

It was time. Nico and he embraced and then with a small bow of the head, he turned to board.

"You must visit London, and soon," he called out from the rail, "there is plenty of room for an enterprising banker there."

"Perhaps. We go to Antwerp, to see my brother Sandro, in the spring. We could cross over to the English side."

As they walked home along Caricamento, they sometimes glanced back to see if the "*George Bonaventure*" had shed her moorings. Then they saw her main mast moving slowly past the last of the buildings on the Molo. Within minutes, she was clear of the breakwater and took on more sail.

"So," began Lisa, leaning on her husband's arm, "it seems that our own clergy are not the only plotters and schemers. Even your 'honest'

English merchants have devious plans up their sleeves." She inserted her arm in his.

"True enough. I never claimed they had a monopoly of virtue. But at least their scheming didn't involve abduction and murder."

"Signore Sutton seems an honourable man. Why would he get entangled in something like this?"

"I'm not sure he had a choice. When Secretary Walsingham asks you to do something he is speaking for his sovereign, after all. Not so easy to say no."

"I don't think I like the sound of *him*."

Nico shrugged. "Maybe not. But he does what he must do. Every prince gathers around them the men who enable them to prevail - or at least survive what their enemies throw at them. Walsingham is no different - just better at it than some of the others."

Chapter Forty-Five

BARN ELMS, PUTNEY, NEAR LONDON:
MID-DECEMBER

Across the park from Secretary Walsingham's study window, the River Thames was draped in a garland of fog. White upon white. Inside, the Privy Councillor sat with Thomas Sutton, in front of a roaring fire. Normally, Ursula Walsingham preferred to keep their riverside home a place of retreat, somewhere her husband could escape the duties that fell upon him, night and day, at their house in Scything Lane. But once again duty had prevailed and Sutton, as soon as he had disembarked at St Katheryn's Wharf, had been summoned upriver to Barnes.

Walsingham scrutinised his visitor's solemn face, when Sutton had completed his report. He parted the bridge that he had made of his fingers, by way of announcing his response.

"I must congratulate you, Thomas, on your notable success."

"I can scarcely claim it as entirely mine, Sir Francis, given it was your proposal."

"Nevertheless, you implemented it." Walsingham paused and stared into the fire. "Although, at the same time, my joy is tempered. By two things. First, it has come at a heavy cost. I mean your own nephew, of course."

"In truth, I would undo it all, not to have sent him."

"I cannot make that right, Thomas, but you have my assurance that the Council will offer what help it can to Mistress Jane Belltower. His widow deserves some recompense for his valiant work."

"I am sure she will take comfort in whatever the Council decides is appropriate. But while we are talking about recompense," Sutton added, "there is another lady who is, in my humble opinion, deserving of our recognition - and sympathy."

"And who is that?"

"Signora Castello. Known as Lisa Della Volta, before she was married to our banker friend."

"But what do we owe her, exactly?"

"We made her an orphan. Or rather I should say Drake did. At Cartagena."

Walsingham listened as Sutton told the story. At the end, he shook his head slightly. "It is of course regrettable, Thomas. But I am sure you understand, there are times when innocent persons are caught up in a fight between two nations. This gentleman was unlucky to be in the crossfire between Drake and the Spanish. And if we offered financial recompense to every civilian killed in this way, the Exchequer would soon feel the burden."

"I'm not suggesting that we offer *money* to Signora Castello. Knowing the lady as I do, she would be affronted and, in any case, her enterprising husband is surely on his way to becoming a wealthy man, again. She has no need of our financial support."

"Then what are you suggesting? An apology implies our guilt. A dangerous precedent."

"With respect, Sir Francis, I see it differently. Even if we hold to the stance that Drake is absolved of any personal responsibility, the fact is that her father's death could have been costly to us. Her antipathy nearly propelled Banco Castello into the arms of the Spanish king. As it was, only timing saved us – that, and the venality and brutality of certain clergymen, which turned the lady against their cause. We were lucky. An apology would cost nothing - and it might just gain us a powerful ally in Genoa."

Walsingham tapped the desk with his fingertips. "You make a good point, Thomas. As I know myself, it is far easier - and cheaper - to keep someone as our friend than to bear the consequences of turning them into our enemy." He glanced out of the window at the mist hovering over the Thames. "We have enemies enough."

He stood up, decision made. "I shall write to Sir Francis Drake and see what he has to say on the matter."

Sutton picked up his cloak and hat. "You said there were *two* reasons that your joy was tempered?"

Walsingham looked bemused for a moment, as if he had forgotten.

"Oh yes. Simply this. Our scheme's success has put off the evil day when Philip launches his army against us. But only for months perhaps. I must ensure that the time is not wasted. With the breathing space we have won, I must make England ready. The Lord knows, it will be no simple task."

HAVING ESCORTED his visitor to the door, Walsingham returned to his desk, pondering what he would say – and not say – to Drake. The man was not the force he had once been, especially in those years after his journey around the globe, but he still needed careful handling to get him to climb down from his pedestal. In the end, he wrote a simple request to the sailor, asking him to visit Scything Lane the next time he was in the capital.

The more immediate question revolved around England's friends and enemies in Genoa. A few of their merchants and bankers were clearly well disposed towards the English. The men representing the civil power, Governor Doria, the Doge and the Gran Consiglio, these men were friends with Spain, it was true, but they were also pragmatists, careful to preserve their own interest and Genoa's independence from its principal debtor, King Philip. So arguably neutral. But not so some of the priesthood. And even Archbishop Sauli, it seemed.

The archbishop, now a cardinal, was effectively untouchable in the Vatican. No doubt he would continue to scheme there, but there was little to be done about it. But then there was that priest, Guido Vacchero. An obsessive enemy, hiding behind his clerical habit, resolute in opposing us. And not a man to be bought with forty pieces of silver.

And now, according to the Castello brothers, he was based in the Netherlands which for Walsingham was rather too close to home. Hostilities between Spain and the Dutch rebels were temporarily halted there, it was true. The Duke of Parma was seemingly content to halt in Antwerp, rather than press on to try and retake the Northern Provinces. But who knew what this Vacchero might meddle in? Someone had to be sent there to find out. If the priest became a threat, someone who could handle it and if need be, ensure that Vacchero vanished from the scene. But who to pick from among his agents? After a moment, it came to him. Francis Needham, currently posing as Leicester's secretary, was the obvious choice. He reached for his quill again.

Chapter Forty-Six
CASA DELLA VOLTA, CARICAMENTO: 31ST DECEMBER 1587

Lisa and Nico walked through the *sala*, checking last-minute preparations for their *festa*. The furniture had been cleared and in an hour's time, the room would be full of friends and family celebrating the end of the year, one which had finished far better than Nico would have predicted just three months earlier. But more than the revival of his business fortunes, Nico treasured the sense that domestic life had emerged from months of doubt and conflict.

Ferro Lercari and his wife were to be among the guests, which would afford Nico and Lisa the opportunity to offer their congratulations: An invitation had just come to join the Lercari family on the following Saturday for the *anellamento* of their son Gino and Nicoletta De Marini, whose wedding was planned for the spring. Nico and Lisa had already got wind of the forthcoming nuptials from an unusual source, Adriana, who had set up a new dressmaking business and had been commissioned to make Nicoletta's wedding dress. Indiscreet as ever. The other news imparted by Adriana was that the new Doge, Davide Vacca, had decided to exercise his right of clemency in certain cases, as result of which Bianca Bastone would soon be released from Santa Maria. The Brozzi confession coupled with Nicoletta's testimony about Monty's incarceration had obviously proved instrumental in engaging the Doge's sympathy for the former courtesan. "She will become my partner in the business," Adriana had announced proudly.

"A pity Sandro isn't here, to share our table," said Lisa, now satisfied with the preparations.

They were about to head to their bedroom, to dress for the *festa*, when Luca came along the corridor bearing a small package.

"A courier has just brought this, signore."

It was written in a hand which looked familiar to Nico, but he couldn't place for the moment. He opened the letter.

"Ah, it's from Tomas Sutton, Lisa. From London."

They sat at the table as Nico scanned the contents.

"He asks firstly, that I express to you his sincere esteem and good wishes," he explained to her. "He had a safe, uneventful return to England. The cargo has been sold and the Adventurers are well pleased with the business. He hopes they will return to Genova next spring. He says that he has spoken to Sir Francis Drake about your father and...."

Nico's voice tailed off as he took in what he was reading. Then he resumed, but more slowly. "He says he is enclosing a letter from ... Drake which he prays will be of some comfort to you...."

He glanced at the enclosed, sealed letter, addressed to "Signora Lisa Castello". The seal displayed the impress of a shield. It bore two stars, one below the other, the fess dividing them in the form of a wave. He passed the letter to Lisa, who opened it with a bemused expression. A small silver medallion fell out of the envelope. The letter was written in Italian, the work of a translator, Nico presumed. Lisa read it aloud.

"Buckland Abbey, Plymouth, Devon.
The first day of December 1587.
To La Signora Lisa Castello
My Dear Lady

I have been advised by Sir Francis Walsingham, Privy Councillor to Her Majesty Queen Elizabeth, whom God preserve, that your late father, Cristoforo Della Volta, was present in Cartagena in the Indies at the time of my assault on that Spanish harbour. And, it is said in certain quarters, that he was struck down by my own cannon, and so died.

Permit me to give you my own account of the matter which, as I hereby do swear by Almighty God, is the plain truth and nothing else. First, let me say that such little fighting as there was before the city surrendered to me, was confined to its harbour, where the Spanish had stationed a few pinnaces, and to the perimeter wall between harbour and town, where there was a small defending force of militia. Although there was some unintended damage to the cathedral during our assault, there was no necessity of firing our cannon into the city itself. The notion that we fetched destruction on the Governor's mansion is merely that, the purest notion. I stayed in the very same house after our troops were landed and throughout my sojourn in the city thereafter.

When staying there, I was told that many of the inhabitants had recently been struck with the ague. This was no surprise to me, as I had lost many dozens of my own men to the fever or flux, many more than ever died during any battle. However, the Spanish did not want it known abroad that the place was full of disease, lest it deter those who were assigned to be stationed there. The Governor was most fearful that this news might spread.

I was also told that there had recently been staying at the Governor's house, an Italian gentleman of middle years. I was informed that he was a distinguished banker from Genoa, there on the business of his own government. But shortly after my arrival there, he succumbed to the same ague as had struck many others. He was therefore interred in the gardens of the mansion. I attended his burial service, which was most respectful

Madam, from what appears to me, I am now in no doubt that this gentleman was regretfully your own father, Signore Cristoforo Della Volta. His clothes and effects *were burned by the household for fear of spreading any contagion, but one item I retained was his badge of office. I kept it out purely out of my own whimsy, because it happened to sport the flag of my country's patron saint, St George. I happily enclose it herewith and pray that it will be a keepsake to you of his memory.*

My condolences for your sad loss and may the Almighty Father, who understandeth all things, grant you His peace.

Sincerely
Sir Francis Drake"

Lisa put down the letter and picked up the medallion. An oval-shaped brooch with silver edging and on its face the cross of San Giorgio, red on white.

She clasped her hand around it. Nico put his hand on top of hers.

THE END

Antonio Semino, *San Giorgio e il Drago*
Genova, Palazzo San Giorgio

Use of Italian and Spanish Terms
(SPANISH TERMS IN ITALICS)

Anellamento: formal ceremony of bethrothal, in which the engaged couple exchange rings as a token of their pledges to one another. Takes place in the future bride's family home.

Asiento: a Spanish legal document, acknowledging entry into a bill of exchange or short-term unsecured loan. Included the promise to pay interest at the agreed rate.

Banca: literally, a bench or table, the simple 'workstation' from which an Italian moneychanger conducted business, from which term 'bank' and 'banker' are derived.

Cambisto/cambisti: moneychanger(s). Hence the modern term 'cambio'. The cambisti provided loans and other financial services, not just currency exchange. 'Cambiale' was the term for the bill of exchange or other finance document.

Canterali: Genoese term for a tall chest of drawers.

Caravani: the porters who worked on the dockside in Genoa harbour.

Caruggio/caruggi: a local dialect name for the narrow alleyways which abounded in Genoa. In Italian, such a passage would be called a 'vicolo'.

Cassone: a wooden chest, a piece of domestic furniture, seen throughout Italy. In principle, these contained bedlinen or clothing but over time they became prized possessions, rather than merely functional items. Often elaborately (and expensively) carved or painted.

Consejo: literally a 'council', but effectively a ministry of the Spanish government, headed by a committee of nobles. Examples were the *Consejo de Finanza* dealing with King Felipe's finances and taxation, and the *Consejo de Guerra*, his ministry for war.

Consulta: a formal report issued by a Spanish minister of state or other official to the king or to a *Consejo,* for their scrutiny and approval.

Credenza: a sideboard, an innovation in furniture at the time, usually in the sala.

Darsena: the naval dockyard in Genoa harbour.

Doge: As in Venice, so also in Genoa, the leader of the civil government. The chairman of the ruling council, the Gran Consiglio, who was elected by his peers and served a two-year term. (But see 'Governor').

Domiductio: the ancient custom whereby, when a woman was married, she would be led in procession (with her dowry) to her new husband's home. Still honoured, ceremonially at least, at the time of our story by citizens lining the streets to witness the bridal pair walking from the wedding church to the groom's house.

Ducal Guard: Genoa's civil police force, in effect. 'Ducal' refers to the Doge and thus incorporates their ceremonial as well as their security function. Stationed at Palazzo Ducale, the Doge's Palace, in the centre of the city, and no doubt elsewhere.

El Draque: the punning nickname, meaning 'dragon', given by the Spanish to Sir Francis Drake. In Italian, 'Il Drago'.

Festa: a party or celebration in a domestic house or in the streets on ceremonial days.

Gagliarda: In French or English, the Galliard. A popular dance throughout Europe, incorporating athletic movements, especially the somewhat sensual but officially disapproved 'La Volta' where the man lifts the woman in the air while their bodies are entwined. Favoured by Queen Elizabeth I, as is often depicted in movies.

Governor: The unelected head of state, at that time, Gianandrea Doria. The Doria family had over several generations maintained the powerful Genoese navy and thereby preserved the Republic against foreign domination. Doria applied the hereditary principle to his succession but was not an absolute ruler (See Doge).

Il Drago: see *'El Draque'*.

Lanterna: the famous lighthouse, bearing the cross of St George on its flank, which still stands at the head of Genoa harbour.

Loggia dei Mercanti (or Loggia di Banchi): the hall with open porticoes flanking Piazza Banchi which housed the tables of the moneychangers.

Majolica: a type of fine tableware for which Genoa was, and is, famous. Fired red clay, it was coated in glazes and typically incorporated elaborate painted scenes in bright, luminous colours.

Merlo: Italian for a blackbird. Bianca Bastone's nickname, on account of her hair colour.

Molo: the name for the long stone jetty stretching out from the Genoa waterfront, against which ships would be moored.

Pammatone: the public hospital in Genoa

Passeggiata: the custom, still popular with Italian families today, of the evening walk. Often, a Sunday affair, but could be done on other days. An opportunity to dress up and to see and be seen. In Genoa, it could have been taken along Caricamento, the broad avenue next to the waterfront. Today, a motorway flyover (the 'Supraelevata') roars above it, so the prospect is less appealing.

Piano nobile: literally, the 'noble floor', it refers to the first floor of the house of a well-to-do family, where the main reception rooms (see 'sala') were to be found. The ground floor would incorporate the courtyard, storerooms etc and the bedrooms were on the upper floors or even (in grand palazzos with double height ceilings) in between floors.

Porta Siberia: the large stone gateway, in the form of a barbican in the city wall, that separated the port from the city. All those arriving by sea had to pass through it and, more importantly, all goods had to be declared and stored there, pending customs clearance. ('Siberia' refers not to that region of Russia, but probably to a grain store, being a corruption of 'Ciberia').

Prottetore: a trustee, or protector of assets. The assignment given to Cristoforo Della Volta by Banco di San Giorgio.

Sala: the principal reception room in a house, which might incorporate credenzas for the flatware and glass, and of course tables for dining and entertaining. In the grander houses, ornamental fireplaces and portraits. A smaller room for more intimate dining, family etc was called the salotto.

Sottoripa: the street underneath the elevated promenade of Caricamento, which housed in its archways, the stores and shops of small merchants.

Sponsalia: the legal document drawn up to record the terms of a marriage contract. It reflected the financial and other arrangements agreed between the respective families of the bride and groom to be. Essentially a business matter, it preceded the anellamento (see above).

Straniero: a stranger, i.e. a foreigner from the Genoese perspective

Studiolo: a male preserve, this was the small study room in the house in which the head of the family would attend (presumably) to his business affairs, keep his library etc.

Zuccoli: ladies high-heeled shoes.

THE SHIPS

Carrack: English version of *carraca*, the Spanish, Portuguese and Genoese word for a large square-rigged sailing ship. The hull was wide with rounded ends, designed to hold substantial cargoes. Not exclusively for merchant use though, it could have a military function or be used for long explorations. The captured *'San Felipe'* featured in the story was one such. Columbus' *'Santa Maria'* and Henry VIII's *'Mary Rose'* are other examples. Being superseded, at the time of our story, by the sleeker Galleon and particularly by the 'race-built' English designs favoured by sailors like Drake.

Demi-culverin: a medium cannon developed for land use but also carried by naval or merchant ships.

Flota: the name by which the Spanish referred to their annual Silver Fleet, the ships that bore gold and silver back to Seville from the Spanish colonies in New Spain (Mexico) and the Kingdom of Peru.

Freebooter: an English term, derived from a Dutch word, meaning a pirate. From this, the Spanish developed their own *'filibustero'* meaning the same thing. (Over time, this morphed into the English word 'filibuster').

Galleass: a composite ship design, developed in Venice in the mid 16th Century, which combined sail and oars. Again, it could have a military or merchant function. Successfully used in the Mediterranean coastal areas for fast attack, it was favoured by Barbary pirates as well as the Venetians and Genoese. Unsuitable for ocean-crossing, six of these took part in the Spanish Armada, but failed to cope with the heavier seas around the British Isles.

Galley: a term for a naval vessel which carries a lateen sail but is primarily powered by banks of oars. Principally for defensive use in mediterranean coastal waters. Genoa had a large fleet of them.

Minion: a ship's cannon smaller and lighter than the culverin or demi-culverin, developed for fast-moving naval warfare. Drake's *'Golden Hind'* carried these.

Privateer: the English term for sailors like Drake and Hawkins, who fought in their own ships alongside Queen Elizabeth's official navy. They were authorised by 'letters of marque' granted by the sovereign which meant that they could undertake military expeditions, takes ships as prizes and generally plunder the enemy's possessions. The Spanish regarded the privateers as, in effect, licensed pirates, but England's sovereign was not alone in the practice of granting these 'letters of marque'.

Author's Notes

DID IT HAPPEN LIKE THIS?

A natural question for the reader of historical fiction to ask is: did the events on which the story is based, really happen? Or is it a work of pure fiction, even if some of the characters portrayed are historical figures? In the case of '*The Alchemist of Genoa*' the truth lies somewhere between the two. There are some footnotes to history which suggest that the Spanish Empire and the English Crown were, at the time, engaged in sophisticated economic warfare, a struggle in which the bankers of Genoa played a part. A 'cold war' which was the prelude to the more famous 'hot' one in 1588, the series of naval engagements which culminated in the defeat of the Spanish Armada, its sorry remnants limping home.

It seems that at least one side used bank finance not merely to pay for war, but as a weapon of war in its own right. But to construct the story, I needed first to 'reverse engineer' the method by which that could have been achieved. It had to be something that was feasible in the context of the markets and methodologies of the time, as well as practical with the modes of transport and speed of communication then available. Fortunately for the story, the bankers of Genoa were at that time probably the most sophisticated practitioners of finance on the planet. Not that they would have so described themselves: they were 'moneychangers', the *cambisti*. But many of the techniques used today for financing international trade had their origins with these men. Their methods will be familiar to their successors in the City of London and on Wall Street.

Early in the novel, we hear a transaction being announced by public outcry in the piazza, as was the practice in Genoa. That transaction is the prototype for what in more recent times would have been termed the ninety-day bill of exchange. Ninety days remained a standard credit period for trade bills for many centuries, but the practice was established back in these days of sail – because that was presumed to be sufficient time for the merchant-borrower to take the cargo from origin - in Genoa or Venice - to their destination, say Antwerp or Paris, resell it and pay his lender back. Another principle of quarterly reckoning was also built into each *cambisto's* own calendar, because Exchange Fairs were held in Genoa and other cities, attracting the merchants of Europe, and that was the time for their finance accounts to be reconciled and bills to be paid. The dates of the Genoa Fairs coincided with events in the religious calendar, being held on the Feast of the Apparition, Easter, August and All Saints.

Genoa, like its great rival Venice, was then at the epicentre of east-west trade. Exotic goods from the East, spices and silk especially, found a ready market in Western Europe. Venice and Genoa financed this trade, using the sophisticated tools they had developed, and in doing so, established a network of relationships with banks in other European cities, their counterparts in these transactions. In times past, the strong links between these two Italian cities and ports in the eastern Mediterranean (which linked them to the Silk Road), had been fundamental to that position. But, by the time of our story, the Portuguese had opened up sea routes to the Far East and these were competing successfully with the overland route. Nevertheless, Genoa's financial expertise and capital wealth enabled it to maintain its stranglehold, even if the ports in Northern Europe were assuming ever greater importance. Once the Spanish (under the Duke of Parma) had retaken Antwerp from the Dutch rebels in 1585, it was Genoese bankers who controlled the financial markets there. But the world was changing. Antwerp had built the world's first permanent financial exchange, the Handelsbeurs, some decades earlier and that practice was copied elsewhere, notably by the Royal Exchange in the City of London. Over time, the presence of a 'bourse' or exchange in a city made the practice of quarterly Exchange Fairs redundant.

As in London a few centuries later, pure trade finance spawned a range of other credit transactions – once the banks had accumulated the capital and the skills to offer them. And not just loans to merchants, but to sovereign borrowers as well, like Philip II of Spain. For many years Genoa was the principal lender to the Spanish crown and her bankers grew rich on the strength of this business. At one time, the value of the city's banking transactions was twice as large as the economy of the Republic itself. An unbalanced position, which has its echoes in the global financial crisis of recent times.

Genoa also had, long before Amsterdam and then later London, an organisation which could supervise this business activity and ensure that it worked to the benefit of the Genoese Republic. The Banco di San Giorgio had been founded nearly two centuries earlier and Christopher Columbus, back from his epic transatlantic voyage, was an early shareholder. The San Giorgio was in effect the city-state's central bank – and more. It licensed the activities of the *cambisti* and acted as the clearing house for their transactions at the quarterly Exchange Fairs. It issued what you could term treasury bonds to wealthy investors on the Republic's behalf. It managed Genoa's mediterranean colonies and garnered the revenues they generated. And finally, it collected Genoa's customs duties and other taxes derived from foreign trade. From all these sources, it provided funds to the Genoese Republic to pay for its policies, foreign and domestic. The building from which this all-powerful organisation once operated still stands today on the Genoa waterfront, looking out to sea, the true source of the bank's wealth. When the Genoese Republic finally collapsed in 1797, defaulting on its debts, the bank did also.

WHO WERE THE CAMBISTI?

The men – and they were invariably men – who transacted finance business in Genoa were called *cambisti*, meaning moneychangers. The modern term in Italian for a bureau de change or currency exchange, cambio, is derived from this word. The fact that they described themselves as 'changers' rather than 'lenders' was accurate in a literal sense, in that they held reserves of foreign currency as a matter of course to facilitate cross-border trades. But it was at the same time a useful euphemism, which glossed over the fact that they were also moneylenders.

Despite the city being a pioneer in commercial finance, the bankers of Genoa operated in a society that was still Catholic and orthodox. Moneylending had negative connotations in that context, and the accusation of charging excessive interest ('usury') was still problematic, even in the late Renaissance. Over the preceding centuries, the position had slowly liberalised across Europe, so that it was no longer a civil offence in most cities. But it was still regarded as breaking the Church's laws and the bankers remained sensitive to that charge. To disguise the true size of their margin, they used exchange rates rather than 'interest' to fix their profit, the difference between what they advanced to a buyer in Genoese currency and what they collected in local currency where the goods were finally sold.

The Loggia dei Mercanti, or Merchants' Hall, was the place where the *cambisti* conducted business. A large, covered space flanked by open columns which gave access to the outside. The Loggia was strategically positioned on the north-east corner of Piazza Banchi which, at the time, would have been filled with stalls on market days. The Loggia still stands proud today, although its open columns have been glassed over in more recent times. Inside, each *cambisto* had his own 'pitch' the spot from where he did business. A simple affair, chairs and a bench on which he would place a suitable cloth and place the instruments of his trade: the ledgers, the abacus and a store of currency. The Italian word for bench or table is *'banca'* and from this term is derived our own 'banker'. Although they probably would not have used that term themselves, I have taken the liberty of using it in the novel.

These Genoese bankers spent some of their profits building themselves grand palazzos, to advertise their dynasties and impress their neighbours. The banker who was pre-eminent in providing credit to Spain at the time was Nicolo Grimaldi, nicknamed "the Monarch" by Genoa's citizens. The 'Monarch's' palazzo and many other impressive houses can be seen today on what is now called Via Garibaldi, but was then Strada Nuova – New Street, because it was.

HISTORICAL FIGURES IN THE STORY

In the scenes set in the English and Spanish Courts, all the characters are historic figures, and the reader will judge if I have captured something of the personality of these leaders of the age.

What is unarguable is that Philip II of Spain was a micro-manager, almost drowning in a bureaucratic sea of paperwork and no doubt a nightmare to his ministers and civil servants alike. A job made no easier by his vanity about his short-sightedness and his crippling gout. At the same time, his convictions, both religious and as regards the absolute authority of his role as monarch, led him into a lifetime of war and not infrequently, debt. Whether Don Juan de Idiáquez, his minister and a member of the ruling triumvirate, was as manipulative and bullish as the character as I have portrayed, is another question. Certainly, he would have supported the principle of the 'English Enterprise', as Spanish courtiers privately referred to the ill-kept secret of a planned invasion. But he was also cautious about the prospect of success, given the huge logistic challenge of coordinating its naval forces (the Armada) with the Duke of Parma's army stationed in the Netherlands, then a Spanish possession.

In the case of Elizabeth I, what stands out is her combination of parsimony when it comes to national defence and vacillation when faced with the toughest decisions. Again, she would have driven her ministers - and Walsingham in particular, given his hawkish views - to distraction. On the other hand, her instincts were for peace rather than war and were well-tempered by her experience. While she was perfectly happy to share in the spoils of her privateers like Sir Francis Drake, she was also fearful, correctly, that bold assaults like his at Cádiz would make peace with Spain harder to achieve. Her Principal Secretary, Sir Francis Walsingham, is an intriguing character (in both senses). The 'footnotes' referred to earlier indicate his possible role in the conduct of economic warfare. Indeed, it is hard to imagine who else could have conducted such a strategy. Despite several fine biographies, the persona of Elizabeth's so-called 'spymaster' remains elusive: perhaps that befits his role. In the cinema or on television, he is portrayed as a somewhat cold and sinister figure, but there is an argument that this stereotype of the ruthless 'man in black' does him less than justice. His tireless work to protect his sovereign and his country may not have brought him many admirers at home, but in Spain there was grudging respect, as is shown by the back-handed compliment paid by Philip II when writing about him, shortly after Walsingham's death was announced some years later.

When it comes to the leaders of church and state in Genoa, I have for the most part, used the actual names of the individuals at the time. That includes the Governor, Gianandrea Doria; the Doge, Ambrogio Di Negro; and most significantly in terms of the story, the then Archbishop of Genoa, Antonmaria Sauli. The personality of these characters and their part in the action of the novel are however entirely imagined. Cardinal Sauli went on to have a lengthy and not undistinguished career in the Vatican, so my portrayal of the archbishop as a self-serving and ruthless operator in his home city, should be regarded as pure fiction.

THE ROLE OF WOMEN

If the politicians, merchants and other leaders identified in the story are mostly male, it does not follow that the women of the time played a domestic role only. England had its queen of course and the Regent of the Spanish Netherlands was a female member of the Hapsburg family. Other women in England had a significant presence in wider affairs. Ursula Walsingham was by all accounts no pushover, and her inner steel is briefly portrayed here. Genoa's may have been a patriarchal society, but Nico Castello's wife, Lisa, has an assertiveness and self-assurance built, not just on her family name, but on the broad education given to her by her enlightened father. And other women in the story, nuns, daughters, even courtesans, have the agency to set the course of their own lives.

THE CITY OF GENOA

The city of Genoa itself is in some senses a character in the story. The broad sweep of Caricamento around the harbour; the 'striped' cathedral of San Lorenzo with its architectural suggestion of a fortress; the bustle of the marketplace in Piazza Banchi; the narrow alleyways in the poorer districts and the grand palazzos looking down on the old city from their elevated viewpoints.

Fortunately for visitors today, Genova's medieval heart retains much of the look, even some of the ambience, it had more than four centuries ago. A delightful surprise for anyone who imagines that a modern city boasting an international airport, a cruise ship terminal and a container port, is unlikely to hold much attraction for the Renaissance tourist.

So: we come back to the key question: did it happen like this? All I can say is that the ingredients - motivation, means and method - were all in place in 1587. And Genoa was the obvious battleground.

Acknowledgments

No novel is the product of its author alone and this book is no exception. Many people have generously given their time, advice and encouragement as I was writing it. I cannot mention you all, but I am grateful to each one of you. I would however particularly mention (in alphabetical order):

Steven Andrew, Tom Barry, Tina Betts, Matthew Breakell, Peter Buckman, Gillian Burnett, John Case, Nat Case (no relation), Wensley Clarkson, Therese Conway, Roger Daltrey, Kerry Ellis, the late Professor Giuseppe Felloni, Guy Fraser-Sampson, Jonny Geller, Angela Hawksley, Liz Little, Louisa Northway, Chris O'Donoghue, Zia Haider Rahman, Frances Rogers, Libby Rothwell, Mary Sandys, Ann Weinstock and Lynn Willcock. Thanks also to those numerous literary agents whose diplomatically worded rejection slips contained constructive advice or the seeds of encouragement.

A list of the works of history that I read or consulted, when researching the novel, is available on the website. I have endeavoured to be truthful to the historic record, but inevitably in a work of fiction, author's licence has been employed. Any inaccuracies or misinterpretations are of course, my responsibility alone.

Very few novelists, it seems, are tempted to make the arcane world of high finance their setting, much less a driver of the plot. Unfamiliarity no doubt. makes that a rare choice. In my case, many years working professionally in that milieu made me foolhardy enough to take it on. And the fact that my professional practice was itself underpinned by the education I had received (but probably failed to fully absorb) at the feet of Francis Reynolds KC (Hon.), my law tutor at Oxford, whose standing in the study of international trade law is second to none. To him, and to the other mentors I had the good fortune to meet along the way, this book is respectfully dedicated.

About the Author

DAVID BREAKELL was born and grew up in Sussex, England. After his schooldays, he read law at Worcester College, Oxford. Despite spending time on student journalism, filmmaking and fencing for the university, he somehow managed to get his degree. After pursuing various other career options with limited success, he qualified as a lawyer professionally and started proper work in the City of London. That culminated with nearly twenty years as a banking partner in a global law firm.

David is married with grown-up children and lives close to the sea, back in Sussex.

The Lanterna, Genoa Harbour by Giovanni Migliara
© NPL - DeA Picture Library/Bridgeman Images